I'll Buy You an

I'll Buy You an Ox

An Acadian daughter's bittersweet passage into womanhood

Betty Boudreau Vaughan

NIMBUS
PUBLISHING LTD

This book is essentially a work of fiction. With the exception of some family members, all other characters are the sole invention of the author and bear no intended resemblance to any individual living or dead.

Nimbus Publishing Limited
P.O. Box 9301, Station A
Halifax, Nova Scotia   B3K 5N5
(902) 455-4286

Cover design: Margaret Issenman
Cover illustration and illustrations on pages 113 and 339
by Gilles Archambault.
Printed and bound in Canada

Canadian Cataloguing in Publication Data
Vaughan, Betty Boudreau.
I'll buy you an ox
ISBN 1-55109-223-9
I. Title.
PS8593.A92616 1997   jC813'.54   C97-950115-6
PR9199.3.V3915

Acknowledgements

Nothing in this world can take the place of persistence.
Talent will not; nothing is more common than unsuccessful men
with talent. Genius will not; unrewarded genius is almost a proverb.
Education will not; the world is full of educated derelicts. Persistence
and determination alone are omnipotent. The slogan "press on" has
solved and always will solve the problems of the human race.

- CALVIN COOLIDGE

A million thanks:

To my lovely daughters, Lisa and Angeline, who so unselfishly put precious years on hold, understanding how much I needed to write this novel. I'll make it up to my grandchildren.

To my husband, Bob, who cleaned the moat, fed the crocodiles, and spent long evenings and weekends alone for the better part of five years while I made passionate love to my computer. I've had the challenge of my life, and I owe it all to you.

To my brother Regi and my good friend Michael Deveau, whose wealth of fishing experience and knowledge proved invaluable to my fishing village setting.

To Marlene and Claire, friends who are woven from the same divine cloth as the fictional Babette. I love you both.

To Art Parsons, who had a similar upbringing in Rencontre, Newfoundland, and knew how to slaughter a pig, make rabbit snares, and skin a muskrat so articulately on paper.

To masters of the trade—Peter Schwenger, Bill Gaston, Bruce Armstrong, Alexa Thompson, Elizabeth Eve, Annette Thibodeau, Michelle Paon, George Steeves—who believed I could and showed me how. Thirty-nine chapters later, I am forever grateful.

To Paula Sarson, whose tact and sensitivity helped polish this novel.

To Cecilia and Jeanne, sisters by good fortune. Your constant encouragement, "*J'peux point jetter*" spurred me on to finish this colossal piece of work.

To my mother, Thérèse à Alpha,
whose greatest virtue is her abiding faith.
Without her spunk and courage,
what would have become
of us?

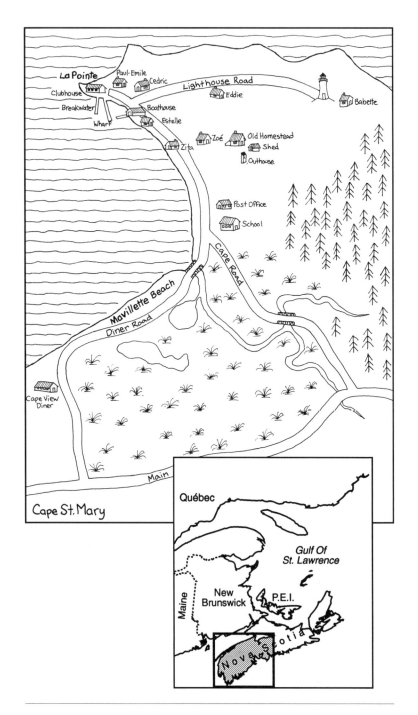

Chapter 1

When the funeral parlour in Meteghan first opened its doors, a chill swept through the neighbouring villages. In my village, Cape St. Mary, the old-timers were not about to gracefully surrender the age-old tradition of mourning their dead at home.

"I'll never go there!" I heard them exclaim. My step Grand-père Dominique ardently agreed. He vowed he'd turn over in his coffin if he were laid out for people from all over creation to gawk and make stupid remarks like, "Doesn't he look good."

When he died, his incessant grumbling ceased, and his mouth was wired shut, hiding ugly brown teeth. Gawkers may have had their chance to say he looked good, but he was laid out at home. So was La Caquette, the village gossip from across the road, Zita's aged mother. That had been her wish, too.

My sweetheart Cedric didn't want his father laid out in the funeral parlour. I was almost fifteen then. Unlike Cedric, who was eighteen, I fancied the idea that a funeral director could rid the widow, his mother, of burdensome arrangements. She had been traumatized enough with the drowning tragedy and didn't need the gruesome reminder in her living room.

Grand-mère Sophie's passing not long after marked a loosening of tradition; she ended up in a funeral parlour in Wedgeport. I remember vividly the cumbersome brooch of rhinestones crowding her black dress and the red ribbon wrapped around her few remaining strands of dishevelled hair. She died at eighty-six, her skin as smooth as a baby's. She was buried next to her first husband, Nicholas, my blood grand-père, whom I never knew.

The funeral parlour became an important rendez-vous, a place to congregate with relatives, and, for me, a place to be spooked by my friend Estelle. It was here that she introduced me to the mystical world through her contrived stories and games.

"It really did happen," she professed, her eyes wild, her chubby cheeks dimpling as she smiled. "In my grandmother's time, some people gave themselves to the devil. Pilotte à Sirois signed up, and at the end of seven years he had to fight the devil to break the spell. People saw him sharpening his sword on an emery wheel and then strike through the air. Bolts of lightning lit up the skies as he challenged his opponent. 'Show yourself, Satan, if you have the power to claim my soul.' "

Estelle's smile turned devilish as she chanted:
I know. I know. That Pilotte went to hell.
Now you must listen, if you want me to tell.
Frozen to my seat, I listened as she continued.

"I woke up one night to this racket at my bedroom window. *Un train du sanava gun.* 'The wind,' I thought, until a dog started howling."

"What did you do?" I gasped.

Her answer was quick. "I pulled the covers over my head. But there was a loud rapping on the pane—a bang like a heavy paw! I tell you, Zoé, the racket wouldn't go away, and I was some bloody scared. I inched my way toward a flickering orange shadow, got a good look out the window and … oh my God!" Estelle's bewitched eyes met mine, "You're not gonna believe this, Zoé. What do you think I saw?"

I gaped stupidly; she lost patience.

"A black dog!" she coached. "Ferocious with its face on fire and a tail so long that it stretched over our lawn, down to the wharf, and hell knows how deep into the ocean."

Her own face was on fire with her desire to convince me. "I tell you Zoé, you would have dropped dead." She leaned her head forward, staring even more wildly into my eyes. "I think it was Pilotte. What do you think?" She nudged me, her voice gruff, "Answer! You think it was Pilotte?"

Hastily, I grinned. "I think you were doing fine, Estelle, but wasn't it too dark to see the tail which was so long that … well, it simply stretched the *tale* too far."

"You don't believe me!" she huffed, and stalked out, leaving me alone in the dimly lit room.

Whether I believed Estelle was irrelevant. Her spirit added excitement to my otherwise boring childhood. Pitiful it was, influenced by Antoine, my illiterate father, who gradually became content to rock in his chair and hum sad songs. His bedtime stories, though popular among his younger children, were born of a limited imagination, centring on the lives of rats in the breakwater. Then there was the iron rule of Martine, my "fusspot" mother, preoccupied with duster and broom to help her forget the problems of raising seven children. Estelle was my escape, but however thrilling it was to follow her, she was downright cunning. I never knew when I would fall into one of her traps.

On another visit to the funeral parlour, she scanned the roomful of bouquets. I should have known by her conniving smile what was coming.

"Let's guess the flowers."

Estelle's backyard abounded with flowers that her mother planted and nurtured every spring. I, on the other hand, knew only of Grand-mère's lupins and of the tiny violets that grew wild in the back fields. Dandelions didn't count.

"What kind are those?" she pointed to a pot of yellow flowers, her voice resounding through the parlour so that all eyes were drawn in my direction.

"Hurry!" she pressed, and I cringed at the mocking look on her face. "*Ma, ma, ma, ma, ma.* I'll give you a hint. *Mom* has that kind in her garden." She allowed me a few seconds, then lost her patience. "Mums, stupid! I practically gave it away."

Her words wounded my pride, and for a long time it mattered.

But now many years later, childish grudges are forgotten. As a young woman returning to that funeral parlour, my hurried pace gives way to short, laboured steps. The door to the funeral parlour is slower to open because I am now reluctant. My breathing comes deep and overwrought. I close my eyes and dull my senses to cushion the blow of that first glance. I've come to see my father.

My heart mourns at the irony of an immaculate body set gently in a bed of silk, silk that has come too late. Somehow it does not suit this man who knew only the silk of dreams, this man who called himself "the Sheik of Araby," this man whose delusions rendered him wealthy.

My thoughts drift back to his kingdom, the kitchen of our house, where he spent most of his life glued to his rocking chair, drinking tea and watching television until the station signed off. Driven by fantasy, he saw himself in one of those shiny Chrysler New Yorkers advertised across the screen—an ironic illusion for a man who worried from day to day where he could find the money to buy tobacco. He once told me that he had been to Hawaii when he was young—also an ironic illusion from a man who hid upstairs, too shy to face strangers.

I didn't intrude much on his fantasy world. It let him own the riches that would never be his and bury the hell he knew when Mam' and the two youngest ones moved to Toronto. Then it had been just him and me, and the ticking of the clock. Yet, I remember in my childhood, he always had a grin. He often grinned when there was nothing to grin about, so that villagers felt compelled to ask him, "Don't you ever complain?"

"No use fussing," he'd answer. And though the ready grin faded, that's how he died—without fuss.

Now in his coffin, he is grinning again, no longer tormented by his fantasies of fame and riches. I don't cry. "People cry when there are regrets," N'Oncle Joseph once told me. I've none. Without fail, I had provided for my father. I had grumbled my way a thousand times to the combined post office and general store to fetch his tobacco, and I kept him company for hours on end as he whittled in Dominique's shed. After Mam', Joel, and Thérèse moved away, I made sure he was fed and that his clothes were clean. And I made his Christmases bearable—the hardest task of all.

I did not arrange for flowers. My flowers I had given when my father's hands could hold them. Those amassed around the coffin are thoughtful tokens, never mind that they merely mark a tradition. There are white and purple mums—yes, mums—from Estelle, and a heart-shaped wreath of red roses from my Cedric, who has just been transferred to Germany from Cyprus and couldn't possibly come home. There is a white velveteen cross of the most beautiful yellow roses, from Zita.

She wants to talk about my father. "Did he die of emphysema?"

I cannot bring myself to utter the horrible word *suffocation*. I merely nod, "The autopsy said bronchial complications."

I look all around the coffin. Flowers, flowers everywhere. They help distract me from the sorrow that threatens to consume me. I have no prayer for him; God has claimed what is rightfully His. "Pray for me when I'm in Purgatory," Dad had jested on occasion. Remembering this, I am touched now by the humility of a man who had done his penance a hundredfold in his long fifty-four years. I know my vigil will be better spent honouring my promise that his grandchildren will know him. Pricille's tiny Agatha is the only one he held. Now my sister is expecting a second child. Pierre's Louise is expecting her first. And someday, ... someday I hope to have two little girls.

I abandon my reverie for there are friends to greet. People from the villages have come to pay their respects, along with a familial circle of aunts, uncles, and cousins who I see only at funerals and weddings. Uncle John from Boston is the only one absent. There was no love lost between him and us, and since our Tante Marceline died, we do not expect to see him again.

Everyone from the Cape is here. I cannot bring myself to acknowledge Paul-Emile's beguiling smile. But I shake hands with Eddie Pockshaw who is crying like a lost little boy. Who will help him drink his homemade brew now, his pockshaw? Wisely, he has left his chewing tobacco at home and is reasonably dressed, save for different coloured socks. He even remembered to zip the fly of his droopy pants.

Charlotte and Basil embark on a detailed story of their grandson's vicious cold which has kept their Estelle at home. I didn't even notice Estelle's absence. I focus instead on Babette, who approaches me with arms open, her mother, Emma, at her side.

A nagging worry clouds her pretty olive green eyes. "What are you going to do? Where will you go?"

I shrug my shoulders to my best friend. "Don't know. Pricille thinks I'd like Boston. You and William have mentioned Halifax. Cedric would marry me tomorrow if I said yes." I sigh heavily in contemplation of the last possibility. "I could always stay in the house. There are enough memories there to haunt me for the rest of my life. I just don't know. For sure, I'm not moving to Toronto with Mam' and the kids."

Emma reaches for my hand. "We'd sure love to have you with us."

I smile at Babette's sweet mother, although her vacant eyes, blind since her youth, cannot see me. "Thank you, but I need to sort out my life."

Emma is one lady about whom Mam' would never tolerate gossip. I remember the day that Zita crossed the road to come and tell, "I saw Emma at the post office this morning. Surely Percy can see when her dresses are filthy."

My mother turned around briskly, almost pricking Zita with the sharp knife she was using to fix mussels. "He makes her see far past a mere stain on a dress."

Indeed, Percy was not only Emma's husband but her eyes. He as well helped her see flowers long after the season was gone, sunsets and rainbows when there were none in the sky, garland and tinsel when it wasn't even Christmas. He made her see the Cape, too—the waves smashing against the cliffs, the sunlight diamonds sparkling on the ocean, the parade of fishing boats leaving the wharf, the faces of the villagers smiling. Today, he helps her see the composure of my father at rest.

N'Oncle Joseph seems to make the same observation silently, that my father is finally at peace. This is the uncle who managed ten children, yet keeps to himself. He and my father became inseparable after their brother, Louis, went to war and never returned, was never reported missing either. No one knew what happened to him, not even his mother, Grand-mère Sophie, who had taken such pains to trace her lost son.

There is little comfort now, for relatives like N'Oncle Joseph for whom roots are planted too deep and time is reduced to a mockery. I walk gingerly across the room towards him. "You all by yourself?" I ask, and he embraces me.

"I hate it when people philosophize at funerals," he whispers. "Idle talk means well, but a firm handshake would say it all." I leave him with his grief.

Moving towards my six brothers and sisters sitting in a handsome row, I smile, for I am fiercely proud of them, and of my mother. She didn't spare the rod. She had raised us well, in spite of the many obstacles, the hard times we had shouldered together. We didn't have much. She had a firm doctrine for us children: you don't have to stay poor. I say her strength came from her abiding faith. When problems seemed insurmountable, she prayed to her *Bon Djeu*, sought His guidance in doing the right thing, asked that her children would love one another. Whether she always did the right thing, I couldn't judge. As for loving one another, there was no question; it was understood.

"It would have been interesting to see the outcome our father's life," remarked my oldest brother, Philippe, "if circumstances had been different, if he had gone to school and his father had not died so young. You know, for a man who signed an X instead of his name, he turned out some fairly intelligent children."

The comment was fitting, coming from Philippe who had obtained an engineering degree with first-class honours. His regrets and consolations were similar to those of the rest of us. We reminisced, except for little Joel, who couldn't interest himself in anything past school in September, and each one of our stories in some way touched on the best in our father.

"I'm a big boy," Joel wanted everyone to notice, but his three older brothers were absorbed in stories of hunting with their father. Though I suspect they exaggerated, I do recall the many times that Dad walked into the house, grinning from ear to ear, clutching half a dozen rabbits in one hand and four or five ducks in the other. If they were excellent hunters, it was because they had an excellent teacher—our father was the best.

My two sisters' stories were less numerous than mine. They had been away far too long; the eldest, Pricille, found work in the States and the youngest, Thérèse, left with Mam'. They stared at a face they could barely recall, each grieving that they had never told their father they loved him. The words "I love you" appeared only in Pricille's *True Stories* magazines that she poured over as a teenager. It was not a phrase openly used in the home, not in ours.

Standing next to my brothers and sisters, I notice my mother spends her vigil kneeling at the coffin, her thumb and index finger marking the decades on her blue rosary. Composed as usual, she is suppressing tears lodged in the corners of her eyes that tell of sentiments too sacred to share.

"I know exactly when Dad died," our ten-year-old Thérèse confides. "Mam' sat up in her bed and hollered his name. When Pierre called to tell us, she wasn't surprised at all. Do you think Mam' had a sign in a dream?" she asks, as I stroke her long, wavy hair and gaze into her young face.

"With every cell in my body, I believe it."

The morning of the funeral, Mam' breaks down and weeps at the funeral parlour. "He's finally at peace." I sense that she, too, has found her peace.

The presence of the funeral director, anxiously pacing back and forth, gives us the silent message. It is time to leave. He approaches the coffin, wearing a kind smile before tearing us away.

"Come," Mam' gestures, summoning her children to her side. But I tarry behind, as if I can possess time. I want to be the last to bid farewell to my father. I am thankful that Mam' has prepared me for the moment with her often repeated advice: "Detach yourself from earthly possessions." Her words are now richly blessed.

As I stand over his body for the last time, my thoughts trace back to the long ago days when my father worked with a dredging crew at the wharf. It was noon, and I handed him a paper bag that reeked of sardines, the oily fish minced between two pieces of soggy bread. I walked down a long flight of concrete steps that were bathed with salt water at high tide, slippery with green algae at low tide. All the men were looking up, except for my father. When he eventually raised his head, my mere presence brought a warm glow to his eyes, "*Ma p'tite Zoé.*"

I wasn't then six years old, because one of the men teased my father, "Who's gonna bring your lunch once Zoé's in school?"

One day, I didn't bring a lunch to the wharf—the day my father slid down the concrete steps and hit his head. One of the men drove him to the doctor. After the accident, I often heard Mam' tell Zita, "Antoine's crazy talk about being rich has worsened since he fell."

My focus drifts back to the coffin before me. I brush a piece of lint from the sleeve of my father's dark green Frenchy's suit, wishing he could see how dignified he looks. The Sheik of Araby, I think, and I smile, certain he can read my mind. I touch his forehead protectively and close my eyes, trying to memorize the grin by which I want to remember him. I, too, grin, my farewell to our good and bad times. I close his casket, closing the chapter of his life on earth.

I am a grieving daughter lost in reverie during the funeral procession. The month of July has welcomed a late summer. Philippe will soon be married and begin a new life. Lush green buds sprouting up from the ground speak of the promise of flowers, sharply contrasting with the hearse in front of me that speaks of a life extinguished.

The teeming emotions around the graveside overpower the soothing of a warm breeze that gently wafts around my face. Seagulls shriek and circle above, then head back to the shore, their curiosity satisfied. A crow perches itself on a nearby tombstone. *One crow sorrow …*

A hushed silence allows me a moment to scan the cemetery. Somewhere, a small cross once marked the grave of my baby sister, but the wood rotted long ago and my mother can't remember where the infant was buried.

I pick up a handful of earth and sprinkle it on the casket before me. As it is lowered into the grave, I bite my trembling lips, meditating on what my mother once said. "Somewhere, flowers will bloom for him."

Chapter 2

In 1955 the American researcher Jonas Edward Salk declared his vaccine against polio safe and effective, two years too late for Babette, the new girl at the Cape. It was also the year, and now, the day that I would start school. I was six years old. Born in October, I could not begin school at five.

I had been staring into pitch darkness for what seemed a lifetime. Though it was still dark outside and the shapes around my bed in the attic had hardly taken form, I knew it was Dad who was tiptoeing to the window on his way downstairs. The glowing end of his cigarette preceded his tall, slim silhouette. I heard the rustle of paper and knew he was reaching into his pants pocket for a peppermint—a morning ritual to soothe his toothless gums. The wind had ceased and, with it, the crashing of the ocean. A calm day beckoned the fishermen to sea.

I hastened downstairs to watch Dad light the fire in the wood stove. The routine was the same every morning. He lifted the cover and stuffed the stove with newspaper while Mam' supervised.

"Get back to bed," she barked, but I stealthily backed away from her cutting stare. Dad returned from rummaging for kindling. Mam' scowled as he carelessly shook his kerosene can, splashing its contents all over her shiny stove and onto the clean floor. Though my attention was on the leaping flames, I caught his furtive grin as he wiped up the spilled kerosene with a swift sweep of his foot.

"Don't wipe the floor with your stocking feet!" Mam' charged, but he didn't listen any more than he did any other morning.

"Yes, yes," he said absently, but as soon as her back was turned, he perfected his aim with another quick stroke of the foot and mopped up the few remaining drops.

After the heat from the stove had permeated the bite of fall air in the kitchen, Dad warmed up his tea and settled into his rocking chair before the pandemonium of school children began. "Dishwater" tea and a quick succession of two or three rolled cigarettes constituted his breakfast. There were no cookies to dip into his cup this morning.

The worn rockers creaked while he hummed Gene Autry's "Silver Grey Haired Daddy of Mine." His humming stopped short, and silence filled the room, indicating he was deep in thought, perhaps reminiscing about his youth. His father's early death had marked the end of a comfortable existence. The scant portions of sugar, flour, and other rations to which his mother, Sophie, was entitled from the Municipality of Wedgeport did little to sustain her and her four children. And Dad's door-to-door begging made little difference. So, at the age of twelve, he entered manhood, weathering the sea to gain his livelihood and to fend for his family.

Dad hummed himself out of his reverie. He drew his fingers through his thick mop of already white hair and lit another cigarette. From the kitchen window, he could see when the fishermen started unmooring their boats, his cue to head for the wharf, though he was reluctant to get up, taking forever to reach the door. He would board the *Little Esther,* and she would follow the parade of small boats headed for the Trinity.

The scene at the wharf never changed: a small fleet of fishing boats bobbing against one another; a cluster of stinky shanties housing fishing gear and bait; a big pier and a small pier built at right angles to one another; and two boatshops standing fifty yards apart, one of them owned by Estelle's father, Basil.

While Dad struggled to leave the house, I could hardly wait to head down the hill to meet Estelle for our first day of school. I wondered if she was still angry with me but that didn't dampen my excitement over this eagerly awaited event. I could finally put away my colouring book and learn important things, like how to write my name.

Back in the attic, I asked Pricille, "Can you print *Zoé à Antoine* for me?"

"Zoé *LeBlanc!*" she corrected impatiently, a holy terror to look at in the morning. She lifted her head from her pillow long enough to peek through the studs to check for signs of life in the boys' section of the attic. "Philippe! Pierre! André! Get up! *Pi décrassez vous.*"

I offered her my scribbler and a pencil, but she gave me a lazy yawn, reached along the bedpost for her bubble gum, and buried her head under the blankets. "Go away!" She wasn't printing my name, and she wasn't getting up, not yet.

I turned to my scanty wardrobe. Mam' had already stored my summer dresses in a cardboard box. My fall clothes smelled of mothballs and hung on nails, except for a pleated jumper and blouse that were laid neatly on the orange crate night table. Its two shelves were reserved for Pricille's prized possessions: a pair of penny loafers, a few Hank Williams albums, a good-luck rabbit foot on a chain, red nail polish that I wasn't allowed to wear, a school photo with a circle around a boy's face, and a signet ring engraved with a P.

I grabbed my clothes and examined Pricille's, hand-me-downs that our Tante Marceline sent from Boston. Mam' spent considerable time mending clothes that arrived devoid of buttons and with broken zippers, adjusting the lengths of skirts and dresses. What had been discarded as American *passé* became *à la mode* for Pricille.

She looked pretty in just about anything, wearing her long, black hair in a ponytail that swung from side to side when she moved her head. Her hair had a natural wave, what I longed for in mine which was straight as a poker. That summer, I had worked hard collecting junk with André to earn money from the junkman. I wanted a perm for school.

"You're too young," Mam' had argued.

I had cried, sitting on the arm of Dad's rocking chair. "But my hair is almost six years old."

I won, but only because Dad had dared dispute Mam's judgement; his laissez-faire attitude normally excluded him from family decisions. "If she wants a permanent, then let her have a permanent! It's her money."

Now I was contemplating the first day of school, and I had a perm. My head was still weighted down with Zita's pink plastic curlers.

"You shouldn't sleep with those," she had warned, but I had feared my poker-straight hair would resist the curl if I didn't. One by one, I removed the curlers, feeling each ringlet tight to my scalp, a good sign that the perm had taken.

"Just like Estelle's hair!" I exclaimed to Mam' when I burst into the kitchen. She reserved her comments, but her stony expression made me uneasy. The more she brushed, the frizzier my hair became, until my head felt heavy, not quite how I had imagined lots and lots of curls. I hastened to the small mirror on the medicine cabinet by the sink. Tears lodged in my eyes and panic marked my face, but my brother André was not deterred.

"Baaaaaahh," he drawled. "Have you seen Deni's sheep lately? I hear he's lost one. *C'est crotté all right.*"

"What an ugly, 'crotty' mess! I'm wearing a kerchief for the rest of my life," I sobbed to Mam', who just stared, her scowl fixed on my kinky curls.

"You wanted a perm. You got one."

In the light from the window, she inspected my clothes to ensure they were properly ironed. It would have been the first time if they hadn't been. She ironed everything: towels, underwear, socks, overalls—all items other mothers ignored. Her obsessive ironing turned washrags into sandpaper. The only one left that morning was a threadbare specimen that Pricille, the eldest, claimed and that Philippe, the second eldest, wanted.

"You wait your turn!" my sister snapped, causing him to narrow his big, black eyes. He grabbed the washrag and flung her comb across the room. A wicked shove won him the mirror on the medicine cabinet.

"You take an eternity to comb your hair," he charged. "I'm first."

"*Hé! Hé! Hé!*" was Mam's bugle call. Though Pricille had a mean temper, she knew to back off; Philippe's was worse.

Clutching a used washrag from the wringer-washer, I approached the sink. "I need to wash my face," I told Philippe, who stopped combing to direct one mean look my way.

"Get outta here!"

Red blotches already burned my face, but I couldn't stop crying, thinking how Estelle would notice my hair and surely die laughing.

I returned to the table, poured milk on my gooey porridge, and ate the guck between sobs, so lost in my misery that I barely heard the gentle voice, "Zoé."

I lifted my face from the bowl. Pierre.

"You know what's nice about your hair?" he gently grinned.

I stopped sobbing. "What?"

His caring hands searched for a handkerchief so I could blow my nose. "It's not straight anymore." My brother Pierre was plagued with straight hair, too, but he was blessed with my father's perpetual grin, which distracted attention away from his hair. His face was never angry. But he was no pushover, as his brothers learned the hard way. When they were younger, Philippe and André were hoarding a train set that Tante Marceline had brought from Boston.

"We had it first!" Philippe had asserted with a shove.

Pierre had hauled off and punched the bully in the stomach. "The set belongs to the three of us," he had announced, ever the diplomat. Pierre's strength became well-known for he could arm wrestle all the boys in the village.

He had spent most of the summer at the wharf. This morning, his attention was more focused on the fishermen leaving the wharf than on his own preparations for school.

Meanwhile, Mam' scurried about doing her chores, one of them making my lunch—a peanut butter sandwich, a Mayonnaise jar filled with milk, and two apples, the one fruit we had in plenty.

Every fall Dad took time off from fishing to pick apples in the Valley with Cedric's father, Gustave. He later confided in me that when he sold them door-to-door in the Valley, he felt like a beggar—the same feeling he had experienced as a child when he set out with his little pail after his father had died.

He distinctly remembered one story from those begging days of his youth in Wedgeport. A nice woman had opened the door. He had asked for a bit of flour, having spotted a sixty-pound bag at the top of the stairs. But before the kind woman could answer, a tall, robust man appeared and lied they didn't have any that day.

After Dad told me this story, I felt ambivalent towards the

people of Wedgeport. But I loved the people in the Valley—they bought his apples—though I could picture him, a grown man with his bashful blue eyes fixed to the floor. Gustave told us about the time that my father knocked on the door of a shack and a mother answered, followed by half a dozen little ones, running barefoot on an earthen floor. Stricken with pity, Dad poured generously until her basin overflowed with fruit. From then on, Gustave said, he gave away more than he sold.

Sometimes my father arrived home from the Valley in the wee hours of the morning. He rarely discussed his travels. Though he was much too shy to tell anyone his name, Mam' still worried about the grog. Even the poorest people kept a shot of rum in their cupboards. She knew that he was with Gustave, and men were men. For those who knew how to drink, a jigger of hard stuff went down easy after a long day's work. But she also knew that liquor had a way of turning her Antoine into a deranged man, and then, heaven forbid, his tongue turned vicious with plenty to say. God only knew, maybe there were women involved. It was best not to question the late nights. We needed the apples; we needed the money.

Apples in plenty. Pricille said they were full of worms that chewed up the intestines. On my way out the door to meet Estelle, I grabbed those from my lunch and tossed them back in the pail.

"Bye Mam'," I called, and hurried down the Cape road to Estelle's house. My friend was all smiles, clad in her new dress from Yarmouth, which strained at her fat bulges. Everything was new, down to the pink nylon panties.

"Are you angry at me?" I ventured, as she turned round and round, sending the skirt of her dress softly whirling.

"Is that why you've been crying?" she asked, peering at my red-blotched, swollen face. Estelle couldn't be called pretty, but two dimples embellished her plump cheeks whenever she smiled, and her long, brown, curly locks bounced when she walked. She complained plenty about her curls when it was foggy, tugging with her comb to straighten out the frizzy locks and bangs.

I now knew how she felt. Not even a steamroller could have straightened my "crotty" mess. I tightened my kerchief self-consciously and she adjusted her gaze to stare me in the face. "Let's see your perm." I froze. "Come on," she coaxed, "and I'll forget about the broken arm on my doll." She crossed her heart, "Promise I won't laugh."

I tugged at the tight knot under my chin, loosened the kerchief so she could examine my hair, scowl at it, smell it, then finally force her hand through my fluffy sheep wool.

"Oh my God, Zoé!" Her smirk also took in my clothes. My navy jumper had faded from too many owners, and Javex had failed to whiten the yellowed blouse. "That was Pricille's uniform," she jeered. But it was now my uniform, and I felt like a real schoolgirl, except for my clumsy brown shoes at which she also sneered. "They're boy's shoes," she scoffed, flaunting her two-toned navy-and-white ones. Not many girls were lucky enough to have those.

I retied my kerchief snugly and diverted her attention to the new girl hobbling down the lighthouse road. "Babette," she said flatly.

I asked with a frown, "Isn't her name Barbara?"

"Babette!" Estelle stammered, stamping her foot on the ground to end the debate. Babette it was, more Acadian sounding, really. We knew the poor girl was still having nightmares about the sting on her leg. Estelle hadn't been allowed up the lighthouse road until she admitted to and apologized for what she had done. I knew that she had tricked the English girl from Argyle into sitting on a bumblebee, but my loyalty was to Estelle.

"Want to wait for her?" I asked.

Estelle was indignant. "She's too slow!"

The desks in our one-room schoolhouse were two-seaters. Who did Estelle end up sitting with but Babette. My friend lasted exactly five minutes.

"Pee-ewe!" she exclaimed to the annoyed teacher, as she made her way towards the empty seat at my desk. "I want to sit with Zoé."

I didn't care much who I sat with, fascinated as I was with my new surroundings. The room was about thirty feet wide and forty feet long, with a stove in the middle of the room, a library of a few textbooks covered with the same oilcloth as that on our kitchen table, graffiti-strewn desks arranged in neat rows, and a clunky machine sitting on the teacher's desk. I gazed at the crank, noticed the big reel of tape and proudly informed Estelle, "It's a protractor. Pricille says it shows pictures about how to brush your teeth."

"A *projector!*" Estelle bellowed, so the older boys at the back of the room could hear her. *Les grands benaits.* There they were, the inseparables: Paul-Emile, blond and handsome, Mr. Charming, with the beguiling smile, and Cedric, tall and dark, Mr. Coy under a tuft of straight hair perpetually hanging in his eyes. It was rumoured that Cedric was as bad as Paul-Emile when they were together. *Y pouven fare sa part.*

"Zoé," Paul-Emile called, his mocking attention on me now, "aren't you gonna take your kerchief off?"

I felt my ears flush. I willed myself not to cry, fixing my stare on the teacher, an old madame with a friendly smile but stern, who scanned the back of the room as if welcoming the challenge of difficult boys.

"You can call me Madame Comeau," she announced, ignoring Paul-Emile's remark. "I'm here to teach. You're here to listen … and *work.*" She opened her folder and flashed holy cards of Saint Theresa and the Holy Family. "If I'm happy with your work, you'll get one of these." She also had sheets of shiny coloured stars, the reward for mediocre work I figured. She continued, "When I ring the bell, you girls and boys will leave the school in separate lines. And you'll raise your hand if you need to go to the *cabinet.* Is that understood?"

"*Oui, Madame,*" the younger ones harmonized.

"Fine," she smiled. "Now we'll begin with our prayer. *Je vous salut, Marie* …"

After the roll call, she zigzagged up and down the aisles to inspect for dirt under our fingernails and pass out cod liver oil pills. When she passed my desk, Estelle was at the back of the class pestering the boys and missed out on a pill.

"I want one!" she hollered, and the teacher turned in search of the source of the sassy voice.

"Estelle! Get back to your seat, and take that gum out of your mouth."

Used to ignoring orders, Estelle continued to chew. So she became the first to discover just how much the teacher loved to put children in the corner—directly in front of the class. Everyone had a clear view of the gum that Madame stuck on Estelle's nose. I threw an occasional furtive glance at the dreaded corner while I practised the fancy alphabet displayed at the top of the blackboard.

I had noticed at the outset that Estelle took an immediate dislike to Cedric, at his constant staring. By the time the bell rang, she had developed a terrible grudge against him, one that intensified when she stood in line and he snickered at her. Even amidst the noise and shoving, the teacher heard the loud smack and stood transfixed with her mouth half open.

"He lifted my dress!" blurted Estelle, now raised on her toes, trying to equal Cedric's height and ready to swing again.

"Hé!" yelled the distraught Madame, scowling at my friend. "I've never seen such a temper from a little girl." She turned her scowl to Cedric, "Nor such behaviour from a big boy. Twenty Our Fathers each, after school."

"I can't recite all that!" sobbed Estelle at recess. "I don't even know it by heart."

I sat snug to her, "You will by the time you're finished. Doesn't it go something like: *Forgive those who trespass against us?*" My gaze was frozen on the bright pink popcorn Estelle held in her hand.

She moved away from me to the edge of the step, sheepishly laying out the rules. "I'd give you some but my mother doesn't want me to." While she looked over, awaiting absolution, I fumbled in my pocket for my linty piece of toffee.

"I don't want any," I said, and she crunched in peace, as little girls also eyeing the popcorn brushed past her on their way out.

Uninterested in the recess snack, Babette wanted to play. "Hi," she said. Estelle only smirked at her uneven legs.

"Did you notice that her right leg is too short," she loudly remarked as Babette limped away, hurt and shunned.

"She had polio," I explained.

Estelle wrinkled her nose. "What's that?"

"It's a disease that makes your arms and legs short. And thin. Like spaghetti."

She moved next to me. "The real reason I didn't want to sit with Babette is because she stinks. I think she peed in her pants and some pee dripped in her shoe. That's why her leg is too short, it shrivelled up like a prune."

Estelle's comment provoked a fit of boisterous laughter between us, which lasted until we returned to the classroom. Madame quickly silenced us. "Stop that right now or I'll separate the two of you."

She turned her attention to the students of nine other grades and soon forgot about us. But we had not escaped Philippe's notice. I could tell he was angry by the dark stare he had fixed on us from across the room.

I lagged behind after school while Estelle recited her prayers, but when we left the grounds, my big brother was waiting by the road. He pinched my arm until I started to cry and confessed why we had been tittering.

"The next time, Mam' will know about your nasty mocking," he warned, releasing his threatening grip. He had witnessed my mother's temper.

Just the week before, she had overheard him imitating the other boys in the village. "Hi Bosco," he had called out to Estelle's father.

"His name's Basil!" Mam' had scolded from the kitchen window. "And that's what you'll call him." She had yanked Philippe into the house by the scruff of the neck and pulled out her "*palette*" from the warming oven. I imagined he gaped at the stick with terrible fear. Mam' didn't tolerate mockery.

Chapter 3

One Saturday at Estelle's, her mother warned, "Don't bother your father," as she headed for the backyard with her watering can. Estelle nodded, waited until her mother had disappeared past the side of the house, then motioned my way, "Hurry! *Décrasse toi!*"

We made a beeline for her father's boatshop and slid open the massive wooden door. Estelle poked her head in, chanced a peek, then yanked on my sweater until we neared the floor opening inside. Below, her father Basil and his men were caulking the underside of a thirty-eight footer.

It wasn't the first time that we had eavesdropped on grown-up conversations, not that two eight-year-olds understood much. We couldn't figure out why the mere mention of the word "Tories" could fire up such heated arguments, draw such fury from Basil. Who was Louis St. Laurent, the "good man" who he praised so much? One of his uncles, we assumed, because he often referred to him as Uncle Louis. Conversations in the boatshop were usually about hunting and fishing. We heard a whole lot of bragging about the longest fish or the biggest buck. What did it mean, to "jack a deer" with a flashlight?

Estelle knew. "The light blinds them and they can't move. And then *kabang*! Right between the eyes."

Often there escaped from below careless talk that stilled our breath. As a rule, gossip did not emanate from Basil's mouth, but this morning was an exception. I caught the whole ugly conversation.

"What a Jesus pest that Antoine is when he's been drinking. Him and his friggin' money. And jealous! I've never seen the likes. When he started talking about Martine with his dirty mouth, I bluntly told him, 'Watch your language around Estelle or get the hell out of my house.' "

Estelle turned to face me. "Wanna go to the Pointe?"

But I couldn't move, my senses were numb. "Why didn't you tell me?" I whispered between clenched teeth.

"Because I knew that Zita would get to your mother fast enough. Your father went to her house too."

The huge sliding door behind us opened. I found myself behind the pop cooler, not knowing how in the dickens Estelle got me there. "Ssh," she threatened. Heavy footsteps bypassed the cooler, moved towards the long ladder and down to the sunken pit. We crept back to the opening. There was a stranger, circling the thirty-eight footer.

"How much would this boat sell for?" he asked, catching Basil off guard.

"Euh ... you mean with engine, ready to fish?"

"Yeah."

Estelle's father paused. "Give or take thirteen hundred dollars. I can check the books."

"How long does it take to build a rig like this?" the outsider wanted to know.

"Oh, depends on the size, and how fancy the order is. This one will take about twenty-one days. It's the *maudit* finishing touches that take time." Basil offered a haughty grin. "We build the best boats in the Maritimes." He backed up his boast, pointing to the meticulous workmanship of his men, then invited the potential buyer aboard.

When the two headed for the ladder, Estelle and I rushed back behind the cooler but we had a good view. At the top of the ladder, Basil was scribbling in his notepad, adding yet another order to his list.

"Canopy or pilot house?" he needed to know.

The outsider narrowed his eyes. "What's the difference in price?"

"A hundred dollars more for a canopy."

"Nah. Pilot house."

"Pilot house," repeated Basil, contemplating a time frame. "If everything goes well, it should be ready in about four months." He extended a firm handshake and a friendly smile to the buyer from

Grand Manan, saw him to the door. He returned to the floor opening to holler to the men below, "I'm going to Lunenburg to pick up a stuffing box and an eight-by-eight for the stern post."

Estelle waited until the door of Basil's truck slammed shut. "Let's look for crab," she decided. I agreed and we ran off to solicit empty cans from her mother. On our way to the Pointe, she happened to notice a gathering on the wharf. Excitement was obviously brewing as we drew near.

"If Mam' sees me on the wharf," I fretted, but there was no changing Estelle's mind.

"That looks like Paul-Emile. Come on! I know it's him."

The excitement of the day was his doing all right—he had thrown his cat over the wharf where a flock of seagulls, pecking at fish and garbage from the ships, terrified the poor thing. It struggled to shore, where it swam right into Cedric's clutches. He delivered the frenzied cat back to Paul-Emile. Then the game started again, the more mischievous boys urging Paul-Emile on.

My brother André arrived in a huff. "You're not allowed on the wharf!"

"Just like you're not allowed in the cliffs!" I reminded the pest. He promptly joined the boys.

Estelle would have been right in there, one of the boys, if she hadn't heard the irate trot of rubber boots heading our way. "It's Gustave!" she exclaimed, and we both trembled at the fuming expression on his face. He would surely maim the rascals.

I caught Cedric's eye and let out a panicked cry, "*Run!*" He bolted, leaping over lobster traps, buoys and nets, with his irate father trailing behind.

"You'll get my number twelve boot in the ass if I can ever catch you," Gustave shouted. But Cedric's long-legged leaps carried him halfway up the hill while Gustave was still on the wharf, gasping. He wheeled around, ready to direct his threats at the scoundrel who had started it all. In a flash, Paul-Emile disappeared. Clearly, he was too foxy for a wheezing Gustave.

Her enthusiasm squelched, Estelle grudgingly walked to the Pointe. My fun finally began. Everywhere I looked, there were mounds of seaweed that the big winds had loosened from the rocks.

I uncovered endless bundles of the brown leafy fronds—I lived for dulse.

"Can you imagine Pricille here?" I shrilled, but Estelle was unimpressed. She choked on the stuff every time she ate it.

"You have to help look for crab," she charged, but I continued to stuff my face. She crossed her arms and posed the ultimate threat. "I'm going home!"

Reluctantly, I joined in the quest, lifting promising rocks and yelling excitedly each time I spotted a crab. "I got one! I got one!"

Estelle had just two tiny ones in her can. She watched my can fill, never at a loss for ideas as she leered at the eight big crawlers to my credit. She located a shallow saltwater pool and issued a new command for the game. "Let's dump them here," she ordered, "and they'll *all* be ours." She could now spare her two meagre ones for experiments.

"They can't walk without these," she determined, pulling the pincers off one of the creatures. She detached the shell from its body and we examined its innards. Nothing much to see. Having dismembered her two, Estelle's interest shifted. "Let's play hopscotch." She proceeded to stamp her rubber boot at random, crushing the remaining captives.

"Don't!" I pleaded, but she pursued the very last baby crustacean crawling for cover.

"Where do you think *you're* going?" she bellowed as she lifted a big rock at her feet. "There!" she asserted, mercilessly crushing the tiny victim to splatters. "Let's go."

The sand by the boatshop was hard, ideal for hopscotch. I drew the squares. Estelle went first. She tossed her stone about, hopping clumsily from square to square, unable to grab the stone but ignoring the rules. "That didn't count," she decided and took another turn.

"You walked on the line," I noted. She simply snubbed me. Now I was really angry: angrier than when she had ripped pages out of her mother's cookbook and blamed it on me; angrier than when she had pushed me into cow shit. I pointed to her sunken footprint on the line. "See!"

"That didn't count," she persisted cooly, and I stamped my feet all over the game, until there was no sign of hopscotch ever having existed.

"There!" I yelled in her ear. "Did that count?"

My arms swung wildly as I scrambled up the Cape road with the spoiled brat on my heels, flaming my fury with her name-calling.

"Skinny Minnie!"

"Sticks and stones will break my bones, but names will never hurt me," I retorted, now trotting up the hill with greater determination.

"Cod face," she hurled—the one taunt I couldn't bear. But I inhaled deeply and kept walking.

When she wouldn't let up with Cod face, there was one insult I knew would drive her mad. I howled it for the whole Cape to hear. "Blubber face!" I drove my index fingers in my ears, shutting out all sound as a sly Estelle crept up behind me. A tremendous shove from her solid frame pitched me violently onto the gravel shoulder. Something stung terribly. I covered my nose, and blood trickled through my fingers.

From the woodpile where Dad was chopping wood, he heard my screams. He had seen Estelle make haste past the corner of her house. "She's too rough for you!" he warned, before my full story came out, in stutters, between sobs. He handed me his scrunched navy polka dot handkerchief, which quickly soaked up the blood and ended my tears. With the hankie pressed to my nose, I sat on the woodpile and watched him split blocks of wood.

"Have you ever had a nosebleed?" I asked, and his grin returned. It was a special moment when he had my attention.

"No, but I broke my arm," he began.

"Arm! How old were you?"

"Nine."

"Can we go to Wedgeport for ice cream?" I interrupted. "It might make my nose feel better."

"Someday, when I buy a car," he smiled in a firm promise. He returned to the tale of his misadventure. As a boy, he had played in a spacious treehouse that dominated the leaning oak tree on the side of his home. "My father made it with scraps of wood from the sawmill and painted it white. My dog Wimpy and I lived in it, waiting for Dad's beam trawler to return from the Grand Banks, sometimes Georges Bank. If the trawler unloaded in Shelburne or in Lunenburg, he brought me something. I had asked for a pair of black rubber boots with red soles like my brother Joseph wore."

Dad paused, driving me mad with curiosity. "Did you get your boots?"

His blue eyes saddened. "No."

"Why not?"

"One day, a stranger arrived at the house. I was in my treehouse, but I could tell something was wrong after my mother came to the door. The man was doing all the talking. She just stood there, crying. I slipped on a rung of the ladder coming out of my treehouse and down I came, landed right on my arm." My father raised his axe, sighed in the middle of his story. "That's how I broke my arm."

"Did it hurt?"

"A bit."

"Well my nose hurts a lot!" I asserted. "What was your mother crying about?"

Dad wedged his axe in a stump and his far-away gaze rolled sideways to look at me. "She learned my father was sick with pneumonia for three days before the boat he fished on made it to port. Mam' went to the Shelburne Inn to see him, but he hardly recognized her, couldn't even put his papers in order. Three hours later, he died."

"Did your mother die too?" I asked.

He grinned, excusing the innocence of my query by pointing next door to where Grand-mère Sophie lived with my step Grand-père Dominique. "You know who my mother is."

Mam' stepped out of the house; I was thankful she hadn't heard my dumb question. Worn out with fatigue, her patience did not accommodate stupidity.

"What happened to you?" she asked, drawing my hand away from my face.

Just then, the meat truck stopped at the driveway. I didn't have time for her inspection. I had to get my free hot dog and ask the nice meatman, "Do you have pig's feet?"

"Yes," he smiled, anticipating my weekly punch line.

"Then it must be hard for you to walk."

He chuckled, stroked my hair. I wondered why he didn't ask about my blood-soaked handkerchief. Instead, he turned to Mam'. "How you feelin', Martine?"

She glanced towards the woodpile, fearful that my father might accuse her of being gone too long. "Pretty good," she replied hastily, then stuck her head inside the meat cabin.

I stiffened, terrified that the smell of raw meat would make her vomit. She wasn't "pretty good." Sometimes she was so nauseated that she didn't care about the housework, or her looks. Zita claimed that Mam' was skin and bones, except for her bulging stomach—another baby on the way. The scoop-neck, flared house-dresses that Mam' wore did not flatter her. The straps of this dress were falling off her thin shoulders. A few religious medals were pinned to the dress, drawing looks from the meatman as she withdrew her head from the cabin.

"Nice mincemeat today," he mentioned, but she declined a treat that was strictly reserved for Christmas pies. She settled on four pounds of baloney wrapped in waxed paper.

That evening, she didn't touch her supper, collapsing instead on the couch while Don Tremaine and Rube Hornstein gave the news and weather on TV—the one commodity we children had fought hard for. Mam' had sacrificed her much needed baby bonuses, tired of hearing Zita complain because we were always at her door, wanting to watch TV.

Pricille was now washing the dishes, having observed Mam' long enough to know the procedure. She swept the kitchen floor, then melted lard on a rag and polished the stove until she could see her face in the shine. She wiped the dirty marks off the cupboards. Mam' pointed to those on the walls.

"Okay now?" Pricille asked, but my mother's brow remained furrowed with some unspoken displeasure.

When bedtime beckoned me up the attic stairs, Dad grinned his *bonsoir*. Mam' *bonsoir* lurked somewhere behind her gaze that darted about the kitchen. What didn't suit her this time?

Chapter 4

The nosebleed incident was long forgotten. Mam's banishment of Estelle didn't matter to Dad. He dared argue with her, "Zoé's a kid. Leave her alone!"

I stood on Grand-mère's lupin bank where Estelle could see me. She waved. I waved back. In a flash, she was up the hill, a smirk setting off her mischievous dimples as she chewed a hot dog.

Grand-père Dominique approached the bank at his usual plodding pace, arms crossed behind his back and shoulders slouched forward, giving the impression he'd fall flat on his face if anyone nudged him, despite his overweight stature. But today his face wasn't twisted by pain, as on foggy days when his bones hurt.

"I'll be darned," Estelle observed, "he even has a smile for us."

Grand-père loved to brag about his full set of teeth—he claimed he never used toothpaste. His smile supported his story. His uneven teeth had outlived their yellow days and had turned a scummy brown. His round, wire-rimmed glasses suited his chubby face, distracted one from his dull eyes. His nose wasn't spread across his face too badly. When his mouth was closed, Grand-père Dominique was not ugly. But there was no trace of him ever having been handsome either.

He shuffled towards Estelle and me, grumbling about Zita and her paintbrush. "Every summer, she paints those front steps. She's gonna wear them out."

Grand-père shuffled through life grumbling—about the price of meat, damned kids, the fog, Zita across the road—about every-thing and every one. Mam' blamed the grumbling on arthritis aches and pains, but Grand-mère Sophie claimed he had always been a miserable old man, the very quality that intrigued Estelle. Her grand-père was too nice. She couldn't get him angry, unlike Dominique, who often fumed at her mere presence.

This time she jeered at his hair, which was always cropped too short, especially at the back, where Mam' had zigzagged her blunt clipper unsparingly across the nape of his neck. Estelle couldn't help staring.

In return, Grand-père stared back at her, but for another reason. He was obviously delighted that she, too, dared defy the church's forbidding laws, foolish in his eyes. Who else but Estelle would feast on raw hot dogs on a Friday? *En plein venderdi*. He ate meat whenever he felt like it.

My favourite church law came straight from God Himself: we shouldn't desire our neighbour's stuff. As for me, I had never once wished for Estelle's red bicycle. And when she retrieved a candy from her pocket to follow her hot dog lunch, I moved closer, but only to see the wrapper—a Sweet Marie for a nasty Estelle. She smacked her lips in my face, savouring each bite with hoggish "uuummms" in my ear.

I made sure Mam' wasn't within hearing range before I glanced humbly at Grand-père. "I don't suppose you'd have a nickel?"

"No I don't," he grunted, scowling like a miser, but unable to look me in the eye. His hands jingled the change in his pockets, as he carried on towards the old homestead.

"A few pennies?" I pleaded, but he shuffled along in silence.

Estelle rolled her eyes, pointing at his clothes, which were disordered and wrinkled, as if he had slept in them. I loved his overalls. They made him look like a Grand-père.

When he reached the corner of his house, he paused to glance towards the wharf and inhale deeply, sucking sunny air into his musty lungs. Hands still in his pockets, he sheepishly looked back at me, then disappeared into the house. If he had change to jingle, it was reserved for my older brother Philippe, the only one who could bring a gleam to the old man's dull eyes.

I, too, glanced towards the wharf, spotting Gustave and Cedric bent over their driveway, busy spreading moss to dry on such a fine day.

"Want to go watch them?" I asked, but Estelle wrinkled her nose. Too boring. "Then can we look for crab?"

"Nah." She didn't want to. Her focus was on the old homestead. A smile filled her mischievous eyes. "I have an idea!"

My grandparents' house was long because of the shed and far pantry attached to it. The shed was used for storing wood for the winter. It came in handy for muffling the sounds of two little girls sneaking into Grand-mère Sophie's pantry. I loved her store-bought cookies, with jelly and coconut in the middle. Estelle loved her stew meat. The carnivore ate chunks of it raw, but gagged at the sight of butter on her bread.

"Gluttons," Grand-père Dominique grumbled to Sophie. "*Une bande de haglettes.*" But he couldn't keep us away. It was too easy to slink into their pantry.

Sneaking up to their big attic was a different story because we had to pass through the kitchen. "Let me think," muttered Estelle. In a matter of seconds she had a plan. There was a small room adjacent to the pantry, with a door to the outside and a set of stairs leading to a small attic, partitioned from the big attic by a lath wall. There was nothing up there of interest: broken chairs, twisted bicycle wheels, sharp pieces of window pane. But on the edge of a step sat a Flit gun.

The old stairs creaked under Estelle's weight.

"Shh," I fretted. "Grand-père will kill us."

She pointed to the Flit gun. "I'm gonna knock this over. Wait for me outside."

The diversion worked beautifully. The hand-pump fly-sprayer plunged to the floor, and Estelle made her getaway outside. Our ears pressed to the door, we heard the stairs creak again, this time under Grand-père's heavy frame.

"You laid it too close to the edge," he growled at Sophie.

"*By the farnell,*" were her curse words and the last thing we heard as Estelle and I raced to the other side of the house, where there was another outside door with access to the kitchen. We stealthily climbed the stairs leading to the big attic, our favourite hideaway.

The house was at least a hundred years old. I knew all about the wooden pegs securing the posts and beam. "Stronger than spikes," Dad had assured me, emphasizing their strength. Joseph and he had weathered many wicked hurricanes in this attic.

Fragments of wallpaper dangled from the lath wall dividing the two attics; lumps protruded from the sloppy job of a gooey paste mixture. To a rafter were nailed tattered pictures of Marilyn Monroe, Judy Garland, and other half-naked female idols. These looked *maladroit* pinned next to an icon of Saint Theresa, the patroness of the household.

Everywhere we dug, there was a hint of l'Acadie. With an old spinning wheel, a butter churn, a rattan carriage, and a washboard, we set up housekeeping. We rummaged through cardboard boxes of abandoned clothes and hats from Boston. Estelle laid claim to a hooped skirt and a "cancan," a triple layer of white net, enough to make the skirt flare delightfully.

"Look Zoé!" She swung round and round like the girls on TV in "Country Hoedown," stirring up settled dust. "Holy Cow!"

My interest was captured by the agitated dust that streaked across the sunlit attic, just like the dust the projector made at the movies, Estelle said. Someday I would go to the movies. When I got big. Like Pricille.

There was an old mirror hanging on a nail which distorted our faces. The more we grimaced, the uglier we became, and the more we had to muffle our giggling.

Grand-mère Sophie's cedar chest interested me most. It held prized possessions that small hands had no business touching. I scanned the boarded attic walls, afraid they might somehow reveal to her that I had opened it. Folded neatly across the top was a colourful, nine-point star quilt. I examined the fine stitching of my great-grandmother's last quilt, so special to Grand-mère Sophie.

I reached down for the box that contained cards from Tante Marceline—the prettiest Christmas and Easter cards, always with lengthy verses, but who cared what they said. There was a secret compartment in the box with cards, a hiding place for Grand-mère's American money. Although we held the strange dollars, we were careful to put everything back in its place.

We didn't dare jump on the beds again. That *faux pas* had hastened Grand-père Dominique up the stairs the last time. Besides, the mattresses were falling apart, one of them a *paillasse*, its flour-bag covering torn, exposing the straw stuffing. Three others were made of feathers, also traps for fleas, according to Mam' who repeatedly warned Dominique, "God help you if the fire ever took up there."

He would just grumble back at her. "Everything up there is good."

There was an antique bureau, with photographs in the top drawer: one of a young Tante Marceline, a yellowed one from Grand-mère Sophie and Grand-père Dominique's wedding that I had seen a million times. Estelle focused on the spats on Dominique's wedding shoes, while I concentrated on a photo of a young N'Oncle Joseph wearing rubber boots on his small feet—likely black with red soles. Tall Dad sported thick wavy hair packed on the top of his head with the sides shaved flat, just as he still wore it, but his hair wasn't white then. His smile displayed a full set of teeth—he once had teeth.

Judging from photos of a young Grand-mère Sophie, it was almost as if she had never changed. Even as a young woman, she was heavy with sparse hair, flabby jowls, although she didn't have stovepipe legs. There was not one picture of N'Oncle Louis; his name was an echo with no face.

There were cut-out cartoons of the Gumps, reminders of the old, old days—something from N'Oncle Joseph's newspaper run. As the first newsboy on the Cape, he had charged three cents for the *Halifax Herald*.

There were records in the dresser drawer warped into the shape of Christmas ribbon candies—seventy-eights of Jimmie Rodgers' hobo and yodel songs—definitely something from my father's past. I picked the least warped of the discs, placed it on the old gramophone nearby and cranked. The sound was hardly audible, so muffled that we couldn't make out the words.

"We can sharpen the needle," I suggested. I told Estelle how Dad sharpened his razor blades. Holding them tight between his index finger and the inside of a glass, he rubbed back and forth.

She rolled her eyes right across their sockets. "And get the glass where? I would imagine they keep them in the kitchen."

I reached for a jar full of buttons. "Why wouldn't this work?" I lifted the gramophone's tone arm to pry the needle loose, but it broke off, lodging in my finger. "*Yoye!*" I started to cry.

Estelle's shallow compassion was absorbed in frantic nerves. "If you don't shut up ..." she threatened, grabbing my wounded thumb. She pulled the needle fragment from my skin. "Two drops of blood and you have to cry. *Pire qu'un bibi.*"

She lent her ear to the stovepipe, sighed with relief at the safe sound of Grand-père's voice in the kitchen below, grumbling about the roof, as usual. She gestured for me to move closer to listen. Grand-mère Sophie wanted it fixed. Grand-père Dominique couldn't have cared less if it fell on his head. A boring discussion for Estelle and me.

But that was not always the case. The two were not immune to gossip. They had their share of contaminating the village with it and using undue exaggeration to embellish their stories. They loved to unmask other people's closet skeletons. With our ears glued to that very stovepipe, Estelle and I had learned that Zita across the road once had a husband. Mam' was enraged when I told her, claiming Grand-père Dominique would do better to clean his own backyard before cleaning Zita's. By the fury in Mam's eyes, I knew better than to mention that he had said all *she* was good for was shining her stove and having babies. If I had snitched, Grand-père would have been pedalling his bike to the barber in Meteghan.

I pulled back from the infamous stovepipe and drew a long sigh, fretting to Estelle, "What now?" We weren't going anywhere, not until she came up with another plan to distract Grand-père Dominique away from the kitchen so we could make our escape.

Chapter 5

M am' called Grand-père Dominique downright low to have
told the men at the garage that Zita's husband had fled on
their wedding night. She judged it a sacrilege that he dared
speculate as to why the poor woman never approached the altar to
receive Holy Communion. "There's gossip and there's gossip," she
said. I understood from the rebuke in her sunken eyes that Grand-
père Dominique's gossip was not nice. But neither was Zita's, who
went around saying, "The old grump would do better to fix his house
than to spend his time counting his money." She was not the least
inhibited to add, "Sophie only married him because there was no
widow's allowance when her husband died."

Nonetheless, the old grump did hang a swing for me in his
workshop, a shingled shed that stood a few yards from the old homestead, providing shelter from the drizzle and fog. There my father
spent his idle hours, whittling on blocks of wood while I watched,
swinging until I felt nauseated. Then I would jump down from the
swing and kneel next to him. On the rare sunny days, he whittled
outside so we could observe the goings-on at the wharf.

There was a slight problem with the shed. Estelle wasn't
allowed inside it, but that only set her dimples in a more defiant
smirk to chance the odds of getting in. One day, Grand-père
Dominique had barely made his exit from the shed when Estelle
burst in, forcing me off my swing. "Once I've recited the alphabet,"
she promised, "you can have it." I fell for it. How long could she
stretch the A.

I slapped her bare leg. "I don't have until Christmas!"

She shortened the B, hastened through to Z, but of course had deliberately left out an R, rushing through Q-S-T. "I have to start again," she argued. I let her drawl another alphabet. This time she missed the N and the O.

I gave the swing a sharp jerk. "That spells *no!* Now get off!"

"You get it all the time!" she yelled.

Her pout did not persuade me. I shoved her off, "Whose swing is it?"

"Mean shit," she fumed.

I charged right back with the reliable standby, "Takes one to know one."

And then her usual threat, "I'm going home!"

"Then go!"

She caught sight of a menacing form in the doorway and had some quick manoeuvring to do. In her haste, she almost knocked over Grand-père Dominique. He couldn't run worth a scare, but he always grabbed the closest maiming object when he chased kids off his property. This time it was a pitchfork. Safely at the road, Estelle turned her chubby face and pitched her infamous sass at Grand-père Dominique:

Dominique. Dominique.
Ha. Ha. Tic. Tic.
Dominique. Dominique.
Mon craaazy luna-Tic.

Now at the foot of the driveway, his blasphemous grumble was wasted, for Estelle was far down the Cape road. While his attention was on Estelle, I fled home, trembling behind closed curtains.

A week went by. I was sitting at the kitchen table, colouring, when I heard Grand-père Dominique's loud rap at the door. Arms crossed behind his back, hands clutching his cap, he shuffled inside. "Your mother home?" The gruff tone melted a crayon in my clenched fist.

Mam's face fell at the unexpected sight of him. "I just *cut* your hair, a week ago!"

I thought Grand-père had surely come to tell on me and Estelle. He took a seat at the kitchen table and leaned back, hands fisted in the bib of his overalls. He opened with idle chit-chat. "We had salted cod ears with pork scraps." The glutton let out a succession of belches. *"D'la graisse de lârd."* Mam' winced. She could hardly stomach half a can of Campbell's tomato soup, let alone his crude manners.

Grand-père Dominique grumbled about the kids stealing Sophie's lupins. I kept my nose in my colouring book, at ease because it wasn't me. I didn't want her lupins; they smelled like dead people. He asked if we had his hammer. We did. The next unrelated burning issue was that Tante Marceline wanted to get them a telephone. He grumbled about that and then arrived, finally, at the real point of his visit. "I wonder if you could call the Harringtons for a cord of wood?"

As if Mam' had heard my sigh of utter relief, she shot a glance my way. "I'll go over to Zita's and call."

At the mention of Zita's name, Grand-père Dominique unloaded his annoyance at Zita, at *yielle*, because she was always at his door begging for the church. Though he never fell short of his ten cents in the collection box every Sunday, he begrudged any extra dimes solicited. When he opened his mouth wide to continue his rant and raise his voice, I saw his ugly brown teeth. "This morning, she was at the door again, for a family in Mavillette whose house burned down. I told her I didn't have any change."

Mam' had spared our last dollar for the cause. Her reprimanding stare towards Grand-père didn't intimidate him, nor did it shift his hands out of his jingling pockets as he shuffled towards the door. The determination of the old man to hold onto his nickels and dimes was summed up in his parting grumble. "Who do they think I am, Vendor Bill?"

In spite of occasional rude receptions like those she received from Grand-père Dominique, Zita loved collecting for various causes. It got her into people's homes. She'd report everything to Mam'. One story was particularly interesting to me. *A yâ toute conté.* "Charlotte and Basil had a riproaring fight about Estelle. I tell you, that one runs the house. Tells them to shut up. Now if that were my kid ..."

Just then, Pricille squeaked by in the shiniest pair of patent leather high heels, having finished polishing the stove, a last-minute chore.

"What's on the flannelette rag?" Zita was curious to know.

"Melted lard," Pricille replied. Zita threw a scowl at the freshly polished stove. The secret for everything shiny around here, she deduced.

She frowned at my sister's evening dress, designed more for one of Tante Marceline's festive galas than for a night out at the Cape. Zita examined the exquisite nylon fabric of the pale blue dress from Boston, rather low-cut at the neck. My sister's face was glowing. Unbeknownst to Zita, Pricille was wearing a brassière for the first time, fastened at the back with a safety pin.

"Where are you going?" Zita inquired.

My sister swung her long, black ponytail sideways. "To the Diner," she announced matter-of-factly, "for an ice cream." Grabbing her coat, she was out the door before she called back, "I'll be home by nine."

Once she left, Mam' got Zita's full sermon that predictably began with the gossip's favourite four words, "When we were young ..."

I had heard this one before. Their dresses had to hide their shins. "And let me tell you," Zita was sure to press home, "we weren't going to no diner at fourteen years old. I was nineteen, and at ten o'clock, Dad started clearing his throat. Tommy à Elisée was my boyfriend back then. He had to leave." She paused for air, gaped at Mam'. "Did you know they have dances at the Diner now? Oh, yeah. They built a hall at the back. That's what draws the boys from all over hell's half acre." Zita wore a busybody's look of deduction. "God only knows what goes on at that Diner."

Mam's face paled, as it did every night after supper when the urge to vomit struck her. Her elbows resting on the table, she supported her head in her hands.

"I have to let you go to bed," Zita realized. She made my father grin when she brushed past his rocking chair with the closing last words, "Not like when we were young, eh Antoine?"

After she was gone, he glanced over at Mam'. "If Tommy à Elisée had to leave at ten, he came back through the window."

Mam', now flaked out on the couch, scowled. "What Zita did when she was young doesn't concern me."

"Why don't you go to bed?" Dad urged. "Don't you worry

none. Zita will be watching for Pricille."

Sure enough, early next morning, the gossip was back at the house. She had seen Pricille come home the night before—in a strange car. She had other pressing news, anxious to draw Mam's attention away from the mackerel she was fixing. Stealthily, she advanced into the kitchen, stretching her neck over the sink. "Have you heard?"

Mam' laid her knife down, irritated by Zita's game. "Have I heard what?"

Catching sight of André and me, Zita lowered her tone, revealed the scandal. "Her daughter's pregnant!" Instead of using names, she pointed to the house on the hill. "Now what do you think of that?"

What did Mam' think of that? She drew a *chopine* of cold water, rinsed her bloodied hands. "Zita," she said, as she dug her dripping left hand into her side, "I have a teenage daughter." With her right hand, she guessed at my height. "And a little girl only this tall, but growing up fast." She then patted her bulging stomach. "And who knows, maybe a third daughter soon." As if Zita wasn't humiliated enough, Mam' was not intimidated to add, "I can't afford to spit in the air. It may fall on my nose."

Zita backed away from the sink, her face as red as the geraniums in Charlotte's backyard. She had no trouble finding the door.

When she next visited, she needed a cup of sugar. Another day, she brought over her expired Eaton's and Simpson's catalogues for our outhouse and unloaded on Mam' her worries about her ailing mother, who seemed to have everything wrong with her.

When the cold and the snow arrived, she came by every day, sometimes twice a day. And when Mam's due date slipped by on the calendar, Zita practically lived at our house, trying to cheer her up. "That baby's just not in any hurry."

Mam' paced the floor and ate chalk by the dozen to relieve her heartburn. She and Dad waited. Zita waited. All of us children waited. Impatiently. But nothing happened, and Mam' turned into a Bolshevik, an extremist. She became nauseous from Dad's constant trail of cigarette smoke and ordered him to smoke outside or not at all, so he smoked in Dominique's shed.

When I spilt milk on her clean floor before bedtime, she raged that I didn't act my age. "A nine-year-old would be more careful," she scolded.

"A nine-year-old shouldn't have to go to bed until nine," I foolishly argued. "Estelle doesn't have to."

"Well you're not Estelle!" she snapped, her anxious eyes fixed on the clock. She bent forward, suddenly gasping, as if she had severe cramps. "To bed!" she ordered, and I knew I wasn't getting my slice of bread and molasses.

Zita showed me to the stairs, but ordered Pricille, "You stay here. We'll be needing you."

I needed Pricille, too. Without the warmth of her body, I couldn't go to sleep. There was too much commotion in the kitchen below; someone had just come in. I lent my ear to the stovepipe. My brothers. Zita went home. Some time passed. When I heard more commotion, this time from across the road, I ran to the attic window. It was my father, banging on Zita's door. I lifted the window a crack so I could hear what he was hollering.

"*As-tu callé l' docteur? Martine en fait d'aour son bibi.*" Had she called the doctor? When he ran back across the road, across our lawn, he failed to stoop. The clothesline seized him at the throat, throwing him down, and he struck the back of his head on the icy ground.

Zita followed, *à la grand race*, out of breath. "Are you trying to kill yourself? *Mon Djeu du ciel. Assaie-tu te tuer?*"

She must have helped him into the house. I snuck down to the foot of the stairs, saw him stagger to his rocking chair. A small crack at the hall door let me see and hear everything in the kitchen. Zita was tearing around, boiling a large kettle of water, balancing an armful of towels to the bedroom off the kitchen. Wasn't Mam' going to the hospital? My eyes grew big, scared. Why wasn't she getting ready to leave?

I heard a car. Docteur Theriault burst into the kitchen. "Where is she?"

In there, my father motioned with a hand gesture, still stunned from the fall. He wasn't frantic like the voices in the bedroom, where everyone was talking at once, until the doctor got the story straight. He took over. He was surely talking to Mam'. "It'll be quick. You have your babies like rabbits." He chuckled, but in another breath, started barking orders for Mam' to inhale deeply and to push.

I was terrified. From the moaning and rapid panting, it seemed like Mam' couldn't breathe. And then she yelled back at the doctor, "I can't push!"

"Yes you can!" he assured her, but she wasn't minding him because he began to plead with her, like one does with a child. "Come on, Martine. It won't be long now. Just a few big pushes and it'll be over." The coaxing lasted until he lost his patience. "You can do better than that!"

I held my breath, expecting a scream of rebuke from my irate Mam', but there were long seconds of silence and then a faint whimper, a tiny moan, so helpless that it was barely audible, followed by a feeble whining—nothing like the strong bellows that Mam' said the rest of us let out when we were born, assuring her of our healthy arrivals.

"A girl!" someone called from the bedroom.

I could see my father in his rocking chair, the wide grin on his face as the doctor finally returned to the kitchen. "Another girl!" On his way out, he reassured my father. "They're both very tired, but all right."

I widened the crack at the door for Dad to hear me. "Can I see our new baby?"

Pricille came out of the bedroom with bloody sheets that she stuffed into the washing machine. "Come on," she urged, then grabbed my arm and led me to my mother, to our new baby. She had such a tiny face, and oh so white, white as a ghost. I caressed her head and her teeny-weeny feet.

"Three girls and three boys," Dad grinned, now standing at the foot of the bed. But my mother's glare made any further advance too intimidating. He didn't embrace her as fathers did on TV when their wives had new babies. Instead, he backed away, looking quizzically at Mam', looking at the baby, looking back at Mam', finally moving aside so that Zita could finish her business.

"Have a good rest, Martine," she ordered. "I'll be back

tomorrow. Okay?"

Mam' didn't answer. I followed Dad back to the kitchen, then watched him pile blocks of wood into the stove—enough to last until morning. His happy grin gone; he gazed out the kitchen window for a long time, looking at what? the solitary light on the wharf? All the houses were asleep. He glanced towards the bedroom as if mustering the courage to go back in, but he went no farther than the doorjamb, perhaps hopeful that Mam' would welcome him in, where he belonged. "You need me for anything?" he asked. She didn't answer.

Mam' didn't like our new baby. I could tell. She avoided the tiny face. She sobbed softly, with her head snug against the infant. Maybe she wanted a boy. I ran up the stairs and pulled the covers over my head. I sobbed too, until I heard Dad's weary footsteps shuffle up the stairs. I followed his silhouette across the moonlit attic. He sat on the side of a bed and lit up a smoke. My brothers clamoured for the news. "A little girl," he told them. "*Une 'tite fille.*"

"Yuk!" André uttered, his disappointment genuine. He had wanted a boy. There was no comment from Philippe and Pierre. In no time the boys were asleep. My father lit another cigarette, then another. My tired eyes followed the red tip of yet another one. He wasn't going to sleep.

Chapter 6

By the time my brothers thundered down the stairs, Dad and Pricille were already up.

"Hurry, Zoé!" urged Pierre, but I counted each stair, purposely stalling on my way down. I had already seen our new baby—the scrawny legs hanging limp from a fat diaper, and the tiny fingers no bigger than my doll's. Like all babies. But the babies I had seen before always moved their arms—when they cried from colic, when their siblings goo-gooed at them, or simply because they loved to wave their limbs about.

Our baby's arms didn't work, and her lips were waxen, like Père Lucien's altar candles. They were such thin lips, translucent, as if there were no flesh underneath the skin. Her eyes were lifeless, showed no interest in the brothers and sisters crowded into the room.

My oldest brother Philippe stood with his back firm against the wall, an icy stare directed at Mam', then at the rest of us, as if to give warning, "This is no bouncing baby girl."

André, well, he had wanted a boy. He threw a last quick glance, then headed off to school. He had important business to discuss with Cedric. The "Commandoes" were building a treehouse that was sure to become the envy of all the boys on the Cape, especially the scoundrel who had fired his BB gun through the pantry window when Mam' was crinkling the edges of her pie crusts. He swore that he was aiming at the pies; she claimed he was aiming at her. Whichever the case, Paul-Emile wouldn't be allowed anywhere near the treehouse, and especially nowhere near our new baby.

"Why is she so small?" Pierre asked as he stood at the foot of

Mam's bed, waiting for the answer she didn't have. He hastened to the kitchen window. Had the boats gone out? If the *Little Esther* was among them, then my father certainly wasn't on board. Mam' felt that he would be more useful out fishing, but soothed by the heat of the stove, Dad wasn't moving. The raw wind that constantly blew over the wintry ocean numbed his face and made his eyes water, was merciless on frozen fingers in wet mittens and on feet in threadbare woollen socks chafing against icy rubber boots. Then there was the chill of stiff overalls against bare flesh. No, not today. He wasn't going out fishing.

Pricille was the one needed at home. Zita was showing her how to bathe the baby. The retired nurse was a pro at delicate details. "Make sure all creases are free of lint, and that you remove the blanket fluff from between the toes and fingers. Rub a bit of baby oil where the skin is parched and peeling. Like this." Our baby was growing a belly button. Zita knew how to dab it with alcohol. "Pee-ewe," she jested, smelling between the tiny toes. "They stink!" But my baby sister just lay limp in her arms. Zita goo-gooed at her as she removed the "*crottes de poules*" from the corners of her eyes, but all she got was a glazed stare. Nobody expected a smile just yet, but surely the movement of an arm, anything to indicate the infant was alive.

Pricille didn't need guidance with household chores; she already knew how to keep Mam's kitchen immaculate. She knew how to bake bread—batches of golden brown loaves, fragrant when steaming from the oven. We all plastered molasses onto thick slices and ate heartily, except for Mam'.

"Rest and eat to get your strength back," Docteur Theriault prescribed. But how could she rest with this baby, an around-the-clock worry? As for eating, she had skipped so many breakfasts that she vomited the first one Pricille put before her, a thin slice of toast and half a cup of lukewarm tea.

"I have to get up," my mother insisted. She seemed determined to breast-feed, thinking her milk might give the infant strength. She attempted to raise herself to a sitting position but grimaced from the pain. Falling back into bed, she sighed in frustration. "I was never this feeble with my other babies."

"Because you were never this run-down," Zita reproached. "Forget about breast-feeding."

Mam' modified her attempt to force food down that tiny gullet—with a spoon, drop by drop, the only way she could get the infant to swallow any milk at all. "She only takes an ounce all night," she reported to the doctor, "and not much more during the day."

The baby was unresponsive, except for a few soft whimpers when Docteur Theriault undressed her in the cold bedroom, poking at her to draw life. Mam' searched his face for expression. "Can we talk in private?" he asked, scanning all the faces in the room. Zita booted us children into the kitchen where we waited, patiently, for the doctor to leave. Mam' was as white as her bedsheets.

"Well. What did he say?" Zita probed.

"Something about her blood," Mam' replied. "Red blood cells." Zita understood that the poor prognosis of our baby involved the Rh factor and a reaction with antibodies. Mam' was thoroughly confused. "He said not to force her to eat."

On the way to school, I told Estelle, "Our baby doesn't have any red in her blood. That's why she's white. And she doesn't want her milk. She chokes and rolls her eyes."

"Then she'll never grow big!" Estelle maintained. "She needs pablum. That's what babies eat."

I told Mam', "The baby has to eat!" But she just stared, her eyes vacant. I couldn't encourage her to do anything. "Take the baby to see Estelle's mother," I suggested, but she said no, the baby might catch cold. I took it upon myself to invite Charlotte. "Aren't you coming to see our baby?"

She did come by, but took a quick peek and cowered, as if the baby had the plague. Cedric's mother, Lina, reacted the same way. There wasn't any of the usual jibber-jabber about babies and diaper rashes, how much milk our girl took, or if she slept all night. Weren't they interested?

Only blind Emma wanted to know everything. Who did the baby resemble, how much did she weigh? I knew the answers to both questions: She looked like a ghost, and she didn't weigh anything.

She could have fit inside a shoe box, though Mam' never left her alone long enough for Estelle and me to check it out.

Babette sat her mother, Emma, next to Mam's bed so she could stroke the baby's tiny feet, but her sightless eyes couldn't see the infant's face, and Mam' wouldn't let her draw any nearer. Emma handed me two tiny undershirts decorated with little pink lambs. I took them out of the plastic, examining them. Unless our baby decided to eat, she would be ready for school before they'd fit her. I played with the baby's things at some distance from Babette. Estelle had said that if I played with Babette, I might catch polio and end up with a short leg and a limp. I didn't even say good-bye when she left. She guided her mother to the door, and then turned around like a little lady, "You have a pretty baby girl."

N'Oncle Joseph and Tante Rosalie dropped by with a gift that was sure to bring a glow to Mam's eyes—a nylon christening dress and lacy bonnet. Mam' asked them to call Tante Marceline in Boston and tell her that we had a new baby girl, doing just fine. Tante Rosalie offered to look after us children, and my mother's eyes turned misty. "With your 'click' of ten at home, you have your hands full."

"Don't worry about the children," Zita intervened, "I can handle them."

"But you have your mother to look after," Mam' fretted.

Zita smiled in a most determined way. "That's why they're coming to my house."

Terror! We were hers to discipline as she pleased. The first morning, we were barely out of bed when she started nagging. "Pricille, those pants are too tight for school.... Philippe, it's too cold for no long johns." Pierre was doubly pestered. "Stay clear of that wharf, and stop licking your plate!... André, stop making Zoé laugh at the table.... No, Zoé, you can't go home just yet."

Zita's mother made me cringe. Estelle and I figured that the old lady must be a hundred. Her spine was curved and she wore ugly brown elastic stockings. We had seen her bare legs. They were scary, with purple veins popping out like grapes where they met in clumps.

The old lady sat handy to the window, with her legs elevated, checking out the villagers walking up the Cape road. She gossiped about all of them, even those who paid her regular visits. Emma Goodwin was the sweetest woman on the Cape, yet the old gripe found plenty wrong with her. Her dresses were either too long or too short, she shouldn't own a cat, and she depended on Babette far too much. Yet if Babette happened to walk up the Cape road, the old woman complained, "Why isn't she at home helping her mother?"

If Zita was a gossip, she had come by it honestly. La Caquette, as she was known, had taught her well. She cackled continuously. She wasn't fussy about us children either, though she let Zita bark the orders.

Estelle advised, "Zita's crazy. Go home if you want." She and I trailed behind the others after school, walking up the path to my house. More quiet than a mouse, I opened the door and walked gingerly across the kitchen floor.

"*C'est Zoé et Estelle,*" I called. Silence. I ordered Estelle to wait at the door, then advanced into the bedroom. Mam' looked like she hadn't slept for a decade, though she had regained her strength; she was back to eating potatoes and fish and *fricot* that Zita brought over. The baby was bundled in a blanket that I loosened when I drew near. "Would you like Estelle to come see you?" I asked her, as I looked up at Mam'. "Can she?"

Immediately, Estelle wanted to know everything—why the baby wasn't in her crib, why she was fed with a spoon, and why she was so white. I walked her right back to the kitchen. "You wait here."

I returned to Mam', saw the tears that had spilled from her eyes. "Zita said the doctor doesn't know what he's talking about," I tried to comfort her. But she rocked back and forth as she stroked the baby's hollow cheeks.

She raised her head and gave a long, hard stare towards the window before she turned, focusing her sunken eyes on me. "How I wish Zita was right."

I was too distraught to cry, too angry. The top of the baby's bureau was bare, save for a bottle of Vaseline, two safety pins, and a diaper. "Where's the teddy bear that Estelle gave us? The fuzzy blanket that Zita got from Yarmouth? The bonnets and sweaters that Lina and Charlotte knit? The ..." I opened all three drawers.

All in there, out of sight, out of mind. The christening dress was still in the box. I raised my eyes to Saint Theresa who was holding roses and smiling at me.

"I don't like it at Zita's," I said flatly.

Mam' dried her eyes. "You want to come home?"

"Yes. I'm scared of her mother."

Her attention taken away from the baby, she smiled. "Why?"

"Because she's all 'shrinked' up."

My mother knew an opportunity when she heard one. "That's because she didn't drink milk when she was a little girl. And now she's missing calcium in her bones. Remember she broke her leg last winter?"

I wrinkled my nose. "Is calcium why her legs are ugly?"

"Varicose veins," Mam' supplied, "from having too many children."

"How many?"

"Fifteen," she said.

My eyes popped. "Did you have too many?"

Mam' couldn't help but chuckle. "What do you think? I'm sure glad I had you."

My grin broadened to a happy smile. "How come Zita got stuck looking after her mother?"

"Because," Mam' replied, "she's the only one without a family. She gave up her job at the Yarmouth hospital." My mother scowled a little. "That was quite a charitable thing to do, and it would be charitable of you and Estelle to be kinder to her mother."

"We are. It's just that … she wears diapers." I made sure Saint Theresa couldn't hear me, "And she pees in her pants."

"Problems with her bladder," Mam' frowned. "Nothing for you to repeat."

"I won't tell, but maybe Estelle will, at school."

"Then you tell her not to!"

"When can I come home?"

Mam' looked sad again, gazing at the little angel lost in her weary arms. "Soon."

"Soon" came the next day. Pricille warned Zita that she was going home. "I can clean the house and go to school, too," she assured her. Then if Pricille was going, the boys were going. And if the boys were going, then so was I! We flooded home at once. The baby didn't want us back. She whimpered all the time, worse in the evenings. Mam' occasionally dozed off to the sound of her moans, until they got weaker and more frequent. Then Mam' kept all-night vigils, while my father rocked in his chair, his question to her uneasy. "Should Zita call the doctor?"

My mother couldn't decide. She came to sit at the kitchen table and monitored the baby's chest for any signs of change. Early next morning, it was time to call the doctor. "Now!" Mam' panicked, and my father was out the door.

The doctor came and gave the baby a needle. He said an awful thing on his way out. "If she's still with us by tonight, I'll give her another needle."

We couldn't stop Mam's sobs. It was mid-morning when her chilling cry came: "She's barely breathing!" Then she bent closer to examine the infant's face. "Antoine! Get Zita! I want the baby baptized."

I don't know what in the heck was wrong with Dad, but he wouldn't move from his chair. It was only when the baby's breaths came farther apart and her eyes transfixed that he grabbed his coat and left, zigzagging his way through the fields. "He's not going!" I cried to Mam'. She called me from the window, "Then you go! *Astheure! Vâ-ye.*"

I hurried, hurried as fast as I possibly could, but the baby had stopped breathing by the time Zita and I came bursting through the door. When the frigid cold water from the pail hit the baby's forehead, she didn't twitch a hair—a sure sign she had passed away. All emotion had drained from my mother's face. Zita ran back across the road to make the necessary calls. Père Lucien arrived, said there was no need for a mass as this little angel was already in heaven. He would bless the coffin, and then he and Docteur Theriault would bury it.

Mam' laid her washbasin on the oven door, where it was warm for a bath. With such fuss, she shampooed and rinsed the baby's few hairs squeaky clean, then anointed the top of her head with baby oil. She cleaned her ears with a swab and changed her diaper, sprinkling it with lots of powder so that our baby smelled nice. She retrieved the undershirt with little pink lambs and Tante Rosalie's christening dress and bonnet. After everything was done, she wrapped her baby daughter in Zita's fluffy blanket, then in many layers of a white bedsheet. The tiny face was lost in the linen, like an Egyptian mummy. The priest was still waiting. Mam' pressed the bundle to her chest, then extended her arms high. Like people in the Bible stories offering their best lambs for sacrifice, she offered our baby. "Take her. *Emmenez-la.* She belongs to God. *A l'appartchein au Bon Djeu.*"

I stormed out of the house, down the road to Estelle's, where I found a cosy niche on the couch in my favourite sun parlour. I stared. "They took our baby away." Then I confided in Estelle, "Zita said that giving up our girl was the greatest sacrifice a mother could make. How would she know? She never had babies."

"Promise you won't tell your mother?" Estelle urged, and I crossed my heart three times to her threatening, narrowed eyes. "Your baby died because your mother didn't feed her."

"That's not true!"

"Not so loud!" she scolded, then lowered her voice. "Your baby didn't have a bottle."

Having already cried a deluge of tears, I knew that if I argued with Estelle, I would throw up. I had the truth within me. Our baby had died because her blood was wrong.

I counted five window boxes set in the winter sun. The same sun that fondled the earth and coaxed the shrivelled plants to awaken rendered my body listless, eased me into a deep sleep and an odd dream. Estelle was a Hula Hoop queen, the only one capable of twirling her yellow hoop for more than five minutes without it sliding off her hips. I was Dale Evans or Annie Oakley (it wasn't clear in my dream) riding in the air on our pig. I was coming after Estelle at full speed with a mean look on my face, meaner than Grand-père Dominique's.

"Zoé! Zoé!" I heard from a million miles away.

I rubbed my eyes, uncertain for a second where I was. I took in my surroundings: the window boxes, the couch I was snuggled on, finally Estelle, sitting in the far corner, colouring. Her long brown hair was restrained in two braids adorned with white ribbons, a style not at all flattering to her chubby face. Her wide smile flaunted her dimples.

"Want to colour?" She was kind to ask, but quickly clarified, "Not in my good book."

I untangled myself from Charlotte's afghan. "I need to go home."

"Not now," pouted a bored Estelle.

Yes! I had to. I had never felt so troubled. I slammed the door behind me and raced up what seemed like the longest hill ever. Finally, I burst into my house, out of breath, out of my mind. "Mam'!"

"I'm here," was the soft reply. "*J'su rinque icitte.*"

I hugged the right arm of Mam's chair. "Estelle said that the baby died because you didn't feed her."

Mam' stopped rocking, a renewed strength burned in her eyes as she gently smiled. "The baby died because she wasn't ours to keep."

"But babies should only die when they're old," I sobbed.

She looked at me more kindly than I could ever remember, paraphrasing a passage that even a nine-year-old could understand: "*He did say He would come like a thief in the night.*"

Her sacrifice to God was buried in the sleepy cemetery behind the church in St. Alphonse. N'Oncle Joseph planted a wooden cross that marked the grave where Père Lucien and Docteur Theriault had lowered the velvet-scrolled white coffin, paid for by Tante Marceline from Boston.

Chapter 7

In his sermons, Père Lucien talked about faith: to believe what we can't see, the rewards of that faith, to someday see what we believe. I believed that our baby was a veritable angel. Estelle argued that everybody goes to purgatory first, but I told her what Père Lucien had said—that all babies go to heaven right away.

My mother went to church regularly and prayed. When everyone else was standing or sitting, she was on her knees with her eyes tightly closed, indifferent to the embarrassment she was causing Pricille.

At night, she knelt for long stretches, while my father sat on the side of their bed, smoking. He wore a happy grin. She was back in the attic, where she belonged. But before, they used to whisper as they went to sleep. Sometimes they even laughed. Not anymore.

The change in Mam' sent me to Dad. I found him whittling in Dominique's shed, an opportune time to scold. "Why wouldn't you get Zita? Where did you go?" I demanded, though I knew his refuge was the woods. Now I only added to the affliction in his blue eyes. "Mam' is angry at you. Our baby's name is Thérèse. She's with Saint Theresa in heaven."

Dad turned his attention back to his pocketknife, continued hacking at a block of wood. He was carving some form of animal.

As I wondered if it was for me, he took me by surprise with the infamous term he used whenever Mam' was on her "high-horse," hell to live with. "Don't bother your mother these days. She's a Bolshevik."

"So is Pricille," I readily attested. "Mam' asked her to help with the wash, and she practically took a fit. *Chaude coumme la graille du d'jâub.*"

I turned to the rusted piece of junk in the corner, an engine-driven saw that still bore the Fairbanks trademark. "Why doesn't Grand-père Dominique throw this thing down the cliff? What is it for anyway?" Dad had told me the story before, but I wanted to hear it again. Long ago, Dominique owned acres and acres of woodland and cut his own firewood. "How did this thing work?" I asked.

Dad pointed to the end of the machine where Grand-père held the logs while someone—sometimes my father, sometimes N'Oncle Joseph—poured buckets of water into the large tank that fed the engine reservoir. All day, under Grand-père's watchful eye, huge logs were diminished to piles of blocks, ready to be split into firewood.

"How did you get the logs home?" I prodded.

Dad remembered, all too vividly. "On bobsleds, pulled by Dominique's oxen." He turned his attention to the small block he was carving and chiselled a few more delicate indents, distracting me from his story.

I became excited. "It looks like an ox!"

He just grinned, talked about Dominique's oxen and N'Oncle Joseph's boldness as a young boy. Grand-père's heavily burdened beasts trudged two miles of rugged, snowy woods, their bells tinkling after a mean flick of the whip. "One time they were slowing down," Dad recalled, "unable to pull the overloaded sled. Dominique raised his whip, and Joseph grabbed it from his hand. I had never seen his face so red. 'Beat those oxen one more time,' he warned the old man, 'and you won't live to raise another whip.'" My father's grin was boastful. "That Joseph wasn't scared of anything." He resumed his meticulous work of putting finishing touches on his sculpture, then raised his head as he heard someone call me. "*Depêche! C'est Mam'.*"

I hastened out of the shed. Dad would finish whittling his ox while waiting for my return.

"Pricille needs help!" Mam' barked as I brushed past the frozen clothes on the line. Inside, my sister was wrestling with the wringer of our washing machine, coaxing my father's heavy overalls between the rollers.

"Don't just stand there!" she directed, "help me pull these

through. And watch your fingers!" She had barely caught her breath when the safety release snapped and popped open, thrusting the wringer in a semicircle so that the heavy overalls dripped all over the floor. Soaking wet, my sister knew how to curse. "*Rig de sacré marde!*" Her black ponytail jerked sideways. "Sweet Jesus! We'll have to wring them by hand."

I stared at the stiff overalls, then at the potatoes boiling over on the stove. I rushed the heavy pot towards the sink and lost my grip on the cover. *Aaaaaaaahhh!* Our dinner landed on the floor. I juggled the hot potatoes back into the pot, shaking my burning hands so as not to cry.

"Don't wipe the floor with the dishcloth!" Pricille shouted as the door opened. I wasn't sure which looked stiffer, Mam' or the frozen clothes she was dragging in from outside.

She squinted, as always when she was annoyed. "By the crackie, what happened to those?"

Pricille, who earlier had flung Dad's underwear into the washer with a red blanket, dared not open her mouth. Mam' hung the pink long johns along with my now pink bloomers behind the stove to thaw. She dug through the rest of the frozen clothes on the table. "Where's the boys' underwear? Didn't they change?"

My sister had to think. "Actually, I haven't noticed any underwear for weeks now."

"But I bet you noticed the boys at school," Mam' charged. "Or your *True Stories*. That's all you think about these days." In a fit of rage, Pricille meant to take flight to the attic but instead collided with the huge rinsing tub. "*Jesus Cramette-a Hell!*" Mam' echoed across the kitchen. She had never used such blasphemy before.

A flood poured over the floor as I raced for the long-haired mop. Mam' tried to lift the cumbersome tub back onto the two wobbly chairs, forcing my sister to yell at her, "No lifting! Didn't you hear Docteur Theriault?"

Don't lose your head, I told myself. When Pricille grabbed one handle of the tub, it made perfect sense for me to grab the other. The thing weighed a ton and I dropped the cumbersome tub—right on Mam's foot.

"*Dâr dine de luck!*" she raged. I narrowly escaped her frantic hand, leaving a tuft of my hair in her grip. "Go back where you were!" she fumed. Crying, I knew to get the hell out of that house. "You should see our kitchen!" I sobbed to Dad. "There's water all over the floor. *Yâ d'leau éparé partout. C'in tintamarre du jâub.*" Just now, I hated his grin over something so serious. "You're always in here whittling!" I accused. "Why aren't you home helping?" Where was the block of wood anyway? "Get rid of that grin and tell me why you're always in here!" I lashed.

An annoyed look came over his face, his answer unusually gruff, "I come here to get out from under Mam's feet."

As I realized that in Mam's eyes, he couldn't do anything right either, my anger dissipated. Sadness came briefly in its place, but the anger returned. My whole head hurt, even the roots of my hair throbbed. When I was troubled, I always retreated to my swing, and Dad wasn't allowed to talk to me. I hated my mother. The more I thought about her rage, the more I wished that she was old, so I could pull her hair, too. My deluge of tears lessened to a trickle, as my ugly thoughts settled. I wiped my eyes and my snotty nose on the sleeve of my sweater. I even had a grin to match Dad's. The grudge was gone. I could now reason, with the help of past sermons from Père Lucien. Even with all the faith Mam' possessed, sometimes grief showed itself as anger. She was having an angry day.

Dad reached into his shirt pocket, scratched the bottom of his flattened tobacco package for a skimpy cigarette, which he lit and crudely savoured, sucking in his cheeks with each puff.

"Why don't you have teeth?" I asked.

An amused expression appeared on his face. "N'Oncle Joseph pulled them all out. He used to tie one end of a piece of string around my loose tooth and the other end to a doorknob."

I figured out the rest. "And slammed the door shut. I lost most of my teeth in toffee," I informed him, but he smoked his cigarette, stalling, staring at the piled woodchips around his feet as if contemplating his next move. What was he hiding under the woodchips? With his large hand, he swept them away. My eyes lit up, Dad told me later, "Brighter than all the stars on a moonlit night."

"You finished it!" I gasped as he picked up his carved work of art. With the proudest grin that had ever livened his face, he passed it to me, "*C'est pour toi.*"

"*Pour moi!*" I dug a fingertip in the creases of the neck and bovine face of the chef-d'oeuvre. "But this is the very nicest thing you've ever made!" A wooden ox was simply divine, far more special than any of my brothers' whistles.

During the spring, when the sap was running and the bark loosened easily, Dad would cut alder limbs for whistles. The shorter the limb, the higher the pitch. Whistle-making was a tedious process with his jackknife: notching cavities in the limbs with the bark intact and then sliding off the bark; cutting away at the naked sticks to make the air columns; and then, finally, sliding the bark back in place. *Voilà!* But these whistles had to be handled with care. Bark cylinders soon slid out of position, or the bark would dry out and contract enough to close the opening of the air channel.

Slip-bark whistles didn't last long; my ox would last forever. It needed to stand up. Dad raided Dominique's nail box and hammered in four silver legs. He then found a piece of twine, and with his penknife, cut a tiny tail. He even made a real yoke!

"I want it painted," I brusquely ordered. I visualized Deni Fournier's oxen. "A brown face with white spots."

My gentle father picked up his discarded cigarette butt and flicked it back on the floor. "First, I need some tobacco."

"Now. Can you paint it now?" I begged, but he kept gazing at his empty package. Away from Mam's gaze, I could shake my head in a daring no. "I want you to paint my ox!" Then I turned downright sassy. "You go!"

Never. Never would Dad have walked to the post office. Grand-mère Sophie could take the blame for that. "I should have made him go to school," she often lamented.

I knew the story. When the trustees went to the house, my father hid in his treehouse. He grew very shy, too shy to climb down for his apple when the *P'tit Démilier* called him. He instead picked his Gravenstein from his mother's pail. He never went to church, not that I remembered. And he hid in our attic when strangers came to the house. But when he needed tobacco, ah, then he came down from his *cachette*, looking for me.

"Hurry," he now pleaded, and I examined my special but pale-looking ox. "Estelle will want one. I just know it." But it needed a rusty coat, and there'd be no paint job unless I agreed to the dreaded mile-long walk to the post office. Drained from the day's anguish, I dragged my feet to the hinged door, could hardly bring myself to open it.

"The ox will be painted when you come back," Dad assured me. I would have sooner collapsed on the floor than undertaken the miserable walk.

"What will you buy me?" I growled, making the deal crystal clear. "I don't want a dirty peppermint from your pocket!"

Dad paused but a moment, looked at me point-blank, as if the promise was perfectly natural to a nine-year-old. "I'll buy you an ox."

"An ox!" I exploded, my energy revitalized. "An ox! A real one?"

"*Un vrai*," he nodded.

I passed him the wooden one that was already mine, resolved that the very idea was just plain ludicrous. "I'll be happy with this one, painted."

I skipped down the Cape road, stopping suddenly on the middle of the white line. I knew the dumb stare of Deni's oxen, as they swung their mammoth heads from side to side. What a strange, strange idea, a real ox. What would I do with it?

Estelle wrinkled her face in a grimace when I told her of the offer. "An ox! A real one? What a stupid idea if I ever heard one. An ox is so slow, so lazy, too lazy to blink its eyes. Slowpoke, that's the only name you could give an ox!" She got her coat, and with her smirky stare she met me at the door. "Why not a fluffy white kitten? A horse to ride? Even a cow. You'd have to whip an ox to death to make it move."

"The tail?" she ridiculed. "This trip will buy the tail?" She did have a point. "You'd think he'd start with the head. *C'est vraiment une drôle d'idée ça.*" She didn't want to hear about my *wooden* ox. She jingled the change in her pocket, calculating how many candies she could buy, and how long it would take me to earn a complete ox. "You'll be as old as Zita's mother."

She blabbed the *drôle d'idée* to the postmaster. "Her father's buying her an ox!" The two exchanged bizarre grins as she pointed to the candies inside the glass case. "Five jawbreakers. Six Bazooka bubble gum."

The postmaster smiled. "Zoé?"

"Twenty peppermints and a package of Export A." My cheeks flushed with embarrassment. "On credit."

Not long ago, Estelle had told the whole class, "At Zoé's, they buy on credit."

I knew I wasn't getting any of her gum, but I was anxious for the Bazooka Joe comic. She waited until we were outside.

"I'm saving these for a flashlight," she said, then brought the tiny print close to her face. "Still want to hear the comic?" I nodded, and she smoothed out the crinkled wrapper. " 'Joe: Mom, what happens when a car is too old to run? Mom: Somebody sells it to your father!' " Estelle slipped the wrapper into her pocket, annoyed at the stupid look on my face. "How *could* you get it? You don't even own a bicycle."

She inflated her chubby cheeks attempting the largest bubble ever. She let it burst, then mumbled between chews, "Tell me about your concert outfit that Pricille's sewing in the 4-H."

She sparked my excitement. "A blue gown to my feet, and a white veil, just like Mary in the grotto at church!"

She scrutinized my poker-straight hair and the bangs which were cropped crooked and too short across my forehead. I knew exactly what she was thinking. Her hair was long, perfect for the part. But she was sugary nice. "I can't wait to see the play."

"Cedric will be Joseph," Madame Comeau announced. I looked back at the tuft of hair hanging in his eyes, felt a pang of disappointment. I had hoped for André. Babette beamed with delight; she had a baldheaded doll for baby Jesus. Paul-Emile would be one wise man, though far better suited as an ass, as far as I was concerned. I fidgeted in my seat, and the teacher settled her gaze on me. Then she looked towards the back at Pricille, again at me, finally at Estelle, as if it were a big deal to make it final. "Estelle will be Mary."

Estelle! I turned to capture Pricille's expression, which was as shocked as mine. Estelle indulged in a smirk, of course. I caught up with her at recess, and she had her arm ever so amicably wrapped around Babette, the lighthouse slowpoke who she couldn't stand the day before.

"I hate you!" I yelled, with all the bitterness of a grudge that would surely last a lifetime.

Estelle simply stared, feigned surprise. "Me? What did I do?"

I rubbed the tears from my eyes. "You knew I wanted to be Mary."

"But I couldn't remember if it was Mary, or if you wanted to be an ox," she gloated.

I hollered into her fat face, "I hate you, and I don't want to see you at my house ever again. *J'veux jamais back ter ouar la grand face chu nous. Never! Never! Never! Jamais. Comprend tu?*"

When the Christmas concert was over, I told Dad that the teacher had chosen Estelle only because her father had built the nativity stable at the boatshop. He stopped whittling, and I asked him, "Did you ever see a Mary with dimples?" But then I remembered the brown, curly locks bouncing out of a flowing veil, and I ached. Estelle made a far prettier Mary. Surely anyone could see that. The teacher did.

I got on my swing and dug my feet back in an angry push. "You know what else Estelle did?"

My father continued whittling. "What?"

"She told Babette that you're loco when you've been drinking, that you tell the whole Cape you're rich. And then Babette asked me, 'Why doesn't your father buy you a bride doll if he's rich?' I told her, 'Because Santa Claus is bringing me one.'" I stopped my swing because I was getting too angry. "Every time you get drunk at Eddie Pockshaw's, you think you're rich!"

What did my father have to say for himself? Nothing. He just grinned, a demented grin that unmasked a deeply troubled mind.

"But I am rich. If only Martine would go to the bank and get my money."

"I'm going to get the mail," I raged, and I jumped off my swing, slammed the latched door nearly off its hinges.

I followed the ditch, hurling rocks to shatter the sheets of ice that had thickened over the trickling water. The postmaster brought me back to reality when he filled my arms with Christmas. I hurried back to Grand-mère Sophie's. Nothing could bring a smile to her face more readily than a parcel from Tante Marceline. This one was filled with jams, hand creams, hair ribbons, and brooches to pamper her—all things that lured Estelle and me into Grand-mère Sophie's bedroom. Of course, there was a heavy woollen sweater for Grand-mère to survive the winter. Perhaps she was always cold because she didn't have much hair on her head.

Grand-père Dominique grumbled over the parcel, about how much Marceline had spent on foolishness. He scowled at all the presents wrapped in pretty Christmas paper.

There was another small package, this one addressed to Mrs. Martine LeBlanc. I hurried home to the vultures gathered around the kitchen table. Mam' had never received a parcel that I could remember. Baffled, she examined the return address.

"Halifax?" She opened the gift.

I could only gaze at the lacy socks and the most elegant matching baby dress in the box—ruffle upon tiny ruffle of pink lace. Mam' rooted for a card, anything to identify the sender, to appease the suspicious stare coming from Dad in his rocking chair. But her face was devoid of any explanation for my father. "Obviously someone who doesn't know that our baby girl died." Jealousy ate at him, while she went about her chores, utterly perplexed. "I can't imagine who in God's creation would have sent that."

The mysterious parcel ruined my Christmas vacation and Christmas Eve. Dad returned from Eddie Pockshaw's with a rage glazing his eyes. "Some old boyfriend, is it?"

The accusation threw Philippe into a foul mood for Christmas Day. "Sit down and eat your dinner!" There was another pair of angry eyes watching—Pierre's. Even André, only ten years old, glared at Dad.

I gobbled my food and made a mad dash for the door, only to be called back to the table. "You're *not* going to Estelle's! How many dirty tricks does she have to play on you before you learn?"

"But she has a new bride doll," I pleaded with my irate mother. I spent the afternoon staring at the Christmas tree, which was bare at the base, except for a matching comb and mirror set from my godmother. I gaped in the mirror, but I failed to see a pretty girl staring back at me. I found Pricille. "My godmother said there's a pretty girl in the mirror. Do you see one?"

My sister grabbed the mirror, took to laughing, "Depends who's looking in it."

"Exactly," I concluded. "*Now* there's one."

I didn't have to go to bed right after supper, but I wanted to. I put on the Mary gown that Pricille had sewn in the 4-H and laid in bed, awake for a long, long time with a gnawing pain in my stomach. Even after everyone was snoring in the attic, I was still awake, terribly disappointed. Santa had missed our chimney. But then our small house had grey asphalt shingles and a black roof, much too difficult to see in the dark, especially in blinding snow.

There could never be a worse Christmas.

Chapter 8

There was a worse Christmas. I was twelve and school was out for Christmas vacation. Staying away from those shanties was foremost on Mam's list of orders. I was blessed with a virtuous face. She would have snapped her black eyes, utterly dumbfounded, if she knew that Estelle had lifted her blouse for Paul-Emile, and that her Zoé had witnessed the incident, in a shanty.

"No big deal," the scoundrel had coaxed. "You lift your blouse, and I'll pull my pants down." Estelle had been too eager. Just because he was unbuckling his belt didn't mean he was gonna drop his pants.

Estelle was enamoured of Paul-Emile, who measured up to the idols in Pricille's *True Stories*—the blond hair and the baby face embellished with rosy cheeks as if he had just woken from a deep sleep. Even the older women turned their heads and were heard to lament, "That I could be young again."

When Mam' turned her head, it was because she didn't trust the scoundrel, not at all happy that he would spend most of his Christmas vacation at my house. The first night, she was shampooing my hair, digging her nails into my head as if clearing lice. Then she shocked my raw scalp with *chopines* of cold water. Fortunately, there were no snarls for her comb to rip through, nothing to slow her down—except for the outside door, which gently opened. She stopped combing.

It could only be Paul-Emile's smooth voice approaching the sink. "André home?" My heart stopped beating.

Brusquely, Mam' pointed to the living room. "In there."

She then cautioned me, "Now Zoé, you better scrub behind

those ears, or I will." Then again, as if I hadn't heard the first time, "You hear me? Don't be scared to scrub."

The humiliation worsened as Paul-Emile stared me up and down. Mam' flashed him one of her looks, and he disappeared, only to return minutes later, looking for a drink. She handed him the *chopine* which he dipped deep into the bucket of water, stalling, taking forever to drink a mouthful. Once she had steered him back to the living room, Mam' transferred the washbasin to the pantry. "Surely I can go to the attic now. Wash behind those ears!"

She left me perturbed, wondering. Paul-Emile wouldn't dare. Paul-Emile *did* dare, and I looked up in shock. The prying snake was back, had the gall to slink right into the pantry. Mortified, I could only shrink from his lustful gaze. Oh how I wished myself in Estelle's porcelain four-legged tub, inside a real bathroom, with a door, a lock. I grabbed the threadbare towel.

"Get out!" I ordered, and he retreated, his wrinkled brow complementing his arrogant smile.

"Estelle has more *tétines* than you. You don't have any at all."

"Get out or I'll scream," I threatened between clenched teeth. The cesspool rat knew to make his escape, just in time.

"What's wrong?" Mam' wanted to know, but all the sharp black-eyed stares in the world couldn't have extracted the reason for my sudden exit to the attic or my explosion of tears as I fell to my knees. I modified my prayer, adding to the long, curly locks that I had been pleading for: *Dear God. I need to grow breasts.* I didn't want enormous ones, like the Vargas girls on the playing cards under Philippe's mattress. I merely wanted to fill the 30-A foam-cupped brassière I had seen at Fred à Bill.

The snake got to Estelle. "Guess what?" she announced on the wharf, for all the boys to hear, even the fishermen. "Zoé doesn't have any *tétines*. Paul-Emile saw her with not a stitch on."

Paul-Emile's sleazy smile and the rhythm of his little chant brought resounding laughter, made me recoil.

Zoé. Zoé. T'en auras jamais assez,
Zoé. Zoé. Un manche à balai habillé.

A broom handle he called me! He had used Mam's very words,

the result of her frustration when the skirts she sewed never hung right over my shapeless hips. Estelle hooted, but not for long. I invented my own little chant:

Your father will be very, very, veeery happy,
To hear you lifted your blouse in the dirty shanty.

Estelle gaped. "Shut up!" she threatened, "or I'll lift you blouse, right here." She thrust her blubber face forward. "And then everyone will surely know you don't have any." She grabbed Babette's arm. "Come on, let's go."

I threw a mean look at Babette. "Estelle's only walking back with you because I hate her." Immediately, I regretted the harsh words of my embittered tongue.

However she laboured to keep up with Estelle, Babette's green eyes gleamed all the way home. She thought she had a friend.

How would I survive the rest of the vacation without Estelle? André wouldn't play with me. Pricille wouldn't play with me either, obsessed with her Clyde and her *True Stories*. Pierre practically lived at the wharf, watching the boats unload, wishing himself in his own boat headed for the Trinity. Philippe was too busy, focused on examining the back of our TV and dismantling radios. Snooping in Grand-mère Sophie's things was no fun alone, and listening to Grand-père Dominique grumble was boring.

We all knew of his dislike for Babette's father, Percy Goodwin, who had brought his library of books from Argyle. He caged himself in the top of the lighthouse, kept company with the seascape and rugged cliffs, the parade of little boats that his lone light beckoned home—inspiration for a writer.

Like everyone else at the Cape, Percy detested the fog that incessantly shrouded our village come spring. He had published a poem in *The Vanguard* about the blighted mist. I read it and deeply appreciated the few lines I understood. Dominique read it and said that *The Vanguard* couldn't be fussy about the stuff they printed. "*Un poète de gâzette*," he christened Percy, and the slander reached the wharf in no time—something to laugh about when the fishermen mended their nets. The poor man would approach the wharf from a mile away, and they'd all grin, "*V'là poète de gâzette.*"

Actually, I liked Percy. He had been to the house a few times lately, having heard that Philippe was good at fixing radios. And he loved toddlers, was quite taken with our *new* Thérèse, my new sister.

To me, she was a genuine pest. Unlike our deceased baby girl, this one had exploded into the world, determined to talk early, making the women in the village stare in disbelief. Her first word was *rât*, having been introduced to them early on from Dad's bedtime stories. Though she was young for stories, she insisted on them, perhaps because we clapped our hands, jumped up and down, and acted them out for her. I had taught her *by-low*, her command when she wanted to rock.

Whenever she noticed my legs crossed, she came and straddled my foot, then extended her little arms to me. "*Ka-jack.*" To keep her out from under Mam's feet, I swung her up and down, until my leg cramped. The load was beyond toddler heavy.

"Amuse her," Mam' ordered, whenever she was baking. No one was allowed near the pantry, lest a speck of flour dot her clean floor. Her sewing machine was also forbidden. I recognized the blue plaid material moving beneath the needle, from Tante Marceline.

"What are you sewing?" I asked.

She retorted, "Either you find something to do, or you're going outside."

"Outside!" I exclaimed. Though it was only December on the calendar, it was frigid as the Arctic out there. Dad couldn't whittle in Dominique's shed, so he sat at the window, watching the white caps pounding the granite boulders of the breakwater.

"There's no lobster this year," he kept apologizing to my mother, who had already spent the few dollars he had brought home for a week's pay.

She growled about the boats tied to the wharf, at my father, at the children. She even snapped at Grand-mère Sophie, "You're getting too old to trek through knee-deep snow to the outhouse. *Dans la neige jusqu'au dârriere.*"

She approached Christmas with worry furrowing her forehead.

N'Oncle Joseph dropped by to cheer us up, but he couldn't find the right words as he gazed at the swells crashing over the breakwater. He returned the day before Christmas Eve with revived spirit. "You have to test my homemade brew," he told my father, lifting a glass of foul-smelling liquid to the light. The yellow scum at the top of the malt glass was far from the clear version he had bragged about; it hardly looked palatable for humans. Judging from the gleam in my father's eyes, it wouldn't be wasted.

Still clad in his shipyard clothes, N'Oncle Joseph meant to stay but a few minutes; however, one foamy glass led to another, and before Mam' knew it, he and Dad were deep into their past, boasting about their father, Nicholas, and his success as a fisherman. I learned that Grand-mère Sophie could cover the top of a double-size quilt with five-dollar bills when he built their house in Wedgeport. I jerked my head back and forth to follow the voices in progress, my interest not on their *tête-à-tête*, but on comparing faces.

N'Oncle Joseph was the handsome one; his neatly trimmed mustache and boyish brushcut kept him young looking. His darling wife, Tante Rosalie, was often heard to boast that, in his army uniform, he had turned more than a few heads. He still could.

My father's face bore the ravages of inclement winters at sea, making him appear much older than his forty-seven years. According to the pictures in Dominique's attic, he, too, was once handsome; his nose was not a serious distraction when he was young. I had heard it said that the nose keeps growing long after everything else has stopped; his had started to spread across his face.

Mam' had a fair-size nose also. We children didn't stand a chance. We all had big noses, even Thérèse, who had not broken the tradition. Nor had she escaped the awful temper that came from my mother's side of the family. She got plenty angry when N'Oncle Joseph tugged on her springy curls. She was exceptionally dark, so dark that he found mistaken pleasure in teasing, "Where did that one come from?" My jealous father invented enough foolishness of his own. Mam' didn't want him thinking the kid wasn't his.

N'Oncle was now dragging Dad into a wartime mishap that was better left alone. I knew the story well. N'Oncle Joseph had sailed from Halifax on the *Isle of France*, which took him and his brother Louis to Amsterdam. Joseph was stationed in England to train forces, while N'Oncle Louis was posted in a different regiment bound for Germany. Fourteen months later, Joseph returned from overseas without Louis. Since he was never reported missing or killed in action, N'Oncle Joseph and Grand-mère Sophie had tried repeatedly to have him traced through the Red Cross, but there was no record of a Louis LeBlanc ever having fought in any regiment. In fact, there was no record of him ever enlisting—nothing.

Now, my father again speculated that maybe their brother had fled the war. Joseph slammed his glass down, splashing froth over the table. "Louis was no coward! He was killed in action. The records were lost." The two couldn't agree on anything about Louis, not even the colour of his hair. A pity there were no photographs.

N'Oncle talked a lot. Dad stared, glassy-eyed, but behaving himself, until N'Oncle got up to leave. "Rosalie's expecting me."

Dad jumped off his chair, his grin threatening. *Y çâ a-piqué.* "Two brothers should be able to enjoy a drink so close to Christmas."

My mother cowered as he brusquely ordered Joseph to sit, and then poured himself a jigger of whisky, a risky combination with the malt beer he had already consumed. Soon his abusive mouth would persecute the people around him.

"Don't you think you both have had enough?" Mam' was starting to fret.

Dad refilled N'Oncle's glass to the brim with malt. "Hear that, Joseph. She thinks I'm drunk. *Plein d'marde.*"

Clearly distraught, Joseph rose from his chair and pushed the glass aside, "*Naoun, naoun, naoun.* I can't drink that. *Y'est tant se raderser.*"

But it was unwise to whet Antoine's thirst and then take away his drink. Dad grabbed the whisky bottle, adopting the same demented expression that possessed his blue eyes every time he drank hard stuff. "*D'la sacré marde.* You sit yourself right back on that chair!"

What else could N'Oncle do but direct a sheepish apology at Mam'. "Look at the mess I got you in."

"You didn't pour it down his throat," she assured him. "Go home to your family."

Shamefaced, he brushed past her and squeezed something into her hand. "It's not much, a little something for Christmas."

The door closed, and fury darkened Dad's face. "Aaaaah! So it's him now. What did he give you, a love letter?" He vocalized a string of raw drunken vulgarities, including a "sonofawhore" for Mam', a "pimp" for N'Oncle, and while he was at it, he sent to hell and back the dirty rotten bastard who had sent the parcel in the mail three Christmases ago! Philippe and Pierre both jumped up at the same time; it was Philippe who glowered fiercely and pointed to the hall door. "You see those stairs?"

The two couldn't get the drunkard up the attic steps before he started a row with Mam'. What was she clutching in her hand? She opened it for all eyes to see. Twenty dollars, to buy the kids candies. Thérèse, terrified of angry voices, started to cry. What a commotion!

My father insisted he couldn't go to bed, not before Thérèse had her story about the rats in the breakwater. *Les rats au tchai.*

Dad had invented the rat character Avarât when the big trucks rumbled down the Cape road, lugging two thousand tons of rock to build the breakwater. The largest boulder weighs over eighteen tons and juts into the ocean. Its granite pink sparkles through the grey, giving the illusion of a two-toned rainbow encircling the rock.

According to Dad's story, this glittering beauty had the fat and greedy Avarât gawking, with his nose pointed and ears *a-piqué*. However, the ambitious, territorial Scrat was also gawking, *les griffes ajussés.*

I finally had Thérèse snug in bed, in the downstairs bedroom, where I promised her a story. Philippe and Pierre had at long last helped Dad to bed. Admiring her springy locks, I diverted my baby sister's attention to the happy season it was supposed to be. "Who's coming tomorrow?"

Her eyes sparkled. "*Jésus.*"

"Who else?"

Again, the sparkles. "*Jésus.*"

For Thérèse, the magic of Christmas was clearly not in Santa Claus. Nor in my story. No one could tell a rat story like Dad. *Le poète de gâzette* could vouch for that.

Percy Goodwin had interviewed my father and listened attentively to several of his rat stories. He had asked permission to take his favourite one, put it in poem form and take it to the newspaper. On the second page of *The Vanguard* had appeared "The Fat and Greedy Rat," the story I would have told Thérèse if she hadn't fallen asleep in my arms.

The Fat and Greedy Rat

It was on a mighty rock that a fat and greedy rat did reign,
boasting of the finest granite to a defeated Scrat,
the territorial shanty cat.
Now the royal Avarât, he sharpened, he sharpened
his front teeth, he did. But of the village rats
drawing near, he quickly got rid.
"Get away! *Va t'en*," he rudely ordered Evâ,
without a doubt, *la plus jolie d'tous les rats*.

Avarât sharpened, he sharpened,
mounds of seaweed he did grind.
But a rat is a rat, and a rat is not kind.
To the starving scroungers, he had this to say:
"If you could sharpen your teeth on my rock,
your bellies would be full today."

He sharpened, he sharpened,
going totally mad,
"You tie me up," he challenged.
Then proceeded to brag, "These razor-sharp teeth,
they'll cut me free. Go on,
try it," he urged, *un vrai point d'esprit*.
"Bet you they won't," dared the quick-witted Scrat,
"Will so," returned the sure and cocky rat.

The eager Scrat, he fetched a rope, he did,
and round and round, haunted by defeat,
he bound Avarât's fat belly,
tied up his naked feet.
Then to the fat and greedy rat, he had this to say:

"Though you have sharpened your teeth on your rock,
You will surely perish today."

"*Sacré Bleu*," protested a distressed Evâ.
"A rope so thick, Avarât will never gnaw."
But the other rats, they cared not a torte
about the dim-witted Avarât, who had grinded too short.
Hastening for food to find,
they left Evâ to tarry behind.
Was it the Scrat, *les griffes ajussés?*
Or was it the crashing waves that made her stay?

Now the royal Avarât, he had sharpened, he sharpened
his front teeth he did,
but when crashing waves leaped o'er his rock,
he just stared. *Un vrai stupide.*
"Cut the rope loose!" mocked the Scrat.
"Or have you sharpened too much, you stupid dingbat?"
One should rise to such a wicked tone, such a nasty beat,
But the rope it was tight around Avarât's naked feet,
He gnawed, he gnawed, but gnawed himself nowhere,
While the Scrat made merry of the poor rat's despair.
"I deserve this," Avarât lamented and wept,
Then he saw the giant breaker,
"Take me, now that I welcome death."

The other rats, they all did agree,
that Avarât he should float down the Bay of Fundy.
But Evâ, she pounced forth in such a raging yell,
"*Vos grudges*," she said, "you bid them to hell."
And with a powerful grip, and a mighty face,
she lifted Avarât from the abyss of disgrace,
And thence, she did scowl, and ordered the king of greed,
"One hundred and one rats you must now feed."

"Evâ. Evâ, there was no sweeter name on the lips of Avarât.
Au Finistère. Au Finistère. He did march,

and there conferred with Monsieur Ratouille,
le chargé d'affaires en Clare.
" 'Tis not the exile that I so terribly dread,
but that the village rats will cease to be fed."

Now Monsieur Ratouille, he knew of the Scrat,
and he pondered justly, in the tall chair he sat.
A month of deliberations, then he scratched a law,
"The granite rock" it read, "it belongs to Evâ."

It was on a mighty rock that the fairest of all rats did reign,
Boasting of the finest granite to all drawing near.
Now the village rats, they sharpened, they sharpened,
their front teeth they did,
but with moderation, and they did find,
that seaweed aplenty was theirs to grind
under the just guidance of who else but Evâ,
without a doubt, *la plus jolie d'tous les rats.*

Thérèse was sleeping soundly. My father was confined to the attic that night, and on Christmas Eve. He was too ashamed to show his face.

Christmas Eve was ours. "Potatoes," Mam' said, and Pierre jumped to orders. I followed him to Dominique's earthen cellar, to the creaking hatch door that he opened ever so slowly, so as not to disturb Dominique and Sophie. He located the light and looked around, contemplating the fall harvest: barrels of valley apples, carrots, turnips, potatoes, salted herring, and salted pork. Our share long depleted, he eyed Grand-père Dominique's jars of Solomon Gundy and Grand-mère Sophie's chow chow.

"I better not," he reasoned aloud, knowing full well that Grand-père Dominique was down there every day, taking stock. He filled his bucket, mindful of his hand, lest he should feel the fur of a big rat gnawing at the potatoes—one with its teeth sharpened just right.

"What's a pimp?" I blurted.

My brother jerked his hand back from the barrel, elbowing me in the stomach. He stared dumbfounded. "Whaaaat? Now why in the name of Jesus would you ask me that?"

"Because that's what you say when you see Paul-Emile walking up the Cape road. And last night, Dad called N'Oncle Joseph that, too."

Pierre could hardly contain a chuckle. "We don't repeat what drunken people say." He walked up the cellar steps and closed the hatch door. "But for Paul-Emile, the name fits well."

Back in our kitchen, a rappie pie was in the making. Chicken and salted shallots simmered in a broth. Little cubes of pork fat sizzled in the frying pan. Potatoes were ready for peeling, but we all preferred grating. We each had a turn, so that the grated potato mush contained a blood sample from everyone. Pierre's strong hands squeezed the mixture dry of its starchy juice, while Mam' measured and replaced the liquid with boiling broth. Philippe stirred the white mush, and with a wooden spoon, Pricille smoothed half of it in a large pan, adding meat evenly on top, and then covering it with the remaining potato mixture. With a happy smile, Mam' slid the deep pan into the oven. "Crust, you six-o-six!" Whatever "six-o-six" meant, one of her expressions, like "seventy-six and a half," what she called Paul-Emile.

She rooted through her bureau drawer for the ten cents that would buy us a ride to midnight mass in the back of Basil's truck.

Christmas morning brought ribbon and barley candies, grapes and oranges, and all the mince pies we could eat. A huge turkey was browning in the oven. If the *Little Esther* couldn't land any lobster, poaching wasn't out of the question. Philippe and Pierre had provided well, all the lobster we could eat over the holidays.

The Christmas meal was a disturbed one for Mam'; the future of her children no longer lay in her hands. Pricille, my sister had already given her word to a lady in Mayflower. Her nose was always buried in her *True Stories*; I couldn't imagine Pricille as a maid. "I suppose," Mam' was forced to conclude, "she can't be tied to my apron strings forever. *Sous la cotte à Mam'*."

As for Pierre, how to keep a boy of fifteen in school when his soul resided at sea. The only arithmetic that interested him was how to weigh all the lobster and fish he'd land at the wharf. He had given his word to the Captain of the *Cape Marguerite*. First nice day after the holidays, he'd be at the wharf bright and early.

Philippe, though, was staying in school. Grand-père Dominique had no problem emptying his pockets whenever my brother complained of no money. His occasional mention of the word "engineer" sent the old man rooting in his attic to examine his dollar bills.

As for me, Mam' didn't know yet that I could never go back to school. I would hide in the house forever to avoid the boys from the wharf and Estelle. The mere mention of her name made me shudder. I didn't care that she was getting a reversible skirt for Christmas either. André said that reversible skirts were ugly, for old-fashioned women like Zita. Actually, Zita looked nice in reversible skirts. She was tall and shapeless, with her short straight hair slicked back, like Miss Hathaway on the "Beverly Hillbillies."

Maybe Mam' was sewing a reversible skirt for Pricille. Whatever it was that she was making, she was obsessed. She had hardly cleared the dishes before she hastened to her sewing machine, adamant that we not approach her corner. When Thérèse began to choke on a ribbon candy, she sprang up, slapped the child between the shoulders, and hurried right back to her sewing.

My father rocked in his chair, his face heavy with remorse. Just because he had a nasty, drunken tongue didn't mean he had to examine the floor for the rest of his life. On the other hand, maybe the floor would help him think.

"Did I insult anybody?" he muttered.

I snapped back, "Like you do every time you get drunk!" I followed André into the living room where we became mesmerized by the lights on the tree, hardly conscious of the continuous pounding of Grand-mère Comeau's antique sewing machine. But when the noise stopped short, we looked at each other, expecting Mam' to walk into the room to savour Christmas with us.

Instead, her roving eyes scanned the base of the tree and, of course, spotted a pile of dry needles on the floor. We couldn't have that.

"What are you doing?" howled André.

One by one, she denuded the thirsty branches of their plastic icicle decorations, making more needles drop to the floor, which annoyed her all the more. The cardboard nativity scene folded like an accordion. It had been spread across a cozy spot between two layers of thicker branches.

"Don't!" André pleaded, but Mam' stripped the tree of its pretty lights, ripped the angel off the top, then pushed aside the wooden stand. She ignored our dejected faces as she squeezed through the door with the tree, clearing our living room of any trace of Christmas, save for a trail of dead needles. Her irrational behaviour was surely out of frustration with my father and him ruining our Christmas.

André jumped up and kicked the TV, cursing Perry Como and his boring Christmas special before he bolted out the door, bound for Cedric's house. I hastened to the attic, found my rosary, and prayed. More fervently than ever I prayed that I would grow a chest bigger than Estelle's, yes bigger than those Vargas girls! And then she could never again diminish me in front of the boys. I lay awake for long hours, thinking, crying. How I hated Estelle.

Mam's sewing machine was pounding below again. I bet there wasn't one string of thread on that floor. A frown creased my forehead as I turned onto my side. Why had she bothered with a tree at all, up on Christmas Eve and down—this one hadn't even made it to Boxing Day.

Chapter 9

With a broad smile that lit up his face, Pierre slapped his earnings on the table. "I have found my good fortune with the *Cape Marguerite*," he announced. The fishermen at the wharf had the reverse story: that the *Cape Marguerite* had found its good fortune with Pierre. Whichever, my brother's determination to drain the ocean of its lobster caused a smile to linger on Mam's lips—until Jubis Brothers arrived at the door with a new couch for our living room. Santa Claus' generosity transformed her smile into a scowl.

"You don't have money to throw away!"

"The couch was falling apart," our Pierre readily justified. He counted out thirty dollars. "When is the last time you bought yourself a dress?"

"I can't take your money!" she protested.

N'Oncle Joseph, who was sitting at the table, chuckled. "Let him treat his mother."

"Thirty dollars is way too much." She half grinned. "But since you're rich, we could use some meat." I took that to mean we'd be getting a change from salted herring.

"Get your coat," N'Oncle ordered my mother. I grabbed mine, too. I wasn't missing a ride to Meteghan.

The meat market was so small that if one of the four men lined against the wall had been staring, Mam' would have surely noticed. But she headed straight to the counter, checking cuts as if she had just landed a job as meat inspector. "Too lean. Too fat. Good price. Uuumm, fresh."

I stared at the fly strip coiled above our heads. Better that the flies were stuck to the sticky molasses than on the carcasses in the back, where Mam's focus had wandered. I tried to tell her that one of the men was staring, but her attention was directed at the employee behind the counter. "Six pounds of stew meat," she ordered.

Another wipe of the dripping knife on his bloodied apron wouldn't matter. "We have nice blood pudding today," he announced.

Mam' shook her head. "We eat enough of that when we kill our pigs." She reached into the cardboard box at her feet, picking up a bone with copious patches of meat on it. "Now, let me tell you, I'm gonna have myself a soup."

"Any dogs?" the butcher queried.

I nodded. "Her name's Lulu."

"Then we'll throw in an extra bone for Lulu," he grinned.

The man leaning against the wall smiled at me, and I tugged on Mam's coat. "That man is still staring."

Finally, she turned her head to the back wall, squinting to be sure that she had seen correctly. Her jaw dropped. "Tommy à Elisée!"

Seemed to me Tommy à Elisée could have expressed his mutual surprise without having to stroke her arm. "Martine! By the Jesus, I thought it was you."

Mam's long bangs were pinned back with bobby pins, making her straggly hair not so straggly. She was wearing her bright red lipstick, and her coat hid the flowered housedress that hung on her frame. If the greying-haired man happened to be an old boyfriend, she was not looking bad. The first question was about Zita. How was she doing? Was her mother still alive?

"Doing fine," Mam' answered, not one to go into details. She didn't appear to mind when her old classmate recalled their school days, with plenty of *te souvain tu*. They both remembered the Jeremie à Benoit who had peed in the nun's flower pot, killing her precious plant. The memory of this scandal made Mam' chuckle, though she nervously focused on the meats at the counter, her chit-chat weighing on N'Oncle Joseph's time.

She grabbed her packaged meats and the man lowered his voice to a mere whisper. "You'll never guess who I saw. Oh, ..." he calculated, "it must be three or four years now. My wife and I were walking on Spring Garden Road in Halifax. You'll never guess," he probed, then waited, but there were no enthusiastic guesses from Mam'. "Philippe Delaney," he said, and her head jerked back. Perhaps there would have been a string of questions if I hadn't been there.

Since the meat saw was so darn noisy, I had to crowd myself in between the two to catch Mam's query. "How was he?"

"Funny," the former classmate grinned. "Philippe wondered the same about you, so I told him you had just had a new baby girl." His eyes met Mam's. "She died, didn't she?"

All colour drained from my mother's face as she rolled her eyes sideways, now understanding the origin of the pink ruffled dress and lacy socks. Pale as a ghost, she backed away, "Yes, she died. I really must be going. Joseph's waiting."

"Give my best to Zita," the man called after us. Mam' feigned a pleasant smile, but knowing my mother, Zita would never find out that she had crossed paths with Tommy à Elisée.

In the silence of N'Oncle Joseph's car, I simply had to know, "Was that Zita's husband?"

Mam's face was stone. "An old boyfriend." The long ago husband was a mystery that she wasn't about to divulge to me. "You must never mention the name Philippe Delaney in our house," she warned.

I recoiled at the alarm on her face. "Why?"

"Because you know what your father is like."

"Then tell me why," I insisted. She resurrected the famous parcel in the mail. "It was from him!" I exclaimed.

She lost no time in setting the record straight. "I knew Philippe Delaney long before I knew your father. Before I got married." Conversation over.

I knew something that Pierre, Pricille, André, Thérèse, and our Philippe didn't know. Even Grand-mère Sophie and Grand-père Dominique probably didn't know that Mam' had a boyfriend a long time ago. Did Mam' care for this Philippe Delaney, enough to call her first son Philippe? I could well imagine the string of vulgar epithets my father would have had for the former boyfriend. I knew enough to keep quiet about that, but I did tell Dad how Paul-Emile and Estelle had humiliated me on the wharf, warning him, "You mustn't tell Mam', or Estelle will never be allowed here again."

No need to worry. He never told Mam' a thing. Sunday afternoon rolled around, and from the way she was beaming, I could tell that something happy was in the making. She disappeared into the bedroom, returning with a brown paper bag which she handed me. "This is for you."

For me! My brothers and sisters were all beaming too, as if they were in on a secret. Pricille was home from Mayflower. "Open it," she urged.

I ripped the bag open, and my surprise exploded, "*Une reversible skirt!*" I did a little tap dance. We took turns inspecting the nicest skirt I had ever seen at school or in Eaton's and Simpson's catalogues. It was nicer than Zita's, possibly nicer than Estelle's. Hers could never be as soft as mine was, flannelette cuddly. I turned the skirt inside out, outside in, ran to the bedroom, and came back to model. "So this is what you were sewing!"

With gentle strokes, Mam' pressed the pleats in place, examining her workmanship. "Not bad for an apprentice. Now, it's not a Christmas gift," she informed everyone. "Just something from Tante Marceline's remnants, a skirt that Zoé desperately needed."

I felt a flush come over my face, a soft flutter in my heart, a sort of affection for my mother. But I had important business to attend to. I skipped down the Cape road, straight to the door of Estelle's sun parlour. She'd *flip* at my new skirt. Out of Mam's sight, I rolled up the waist until my knees were showing, but just then, I saw something that squelched my enthusiasm. Paul-Emile was walking up the hill with Cedric. The very sight of his face rekindled my anger. I backed away from the door. I'd detest Estelle a bit longer. I'd hate him forever.

When I returned home, Pierre made the taunting observation, "Aaaaah, Estelle has a new friend now. I hear she's been spending a lot of time with Babette."

I merely grinned at the tease, "I don't care."

He moistened a flannelette rag with 3-in-1 oil, tied it with a long piece of twine and pulled it through the barrel of his 12-gauge until the gun shone. Then he counted the cartridges on the kitchen table. "André, come, if you want to learn how to make rabbit snares. You cut the wire into one-foot lengths," my brother demonstrated, as he twisted a sample wire into a hangman's noose, just like the lassos Zorro used to catch stray horses. "You leave a tail to attach to the branches. Like this." The expert flashed a boastful grin. "You clear yourself a nice little path, and when the rabbit comes hopping through the first lucky snare, head first, of course, the noose will tighten around its neck, and you got yourself a *fricot*."

I could almost smell the rappie dumpling stew, Philippe's favourite. He was being awfully quiet, his keen eyes examining the back of a transistor radio, though he did stop to caress Lulu's ears and pat her fat belly. "How many puppies in there anyway? Ten?" Lulu stared blankly at the aspiring engineer at work. "Uh huh," my brother muttered, and suddenly he had the whole kitchen's attention with his breakthrough. "I found the *problème*." Philippe picked up his soldering gun, but just as he attempted to weld a cold solder joint where one of the speaker wires joined the printed circuit board, André stood in his light. Philippe controlled his temper. "Move."

"Move me if you can," André challenged, and Philippe gave the smart alec a shove.

"I said move!" He wrestled his younger brother to the floor, seized him in a headlock. "Now what can you do, eh?"

"This," said André, and he wiggled to his feet, leaving Philippe stunned as to how he had lost his grip. Fists clenched, André bounced up and down, moving sideways, forward, backward—quite impressive. "Step into the ring, and I'll show you how you don't mess around with Sonny Liston."

The two swung at each other, playing at first, until Philippe jabbed a sensitive nerve in André's jaw, causing André to retaliate with a sharp left punch. They were striking blows that were a bit too bold for Mam's liking, and when André swung his upper cut and caught Philippe hard on the chin, she got on her high horse. "*Hé* ...

hé ... hé! Now that's nice between brothers, isn't it. *Aie bonne ... aie bonne ... aie bonne!"*

Pierre rolled up his sleeves, strode over to hold Philippe at arm's length until the rage in his eyes subsided. A sinewy lump of flexed muscles rippled the surface of the fisherman's arm, the result of pulling traps every day. "How about I take the two of you?" he invited.

"Sonny Liston" scanned the size of Pierre's arms and stepped out of the ring. Philippe was clearly no match either, with his frail, thin frame. He had not been blessed with the sturdy builds of either of his brothers, but he made up for it with his temper. "I'll get you next time," he promised André.

He soldered the troublesome wire, slid the back cover onto the transistor, and *voilà*, we had music, music from the radio, and music from Lulu—a lingering whimper, with intermittent low, lamenting howls. "*Oké. Oké,*" Philippe pressed as he put his things away. "It's hard to get attention around here, isn't it?" Like the weightlifters on TV, he braced himself for the effort. "Ugh! She weighs a ton! *A peusse une friggin' tonne.*" He carried Lulu to the attic. The attic? That wasn't where she slept.

Gusts of wind started howling at the kitchen window, and the falling snow turned blustery, sticking powdery-soft to the panes. André paced the floor. "I wonder if Dad is still in the marsh."

Thérèse had been perfectly content to watch Philippe and play with my wooden ox, but as soon as supper was finished and darkness had crept around the house, she decided it was time for her story. "*Les rats,*" she insisted. I sighed at the flickering lights, at the heavy snowfall that had everyone worried. Dad never knew when to come home.

"No story tonight," I told the child, who flung my ox across the kitchen floor. I marched her straight to her bed. "You're a nasty little girl, and you're never playing with my ox again!"

"*Les rats,*" she pleaded as I roughed up the blankets under her chin.

"There's a storm outside," I told her. "*Les rats* are hiding in the breakwater, sleeping in their beds, where nice little rats should be."

I snuggled her doll next to her face, but she started crying, "I want Dad."

"Dad's in the marsh hunting ducks," I explained, gazing at her darling little face. "Well, maybe one short story." It was about ducks coming down, one by one. "Bang! Bang! Bang!" Before I could finish, Thérèse was sound asleep … where nice little rats should be.

I hurried back to the kitchen, to the pounding on the storm door. André fought a raging gust of wind which almost blew the door off its hinges. My father entered with icy eyebrows, weeping eyes, and a grin, frozen in place. But he was fine, huddled inside his black army overcoat, his head well protected in a Russian fur hat with flaps that covered his ears. He had warm mittens, knitted with Zita's extra thick wool. He handed his gun to André, dropped to the floor four frozen rabbits from his snares and five ducks from the marsh. The depths of his blue eyes registered a provider's joy and pride.

Mam' rushed to hang his dripping clothes behind the stove and to spread newspaper over the floor. There were ducks to fix, but not before my father had rocked in his chair and enjoyed two cigarettes. He fumbled in his pants pocket for a peppermint, knelt on the floor to gloat over his trophies, which the boys were busy dressing. He had trained them well. They knew how to hold a duck, by the neck, plucking feathers in the same direction that they lay over the breast so as not to tear the skin.

Philippe was not his usual meticulous self, leaving clumps of down behind as his mind wandered to a spring brook. His passion was trout fishing. "Last spring," he told Pierre, "I caught a trout this long." With his index fingers he measured well beyond a foot, making my father smirk.

If there had been any trout that size taken, it had surely been caught by Pierre, the boy who went handlining at age twelve and came in with his dory overflowing with pollock. Pierre never tired of telling the story. "By the Jesus, the first few times, pollock were jumping everywhere, but wouldn't bite. I'd end up with a dory full of herring. Then a fisherman at the wharf told me, 'Pollock go for red, when the blood's in their head.' I started rigging my hook with herring gills…." When Pierre got excited, his voice thinned out into chuckles. He leaned back in his chair. " 'Sus Christ, they bit like hell, faster than I could reel 'em in. One day I came home with eleven hundred pounds."

Though Mam' was busy at the sink and collecting feathers all about, she took time to boast about her fisherman son. "Eleven hundred pounds. The men at the wharf weighed his catch. *J'lai vuz gréer c'matin là.*"

She had a mess of feathers to clean up and our bedtime routine to prepare. The Lambert's syrup and hot peppermint were ready on the table. Surely someone had the grippe. She plugged in the iron, put a few bricks in the oven to warm, and filled our "piggy" with water from the boiling kettle. That piggy, or foot warmer, was the source of many quarrels. The thick metal tank warmed some lucky person's feet long into the night. It was André's that night. He had claimed it first.

I ended up with the iron wrapped in a towel. I had to coax myself up those attic stairs. My nostrils dilated as I deeply inhaled frigid air, exhaling a trail of vapour before me. I jumped into my pyjamas, trembling until my body adjusted to the arctic climate. Once my teeth had stopped chattering and my limbs had stopped twitching wildly, I decided to check on Lulu, feeling apprehensive as I approached the warm stovepipe. She was making suckling noises. What's all the racket in here? I wondered, as I peered into her box.

"What in the dickens? Hein? *Quosque dans'l'jâub!*" Four fussing puppies were clinging to her drooping belly. "Somebody! *Ched zaun!* Hurry! *V'nez vite! Grouillez-vous.*"

Holy thunder roared up the stairs. Philippe was the first to appear in the studded doorway. "*Aâââh* ... she had her puppies."

André flashed his bright light on the little darlings that were soaked in a greenish, black fluid. "Holy frig!" he gasped. "What a mess!"

"Ma ... ma ... ma ... ma ... ma, " I called to Mam', who wasn't far behind. "There's molasses all over the blanket!"

She just grinned. "We'll have to put them downstairs until this cold snap is over." She fetched a couple of tattered blankets.

"When will they open their eyes?" I wanted to know.

Philippe answered, sweeping everyone away with his long arms. "In about two weeks. You'll see them in the morning." He moved the new family downstairs.

How could I sleep lying on a block of ice, with the iron at my feet barely lukewarm? Mam' threw Dad's hunting overcoat on top of me, adding another ton to the weight of my covers. Having picked up momentum over the ocean, the wind now raged at the windows, whistling drafts through every crack above my bed. The force of the gales made my bed rock. If Grand-mère Sophie had been in our attic that night, she would have been praying her rosary, especially when a powerful gust made the whole house shake, forcing the boards to creak. The roof! "Could the roof lift off?" I fretted, to André's great amusement.

"It certainly could, and we would all be blown into the ocean."

"If the rotten roof on Dominique's shed can withstand the likes of our gales," Dad assured me, "then you have nothing to worry about. Might lift a few shingles." I could see the red tip of his cigarette. He must have drawn a puff, pausing before he explained. "When the wind shifts to the northeast, you can expect this. It's nothing. It's only blowing sixty miles an hour."

But a gale of that velocity was more frightening at night. The most horrible feeling overtook me. "I don't want to die in the night," I called across the attic.

Dad didn't take any time to answer, always to the point. "There's no sense fussing about something we have no control of."

"I don't want to die on a rainy day either," I made it known. That was okay for Jesus on the cross on Good Friday, when it's supposed to be rainy and terribly gloomy.

The windows rattled. The cold and gusty winds raged. Every time I got a niche warm, my hip ached so that I had to turn over and freeze again. I tossed and turned until I was so exhausted that I finally dozed off, only to be awakened by Pricille, who shoved me over for my warm side of the bed.

"You woke me up!" I stammered, now shivering in my newly assigned icy patch. "Where in the world were you in a storm like this?"

"Playing cards at Zita's," she said. She talked about her job at Madame Thibault's. It sounded so exciting—baking bread, looking after kids, and washing dishes, floors, clothes.

"Do you know how to use the wringer washer?" I asked. "I hope you don't put the man's underwear with red blankets."

"Madame Thibault's not as fussy as Mam'," she assured me.

I rolled my eyes in the dark. "Is anyone? Hey, we have new puppies!" I exclaimed.

But Pricille sank her face in her pillow, yawning herself out of our conversation. "Tomorrow."

She was far too passive about our new suckling family of four. She deserved an elbow in the ribs. "I bet they're cuter than Clyde."

"Are not," she grunted.

I elbowed her again. "Then why don't you ever bring him home?"

"Because, ..." she yawned, "because I don't want him to know that Dad eats rabbit heads."

"Will we ever meet him?"

No answer, just the creaks and cracks and bangs of the angry wind. I got up and listened intently at the stovepipe for whimpering from the kitchen below, but our canine family was fast asleep. I returned to bed to agonize over a grudge that had lasted far too long. I simply had to make up with Estelle. As soon as morning broke, I would jump into warm clothes and trudge down the Cape road. She just had to see our new puppies.

Chapter 10

The cold wind had blustered all night long, chilling me to the bone. Metal rods were at war; their clattering was rhythmic and increasingly intense with each burst of the howling winds that should have died down at dawn. My father feared for his shingles. His trail of tobacco smoke already cut across the attic. If anything, the gusts had become more powerful, each assault more threatening, causing an occasional snap, a steady rattle, and then the crescendo— a violent *bang!*—as if an airplane had crashed on our roof and smashed to pieces. Collapsed metal rods scraped against our asphalt shingles on their way down.

Pricille's drowsy head surfaced from under the covers. "What in the Christ was that? *Quosse que dans l'enfare était çâ?*"

Alarmed, my brothers were energized like bolts of lightning, their thundering feet as overwhelming as the crash. Even my father could fly down those stairs when worried about his shingles.

I had more pressing concerns on my mind. Estelle. The puppies. But my attention was briefly diverted. The insulating plastic on my window billowed with the ruthless Cape St. Mary winds; somehow the snow always got in. There was a sizable snowbank on the floor below the window. I reached under my bed for the chamber pot and covered the frozen urine with the infiltrating snow. My thoughts grew fuzzy, the way Percy maintained that he had learned to think above sea level while gazing out of his lighthouse, his thoughts at times electrifying, to the healthy advantage of the pen. I gazed at the chamber pot, saw snow-white frosting on a piss-coloured cake. I gazed at my sleeping sister Pricille, saw a young woman in love, no longer a girl in the world of younger sisters and puppies, bubble gum and *True Stories*.

I put on my very special reversible skirt and raided the attic for my woollen snowpants. No bloomers for me. I was too old. I rushed down the stairs to Lulu's box, examined the tiny puppies nestled against their mother's warm belly. "Estelle's gonna come see you," I told them. They kept on whimpering.

The kitchen was fiercely cold, numbing—even with a crackling fire. I licked a peephole through the frost on the window. Wow, snowbanks up to the power lines! My father entered the house with joyous news. "No school today," he figured. "The snowplough will be on the main roads forever." He had verified his suspicion about the crash on the roof. "*J'shavais c'était l'aerial du TV.*" My brothers brought in the jagged remnants to show Mam'. She gave our porridge a long, hard stir, no doubt tallying how many baby bonuses it would take to buy a new aerial.

My father counted three peppermints in his bag and emptied, onto the table, the contents of his Export A package, enough tobacco to stretch two lean cigarette makings. His worry was clearly not about the aerial. "*Ma p'tite, Zoé,*" he addressed me; he used the full title whenever he wanted tobacco.

I lowered my face to the porridge before me, getting a bit too lippy, according to Mam's glare. "Not even an ox could make me walk to the store in weather like this, so you can stop staring."

"But this time will buy the two horns," he urged—a meagre incentive, given the sure struggle to the post office.

I shouldn't have looked up. Those pleading blue eyes got me every time. "First I want to watch you fix the rabbits," I compromised.

My father and I bulldozed our way through billowy drifts, arriving at Dominique's shed to fix the four bunnies already hanging on nails. It didn't take Dad long—a few swift cuts, and he had their furry coats peeled off. Then he slit them their full length from the groin to the front of the breastbone. He removed the entrails, reserving livers, kidneys, and hearts for his children to fight over. The ribs were definitely Pricille's. Nothing would be wasted. Even the heads were spoken for, whatever it was that my father sucked through the eye sockets. What a splattering mess he made. Guts were landing everywhere, except in the box at his feet. *Splat,* on my arm!

I shrieked, just like when Estelle and I had seen a mouse in Grand-mère Sophie's pantry, "Uuugh … yuuuuk!" The slimy stuff wouldn't shake off. *"Loutte ste marde d'la d'su ma manche."*

My father merely grinned, as if it were perfectly natural for my sleeve to be decorated with rabbit entrails. "I guess I missed the box."

"Well, you better not miss again," I warned him, "or you'll be passing the day without tobacco." He repositioned the box and perfected his aim. I left him to his rabbits and attempted the towering snowdrifts down the Cape road. I let myself fall on my back, flapping my arms wildly—a snow angel gone mad for Estelle. What fun we would have. I banged at the door, which brought her running to the sun parlour. "Wait till you see the snow!" I gasped, and her whole face brightened. I waltzed into her kitchen as if there had never been a harsh word between us. "You have to come to the store with me."

"Let me guess," she mused, "this time will add two legs to your ox."

"Two horns," I corrected. "We're still on the head." She went to root for heavy clothes.

We were halfway up the hill when I divulged, "We're going to Grand-mère's house first. I have two secrets to show you."

I had her going crazy. "You have to tell me now," she implored.

"Naoun, naoun, naoun," I persisted.

"Oué, oué, oué," she insisted.

Pointing to my snowpants, I slipped a clue. "Something new, something blue."

We stepped inside the shed of the old homestead and Estelle could barely keep her eyes closed. I pulled down my snowpants and, as gently as Mam' had, I ironed out the wrinkles in my new skirt.

"Can I open my eyes?" she pestered.

"Jette une minute," I answered. "All right. *Tu peux t'les rouvrir astheure."*

"Aaaaah," she exhaled from deep within her throat, making me turn around several times and admiring what I figured was the prettiest reversible skirt ever.

Her face grew dull as she coldly inquired, "Who made it?"

I couldn't look her in the eye. "Mam' bought it in Yarmouth."

Her dimples now set in a jeer, she drew back a few paces. "You're lying."

"Honest the God," I desperately pleaded, "I'm telling the truth."

"You're lying!" Estelle knew. "It's homemade. Your mother sewed it. Zita told Mam'." I could only cringe. That witch of a snitch! "Now what's the other secret?" Estelle probed.

"I'm not telling you!" I snapped.

She snapped right back, "Then I'm going home!"

"Then go home!"

The kitchen door opened, forcing a truce as Grand-père Dominique emerged, holding a poker in his right hand and glaring at the sight of Estelle. She gawked at the black poker and instant honey poured from her mouth. "Zoé told me that you have a new Boston Breeze. Dad's buying one. He sent me here to see if you like it."

Grand-père Dominique's expression changed instantly. Turning, he shuffled over to the stove and, surprisingly, responded in a civil manner. "Then come see."

He turned the knob of his new rig to ten, and with his poker, lifted the cover. The ejecting oil flame looked like the blow torch at the boatshop. Estelle knew how to feign utmost interest. "*C'es'n quite-a rig.*"

My father sat rocking by Dominique's kitchen window, his gaze fixed towards the wharf. The *Little Esther* had about three hundred traps at risk. Had any withstood the gale?

Grand-père Dominique grumbled about too many traps too close to shore. He grumbled about Grand-mère Sophie taking too long. She came out of her bedroom with her slip hanging inches below her dress. She was wearing two sweaters. I helped her button her coat, knotted her kerchief tight under her chin and fetched her tall boots. What if she fell? Even I had to scowl at the woman's stubbornness. "Why don't you use your new toilet?"

Her jowls turned red. "I can't do anything on that thing." She shuffled past the tiny bathroom where the infamous seat was installed. The necessary fixture caused her far too much anguish. She hadn't been averse to Tante Marceline buying a rig for the stove, or installing a phone, but a toilet had surely been Uncle John's idea, the braggart too highfalutin to use the outhouse for two weeks in the summer. Well she wasn't gonna use that toilet. Not for him, not for Tante Marceline, and certainly not for Dominique. He could grumble all he wanted.

"She'll use it someday," my father figured, always with a grin. He didn't mind shovelling a path to the outhouse.

Estelle and I were free to invade Grand-mère's bureau, which was covered with hand creams, brooches, ribbons, a saucer with a toothbrush to dye her hair, holy water, and a rosary. The latter was her security against the wind and the thunder, and her source of hope that her son Louis would someday return after a sixteen-year absence. I opened the top drawer and discovered Tante Marceline's wedding picture. She was so pretty in the satin crepe dress. Tante's inherited sparse hair was her agony, but it was an imperfection well-hidden under a brimmed hat decorated with a band of bugle beads. There were other pictures of Tante Marceline, in tailored suits and brimmed hats hiding her scanty hair. The high society clothes camouflaged the poor life she had known before she met Uncle John.

He was a braggart who came to our home for the sole purpose of finding fault with everything, barking his orders of what should be fixed on the old homestead, but never offering a "black penny," as my mother put it. His suggestions fell on deaf ears. Dominique wasn't Vendor Bill; he was far too cheap to replace even a nail. My father and N'Oncle Joseph shared a foul dislike for the light-haired, well-fed American. In the wedding photo, he is plump, dressed in a black jacket with satin lapels, and a ruffled shirt that looks like the blouse Zita wears with her reversible skirt. His dark trousers and bow tie are sissy looking, too. N'Oncle Joseph used to cringe at the picture, the reason Grand-mère removed it from the kitchen shelf.

On the braided rug by Grand-mère's bed is a bottle of Minard's Liniment for her rheumatic knees and a can of Dodd's Kidney Pills for Dominique's ailing kidney. The new Boston Breeze killed some of the mold and dampness in their bedroom, but the walls were still sweating, chunks of plaster having fallen from the cycle of freeze and thaw.

"How can two big people sleep in such a small bed," Estelle

queried, "when they're so fat!"

"Sssshhhh," I scolded. "Grand-mère Sophie's coming. Now watch your mouth."

Grand-mère loved it when Estelle put pincurls in her hair. My friend had a knack with sparse hair, gently securing the scant, wet strands with bobby pins, then making us wait for the few curls to dry.

"Couldn't we come back later?" I fretted, anxious about Dad's tobacco and the other secret waiting at home. But brushing the curls was the fun of it. With a hundred strokes of the brush, Estelle effected a thicker look for Grand-mère's hair, tying her favourite red ribbon snugly around the fluffed hairdo.

"You're gonna be quite the hairdresser," Grand-mère praised, and Estelle simply gloated. Away from Dominique's scolding eyes, Grand-mère admired the younger look in the mirror as if she might stop the clock from racing. "I'm sixty," she'd snap to the village ladies who themselves had enough wrinkles to inquire about her age. "*Y ont la fasse épaisse.*"

My father guessed she was eighty-two because the old Céline in St. Alphonse was rumoured to be around the same age.

"The old Céline finally died," I mentioned and Grand-mère simply stared. Her face was pale by nature, and now her droopy jowls turned red; she was upset at my repulsive remark. Though herself harvesting the scent of death, the thought of dying terrified her. She opened wide her blue eyes, her old hands fidgety. "To think where we end up." Six feet underground, I presumed she meant.

Estelle's eyes were fixed on Grand-mère's rheumatic knees, which were bound with turns and turns of brown gauze secured with big safety pins. My Grand-mère's swollen legs bore no shape, not even at the ankles. Her sneakers looked odd but were a must for such swollen feet.

"Her legs look like stovepipes," Estelle whispered as I coaxed her outside, rapping her on the head.

"She's not totally deaf you know! She has already complained that you're always staring." I steered her towards my house. "Now for the other surprise."

The fussing puppies' tiny grunts came from behind the stove. Estelle reached in the box. "Let's take them out."

"When we come back from the store," I stalled.

But she begged, "Come on. *Rinque une minute.*"

Even Mam' fell for the appealing dimples. "I can't see what harm it would do."

We watched the puppies' fat bellies wobble as they crawled to make headway. "Are they boys or girls?" Estelle asked, flipping them on their backs. Two males and two females. She baptized her girls Esther and Aggie.

I baptized one of my boys Bosco. The other one baptized himself when he bumped into a saucer of Lulu's milk—Clumsy. "I'll feed you herring and potatoes," I whispered under his floppy ear, "so you'll grow big and strong."

Estelle wouldn't let go of her beautiful Aggie, bringing her next to her face. "Pee-ewe! These puppies stink!"

Oh, oh! Madame Lulu was staring from her box. I took the puppy away from Estelle, lowering it back in with its mother. "Time to go to the store," I decided. "I think Lulu wants us to leave."

Estelle didn't forget that the puppies stunk, and waited for her chance to implement her plan.

When Philippe transferred them to Dominique's shed, she dragged me in there with a grin, determined to defy hell if she had to. "Let's give them a bath!" Dumbfounded, I could only stare. "Oh, come on," she urged. "They're big enough."

They didn't look it to me. "What if …"

"Don't start!" she cut me off. "Nothing will happen."

She fought the drifts to her house, out of breath by the time she returned with powdered soap, a basin, and a towel, all in a burlap potato bag. "And now the problem is water," she said, handing me a nearby pail. "Take this to Zita's."

"Zita!" I exclaimed, then contemplated the alternatives—my house or the old homestead. That would be inviting Mam' or Dominique to the shed.

"Learn how to lie," coaxed Estelle.

I anticipated Zita's response to my request for water. "What on earth for?"

Easy came the lie. "Estelle and I decided to clean Grand-père

Dominique's shed."

"Since when do you go around cleaning sheds?" she inquired, eyebrows raised, and I had reason to sweat. "My father fixed rabbits and made a mess. We want to swing in there but it stinks."

She was perhaps a bit hasty to grab the pail and fill it to the brim. "I think you two are up to no darn good."

I fled before she changed her mind.

Estelle filled the basin and partly submerged her Aggie in the sudsy water, rubbing her fur gently. "See, she likes it." The next puppy, Esther, didn't like it so much.

Estelle handed me Bosco, and I cupped my hands to the shivering body. "We better hurry! I think they're cold."

I grabbed the towel and dried the trembling puppy back in the box, covering him cosy in the folds of the old blanket. "Never mind Clumsy," I panicked, "I think something's wrong." I called Lulu back to the box. "*V'in t'en citte.*" She wouldn't budge. Madame Lulu was fixed in the corner of the shed where she had retreated.

Estelle gathered the evidence back into the burlap bag. "Come. She'll go in after we leave."

But rigor mortis had set in my limbs. "I can't move," I gasped, "not until they stop whimpering."

"That's their fussy period," Estelle reproved, her expression serious, believable. "All puppies do that. They'll settle down when their mother goes back in. She's waiting for us to go."

Terror-stricken, I looked around for the least trace of our despicable deed, which annoyed her all the more. "I got everything! Come on." She hid the burlap bag behind the outhouse and proceeded to babble on about a lousy kitten that her father didn't want her to get. "I already got a name—Foufou."

"Your father's not buying a Boston Breeze," I accused, completely changing the subject.

Her head swung sideways, her dimples showing again. "Smart, aren't I?"

"What if the puppies get pneumonia?" I pressed.

Her annoyance quickly turned to anger. "Pneumonia's for people, not dogs!"

She jumped into an inviting snowbank, surfacing in time to

catch my next concern. "What if Lulu doesn't go back in the box?"

"I bet she's in that box right now!" Estelle snapped. "And the puppies are all cuddled under her belly, nice and warm." She crossed her heart. "I saw Lulu move towards the box when we unlatched the door."

I had seen no such thing. An uneasy feeling started to knot in the pit of my stomach, gripping me in the chest. I could hardly breathe. Estelle chattered on about a fluffy white kitten. I fretted about four shivering puppies. Zita was right. The two of us were up to no darn good.

Chapter 11

There was a breathless calm in the attic the next morning. I turned my head. No rattle at the windows. The icicles were melting off the eaves of the house. The ray of sunlight that streaked across the attic warmed the morning air, a welcome change from the raging winds that had uprooted the aerial and lifted shingles from the roof. And now the aftermath—ravaged lobster traps, dismal faces among the fishermen. Pierre had heard at the wharf that a fisherman in Meteghan had lost his boat. "*C'est çâ qui l'on ramâché' au tchai.*"

The sun should have brightened my spirits, especially after a succession of such frigid winter days. It should have dragged me out of bed. But I feared getting up; my head was filled with a gnawing guilt. I could well imagine Estelle, nestled under her covers, unconcerned as to whether Lulu had gone back to the box. What if she hadn't? What if she had ignored the puppies' whimpering? I rolled the covers off me. I just had to face the day. I'd hurry to the shed and check for myself. The stairs creaked eerily on my way down. I had barely swallowed the last bite of my porridge before Mam' reminded me of the detestable job at hand. "The chamber pots are getting full." She already had her coat on.

She led the way through the snow drifts, spills from her pot dotting a yellow trail to the outhouse. I stopped and listened to the crunch of snow under her feet. I gazed at the white, soft blanket covering the countryside. The snow was blinding. Crystalline diamonds glittered everywhere, as far as my eye could follow the fields. The ocean was tame, absorbing blue from the sky. What a poem for Percy!

"What a day for washing!" Mam' exclaimed, the clear skies diverting her attention. In an ill-timed move, she turned her head to Grand-mère Sophie in the window and her arm jerked back, propelling a pisspotful of urine in my face and down my coat. Now on her knees on a patch of ice, Mam' cursed, "*Gee whisker de luck!*"

I dared not laugh, until an echo hooted from behind. "You need a slop pail with a lid!" Zita was in a bit of a hurry herself, breaking through the crusty snow with ankle-high boots. "I couldn't wait." She lifted her masterpieces for Mam' to see. "I just finished the boys' sweaters. *J'fais rinque d'les finir.*"

My intention was to sneak to Dominique's shed, but Philippe was coming, hastening through the path with a dish of food, a container of water, and a frown which worried me, though my brother was forever consumed in deep thought. When we crossed paths, I avoided eye contact. I followed Mam' and Zita back to the house. Better if I had fled down the hill.

Zita's knitted cardigans had long zippers in the front. "I think this one's the nicest," she said, examining the ducks in flight across the back of Pierre's. "Then again, ..." she contemplated the back of Philippe's. The dog was a replica of our Lulu, brown with a patchy white belly. Lulu! How long did it take to fill her bowls with food and water. What was taking Philippe so long?

I stared out the kitchen window. Such a lovely day, and the *Little Esther* and *Cape Marguerite* were tied to the wharf. Cedric was walking up the road. He bypassed Estelle's house and headed straight to mine. The poor boy took long enough to open the door, only to be greeted by a sarcastic Zita. "Look what the sunshine brought up the hill. I'm surprised you're not with Paul-Emile, up to no good."

André urged Cedric in. All in one motion, the boy grabbed a chair, spun it around, straddled it, and rested his elbows on the back. Wow! My brothers couldn't do that. Cedric had a strapping frame clad in an oversize army jacket—a fifteen-year-old seduced by the glory of someday joining the army. There was something about him. Perhaps it was the tuft of straight hair always in his eyes which made him look tough, or the nonchalant tone when he finally opened his mouth to speak. "I guess the *Little Esther* lost more traps than they thought."

André made a run for his jacket. "Then we have to go see! Was Dad at the wharf?"

"Yes," Cedric attested, then he abruptly raised his head. "Where's Philippe?"

Philippe. I could feel the palms of my hands begin to sweat.

"Gone to feed the dogs," André answered. "Why?"

Cedric was clearly embarrassed by my presence. "Dad was wondering if he could look at our TV. We've called a repairman for three weeks now."

With his keen eye for electronics, Philippe had earned himself a reputation. He could fix any TV. But when he stormed into the house, Cedric didn't open his mouth, and from his murderous eyes, Zita knew that my brother was in no mood for modelling cardigans.

"Zoé!" he bellowed, and I knew I was in violent trouble. He was shaking with rage. "Grab your coat and come with me!"

Mam' didn't say a word, her question silenced by the fury in her son's eyes. Dad couldn't save my life; he was at the wharf. The embarrassment of having to pass by Cedric in my urine-soaked coat was a humiliation I would live to remember.

My outburst of tears didn't generate the least pity in Philippe. When we got to Dominique's shed, he shoved me inside, pointing to the four puppies lying stiff in the box. "Did you have anything to do with this?"

Lulu was huddled in the corner of the shed, as if she had never moved. I stared at the frozen puppies, at the sprinkled detergent on the floor. "I don't know what you mean."

My brother picked up a few grains of the white powder on his finger, smelled them and dabbed the tip of his tongue. "You and Estelle washed those puppies, didn't you?" He yanked on the collar of my coat. "Didn't you!"

In broken sobs, I stuttered something about stinky puppies, Estelle, me, all the while watching the latched door. He released his grip and I ploughed through the tiny door, through the shovelled path as fast as I could, but not fast enough to escape his heavy lumberman's boot that struck me in the backside as I burst into the house.

My father, who had just walked in, grew enraged when he saw me doubled up, holding onto my lower back. "Leave her alone!" he ordered, and Philippe let go of my arm.

I hid behind the stove and cried, away from Cedric's stare and out of my brother's reach. Philippe's reasoning took another turn. "I bet you anything it was Estelle's idea. She's always up to no good, that one."

"And they can't wait to be teenagers," was Mam's troubled reproach. "*Des grand bringues coumme çâ.*"

"Only Estelle could scheme up something like that," Zita agreed. "So that's what the pail of water was for! Should have known."

"Even if it was Estelle's idea," Mam' hastened to point out, "Zoé didn't have to go along with it."

Philippe turned his fury towards Mam'. "I don't want to see Estelle around here ever again. Never! *C'es'n sacré folle çâ.*"

Pierre arrived home shortly thereafter, met at the door by my irate brother. "You can forget about your hound!"

Pierre dropped his soaked mittens on the oven door, got himself a drink of water, and listened to the drawn-out story. He simply raised his head to Philippe, grinning, "Then I guess we'll get our hound from the next litter." He had a story of his own, one of a far greater loss. "There's red-and-white buoys and broken traps everywhere." The two boys donned their new cardigans to patrol the shore.

I approached my father's rocking chair, saddened by the deep lines in his brow. "Did you lose all your traps?" I asked. It took him a long time to lift his white head. I could read the solemn expression. Too many. "Can't you fix them?" I fretted, but he didn't answer, just scratched the bottom of his tobacco package. I was sweeter than a buttercup in our spring meadows. "You need tobacco?"

He just stared, a void in the depth of his blue eyes.

"This time will buy the eyes for my ox," I persisted, and his blue eyes brightened. Lo and behold, I had enticed a grin.

Mam' rooted through her top drawer, shaking her head in disgust as she counted the last of her change. "I always thought you had a bit more sense than Estelle. Two peas in a pod," she scolded. I grabbed the change and attempted a mad dash out of the bedroom but ran smack into André's stretched arms across the doorway.

"Seems like Madame Lulu doesn't like the smell of Oxydol," he sneered.

I heard a loud snap when I ploughed through his barricade. "I hope I broke your arm!" I screamed and stormed out of the house, bursting into a renewed ocean of tears. Standing on Grand-mère Sophie's bank, I grieved over the long walk to the post office without Estelle. I glanced towards her house, contemplating Philippe's harsh decision, its severity unbearable. Never again allowed up the hill! Nothing could have lifted my spirit then, not Cedric with his compassionate shy smile, certainly not André with the mocking smirk on his face. Not even the sun shining brightly on the snow, making the sparkling surface dance. I cried, and the beauty of the countryside blurred before me. The sun only filled my head with a dread of the gloomy days that would surely follow.

Chapter 12

I was never so glad to board the school bus and could barely wait for Estelle to claim her spot by the window. "The puppies are dead!" I announced.

She nudged me in the ribs. "Keep your voice down. *Point si fort!*" She turned around, giving Babette one of her fatal glares. "Don't be so nosy."

The sweet girl with the honey-blond, shoulder-length hair and olive green eyes pulled her neck back, turning her head to the boring countryside.

I whispered the horrible sentence passed on Estelle. "You can never come to my house again!" My eyes grew teary as I reported, "Philippe put the puppies in a potato sack, said I couldn't bury them in frozen ground." Estelle understood that he had looked after them himself, down the cliff. For a moment, I thought I might start crying. "If you can't come to my house, I'll just die." Estelle appeared far too nonchalant. "You know Philippe," I warned her, "he means what he says."

"He'll get over it," she figured, not easily intimidated. "How many times has he sent me home? I always came back, didn't I?" I pointed to where the angry boot had left its mark, but it didn't wipe the smirk off her face. "You're just gonna have to learn how to run."

I mentioned the name Zita and *then* she stiffened in her seat. "Don't tell me that big mouth was there!"

I nodded. "She told Philippe that it was all your idea, that you were the one who had gone there looking for water."

"And what did you say?"

"Nothing. It was your idea, wasn't it?"

"But I didn't get the water," she flung back.

I cringed at the malice in her face, but defended, "I got the boot. Shouldn't you take some blame?"

She turned her head to the window. "I'll fix that witch."

I feared for Zita. When Estelle had a fix for someone, she was not nice, at all.

"I don't want to hear one more word about the puppies," Mam' ordered. The boats had left the wharf and she wallowed in annoyance, shining the stove when it already gleamed, sweeping the floor when there was no dirt to sweep, not listening when we spoke. She was preoccupied with the duster and broom that helped her forget her problems.

The captain of the *Little Esther* had gathered in his backyard the salvageable traps, and he and my father had embarked on the arduous task of fixing them and building new ones. It wouldn't be long before another three hundred traps hit the water. But this hopeful view to spring didn't put bread on our winter table. According to Pierre, no one would starve. Not as long as he had his health and the weather permitted the *Cape Marguerite* to leave the wharf.

"We can't take your money," Mam agonized, provoking one of my brother's teasing grins.

"Then what would I do with it?"

"Buy a guitar," she suggested. "You always wanted one. Someday you'll want a car. A house." She lightened up for a little tease of her own. "You'll want to get married."

My brother ignored my mother's pride, seeing to it that there was lots to eat, that lunch cans were amply packed for school. He offered me the excess change from his pockets, but I shook my head, just as Mam' would have. "You need your money."

Philippe offered me a quarter, and I gazed at it, envisioning a bagful of jawbreakers. "I guess I have a bad temper," he grinned, and I knew he must have agonized over this apology. "Take it!" he insisted. It made good sense to smile and grab the quarter, the apology not to be misconstrued as a go-ahead to run down the hill—anger still darkened his face when he gazed towards Estelle's house.

He said I could accompany him to Gustave's house after school.

"Me?" I caught myself exclaiming. I passed the day at school in a twitter, causing Estelle to lose her patience.

"What's gotten into you?"

I couldn't tell her. She would have wanted to come.

The smell of shallots simmering in Lina's kitchen was enough to tempt me to invite myself for supper. She was up to her elbows in *poutines râpées*. She lowered the potato dumplings into a large pot, filling it to the brim, so the lid danced when the *fricot* started boiling.

"Where's Cedric?" I asked, and she looked at me as if it were an odd question.

"Gallivanting the shores with Paul-Emile," came the answer from the parlour. Gustave advanced into the kitchen, a happy smile on his face when he saw Philippe. "Come to fix my TV?"

There was no need to waste time. "Cedric told me the problem," my brother answered.

Gustave moved out of his way. "Pretend I'm not even here." That was difficult to do. "By the Jesus," he couldn't wait to boast, "I got a rig in the barn that will take me mossing this summer. *Ça vâ fare la mousse e-stanné.*"

Philippe clicked the TV on to a screen full of snow. He wiggled the knob, getting a picture for about three seconds. Again, he wiggled the knob, and the picture returned, then faded back to snow. "I see," my brother thought out loud. "It's probably the tuner." He yanked the knob loose and removed the back of the TV set.

"Basil's men did one helluva job," Gustave beamed. "The caulking is some tight."

My brother merely grinned; he had seen the dory at the boatshop. "Those guys are good," he readily agreed. He blew on the tuner and surrounding tubes to clear the dust. "Dirty contacts," he mumbled, pulling a clean hankie from his pocket.

"You think?" Gustave anxiously probed.

Philippe grinned. "I'll tell you in a minute." So utterly meticulous about everything, he fussed, re-examined his work before he let out an accomplished sigh. "Let's see if the problem's fixed." He contained a few curses under his breath. Putting things back together was always more difficult than taking them apart. He wiggled the channel selector back in place and bounced to his feet, "Turn it on. *Yiell'tant tester les affares.*"

Gustave switched channels half a dozen times, mightily pleased. "How much do I owe you?"

Philippe closed the back of the TV, sporting a wide grin of his own. "Nothing. I may need you to guard the wharf this summer. *Meque'haul mes p'tit jumârds.*"

An avid lobster poacher himself, Gustave displayed a full set of teeth in a furtive smile. "Sure thing." He invited Philippe to the barn to check out his mossing rig. The dory was painted bright red. Philippe couldn't help but chuckle. This Noah's ark would surely gleam through the thickest fog.

I, too, had a rig worth bragging about—the best present Tante Marceline had ever brought us kids from Boston. The long wooden sled had narrow metal runners, faster than any skates, and a heavy black steering bar, fashioned for skilled manoeuvring, although André claimed that the trick was in the movement of the feet.

I hurried home to the fastest sled in Clare District. "Philippe's still at Gustave's," I informed Mam'. "I'm going sleighing."

Of course, Thérèse was right behind me, waving two tiny boots and looking for her snowsuit. "You're not coming!" I made clear, and Mam' flashed me one of her glares. I ended up dressing the pest.

Once outside, she immediately pointed to the fields. "*Les vaches.*"

"The cows are in the barn for the winter," I told her. I scanned the fields, imagining the rust-coloured coats beautiful against the white snow. Another poem for Percy.

I had to untangle our sleds from under broken aerial remains. Here was a foot-long antenna rod. I knew the skiers on TV picked up speed with the help of their poles. I figured the antenna could be my pole.

"You like to go fast?" I queried Thérèse, my voice almost threatening. "You're gonna go down that hill like you never have." I started up the long field, pulling two sleds with one hand and dragging her with the other. The antenna rod was clenched between my teeth. "You're too slow!" I growled, and the little tyke started to cry. She had short, chubby legs—adorable she was, really, with her long curly locks bouncing out of the hat Zita had knit for her. She made it to the top of the hill, stopping every few breaths to rest. I positioned her small sled behind mine and hooked the toes of my boots snug into her steering crossbar so that all she had to do was hold on tight. Her happy face added brightness to a dull afternoon. "All set?" I asked, and she nodded with an anxious chuckle.

The narrow runners of my sled were breaking through crusted snow, coasting downhill rather slowly at first.

"*Pu vite. Pu vite,*" Thérèse cried and I dug my pole in the hard snow, accelerating our pace to her kind of speed. But then we hit old tracks, and we were going *too* fast. I looked back, taken by the child's innocent laughter as we plunged down, down, down the steep hill. My sled lunged forward—I saw terror in the making. We were headed for the fence below, and I didn't know any dexterous tricks with my feet. In a frantic attempt to free my hands, I held the antenna rod between my clenched teeth, but nothing could have halted our race downhill. We were doing record speed, straight for the fence.

Pray! Mam' had drilled us, so I begged for sweet mercy. If the heavens were listening, they failed to remind me of the rod, its jagged end pointing down my throat. The other end protruding from my mouth collided with the fence. Thérèse's sled rammed into mine, and my head jerked back violently, bringing the nightmare to a dead stop.

Blood! Blood everywhere. The antenna rod had ripped a jagged wound down to my very tonsils, I could be sure. In slower than slow motion, I crawled away from the fence. "Thérèse!" Luckily, she had been hurled clean off her sled.

"*Es-tu all right?*" I gurgled from deep within my throat.

My small sister pointed up the field. "*Les vaches?*" As if she knew that talk about cows was grossly out of context, her face grew serious. "*Babo.*" Confused, she could only stare at the blood now gushing from my mouth and painting the snow red. "*Zoé morte!*" she cried, and I felt goose flesh crawl up my spine. There was no surer way to send me running home than to hear her morbid cry that I was dead.

Mam' opened the door, and her face turned pallid when she saw the blood dripping down my coat. My legs buckled and she had to support me to the kitchen sink, where a terrible fear masked her dark eyes. "Can you talk?" I nodded a sure yes, and she shook me. "Then say something!"

Words were muffled, gurgling from deep within. "*Bumpé dans la bouchure.*" Good! She understood that I had hit the fence. "*L'aerial,*" I said, pointing to my throat.

"You had it in your mouth?" she probed. I nodded. The blood splattering into the washbasin told the obvious.

"It ripped down your throat when you hit the fence," she quickly determined. I gave a nod, relieved that the ordeal of communicating the story was over.

"Does it hurt?" Mam' wanted to know, and I set her mind at ease with a simple shake of my head. She gaped at the blood splashing her enamelled sink. "By the crackie," she well figured, "*tu teulle l'âs collé.*"

Philippe approached the sink and noticed I was swallowing the coursing blood. "Spit it out!" he ordered. "Spit it out, or you'll choke!"

"But I won't have any more," I sobbed, holding onto the sink, frightened by the rapid loss of my precious blood. "No doctor. Don't make me go."

My father approached the sink, examining the oozing mess. Mam' must have prayed like she never had before because finally, finally, the flow calmed to a trickle and I stopped sobbing. She wiped her forehead with her apron then raised her eyes to the ceiling, "*Marci Djeu misarécorde. C'etait'n quite-a geste çâ.*"

She relaxed her tense shoulders and helped me to the downstairs bedroom, where she propped me up with an extra pillow, covering it with a folded flannelette sheet. She turned my face sideways to drain the trickle of blood. Then she returned to the kitchen, and I could almost see her with her Bon Ami, scouring her sink back to a sparkling white. I could hear the rapid rocking of my father's chair and his concerned voice. "Shouldn't we call the doctor?"

We were behind in bills that dated back to when our baby girl had died. Mam's answer was long in coming. "Zoé doesn't want to go." My father should have pressed the issue.

Mam' lay next to me all night, refolding the flannelette sheet clean whenever it became sodden with red saliva. Every time I awoke, she was leaning over me, her ear attuned to the sound of my breathing. Morning had hardly broken before the bedroom filled with people, Grand-père Dominique bent over, peering at my swollen right cheek, which he said was turning blue. The putrid smell of his breath filled my nostrils as he shook his head in disbelief. "Not good. Not good."

Grand-mère Sophie's lips were moving to the sound of rosary beads clicking in her pocket. Even Cedric entered the bedroom, seemingly shaken. Pricille was home from Mayflower. Everybody spoke in hushed tones, so nice to me. The whole scene reminded me of a wake. But I was alive! Very much alive, especially when Charlotte walked in and bent down to whisper in my ear, "Estelle can't wait to see you. I wanted to check with your mother first."

I swung my head sideways, the gurgle in my voice was still audible. "Can she Mam'? A *peut-ti?*"

She glanced over at Philippe and he smiled his agreement. She could.

But before Mam' had a chance to answer, N'Oncle Joseph walked in, cringing as he coaxed himself near the bed. "Open your mouth," he ordered, the only one brave enough to look at the blackish mess curdled inside. He pulled back, grimacing. "It's too swollen to see anything. How much blood did she lose?" Mam' talked about full washbasins and a flannelette sheet soaked through and through during the night. He grinned at the exaggeration. Even I knew I would have been dead had I lost that much blood. "That girl's going to the doctor," he determined. "Pack some clothes Martine. He'll be ordering her to the hospital, or my name's not Joseph."

Mam' neatly folded a few pieces of clothing in a tattered brown suitcase that she found in the attic. Pierre opened his wallet, slipping lots of dollars in her purse. She didn't argue this time and appreciated Zita's help in dressing me. I had my coat on, but my brothers and sisters had crowded around, as if Mam' needed their blessing before we could leave. "This is probably best," she assured them, and they all followed to the kitchen. Where was Dad? The empty rocking chair looked out of place.

"You want me to check in Dominique's shed?" N'Oncle asked, but I knew Dad escaped to the woods when his mind was troubled.

Suppressing tears of disappointment, I turned to face the door. "I want to go now."

Chapter 13

I lay in my narrow bed, totally bewildered by the activity in the halls. Nurses with preoccupied faces were hurrying every which way, carrying trays with pills and needles, bedpans, plastic bags filled with blood, long rubber tubes and pitchers. *Aaaaaahh!* Zita had told me all about enemas and had strictly warned, "Every morning a nurse will ask you if your bowels moved. Just say yes."

My wrist was hooked up to a plastic tube that filtered clear drips from a hanging bottle. I needed special care.

"Where you from?" the nurses wanted to know. When I told them from the Cape, a few of them frowned, but most remembered at one time or another having been to Mavillette beach and marvelling at the quaintness of Cape St. Mary, the little village perched atop a rocky cliff that overlooked the western tip of the beach.

"I'm from West Pubnico," my favourite nurse said. "My name is Adèle." Her auburn hair was tucked in a bun under a white hat adorned with a black velvet band. She tightened a grey cuff around my arm and felt my wrist to count heartbeats. Then she stuck a thermometer in my mouth, cranking my bed to sit me up. "Do you like it this way?" She cranked it down. "Maybe this is better." I could never have imagined such fussing. Adèle was a *par-en-bas*, with a similar French accent that I couldn't get enough of, saying "ting" instead of "thing," "dis" instead of "this," and "doze" instead of "those." She told me "dat" she had three sons, and talked, talked, talked, about her nineteen-year-old, who was attending Saint Mary's University. She asked me the odd question and had to listen closely since my words were still muffled. It was easier for me to point. "I know," she acknowledged. "You have a hard time opening your eye." She brought her freckled face next to mine. *"Ouain, c'est pretty swollen çâ."*

The tube attached to my wrist was feeding me and pumping medicine to fight a vicious infection. The surgeon arrived to scan my chart. He moved my face to examine my swollen right cheek, scribbled a bit, then pressed on my inflamed throat with what looked like a stir-stick until tears welled in my eyes. Again, he scribbled on the chart and bent down, polishing his manner with a smile. "It's swollen because of blood poisoning." He started towards the door, telling Adèle, "The swelling has to go down before I can operate."

They left, and the curious princess in the next bed jumped to the floor, coming to examine my cheek. Her nose was wrinkled to match the furrows in her forehead. "You can't talk much, can you. What's your name?"

"Zoé," I managed to say.

"Mine's Anna. Can I?"

I nodded, and she picked up my wooden ox, inspecting it closely. "Who made it?"

"Dad," I said.

"Ooooh! Your father's very clever."

She must have noticed my blank look at her fancy word. "Special," she clarified. "To have carved this for you. What's his occupation?" I didn't answer, so she asked, "What does he do?"

"Fixes traps," I replied.

"A fisherman," she smiled. "My father's an RCMP officer," she beamed proudly. "I saw yours. He has a brushcut and a mustache. His name is Joseph, isn't it?"

I stared at her innocent round face, lowering my gaze to avoid her eyes. "Yes."

"I'm having my tonsils out," she informed me, "so you must be, too." I nodded, dodging a long story. "I'm getting a real pony if I pass," she said, adding that she had already skipped two grades along the way. "Do you still play with dolls?" she wanted to know.

I grinned at the thought of my boring *catonnes* with which Estelle never wanted to play. "No. I don't."

Anna had a winter doll, dressed in a maroon velvet coat with white fur on the sleeves and encircling the collar. "She's Porcelain," she volunteered. I found that a rather strange name. When she noticed me staring at her silver locket, she drew nearer, opening it. "This is my dad." She suddenly closed the locket and jumped into her fluffy slippers and pink housecoat, leaving to travel the halls. Her bushy, blond curls bounced with each skip. I wondered about the locket's empty space. Where was her mother?

My own mother's eyes widened when the surgeon attested, "One more day at home and your daughter would have died of blood poisoning." She paled at the raw facts. "The aerial ripped her right tonsil. I'll have to take it out. But don't worry Mrs. LeBlanc," he assured her, "we're clearing the infection. The swelling's going down."

Mam' relaxed her tense expression. "She does sound a lot better today." Her red lipstick drew attention away from her sunken eyes. She fumbled in her paper bag and handed me something rectangular and prettily wrapped. This drew an excited screech from my throat. "From Estelle!"

"No," she grinned, but I still frantically ripped the paper off. It was a copy of *Black Beauty* with an autograph inside the back cover.

"Babette!" I corrected, baffled. "How in the Moses, ... how did she know that I wanted this book?" I held the gift to my breast, felt a stir of affection for the sweet girl with the olive green eyes. "I don't have pretty paper to write her a thank you," I fretted.

Mam' smiled sweetly, "When you come home, you can tell her in person."

I loved it at the Yarmouth hospital. Mam' was so nice. "Now," she pressed, "you haven't told me yet what I can get you that's special." Minutes passed as she rearranged cards on the window sill and refolded the blanket at the foot of my bed. "Well, have you thought of anything?"

I scanned the tiny room, my gaze landing on Anna's Porcelain. No. Thérèse would break a doll like that. "Anna's very nice," I told Mam', "but she uses words ... an English dictionary! That's what I want, a dictionary."

Taken off guard, Mam' glanced over at N'Oncle Joseph. "A dictionary!"

"*Oué*," I blurted, "more than anything else in the whole world."

There wasn't the least surprise on N'Oncle Joseph's face. He rose from his chair, accorded me one of his relaxed smiles, then gestured for Mam' to follow. "There must be dictionaries here in Yarmouth."

I told Père Lucien, who was always pressed for time, "I got this from Mam' and I'm gonna read it from cover to cover. And when I'm through, there won't be one English word that I don't know."

Père Lucien smiled as he lifted the heavy dictionary. "How about you start with the word 'confession.' " He drew the white curtain around my bed and spread his black soutane neatly over the easy chair in the corner. "So," he said, his bushy eyebrows moving up and down, laden with important business, "you're having an operation. How about a little confession, or does it tire you to talk?"

"Only to Anna," I whispered. "She wants to talk all the time."

The kind priest chuckled, dragging his chair closer. "I'm sure you don't have volumes of sins. Take your time."

I did take my time, long tense moments before I could bring myself to divulge, "Zita lied to Philippe about who got the water."

Père Lucien's subdued chuckle mushroomed into a hearty laugh. "Even in sin, there is comedy. Then she's the one who should confess."

I cleared my slate of a tobacco-related sassy incident. When he wouldn't stop probing, I fabricated a few swear words at Estelle, at which he lowered his brows.

"Your *pénitence* will be three Acts of Contrition."

Anna wanted to know what I had confessed. "That's between him and me," I rebuked, making her retreat to her bed.

"You're odd."

I asked nurse Adèle, "What did Anna mean, that I'm *odd*?"

She grinned. "In this case, it means you're different, sweeter than any girl she's ever met."

When Anna next came to my bed, I had oodles of friendly

smiles, and I talked as though my throat wasn't tired at all. She asked what we ate at my house and I itemized: rappie pie, *fricot*, lots of fish chowders, potato pancakes, and blah! salted herring. She had no problem with boiled dinners, and told me that they ate shallots, but called them green onions. She smiled at my description of our Hallowe'en cabbage soups and could even admit to having eaten the big clams that we called quahogs. But *yuk* is what she thought of our blood pudding and the stinky dry fish that we tear into edible strips with our teeth. She grimaced at the mention of rabbit, so I felt it best to leave out porcupine and eels.

"Do you know any jokes?" she asked, and my favourite came to mind, about the two flies hovering around a flystrip.

"What did one fly say to the other?" I asked, and she blinked, unknowing.

"What?"

" 'With all the cow shit in the pastures, there's no sense sticking around here.' "

"That's not very nice!" Anna scolded, and I wished that I could dissolve into my IV. She took to the corridors.

"Do you think Anna's mad at me?" I asked nurse Adèle as she rested her washbasin and white towels on my night table, the customary smile on her face. "Who could be mad at an innocent face like yours?" She proceeded to bathe my exposed parts first: my face, neck, and arms, and then with a sweep of her hand she groped under the white sheet, choosing this awkward moment to reopen the case of the frozen puppies. "Tell me the story again."

I got so involved in my story that she had me dressed in a green gown with matching hat and booties by the time I realized I was being wheeled away. I ended up in a large room with glaring lights on the ceiling. I was lifted onto another bed surrounded by lots of doctors and nurses, eager, I knew, for me to go to sleep so they could poke down my throat. Nurse Adèle came over and squeezed my hand, but she had to move aside to make way for the clown in a white coat who was wheeling in an oxygen tank and holding a green mask, which he fitted over my face.

"Want to go diving?" he jested. "If you can count to twenty, we'll all sing you a song."

Determined to witness the entire ordeal wide awake, I smiled back at all the faces, "One ... two ... three ... f o u r ... f i ..."

I opened my eyes to a blurred form standing over me. "It wasn't so bad now, was it?"

"Mam'?" I uttered groggily. Another form approached, dressed in a white shirt, and tall, tall, tall, with bushy hair heaped on top of his head, a big nose. I blinked a couple of times, bringing blue eyes into focus, a grin. "Daaad!" He was just in time to watch me vomit the insides of my stomach.

"The ether from the anesthetic," the surgeon explained.

My father was dressed handsomely, down to a pair of brown suede shoes. No doubt he had scrubbed under Mam's scrutiny because the creases in his neck were clean. But sweat poured down his face, and he huffed, "Phew! It's hot in here!"

"Who's getting your tobacco?" I asked, but he was too shy to answer with white-coated professionals crowding our space.

With his thumb and index finger, the surgeon measured the width of a hair, looked at Dad, then at Mam'. "She's a lucky girl. This much more and she would have bled to death or never talked again."

I understood that if the jagged rod had ripped my jugular, it would have been all over. That was the only time I ever saw my father turn pale. I wondered what it had taken to pry him loose from his rocking chair. God had surely spared me so I could witness this moment —my father in a hospital! Back in my room, he fidgeted on his chair, gasping for air. He ripped open the top button of his shirt, and lamented the heat until Mam' walked him to a well-ventilated lounge where he could enjoy a smoke with N'Oncle Joseph.

Had Anna seen his toothless gums, I wondered. She sat in her bed transfixed, a myriad of questions brewing. But she kept them to herself until the room emptied. "Why did you lie about your father?" she rebuked. "Joseph is your uncle."

Guilt coursed through my veins. The cock should have crowed three times: I had denied my own father.

"Tell me about where you live," Anna pressed.

I merely smiled, "I'm too tired." Princesses lived in rich houses. She could never appreciate snow infiltrating the windows in the attic, urine freezing in our chamber pots, or Dad wiping the floor with his stocking feet. I fell asleep with a grin on my face.

When I awoke the next morning, the inquisitive Anna was standing by my bed, as if she had spent the night watching over me.

"How long have you been staring at me?" I asked, a bit irritated.

"Just now," she said. She insisted that I open my mouth wide, figuring that if they had taken out her two tonsils, then surely they had taken both of mine. As she ate her breakfast, I described the sleighing accident. This led to a dictionary game. She chose words. I looked up their meanings. Then she dug through a pile of her books. "Do you like poetry?"

"No," I regretfully admitted. "I don't understand it."

"Oh, but you'll understand Robert Frost," she assured me, flashing the title in my face—*Favourite Poems for Young Readers*.

Anna insisted that she read to me, and I was glad she did. During the course of a few hours, Robert Frost led me through the woods on a snowy evening, invited me along to choose a Christmas tree, gather rustling leaves, pick apples, stroll through blueberry pastures. We even travelled to Vermont in the United States. Mr. Frost made me laugh. He made me cry. He made me think. He cautioned me that I should make time for friends. He rushed me through four seasons, all possible weather conditions. He made me appreciate ants, even lizards. And he didn't leave out my precious feathered friends, winning my admiration with "A Minor Bird."

"Read it again!" I pleaded.

Anna threw the poetry book on my bed. "Take it home and fill your head." She removed her father's photo and threw her locket on my bed as well. "Oh Anna!" I almost cried, "are you sure?"

"Take it," she insisted. "I have another one home."

I fondled the locket a fair while before I dared ask, "What happened to your mother?"

She gave me a surprised look. "Now, why would you ask me that right this minute?"

"Because she wasn't in your locket," I said.

"Very observant." She slapped my hand away from the dictionary. "Means you notice everything."

"I was five years old when she left," Anna began. By the time she finished the story, tears were rolling down her round face. Rage soon stopped her crying. "It took me a long time to realize that her promises to return were lies."

Somehow I, too, felt that the runaway didn't deserve a space inside Anna's silver locket. I fastened it around my neck, knowing I would cherish it for the rest of my life.

When the time came for Anna to start gathering her things, I fought the urge to cry. She made a soft bed in her folded pyjamas so that Porcelain's face wouldn't break. She arranged her jewellery inside a leather box. She patted the dust off her fluffy slippers and neatly packed them next to her pink housecoat. And then there were all her cards lining both of our window sills.

"Why are you crying?" she asked, noticing my tears. I understood then that she had lots of friends waiting. She had changed my life forever, yet, all she could say was, "Hope you get to go home soon." She had a new canopy bed in her room, a good reason to race down the long hall.

"Thank you for Robert Frost," I called, but the princess kept right on going. She was in a hurry to return to her palace. She'd even forgotten the flowers on her night table.

Had it not been that Estelle had something very important to tell me, I might have cried the day I left. I would miss the pampering from the kind nurses, especially my Adèle, who relayed her deepest regret. "How I wish you were older, to meet my son." I blushed, taking her to mean the one at Saint Mary's University.

Estelle. Estelle. She was all I could think of.

I have something very important to tell you, she had underlined in her card, on which red flowers were painted, geraniums Adèle said. Estelle had enclosed a photo taken in front of her N'Oncle Edwin's house. I wore a kerchief tied snugly under my chin, the long grass hid my skinny legs. How I envied Estelle's thick curly locks and the two dimples that embellished her chubby cheeks. She favoured tight sweaters to flaunt her developing bosom. She had written a short note in the card, the story of her revenge on Zita. By the time I had removed all the staples, I could hardly read the punctured message:

I waited until dark, then took all the things off Zita's line and threw them down the cliff. The next day, the ocean had swallowed them. I heard she was sick to her stomach about her lace tablecloth. She's blaming Paul-Emile and Cedric. Cedric got in a lot of shit. I know you won't tell. You never tell. That's why I trust you.
DE TA BEST FRIEND ESTELLE
P.S. I have something very important to tell you. It's a secret.

N'Oncle Joseph's car was too old, crawling along the country-side like it wanted to die. Estelle must have been watching for it. I was barely in the house before she stormed in. There was a gleam in her eyes that I attributed to pressing news. But Thérèse trailed along behind me, unwilling to release her grip on my skirt until I stooped down and opened my mouth wide. "See, the nice doctor took my *babo* out."

She followed Estelle and me into the downstairs bedroom where she laid her doll on the pillow. Estelle wanted her out, and didn't want to know anything about Anna, nurse Adèle, and most of all, Robert Frost.

She sat on the bed, broaching her own subject with excessive fuss. "The day after you left for the hospital, ..." She stopped, her eyes fixed on the door she wanted closed.

"Mam' doesn't like it when we close the door," I warned. "Now tell me, quick."

Again, she hesitated, causing me to lose my dwindling patience. "Tell me right now, or I don't want to know! *Arrête de frigger.*"

Flipping her long beautiful hair, she played the sophisticate, savouring her big news. "The day after you left for the hospital ..." she reiterated.

I got so stinking mad that I no longer wanted to know. "Say it or shut up!"

"*Oké. Oké.* I'm menstruating," she blurted.

I could only gasp, "You got your period!"

Ceremoniously, the sophisticate took out a sanitary napkin from her pocket, "These are called Kotex."

"And I have a sister called Pricille," I reminded her. "She always had a blue box in her orange crate by our bed. André calls them monkey hammocks. *Des hammaques à singes.*"

Apparently, there was serious etiquette attached to turning into a young woman. Estelle now had to sit right, bathe and change her clothes more often, and ignore all the boys who would surely fight for her. The boys! Her mother warned her that she could now have babies.

I felt a pang of jealousy at Estelle's good news, but just as ceremoniously I began to describe what I had witnessed through the cracks of closed curtains at the hospital: a lady with the ugliest scar where her breasts used to be; the strange gowns with a slit in the back; the old man trying to hide himself while a nurse rammed a needle into his flabby backside. "When she turned him, ... oh my God! I saw everything."

Starry-eyed, Estelle held her breath, examined herself in the mirror, her deep breaths thrusting her chest forward. "So! I've seen one before."

My eyes nearly popped out of my head. Of all the secrets we had told in the outhouse, she had never divulged this one. "Where?" I instantly wanted to know, and her old smirk reappeared.

"You mean whose."

"Tell me, tell me," I begged.

She raised her head snottily, revelling in my torture. "I already told you."

Silence. Of course! It was her N'Oncle Edwin, when the pervert had exposed himself in the boatshop. How could I have forgotten.

Chapter 14

In the winter of my fourteenth year, Robert Frost died. Babette's clipping from *The Vanguard* said that the four-time Pulitzer Prize winner had passed away at the age of eighty-eight, in Boston. I wondered if Tante Marceline had heard of him.

By then I was infatuated with reading. Babette lent me whole series of Anne of Green Gables, Trixie Belden, and Nancy Drew. She lugged the books to school, always with the gentle reminder, "We have a library that takes up a whole wall. Why don't you walk up the lighthouse road and choose for yourself?"

Someday, I thought. I had reading material for the rest of my life.

In the Lent of my fourteenth year, I became a young woman. I was bursting to tell Estelle.

Recitation of the rosary was a cardinal rule at my house, and if anyone should visit when the household was humbly kneeling after supper, then they knelt too. Estelle had been warned that she distracted our ritual, but I had something very important to tell her. The kitchen door hesitantly opened, and she walked in. The rosary not yet begun, Mam' ordered the girl on her knees, and then scowled a forbidding look my way. "You two had better behave. *Vous ferriez mieux d'vous cheind tranchille.*" Mam' was in the late final trimester of her eighth pregnancy, drained of patience, too tired to enforce laws. "You answer too," she alerted Dad. "It's hard enough to get those boys on their knees."

"Yes, yes, of course," he agreed, then sneakily moved his rocking chair to the bedroom. His low humming sounds were not those of the second half of the Hail Mary, but of a Hank Snow cow-boy song. I knew the "Rhumba Boogie" when I heard it. A nervous giggle from Estelle desecrated an Amen. Mam' threw her first cutting glance, then returned to counting beads.

"I can't help it!" Estelle whispered. "Your father makes me laugh."

I pointed to my pants pocket and she understood that I had collected his cigarette butts. Her cheek was bulging so much, I had to ask how many bubble gums were in there. Of course, she had to take the wad out and show me. The aged gum anchored like glue, threading across her fingers a pink web which she tried to lick back onto the chunk. She smeared the sticky gum across her chin. When she fumbled in her pockets for a Kleenex, she smeared her new jacket too. How she ended up with the chunk knotted in her hair I couldn't figure out. Neither could Mam', when she turned to our giggles and observed the holy mess. Estelle would have been put to the door instantly if my mother had been feeling well. Instead, she calmly ordered us to leave the kitchen. From the look on Philippe's face, we thought it best to leave the house.

"I can't believe your mother didn't take a fit," remarked Estelle, once we were safely inside the outhouse. "A çâ point vargé."

"But you better not show up tomorrow night," I warned her, then heaved a tremendous sigh of delight. "I have very exciting news." Unlike Estelle, I didn't tarry. "I got my period," I announced, nervous that she might fall down the two-holer pit. But if the look on her face could have maimed, I would have been permanently scarred.

"That's what you wanted to tell me?"

She grabbed the tobacco butts, filmy white papers, and matches from my hand, then snorted a sigh of disdain. "Big deal!" Her hands still gummy, she fashioned a lumpy cigarette, which she pinched between stiff fingers like the rich dames on TV. Lighting it, she sucked a modest first puff. "Aaaah," she smoothly exhaled, "Virginia Slims. Quoi, Madame?" she addressed my frown. "You've never heard of Virginia Slims? Why it's the only brand I smoke." She slapped my hand away. "Patience! You'll get your turn." In haste to fill her lungs with half a dozen short puffs, the young sophisticate quickly lost her *savoir-faire*. She wasn't supposed to swallow the smoke like an addict starved for nicotine. She fell into a coughing jag, spitting out stringy fibres of tobacco and clutching her stomach. A noise distracted me.

"Someone's at the door!" I opened it a wee crack. Nobody. "Must be André and Cedric. They know we're in here."

"What?" In her panic, Estelle dropped the cigarette in the deep pit. Her only excuse was, "What else could I do?"

"You could have saved me a turn."

She kicked open the door, stumbling outside for fresh air. Her face was turning awfully pale. "I don't feel well," she was reduced to admitting, hunching forward with a sickly grimace on her face. "I'm gonna throw up."

"What about that mess in your hair?" I reminded her. She straightened up but her expression was blank. "I'm going home." She rushed away.

I called after her, and she turned in slow motion, her insides obviously churning.

"What?"

"I think you better change brands. Those Virginia Slims turn your face green."

When I told Mam' about my period, she didn't exactly fall off her chair either. "I figured it had to come sometime," she concluded, then called me to the attic where she kept her flannelette rags, folded thick like diapers. "You'll have to use these until I can afford Kotex." She wouldn't be needing the rags herself, pregnant and harassed instead by a burning sensation beneath her breastbone, causing sour belches. She chewed chalk by the boxful, dragging around the house as if the doctor had never mentioned the word "rest." As she swelled up, her wedding ring came off her finger, her shoes off her feet. She no longer had to worry about the straps of her housedresses falling down her shoulders. "Toxemia" is what Docteur Theriault called her retention of fluids and her abnormally elevated blood pressure. I was in his office when he raised his voice to her, "Total bed rest or the hospital. Which is it?"

Pricille came home and confined Mam' to the downstairs

bedroom, or tried to. Mam' insisted on doing "harmless" tasks, such as pulling clothes through the wringer, polishing her stove, and when Pricille wasn't about, sweeping the floor. She would have succeeded up the flight of stairs to the attic if Pricille hadn't caught her. "Get down here!"

Holding on for balance, Mam' turned to address her gnawing concern. "There might be dirty underwear up there."

"All in the washing machine!" Pricille growled. Mam' retraced her steps, but collapsed at the foot of the stairs.

"I got a dizzy headache," she said, and I knew to run to Zita's and call the ambulance. Then I charged down the Cape road, past Estelle's house, up the lighthouse road. Panting, I rapped at the bent screen door of Eddie Pockshaw's shack, causing him to ruffle the curtains before he opened the door.

"Haw'dam de haw'dam," he cursed when he saw me. "I thought it was the cops. Antoine. Quick! Zoé's here." A runt of a weasel, Eddie Pockshaw's daily calorie intake was measured in glasses of pockshaw. He stood with his fly open, a week's stubble stiff on his face, and froth at the corners of his mouth. "Come on in!"

I squeezed myself past the runt, having to pinch my nose at the stench. "Dad. You have to come home!"

My father rose from his chair, staggering a few steps towards the door. "*Ma p'tite Zoé*," he grinned, but then he fell back on the chair, splitting it in two and causing Eddie's nerves to flare.

"Haw'dam de haw'dam, are you drunk?"

Dad sat on a tree stump this time, eyeing the glass of half-brewed malt at his feet. The poison of darkened tar brought a venomous sting to his tongue. "To hell with 'come home,' I'm rich." A demented look glazed over his eyes as he steadied his head. "You have to get my money, Zoé. Today! Joseph will drive you. Just walk right up to the bank manager and tell him, 'I want Antoine LeBlanc's money.' "

"You better get home!" I warned before I ran down the lighthouse road, back up the hill, panting and sobbing. Estelle's mother was in her yard, had seen me coming. She wanted the whole story.

By the time I made it home, the ambulance had come and gone. Thérèse greeted me at the door. "Mam's gone to get a new baby." Pricille was shaking, crying. The boys were out gallivanting, God only knew where, likely roaming the shore.

Zita kept in contact with the hospital, bringing home favourable news about our mother. Her blood pressure went down. The swelling eased. She delivered a ten-pound baby boy. It was a difficult birth we found out when Mam' came home.

She told us all about the thirty-six hours of agonizing labour. "A stubborn boy," she could grin after the fact. "He had to be forced out. The cord was around his neck." When Docteur Theriault visited our new baby at the house, she asked him, "Why were his lips so blue?"

"Lack of oxygen," the doctor replied, who then told us the shocking reality of how some babies like ours end up with brain damage.

Mam' turned ghostly white at the disturbing words. "They checked him at the hospital. Look at him, fat and healthy as a little pig." His arms and legs flapped all over the place. But the baby did have an elongated head. "Look!" she pointed with her index finger, "these bruises aren't going away."

Docteur Theriault had a bit of a drawl and he almost always wore a silly grin when he spoke. "If you had passed where that baby has, you'd have bruises too. The bruises are from the forceps," he clarified, assuring Mam' that the baby's head would take shape to match the cute little face. He examined the baby from head to toe, choosing this moment, with the room full of wide eyes to caution her. "This child should be your last."

The resoluteness from Mam's weary eyes was uncompromising, to the point. "That you can be sure of!"

Though bred and instilled with the Catholic doctrine—*we must not stop the family*, an order direct from the Pope—my mother stood at the window that night, glaring towards Eddie Pockshaw's shack. She dared challenge the divine order. "No more. I have a duty to live and raise the ones I got."

My father had lingered over the new baby's tiny hands, *les p'tites minines*, the tiny feet, *les p'tites pattes*. But he didn't attend the church ceremony when the little scrimp, as he called him, was baptized. Having announced the birth of Joel Matthew LeBlanc on a drunken spree the night before, he was hiding in the attic. Of course, he had landed at Zita's to mouth off, as if he knew how to get to the core of Mam's pride. Telling Zita anything was like printing it in *The Vanguard*.

The gossip came over to repeat word for word what my father had said. "What's this thing about a fortune in the bank? Why does he think he's rich?" she probed, as if Mam' had lost her senses and would tell.

It was imperative to arrest the story before it spread through the whole village. "You wouldn't repeat what you've heard from a drunken man?" Mam' reproached, and Zita turned a few shades of red.

"Well ..." she mumbled, "eh, I'm just telling *you*."

Mam' must have been extremely angry to have confided to N'Oncle Joseph, "He told Emma and Percy, of all people, that he was rich because of Zoé." N'Oncle frowned in confusion. "Because he says Zoé's not his," she clarified. "If you can possibly imagine that!"

N'Oncle Joseph simply shook his head at the scandalous nonsense. A "pillar of the church" he called Mam', trying to ease a tense moment. "Kind people like Emma and Percy Goodwin would never repeat a story like that." But then he wrinkled his brow, "How do you know that Antoine said that to them?"

"Because Babette was home when he was mouthing off and she told Zoé." In sheer disgust, Mam' threw her hands in the air. "Thank God he never mentioned the part about Zoé to Zita. Can you imagine, all of Clare knowing that?"

N'Oncle Joseph's face mirrored his afflicted soul: he bore a tremendous fondness and respect for Mam', but he loved his brother more. "That's the liquor," he rationalized. "You know he doesn't mean the stuff he says."

But Mam' was older and more tired now, which began to breed intolerance, almost a grudge towards N'Oncle Joseph for playing blood defence. It was surely her growing frustration that made her lash out at him. "A drunken man says what he's too shy to say sober."

Chapter 15

Spring brought a lush growth of tall grass for Deni Fournier's woolly sheep and rust-coloured cows. It graced the telephone wires with birds harmonizing their sweet praises in warm, delightful notes. It scattered bunches of violets across the fields for Grand-mère Sophie. But for an ailing Grand-père Dominique, it brought the cursed fog, *la maudite brume*, that engulfed the Cape—a dismal, grey mass so dense that he continually grumbled, "You could cut the damn thing with scissors."

He rarely made it to Vespers in the fog; his aching bones reduced him to hunched shoulders and a permanently twisted face. It was as if his knarled and arthritic joints were the ones lamenting, "The stuff goes right through you!"

Plane in hand, Dominique shaved the swollen windows and doors that refused to open and shut properly. This he did while Grand-mère Sophie shuffled around the house, her rheumatic knees always bound in thick wraps of stretchy gauze that smelled of Absorbine Junior.

"*La sacré brume*," she also cursed, upon opening the chest Dominique built, sighing at the offensive musty smell of her mother's quilt.

The blighted mist rolled in thick from the ocean, shrouding the Cape for days at a time, hiding the wharf so that the small fishing fleet disappeared in the haze. Spirits sodden with the dampness, the atmosphere at my house was testy.

When the *Little Esther* left the wharf, my father stayed fixed to his rocking chair, smoking, humming cowboy songs, and thinking, nurturing his delusions that he was rich. When he did board the small fishing boat, his week's pay hardly paid for his tobacco and peppermints. Even I couldn't resist the mocking dig, "If you can't buy tobacco, how are you gonna buy me an ox?"

"I'll go fishing with Pierre," was his evasive solution.

When the *Cape Marguerite* went on sale for a hefty thirty thousand dollars, my brother came home resolute. "I'm buying it."

He needed six thousand dollars in a hurry. Who had that kind of money but Uncle John, with his lucrative chain of restaurants. The down payment wouldn't even dent his bank account, not that he was so generous with his money. But Pierre was Tante Marceline's favourite. At seventeen years old Pierre bought his first boat, and instantly became the master of the Trinity fishing grounds.

"Lobster don't like salted bait in the spring," he reasoned. He fed them fresh bait, hauling them by the trapful so that Eddie Pockshaw and other hawks were always on the wharf, waiting for his generous grin.

"If you give them all away, you'll have none to sell," the other fishermen cautioned, but Pierre was resolved. "The more I give away, the more I catch."

Mam' wrote to Tante Marceline and assured her, "Before the year is over, you'll get your money." She spent her days scrubbing and fussing. It was a godsend that our new baby Joel was so good. With explosive smiles, the child greeted all heads that stretched over his crib, kicking and pushing forth a string of drooling gurgles at a game of peekaboo. I had my face within a few inches of his as I cooed, making him strain for variations of baaaaaa, anything to keep me there. But when I stopped cooing, Joel stilled his arms and feet, and we both stared, locked in a silent gaze, causing tears to spring to my eyes. I'm so glad I'm not Estelle, I thought. She doesn't have a baby brother.

I hadn't noticed Joel's arm reaching up, so that when his tiny hand stroked my cheek, goose flesh sent me running to the stove.

"Joel did *this!*" I gasped, as I stroked my mother's cheek, causing the teapot to escape her grip and crash into a thousand porcelain pieces. Of course, she had to sweep the shattered glass away from a red-hot stove, setting her duster ablaze. Terrified by the alarm on her face I jumped back. She grabbed the poker and banged on the blaze until, finally, she smothered it. She let go of the poker, dropped in the stove the black strip of remaining duster.

"*Stupide de stupide!*" she rebuked, and I knew that look. At that particular moment, she despised the sight of me.

"Why do you need a fire on a muggy day like this?" Dad scolded.

She glared at him with the same killing look. "Spring or not, I still have to bake bread."

I retrieved Joel from his crib, bringing a moment's truce. Dad and Mam' both gazed at their beautiful son. The two would never again make babies.

Abstinence was the only birth control Mam' knew. Dad wasn't welcome in the downstairs bedroom, and she stayed away from the attic. Not that Dad didn't try his best to tempt her up there. I remember one amorous overture in particular.

"Martine," he called down from the attic. Mam' was in the kitchen. I was in the pantry, not breathing a stir. A squall of rain was beating on the window. I heard Dad coax, "Come listen to the rain on the roof. *Écoute ouar ste puit là su la couvarture.* You should sleep up here tonight."

"By the crackie!" my mother exclaimed, and there was a bang on the table as if she had dropped a heavy pot. "I forgot to cover the beds!" She charged up the attic stairs. Minutes later, I heard heavy footsteps through the kitchen and then the storm door creaked open—my father was braving the downpour to Dominique's shed. I joined Mam' in the attic. With the plastics that normally insulated our winter windows, she covered all the beds. Then she positioned the chamber pots where the rain was splattering on the floor. She caulked the cracks around the windows with rags. "There," she said, and I knew it could pour all it wanted.

That night, my father listened to the rain on the roof by himself, sitting on the side of his bed, smoking one cigarette after another. Mam' came up the attic stairs, and for a moment ... No. She came to root for something, an extra baby blanket. On the way down the stairs she must have glanced over at the chain-smoker, something worth growling about. "One of these nights you're gonna put the house on fire, with all these kids up here. *Tu vâs mette la housse en feu.*"

Thérèse caught the whooping cough, and my mother wasted away to her pre-pregnancy skin and bones, with the probability of losing even more weight if my sister didn't get better soon. Mam' boiled chicken fat and mixed it with molasses, stirring up a beastly potion which my sister spat out, along with anything else home-brewed that entered her mouth. When coughing attacks left her gasping for air, Mam' opened the bedroom window and held the child to the outside air to fill her lungs. "I'm gonna give her away," she threatened, after a solid month of sleepless nights.

But Thérèse did recover, and then she practically lived outside. She loved to sink her rubber boots in the soft mud of Grand-mère's lupin bank, inching her way to the ditch until the swift current of spring rains gushed over the top of her boots, soaking her skirt to the waist.

This kind of childhood fun, once shared with Estelle, was now behind me. I was more interested in trying on Pricille's old brassieres which wore all wrinkled on me. I could only conclude that the fog was stunting my growth and that, unless I found a job, I'd never get the money for the padded bras at Fred à Bill.

The fog certainly hadn't stunted Estelle's growth, but it frizzled her hair to madness. "Here comes the frizzy belle," Paul-Emile hollered so that everyone on the wharf could hear. She didn't mind when his bulging eyes roved over her bust, but to be called frizzy belle!

She stormed back to her house, ripped a large piece off a brown paper bag and handed it to her mother. "I want you to iron my hair."

Always eager to indulge her spoiled daughter, Charlotte hastened to the ironing board and Estelle bent over backwards into an arch, *pléer en trente-six*, the back of her neck resting against the board so that her hair spread nicely under the brown paper. Back and forth Charlotte pressed with her iron, until the long locks had straightened from frizzy to wavy. But the minute Estelle stepped outside, the locks coiled back to frizz. A thousand angry strokes of the brush were a waste of time.

One lazy Saturday afternoon I had a brainstorm, something that was sure to rearrange the face of boredom. "Short hair would make you look older!" I exclaimed. Estelle considered the proposition seriously. Her mother was gone to town. Her father was off to Shelburne, supposedly. And the gap left where the chunk of bubble gum had been cut out was still unsightly. Perfect timing.

"Let's do it!" she decided. I stood paralysed, terror-stricken by what I had suggested.

I looked hesitantly at the scissors. "Are you sure?"

"Sure as I'll ever be. Or are you waiting until I change my mind? *Quosque tu jettes.*"

"Maybe this is not such a good idea," I fretted. Then I scanned the beautiful locks that I had always envied. With the devil's pitchfork prodding me on, I drove my scissors through her thick mass of wavy locks, grasping clumps of the long mop and simply hacking, until the floor was covered with curls.

Estelle ran to the mirror. "It's not short enough." Lucky she didn't have eyes in the back of her head.

"I need to even it up," I said, as I snipped here, snipped there, with a result far worse than the gap left by the bubble gum removal. Cutting hair was such fun, though.

"Shorter!" she urged. But I drew in a quick breath, rather edgy from the sudden noises outside and then the sun parlour door creaked open. Basil! Neither one of us had expected him back so soon.

"Get me the ledger in my office," he called from the sun parlour.

Frozen to her chair, Estelle managed to mumble something. "Well ... euh ... Zoé will."

"Zoé!" he yelled, annoyed as hell. "How would she know where I keep my books?"

He stormed into the house, hurled a nasty look my way, then stopped short at Estelle. "What in God's name, ... Jesus de Jesus!"

His stare fixed on the scissors in my hand, he screamed, "You cut off her hair!" Well yes, so it appeared. He hastened to his office, returning with his ledger, his eyes watery with rage. There was no misunderstanding his expression. "Estelle, outside! Zoé, go home!"

Estelle sprung to her feet, sobbing, when he grabbed her arm to inquire, "Where does that hairdresser in Meteghan live? Josette." He shoved her outdoors. "Get in that car!" he ordered, and then he hurried off to the boatshop. Estelle rolled down the car window. There was no smirk on her face this time. "You better go, in case he returns with a two-by-four. *Y est libel de fetch'a'vec un deux par quat.*"

Sunday morning was crazy with everyone rushing about, getting ready for church. The chaos was compounded with talk about, what else, but hair.

"I hear the scissors were mighty sharp," André scoffed.

Mam' cut him off. "Go wash your face. You're not even awake yet." She was fuming, her voice acid with judgement, "No doubt Estelle's doings."

Utterly frustrated, I started to cry. "I already told you! It was my idea."

Joel bellowed from his crib. A taste of Thérèse's peppermint failed to appease him. My young sister wore a pretty dress, her curly locks flowed to her waist. "Will you cut *my* hair, Zoé?"

"No she won't!" Mam' exclaimed, suddenly stricken with the most curious frown. "Where was Charlotte anyway?"

"Who gives a damn," Dad retorted, getting irritated himself. "What's the friggin' fuss? Hair grows back."

Now in front of the mirror, Mam' sparingly applied red lipstick and smoothed her straggly hair back with bobby pins. She moved to the table and gathered the breakfast dishes in a pile, had barely fed baby Joel before cars began backing out of their yards. N'Oncle Joseph's car drove up Grand-mère Sophie's driveway and she grabbed her coat, ordering Thérèse and me to find ours.

Tante Rosalie was rather surprised when I plunked myself down in the back seat. "You're not going with Estelle today?" When she noticed my tears she turned her attention on sweet Thérèse. "How's my big girl today?"

André had noticed Mam's icy stare and kept his teasing to himself. Somehow I made it to church, bypassing smiling faces without offering a single "Hallo." Estelle wasn't at church. I saw Basil. I think he wanted to kill me with his stare. I wasn't very atten-tive during Mass, but I sure as heck wasn't in any hurry to go home.

The afternoon was the hellish stretch when all the cars left the Cape and just drove—up the line, down the line, *par-en-haut, par-en-bas*—to visit relatives, friends, explore the back woods, just drive, anywhere, to get away. Sunday drivers always found the sun the instant they left the Cape.

Every Sunday, Basil drove his family to the soft ice cream stand in Meteghan River. And he always invited me along.

"Can I go to Estelle's?" I asked, setting Mam' off all over again.

"You'd be foolish enough to show your face down there!"

There was nothing in her answer to indicate a definite *no*, so I fled the house and ran down the Cape road, scared stiff at Estelle's sun parlour door. Charlotte was as friendly as ever, she even made a little joke. "I guess Estelle won't be worrying about frizzy hair for some time."

Holy mackerel! To remedy my hacking, the hairdresser had cropped Estelle's hair to the scalp, making her look older all right— like an older boy. Basil was clearly sickened, too angry to talk, and when the three of them were ready for their outing, he didn't invite me—the first time ever. I stalled outside, hoping, praying. But they all climbed in the car, leaving me standing there.

Devastated, I started up the long hill, my fingers still crossed. Maybe, just maybe, Basil wanted to teach me a lesson; he would stop the car and show a little grin, order me in. But he sped right by. Estelle waved. The hair was a stranger's, but the two dimples were definitely hers, pronounced from her terrified stare.

I walked into the house and headed straight to the window. The fog had rolled in from the ocean, obstructing the view of the small boats at the wharf. My father was rocking in his chair; his low humming moans echoed the eerie call of the foghorn—its monotonous sound made isolation hell for those with no cars. The boys were on the cliffs somewhere. Mam' and baby Joel were resting. Thérèse was at her friend's trailer in the dunes. I checked the cupboards. Nothing to eat.

I walked back to the window and pressed my face against the pane. The dense, grey fog that now enveloped the village intensified my aching loneliness for Estelle and my desire to get the hell away from the Cape and never come back. The day would drag on forever.

"I hate the fog!" I muttered to my gaping father. *Mon pauvre*

Antoine. He would surely die to the eerie sound of Cape St. Mary's foghorn. Not me. I would one day up and move away—to a town, to the city. And then maybe *mon pauvre Antoine,* terribly *ennuyé,* would finally attempt the long trek to the post office and beg the kind postman, "S'there a letter *d'ma p'tite Zoé?*"

Pen and dictionary in hand, I sought the solitude of the attic, where I could express my profound loneliness on this Sabbath day: I riffled through the pages of my fat dictionary, wrote haphazardly: I hate the fog! I hate the fog! I hate the fog!

I halted my hasty pen to ponder. What a damp, boring monologue. But there were no words in my dictionary forceful enough to curse the fog. Perhaps in French: *La maudite brume! La sacré brume!* So-so. Far too mellow, ... malapropos.

Perhaps the fog could be better described in English. Groggy. Soggy. Humid. Wet. Bone chilling. Downright depressing. Again, I stopped my pen. It is more ... freezing, ... disturbing, ... dripping. Presto, I've got it! The fog makes me feel like shit!! Yes, that's it!

I put my pen down. I quit.

Chapter 16

June arrived and the banks on both sides of the road turned into a palette of purplish blues and pinks, tall clusters of colourful lupins competing for every square inch of space. Grand-mère Sophie claimed a permanent spot at her living-room window.

Mam' covered our fields with white sheets that bleached in the sun. She rampaged through the attic, flinging down the stairs mittens, scarves, snowpants—everything landed in the washing machine, in a heap of bubbling suds—even Grand-père Dominique's heavy trousers that smelled of urine and Grand-mère's large silk underwear, which she had brought over, her face flushed.

"I don't know if they'll whiten." But she was talking to Martine LeBlanc, whose Javex transformed the dullest greys into magic whites: my father's long johns, our long-haired mop, the only two blouses I owned, Philippe's yellowed undershirts.

Mam' slammed her clothes basket on the table and simply glared at Philippe, who was standing over the stove, still half-asleep, with a shiner under his left eye the size of the egg he was frying. When he had left the house the night before, his hair was slicked back with Brylcream and he wore a handsome red V-neck pullover against his dark skin. He looked the very picture of the engineer he would someday be. But this morning, he was a tasteless, militant fool, who had turned an innocent Comeauville dance into a Friday night brawl between our guys and those from Weymouth and Digby Neck—all rival gangs for the cutest girls.

The whole story was digested over breakfast, as Philippe narrated with an impish grin. "I had this girl lined up for the last waltz, when this bastard showed up. The next thing I knew, there were eight of us against fifteen of them."

My brother's adrenaline was starting to pump. "Imagine that! Eight against fifteen! Then I saw Pierre coming and I told them all to step outside. By the Jesus, we were ready for a powwow." I could well imagine Pierre, laid-back and wearing a come-on grin, his shirt sleeves rolled up. "He walked smack into the middle of the brawl," Philippe confirmed, now demonstrating with his fist. "Hauled off and *kabang!* One after the other, except for the one who was after my girl. I gave him an uppercut that loosened the fillings in his mouth. But then he hauled off ..." We could see the shiner for ourselves. Philippe was the only one chuckling. "I tell you. If they hadn't gotten the hell out of there, there would have been a few open skulls outside that dance hall. Nelson *d'la Mâchouaire Tordue* had an axe in the trunk of his car."

"Nelson *d'la Mâchouaire Tordue?*" Mam' grimaced. "Never heard of him."

"You know," Philippe pressed, somewhat annoyed. Who hadn't heard of Nelson? "The one whose mother was in a car accident and broke her jaw."

Mam' couldn't place the boy. "Anyway," she scowled, annoyed with herself for getting drawn into the story, "was the girl worth it?"

Philippe sat back in his chair, his dark eyes fierce, defiant. "That wasn't the point."

Mam' grabbed her basket. Joel had kept her up all night and she looked like she could chew the Gyproc off the walls. "You're gonna look some cute for the graduation," was all she had to say to her fool son. She knew of his plans for September—the University of Toronto. She knew also of Pricille's plans—to high-tail for Boston. As a maid for a houseful of brats, my big sister was disillusioned with washing floors and wiping dirty faces.

Uncle John could certainly use an extra waitress, Tante Marceline had written her. We'd love to have you. My aunt had also mentioned Boston's suffocating heat, and that she was anxious for August, to come home. She needed the vacation. Estelle and I truly hoped that the fortune-teller would remember to pack her cards. And who was that blond nephew of Uncle John's who was eager to meet our beautiful Pricille? From the fickle look in her eyes, I feared for her Clyde. Pricille had definite plans for the big city.

I, too, had plans. I desperately needed a job, and one was available at the clubhouse.

Mam' had flashed me one of her daggered looks. "With drunken men frequenting the place! We'll see about that." We were down to salted herring every day; even she found them hard to swallow. She'd bend.

As for my father, I found him sprawled in the grass behind Dominique's shed, soaking up the sun. I flashed a meagre pan of swill in front of his face. "There's not even scraps for the pig," I remarked, fuming at his leisurely grin, as if he had it made.

"You don't like it when Mam' talks to the meatman," I reminded him. "What are you gonna do when she works at the Diner?" His grin disgusted me. "Don't look at me like that!" I harshly rebuked. "You know she's been talking about going to work. I thought you were gonna go fishing with Pierre. When?" Dad just lay there, so I let him have it. "From now on, you can get your own tobacco!"

From the deranged expression on his face, I knew that something was terribly out of whack. "Why would a rich man work?" he asked. Clutching my pan of swill, I backed away, disturbed by his clouded blue eyes.

I echoed Mam's frustration, "Why would any man work? Because you have a family!"

I took my pan to the fields. The pig snorted as he gobbled his precious food. I wept as I contemplated how I could ever walk down the Cape road again. Everybody would be staring, after all the stories my drunken father had spread in the village. And now he was perfectly content to whittle all day and watch his family starve. Villagers were surely talking.

My father believed all sorts of stupid stuff: that he was rich— little comfort when the cupboards were bare—and that I wasn't his child. Now *that* was an interesting paradox. Infinitely timid, he had come to the hospital to see me. He had stuck up for me ever since I could walk. And he continually kept watch at the latched door of Dominique's shed, lonely for my company—his eyes would glow at the sight of me. And I wasn't *his!* Some people claimed I was the only one who looked like him.

Not even Mam' could figure out the man. I found her in the attic. One sniff too close and the pungent odour from her pail of sudsy water seized me at the throat, constricted my nostrils. "We don't want any fleas and lice up here," she stressed, as if the fittest parasites could possibly survive her lethal dose of Lysol.

Scrub everywhere the hand can reach, was the idea, so I crawled through the attic, lodging splinters in my knees from the bare wood where the linoleum ended in the dark crawl spaces under the eaves. Sharp nails gouged into my flesh, but something lured me to the end of the narrow confine on my side of the attic, something that escaped Mam's puritan hands—Pricille's *True Stories*. I grabbed one of the forbidden magazines and brought it to the light, flipping to the advertisements for special creams promoting big busts like Estelle's. A girl at school had ordered the cream and it had worked. But when her supply ran out, her chest deflated again. Even if I had a job, the bottled cream would cost too much. Exotic wigs of long, wavy curls were forty-nine ninety-five. Maybe someday.

I flipped back to the mushy love stories, "Passion at Midnight." What was that about? I read a paragraph then a whole column of the fine print, became totally enraptured by the Hawaiian romance that kept me on the edge of my bed with provocative scenes involving a tall, strapping lover, baked brown by a tropical sun. I pictured an army jacket, a tuft of straight hair hanging over brown eyes, and conjured up intimate imaginary moments with Cedric, lusting for his touch on my velvety skin, and—oh my God!

"What?" I hollered, just in time to hurl the magazine back in the cubby.

Mam's head popped into view at the top of the stairs. "Are you done?"

"Yes," I replied, giving the floor a quick inspection. "I didn't miss anywhere."

Mam' collected the empty chamber pots and poured Javex straight from the bottle, the smell strong enough to dissolve the enamel off the granite pots. "These smell in the summer," she said, adding Javex to the Lysol in my pail. "Go empty it in the outhouse."

As I strolled along, my thoughts returned to "Passion at Midnight." I imagined I was sitting in the midst of a huge plantation, a paradise of all the pineapples I could eat. I reached the outhouse and rested my pail, sat on the two-seater, and with my eyes closed, I imagined a night of passion in Hawaii. The Cedric of my fantasy wasn't shy at all, whispering seductive endearments in my ear. He took me to a beach of black volcanic sand, where we walked and walked, ours the only shadows in the moonlight. Then he held me, oh so tightly, and voluptuously kissed me, almost swallowed me up. What a kiss!

"Zoé!" I could hear from far, far away. My mother!

I picked up the pail. "Coming!" I called, but I first needed to fabricate a happy ending. Cedric was my lover, the Cape our romantic island—our very own Hawaii—where no one had ever heard of fog, where dementia didn't cloud my father's eyes, and where Mam' could never, never call me. She could be so impatient!

I splashed the two-holer seat with the contents of my pail which poured down the dark pit where masses of the toughest germs would stiffen in instant death. An army of bugs were crawling across rotting floor boards. I crushed as many of the hard black shells as I could, then hastily started home, back into broad daylight, reality.

I regretted each laboured step back to the house, but then, I no longer felt amorous. Mam' was in the doorway, barking at me to hurry. Joel was behind her, screaming. My bones were aching. And a grey mist wasn't far off on the ocean.

"Grand-mère Sophie wants you to air her quilts," Mam' informed me. If I hadn't seen Estelle coming up the Cape road, I might have collapsed from fatigue, but a second wind infiltrated my lungs. Come, I motioned to her. Estelle loved going to the old homestead. Grand-mère Sophie hinted at how dusty the braided mats in her attic must be, but Estelle made it perfectly clear when we got up there, "I'm not broom-beating the hell out of rugs all afternoon. We'll take the quilts."

Her ears finely attuned to boys' voices, she hastened to the window overlooking the road. "It's Cedric! With Paul-Emile and André! They're walking up Dominique's driveway. Coming from the boatshop. Come see!" They each had a bottle of pop. In one gulp, Paul-Emile guzzled the contents of his while the other two watched, impressed with the scoundrel. So was Estelle. "Let's go!" Curious about the boys' intentions, we didn't need a year to hang quilts on the line.

"Where did they go?" Estelle fretted, dragging me up the fields. The pig sty smelled of fresh straw for the mannerless porker, tramping his front hoofs in the table scraps he was voraciously consuming. Clearly, he was not the least interested in the boys' whereabouts.

"Come," Estelle urged, "I have a sneaky suspicion."

We headed towards the outhouse, entering it on featherweight feet. Estelle climbed onto the seat and perched herself between the two holes, clearing a space for me. "Here. I see them!"

A generous crack in the boarded wall exposed the rascals, who were playing bets behind the outhouse. Their bladders filled with pop, the stakes were high.

"I bet my jackknife that I can reach higher than the two of you," André wagered. Cedric risked his army jacket. Then he changed his mind, his leather belt. No one could ignore Paul-Emile's comeback. "Oh yeah? I bet my wallet, with all the money in it." However much that was.

Estelle held her forehead cemented to the boards, watching the boys splashing their figure eights on the sun-dried shingles. I tried hard to keep my focus on Cedric's army jacket, not an easy task but a necessary one if a Catholic girl was to evade the confessional. Even after Paul-Emile had won the bet, Estelle wouldn't jump down. Her smirk told of a thrill far surpassing anything we had ever experienced.

"What's the big deal!" she snapped, standing over me and mocking the disturbed look on my face.

"André's my brother," I stammered as a sick feeling came over me.

She flipped back her hair, which was growing in beautifully, with the promise of restoring every curl to its original splendour. "You have to stop your panicking," she warned, "or you'll get us in trouble." There was a deal in her cunning, wild eyes. "They're going to the cliff …"

"And you want to follow them," I concluded.

"If you come," she promised, "I swear that I will never, never tell about this. Not even if they burn me at the stake." She crossed her heart and my breathing stabilized. The eventful afternoon further unfolded.

We hid behind sheds, trailing the boys until they disappeared into the fields. Then we crawled through prickly shrubs, terrified that they would suddenly turn and spot us. Safely arrived at the cliff, we hid behind a huge evergreen, affording us a perfect view of all three boys. Were they contemplating the cliff's steep descent? Pretty dangerous. Deni Fournier's cows had their necks stretched through a barbed-wire fence, ripping and ravenously chewing bunches of the lush, untrampled grass outside their enclosure. Paul-Emile approached the fence and, with his heavy foot, stamped a section of it to the ground. "Moo-oooou," he coaxed the closest cow and she obeyed, coming right to him. He grabbed her leather collar and pulled her through, then released his foot for the fence to bounce back, warding off the other cows that would have surely followed.

Now what's that jackass up to? I asked myself. Waging high bets, André and Cedric contemplated the cow's next move. Would she want to rejoin the others inside, or would she welcome the freedom of grazing at large? What they didn't consider is that a cow doesn't have a good sense of footing and could certainly wander too close to the edge of the cliff. I poked Estelle in the ribs, but she didn't want to go, not with Operation Terror in the making. The cow's greed led her to taller grass close to the edge. She set one hoof on loose sod, causing an avalanche of dirt under her massive weight.

"Moo-oooou," Cedric coaxed, hoping the stupid cow would retreat, but she just stared, with large, glassy eyes. I watched in horror as she dared the odds for a lousy thicket of dry weeds rooted to the very edge of the cliff. All four legs buckled under her and, unless she could walk on air, it was all over. Too far away to witness the full plunge down the cliff, I could picture a ton of cow rolling down the slated rock below, no doubt landing full flank. She wouldn't bleed through that thick hide. She would just lie there, flat dead. A mouse would have likely scurried away with minor bruises, but not a cow. The force of the fall would surely rupture every internal organ. The stakes had been foolishly high; the sacrificed cow would never graze again.

"I'm telling Mam'!" I gasped.

Estelle was not willing to let me go. "At least wait until the boys disappear."

"I'm telling right now!" I argued, and she had to get rough, pulling me back by the hair.

"Aren't you the one who can't wait for Clare District High in September?"

I half nodded, but what did school have to do with the atrocity at hand?

"There's nothing," she said, warning me, "*nothing* that Paul-Emile doesn't find out. And he sure hates tattletales."

I understood the rest. "I may never get to see high school." Exactly, her smirk read.

Chapter 17

Someone had seen the three misfits walk up the fields on the afternoon in question. No, it wasn't Zita, and Deni Fournier had no intention of divulging names. He was far too grateful to be led to the ring leader. Farm work was very taxing at his age.

"You can go straight to hell!" Paul-Emile raged. "If you think I'm gonna work all summer for nothing, you're crazy."

At that Monsieur Fournier replied, "Then we'll visit you in the Reform School."

The eager Fournier arrived at our door with the same terms, and I had no choice but to break my silence. "André had nothing to do with it."

"The one who holds the bag is as bad as the one who stuffs it," Monsieur Fournier stiffly retorted, and he left. André was also sentenced to hard labour—in cow manure.

Gustave needed Cedric for mossing, but at a dear price: one-third the worth of the cow, one hundred and fifty dollars, or he must work in the fields all summer.

"One hundred," Gustave dickered, but nothing doing. Deni Fournier ran a hard bargain.

"She was a darn good milking cow."

After the cow incident, Mam' would have rather starved us of groceries than entered Fred à Bill's, paranoid as she was that everyone would stare at her. She could barely look André in the face, instead glaring out the window, venting her disappointment. "You followed Paul-Emile up those fields knowing very well what he was up to. You'll have a good one to confess this time."

I was seized with the guilt that I had a full slate of my own confessions, mooning over *True Stories* every chance I got. Père Lucien's gruff voice reverberated through the round panel holes of his cubicle. "Those magazines are filthy, a sin against morality. You *must* destroy them." I left the cubicle knowing very well that I'd go back to the crawl space. And that I would disobey my mother—I was getting a job.

I ran down the hill to the Pointe, straight to the poster nailed to the front door of the clubhouse. CLEANING JOB AVAILABLE. SEE MANAGER INSIDE.

A fair-size establishment, Cape St. Mary's Anglers Clubhouse was built on the edge of a rocky cliff. It had a spacious observation platform at the back, and a large picture window overlooking the wide-open Atlantic.

The manager was friendly enough, though he had to shout above the blaring static on the ship-to-shore radio that kept in touch with the sports fishing boats registered with the club.

"Tunas are schooling in great numbers," Captain Melbourne Comeau radioed in. "Unless heavy gales arrive, they should remain for some time."

With cheering hoorays around me and crackling static in my ears, I had to yell above the noise. "I'll clean the clubhouse."

Mr. Muise turned down the volume on the radio and stretched his neck out of the cubicle. He looked me up and down, down and up, peering at my face, obviously trying to match a resemblance. "Who's your father?"

"Antoine LeBlanc," I said.

He creased his brow. "Don't believe I know him."

He scanned the size of my lanky arms. "A girl," he grinned, "stacking cases of beer, washing and waxing this floor? Look at the size of it. Who'd want to clean this thing for three dollars?" he scowled, perhaps thinking the low wages would send me running back up the hill.

"I need the money badly," I practically begged. My whole face flushed with excitement when he shook my hand.

"Then I guess the job is yours."

Truth was, nobody else wanted it.

"I'm helping with the election," he said. "You'll need a key."

I loved the commotion of election day, the only time that hunting and fishing didn't dominate conversations. Staunch Tories huddled on one side of the small schoolyard at the Cape, the captain of the *Little Esther* doing his darnedest to solicit Tory votes.

Had my father still been fishing for the *Little Esther* he would have downed a shot of rum for Zano, promising him a Tory vote to keep his job. And then he would have voted Liberal. But my father wasn't voting. He was gouging his Xs on blocks of wood in Dominique's shed. Grand-mère Sophie wasn't voting either. She said that voting was for men. Odd thing about Zita. She had the biggest mouth, yet no one knew how she voted. Grand-père Dominique grumbled that how he voted was nobody's business, but everybody knew—he was a Tory right down to the gristle. The polling clerk would have to read the four choices to Eddie Pockshaw, showing him how to mark his X.

"X the Liberals," Basil jested, and Eddie spat his chunk of tobacco on the ground.

"Haw'dam de haw'dam, they're all crooks, whoever you vote for." He disappeared into the school.

Percy Goodwin was a sure Liberal vote. The peacemaker justified, "With civil war threatening the Greeks and Turks in Cyprus, I support Pearson's push to improve Canada's contribution to NATO. And I totally agree that Canada shouldn't get involved in the Vietnam war."

Having experienced the raw front in the Second World War, Gustave couldn't have agreed more, though his son didn't wear an army jacket merely for looks. "*I* think Canada should fight in Vietnam," Cedric remarked. Percy merely sighed at the young man who was restless to pick up a gun, obsessed with the army.

"It was Pearson's U.N. Peacekeeping force that avoided a major war in Egypt when Great Britain and France invaded the Suez Canal," he praised. "First Canadian to win a Nobel Peace Prize."

Just then a brusque voice bellowed from somewhere in the back. "What ta hell is a Nobel Peace Prize?" Estelle's N'Oncle Edwin, the pervert, marched forward and pointed his forefinger in

Percy's face. "I'll tell you why I'm voting for Pearson. And it's not because of your crap about wars. It's because he speaks for French Canadians. It's about time those friggin' *Anglais* learned we exist down here."

Percy's head fell. He knew the origin of the vengeful grudge—ever since he had been hired as lighthouse keeper ten years ago. And it wasn't just Edwin who held a grudge. As nice as he was, Percy was ousted from all conversations. From reading his poems, I knew he wrote Acadian well, but the *poète de gâzette* was nothing more than a good laugh for the men on the wharf. They made fun of his poetry, the way he walked, the fact that he wore pajamas to bed. However they got ahold of that one was beyond me.

I had become intrigued with the *poète* and with Babette, so much so that I had decided to visit their library. But I carefully considered my decision, since it caused a tiff with Estelle. She had gone into spasms at the very thought of my becoming chummy with Babette.

"If you go up there," she threatened, "you're not my best friend anymore."

I bypassed her house, seized with the fear that I'd turn into a pillar of salt if I looked back. I kept going, past Eddie Pockshaw's shack, all the way up the lighthouse road to a white, box-shaped, one-storey house—government-built and plain. Inside, the house was cheery, with frilly curtains, bowls of candies here and there, and delicate China cups smiling from Emma's cupboards.

"Would you like some tea?" Emma offered.

"No thank you."

Embarrassed by her mother's obsession to touch, Babette tried to describe my features, embellishing them, "Lips like a valentine, set in a perfectly shaped face. Lovely hair," she depicted, studying the fine strands of my very straight bob usually hidden under a kerchief. "Beautiful like silk," she specified.

I chuckled, "You must be blind."

"No, but my mother is," she whispered, and I sensed a sudden connection, a strong liking for Babette who I had shunned for so many years. She introduced me to the famous parlour where Percy spent much of his time with his nose in encyclopedias and voluminous dictionaries. He and I had a common passion, poetry. But his treasured collection of classical music held no interest for me; my ears were accustomed to Country and Western hits. Percy claimed that Mozart and Beethoven nourished his soul and that the ocean helped him think. I could certainly relate to the ocean.

There were books, books everywhere, a whole wall of them—children's books, grown-ups books, strange-looking books. Babette explained, "My mother reads these."

Wow! Raised dots that told whole stories, a magic alphabet for the sightless. Louis Braille would have been proud of me—a quick lesson from Babette on the six dots comprising a braille cell, how they combined to represent letters, and I had myself a word.

"All those dots to spell *trees!*" I exclaimed, and Emma grinned.

"Blind people are quick. They learn to read fast." She glided her slim fingers over the scrapbook-like pages, reading me an excerpt from Antoine de Saint-Exupéry's *The Little Prince*.

Though Robert Frost's works graced one of the shelves, I got sidetracked by Babette, who handed me a biography she had recently read—*Gloria Vanderbilt*. "I enjoyed it tremendously. Want to read it?"

I grinned at the wealthy heiress of railroad and steamship fortunes in New York who was well known by Grand-père Dominique at Cape St. Mary. I explained. "Every time he gets in a huff about having to fork out money, he grumbles himself out the door, 'Who do you think I am, Vendor Bill?' "

Babette flashed her green eyes, fascinated. "That's astounding."

Astounding? She used big words, just like Anna at the hospital. I told Babette about Dad calling Mam' a Bolshevik whenever she was being a "pictor," a nag. The expression baffled Babette. How such a cultured word had ended up in an illiterate household was a mystery to me, too. Babette read the definition in her big dictionary. "An extreme radical of the Russian Community party." For those of us familiar with Dad's sick jealousies, the idea of Mam going to work was not a good one at all—extremely revolutionary, Bolshevik to be exact.

Babette pointed to an Acadian classic. "I've read *Evangeline* so many times that I know it by heart."

"I haven't read it," I was embarrassed to admit. Trixie Belden was admittedly more interesting to me than my Acadian roots. "But I plan to," I promised and I scanned the shelves, overwhelmed. Which books to bring home? I looked at Babette. "I'll have to come back. For now, I'll take this one by Robert Frost."

"Do come upstairs," Babette pleaded. Why not? She showed me to her bedroom which was furnished with more shelves and more books.

"Why do I get the feeling you like to read?" I queried, and the saddest expression I had ever seen crossed her face.

"Because no one ever visits.... Don't you and Estelle like me?" she asked, the question catching me off guard. "It's because I'm too slow, a snail in my walk," she surmised.

I countered in a teasing truth, "But one could get used to snails." I got her smiling.

There was a diary on her dresser, with a snap like a wallet and a lock requiring the tiniest key. I couldn't resist asking, "Is this to write secrets in?"

"Yes," she confirmed, "and now I can write about you." Her face flushed with genuine delight. "Want to read it?" Not really. I scanned her walls, which were overdecorated with childhood pictures, a pampered little girl in lacy dresses and ribbons. She reminded me of Anna the Princess except Babette had an imperfection—a short leg uglified by a boyish brown shoe.

"I got a job cleaning the clubhouse," I told her. There was a silence that could have cut through the glass in her picture frames when I added, "On Sundays." A strict Protestant, she didn't even play cards on Sundays.

"Why not Saturdays?" she asked.

"Because that's when the members get drunk and party," I told her. "The next day, I have to clean their mess."

She noticed me staring at the only family portrait on her wall. "My Grandpa Goodwin," she pointed, and I studied the stern face, prim and intelligent looking. According to Babette, he didn't have olive green eyes.

"I never knew my blood Grand-père Nicholas," I divulged, with much regret in my voice. "He died at sea. My Grand-père

Alphée on my mother's side I hardly knew either." I explained, "We had no car to go to Meteghan, so I saw him maybe three times a year. And even then, he spent hours in his bedroom, so religious that I think he drove himself mad."

Babette was curious, so I told her how I had eavesdropped on his arguments with the Virgin Mary, what he used to say, pounding on his bedroom wall. "I promise you that this rosary will never leave my hand!" I looked up at Babette. "He died with the rosary tangled in his hands. Other than that," I told her, "he had a tool shed that my brothers loved to invade. That's all I remember."

"What did he do?" she asked.

I was embarrassed to tell her about the illegal trafficking, so contradictory to his religious fanaticism. "He worked on rum-runners. That's how he met my Grand-mère from Québec. He married and moved her to Meteghan where they had a huge family—a hard-headed, strong-minded girl, ..."

Babette was sharp on the comeback, "Who is now your mother."

We both grinned.

Our time together was so pleasant, but all visits must end. A forlorn look came over her face. "You won't come back. I just know it."

"Of course I'll come back."

"No you won't. You and Estelle hardly ever talk to me." Then her tearful, sad eyes brightened. "Can I see your locket?"

I told her the story of Anna who had given it to me. She was intrigued by the little princess, but more so with the silver locket that she fondled in her palm. She clenched her hand into a fist, then beamed with a hopeful smile. "If you want it back, you'll have to come get it, won't you?"

I could do nothing but grin at such a clever girl. "Sure seems like it."

She opened the locket and peered inside. "That's a really nice picture of you, Zoé. But aren't you supposed to have your best friend beside you?"

It had never occurred to me to put Estelle's photo next to mine. I had no answer. "I really must go."

When I passed through the kitchen, Babette's mother was stroking her huge but seemingly gentle cat that lounged lazily on her lap. His eyes were dark brown with an outer circle of green, and they were fixed on me.

"Do you want to hold Angus?" Emma asked and I pulled back. I only liked kittens, little balls of fur soft against the face. This cat had stiff-looking, ugly faded grey fur. Conscious that temporary competition had arrived, he moved his head back and forth, following our voices. I tried to pat him, and he recoiled. Yikes, the claws! When I touched Emma's hand to let her know that I was leaving, he let out the most vicious *mee-ow* and jerked his right paw forward, to gouge my eyes I figured. He surely would have aimed for the jugular if Emma hadn't flinched, "Angus! That's not like you. You tell Zoé you're sorry." As if the feeling of indifference was mutual, he just stared with a blank look in his eyes.

"Nice Angus," I muttered, and I slammed the door behind me. I gazed through the small pane and distorted my face into the ugliest grimace possible, the way Estelle and I often did in the mirror. I waved good-bye to the miserable cat and whispered, in case he'd hear me, and God forbid, try to claw the door down, "I don't like you either."

Chapter 18

Grand-mère Sophie could barely shuffle around her kitchen let alone attempt the long trek to the outhouse by herself. Villagers had seen Docteur Theriault's car turn up her driveway and had caught wind of her fall. The whole Cape knew, and rumours were rampant. Lina à Gustave understood that Grand-mère had missed the tall step at the shed door and landed flat on her face. Her Cedric had brought home the wrong details. *Charlotte à Basil* delivered the news to the post office that Grand-mère had tripped outside, which was partly true, but it was not over a buoy behind Dominique's shed. How Estelle had come up with that one, I wasn't sure.

Eddie Pockshaw arrived at our house all in a huff, wanting to know how Grand-mère had broken her leg. Pierre had to grin. "She tripped on her way to the outhouse," he told Eddie, "on bare clay to be exact. She didn't break her leg, and she's not in a wheelchair. You can go see for yourself. She has bruises all over, that's all. *Blacaillé partout.*" And I'm gonna tear that friggin' outhouse down," Pierre resolved. "That's the only way we'll stop her from using it." He opened our hall door, checked under the attic steps and came back with an idea. "We're getting a toilet. I'll cut a door through the wall in the living room. You'll have a nice cubby under the steps to put toilet paper, towels, anything you want."

Mam' almost beamed. "Sounds great, but with what money?"

"Never mind the money," my brother assured her. "Can't cost a fortune for a sink and a seat." His *idée* was fixed. The outhouse was coming down.

And we needed some chickens—he was sick of herring. Mam'

couldn't have agreed more. She moved at a gallop, her stride towards the post office full of purpose. "I suppose there's no sense in having an empty chicken coop." Her limbs jerked forward aggressively, and she had to turn her head to speak as I trotted along to keep pace.

We were so rarely alone that I thought it safe to broach the subject, "When can I start wearing nylons?"

She halted her gallop. "When you turn sixteen."

"Estelle's been wearing them for a year," I groaned. The very mention of Estelle threw Mam' into a fit of temper.

"Estelle! Estelle! If I hear that name one more time.... You may have won in getting a job at the clubhouse, but you're not wearing nylons, and that you can be sure of! Estelle's wearing them all right, and people are talking about her in the shanties with Paul-Emile." Of course, she had to point the finger. "Don't you ever let me hear such things about you, or I swear you'll never leave the house again."

Gee. So much for an intimate walk. Mam' resumed her hurried gait, and I let her go on ahead.

A beautiful day it was. The fishing boats had long since gone to their trawls. I watched them along the ocean's horizon. I could tell which one was the *Cape Marguerite*. The *Little Esther* no longer mattered to me. My father was in Dominique's shed, whittling on blocks of wood. What choice did Zano have? He needed a partner on the boat. Paul-Emile was willing and eager. Zano hired him.

I gazed at the rippling waves and wondered, for the love of level-headed dignity, what Estelle saw in Paul-Emile. If people were talking about her frequenting the shanties, I had to warn her before word got back to Basil. Estelle was lucky that her mother was so easygoing. Sixteen was an eternity to wait for nylons. Again, I gazed at the ocean, well aware that my friend had emerged over the hill, looking very cosy arm-in-arm with her cousin from Salmon River. I played a little game. I started walking and when their shadows got too close, I turned around and *boooou!* But I hadn't braced myself for jeers from the two of them. They quickly reminded me of my attire—orange jeans from Tante Marceline's care package.

"Look at the boy's fly," Estelle mocked, and her cousin tittered at the American fashion that would only hit Clare many, many years later. Estelle and her cousin were kindred spirits, both blessed with the same permanent smirks. "Hey, Zoé!" Estelle sneered. "What did you and Babette do, read Shakespeare?" I knew of the jealousy eating at her.

"Among many, many things," I said, and then graciously complimented, "I'm pleasantly surprised you can pronounce the word. Now I really have to run. Mam's waiting."

It took no time for Estelle to grab her cousin's arm. "Let's go back to the wharf. Who wants to stick around here?"

"Good idea," I called after her, "you might get lucky and see Paul-Emile. Try the shanties."

Estelle could scowl all she wanted. I reached the post office fuming, but one look at our baby chicks and my heart turned to mush. They were all huddled together under a spotlight. I poked my head inside the box and grabbed one. It was weightless in my cupped hands, its pale yellow down soft against my face, its helpless body struggling as I caressed it. Mam' merely had to pay the post-master and we'd be on our way.

"I have to put you back," I said, and the baby chick wiggled free, plunging back into the box to peep with the others. All of them smelled of sulphuric acid. "They stink like fertilizer!" I told Mam'.

She still carried the memory of an old incident. "Well you and Estelle aren't gonna bathe these."

"What did they do?" the postmaster was itching to learn.

"Nothing!" I blurted, then reached into my pocket for the change that Grand-mère Sophie had scrounged. "I mustn't forget Dad's tobacco."

"I suppose this will buy a leg for your ox," he teased.

Stiff-faced, I passed him the change. "It will buy tobacco."

One look at Mam' told me to curb my sassy tongue. "We'll take good care of these," I smiled, ever so sweetly.

The postmaster smiled back. "What for? You'll fatten them up so that Antoine can chop off their heads on the wood block." The chill of the statement made me shiver all the way home, so much so that I simply had to stop and tell Zita.

"A strange creature," she said about our postmaster. "*Une drôle de carcasse çâ.* I have to collect for the church picnic and I dread it. He's as stingy as Dominique."

I was at Grand-père's house when she went looking for money. He paid his dollar and ten cents in church tithes without a grumble. *Faut payer la dîme.* "I'm not buying no lottery ticket," he told Zita, who was persistent, the main reason she was so good at collecting. "There are lots of nice prizes this year, a lovely quilt for Sophie."

"She's got too many already," he groaned, and the gossip scowled at his ungenerous face. "There's electrical appliances." She grinned. "A chance for a trip to heaven." Boldly, she extended her hand. "What's fifty cents?"

"Fifty cents wasted!" Grand-père grumbled weeks later, when he saw the scrawny goose he had won. "Take that out of here!"

André happily obliged, welcoming Amos to the small zoo he had begun—a turtle in the pond up the field, a raccoon in a pen, a squirrel in a cage, and a crow tied up beside the well—curious playmates for Thérèse to pester. After André trimmed Amos' wings, she tormented the long-necked bird, chasing him up the fields. The crazed bird started nipping at her bare hands and legs, and gave one sharp nip which drew blood from her poking finger. She found a mean stick and clunked Amos on the head, pressing forth the arrangement. "I'm your teacher so I have to teach you how to act."

The rebellious pupil honked, stretched his neck and flapped his wings, then flew wildly across the blue sky. He headed for the beach area, with all the boys from the village chasing after him. I watched in amazement as André trotted back less than an hour later, clutching the goose.

"I'll fix him," he said, and with Mam's scissors, he snipped and trimmed at the flight feathers until the goose couldn't flap at all. The handicapped bird was reduced to scavenging field and kitchen scraps closer to our house, where everyone passing by patted him, even Pierre on his way home from fishing.

I overheard him tell Amos, "I know you like to hang around the outhouse, but soon it will be gone, maybe next Saturday."

I tore down the hill to Estelle. "Saturday!" I exclaimed. "They're tearing the outhouse down."

She paled. "They can't do that! You don't have a bathroom!"

"We will soon," I informed her. Pierre and Philippe hammered non-stop, partitioning off a small compartment barely large enough to fit a sink and a seat. Oh, but what a luxury when the door was finally hinged, to take a sponge bath and not have to worry about someone walking in.

"A real bathroom," I told Estelle, but the girl was broken-hearted.

"You've got to convince Pierre not to tear the outhouse down. He could nail a board across the seat. Can't you see? We'd still have our hideaway!"

I told her about Pierre's comment, " 'If we leave the outhouse standing, Grand-mère will find a way to use it.' "

"Then move it to the fields," Estelle pleaded. She kept on about the outhouse, mourning our childhood inside its confines. "Remember how your mother didn't want me in here?"

"Not that it ever stopped you," I recalled.

" 'Member the time we threw the catalogues down this pit and she yelled at us, so angry that her false teeth fell to the ground?"

"Yes, I remember. That was our year's supply of toilet paper."

"And the time my doll fell down this hole," she said, "and that mean brother of yours wouldn't get it for me." Couldn't say I blamed André, but I let her talk and could have sworn that I saw a mist cloud her eyes as she reminisced. "How many secrets have we told in here? Plucked how many petals off daisies—loves me, loves me not. And then there's the last secret inside these walls," she said, as a mischievous bliss overtook her face. "The most important secret in the whole world."

I let out an impatient sigh. "If it takes as long as the one about your period, our chickens will have teeth."

"I'll make it quick," she assured me, but then fell into a reverie, reliving the magic moment with an ear to ear grin. "I've had a crush on Paul-Emile since God knows when. Can you imagine?"

I rolled my eyes a full one hundred and eighty degrees. "No, I can't imagine. Now what's the secret?"

"He kissed me," she said, her face dreamy. "But I think I might be in trouble." She explained. "Zita was on her way to the clubhouse. You know her, she has to poke her neck in all the shanties. We pulled back, but I think she saw us."

My eyes widened. "I heard! People are talking. Even Mam' knows. You best go charm Zita, before your father gets wind of it."

A vile look crossed Estelle's face, but then important business returned to mind. "They *must* move this outhouse to the fields. I just have to convince Pierre."

Greater miracles were known to happen. She could be quite charming when she put her mind to it.

All in one piece, the decrepit building was hoisted onto logs and tow ropes were fastened to Deni's yoked oxen. They ambled up the field with an army of men following behind. Estelle and I feared for the creaking walls, praying all the way. "Just a few more feet. Just a few more feet." There were fifty yards of lumpy terrain left to go.

When the time came to lever the shingled building off the logs, Paul-Emile braced himself, causing Estelle to blush. "Piece of cake," he boasted.

Cedric winked at me, ever so shyly. "That's because everyone else is doing the lifting." Sweat poured from under the tuft of hair hanging in his eyes. Hot or not, he wouldn't part with his army jacket.

There they were—Philippe, André, Dad, Eddie Pockshaw, N'Oncle Joseph, Cedric, and then Pierre who gave the command. "All together!" Muscular arms, levers in a combined effort, exerted full vigour, and the structure slid off the logs as two of its rotten walls crumbled flat to the ground! A mild kick from Pierre's lumberman boot and the other two followed. I could tell Estelle wanted to cry as she stared at the fallen walls—walls sworn to secrecy, walls that had borne mute witness to the most exciting moment of her life. She walked back to my house, not a word to share. I failed to understand such desperation over a lousy outhouse.

My family now had indoor plumbing. No more glossy catalogues. No more cracks saluting winter sleet, and on wintry icy mornings, Mam' would no longer have to caution her pace lest she slip on the ice and urge chamber pots in my face. Having frozen my behind far too many winters, I felt nothing, ... well, perhaps a moment's pang of sentimental something, as I looked back at the toppled outhouse—the heirloom of my Acadian passé. Elated! That's what I truly felt. It seemed an appropriate occasion for a poem:

> *Now of the growing* élite,
> *who had acquired a real toilet seat,*
> *what would I say, if I were*
> *proclaiming o'er the deep, germ-infested pit?*
> *"C'est nice that I am now blessed,*
> *with a more noble place to s-it."*

Chapter 19

It wasn't every year that the Tuna Cup Match attracted a Habs pro to the area. With admiration in their eyes, little boys followed Jean Béliveau everywhere, their dream of holding a hockey stick that much closer with his presence. With their young faces glued to TV screens, they idolized the professionals on ice. And now one of them was here in person, at the Cape.

Estelle and I were more intrigued with another visitor, Mrs. Coney. She gave handsome tips in exchange for favours, so we ran every time she wanted something. We strolled the shore for odd-shaped driftwood, seashells, a broken trap that had been hurled down the cliff—all of which she crammed into the back seat and trunk of her car. Mr. Coney wouldn't touch any of her junk; he wanted to keep those pants of his white.

"We're from New York," he said. Then he wanted to know, "Have you two ever been?"

Estelle stood there looking stupid. "No," I politely answered, "but I know of Gloria Vanderbilt."

I figured the Coneys were rich, imagining one of those Beverly Hills homes, the backyard soon to become littered with Cape St. Mary's seashore. Mrs. Coney was clad in bright colours, and dripped in fine jewellery that was wasted on old hands sun-baked with dull age spots, her veins bulging like cables. The elegant dangling bracelet, along with the gorgeous ruby ring would have far better suited Pricille's dainty wrist and finger.

"My birthday's in July," Mrs. Coney said.

I felt it appropriate to add, "Mine's in October."

"Then your birthstone is opal," she smiled.

Estelle nudged me, "How many opal rings would you like?" I could have whacked her on the head. Mrs. Coney didn't like kids whispering.

Her first week produced nothing but blue skies, so she lived on the observation platform at the clubhouse, focusing her binoculars on the anglers barely half a mile away. "I think that boat's got a strike!" she'd cry, causing all the tourists to come running at a false alarm. She clicked her camera at everything and anything. Estelle and I played movie actresses, posing this way, posing that way, big smiles on our faces when she snapped us perched on the granite boulders of the breakwater. She shot a whole film of the three "small fries" hanging from pulleys at the wharf, such a waste, considering the size of the tunas that had been caught weeks prior to her arrival.

"A paradise," she raved, enchanted with the picturesque fishing village—the sweeping view of the sea, the steep, rugged cliffs lined with evergreen trees, and the crescent-shaped beach of the finest sand in the Maritimes. It was the sand dunes molded by the beach that possessed her, the perfect place to sunbathe where no one could see her old-age bulges. Estelle and I sunbathed with her. She was full of questions, and I was delighted to answer them.

"Nobody knows for sure who the first settler was on the Cape," I told her. "Some say it was Oliver Frontain who built a log cabin on the Pointe in 1804. The Pointe is where the clubhouse is," I specified.

She nodded. "I know."

"Anyway," I continued, "his father was one of Napoleon Bonaparte's soldiers, a native of St. Malo, France, who fled to Halifax during the French Revolution."

She posed another question, to which I also knew the answer. "The first tuna," I informed her, "was caught in 1950, a four hundred and sixty-five pounder."

"Why's it called Cape St. Mary?" she asked, offering her own answer. "Makes perfect sense, seeing how this is a *cape* projecting into the ocean."

I could almost hear my deceased Grand-père Alphée pounding on the walls up above. Rosary in hand, he would have set her straight—God forbid, a name of such lowly significance!

"It was named after the Virgin Mary," I told her. From the next question, I could tell that she hadn't visited any of the beautiful churches along the French shore.

"Is everybody Catholic?"

"Very Catholic," I replied. *"Very* Catholic."

"You and Estelle don't know how lucky you are," she sighed. "There's such a freedom here, with no boundaries. A child can stroll the woods, lie on the beach, walk the fields, or even ramble in the dark in perfect safety."

I understood that New York was not a place to bring up children. And yes, I did appreciate what I had, for while she complained about the fishy smell around the wharf, to me it evoked a sense of pride and belonging. Sure I lamented the *maudite* fog, the loneliness at times, but the temple of my soul would always be Cape St. Mary.

"There must be millions of things to do in New York," I remarked to Mrs. Coney, concerned that she'd get terribly bored if she stayed at the Cape too long. But the best was yet to come. She saw a giant tuna enter the cove at the wharf for a couple of hours before it was finally guided back to sea. Like a madwoman, she ran in every direction, as if the stray fish would suddenly leap into the air for a perfect photograph. The giant tuna merely circled the cove, its massive black back only visible when it drifted into shallow water. Finally, to her dismay, the revving boat motors frightened the tuna back to deeper water.

"But it was such an easy catch," she wailed to one of the rescuers.

His grin was steady. "Could any angler brag about having caught a fish that jumped right into his boat?"

"What a day!" Mrs. Coney exclaimed, but it wasn't over yet. That evening, she caught a magnificent sunset behind the light-house.

Babette came over with a gentle reminder. "I still have your locket."

"I haven't forgotten," I whispered back. "Estelle and I are showing this lady around. Want to come?"

One look at Estelle's sour face and Babette shied away. "I don't think so."

It was after this rosy-hued sunset that Mrs. Coney became convinced she should buy one of the older homes hugging our rocky coastline, charmed particularly by Estelle's house because of its sun parlour which held one of the best views on the Cape.

"You'd have to buy the boatshop with it," Basil jested, staring her in the face. "If I were you, I wouldn't run to the bank just yet. Hang around until we get a couple of weeks of fog when you can't even see the tip of your nose."

"A loner's escape from the outside world," she still raved, until two solid weeks of fog arrived. She kept adding days to her visit. "It can't last forever."

"How long do you have?" I asked. "It leaves in the fall when the cold drives it away."

But she was determined, until the afternoon she met the likes of Eddie Pockshaw. He came trotting down the hill, screeching as he greeted locals, "A person could get moldy in this haw'dam de fog." He stormed towards the clubhouse, cheeks bloated and flushed from too much pockshaw. I grimaced at the black saliva and the chunk of tobacco that he spit on the ground, inches away from Mrs. Coney's feet.

A strange car drove up to the front steps and his eyes bulged out of their sockets. "Haw'dam de haw'dam, what's that?" He circled the car, staring at the people inside as if they were dinosaurs that had risen from sunken pits. He poked his nose at the driver's window; the man rolled it down a crack.

"Can you tell me please," he asked, "how far to Yarmouth?"

Eddie pointed "down the line," *par-en-bas.* "Keep right on going."

"About another twenty-five miles," Percy Goodwin clarified, affording the stranger a friendly smile. "I'm from Argyle myself." He sent the family politely on their way, then, with his face crimson angry, he walked straight over to Eddie Pockshaw. "Haven't you ever seen coloured people?"

Piqued by the sudden attack, Eddie bounced forward, the black saliva showering Percy's face. "Haw'dam de haw'dam, it's a man's business if he wants to look."

Percy backed off, but Mrs. Coney didn't have that kind of

sense. "I've never seen such an ignorant person in all my life," she said.

Aware that the word "ignorant" was no compliment, Monsieur Pockshaw sent her back to New York the fastest way possible, riding on a string of curses. "We don't need no highfalutin broads around here," he said, and her eyes filled with rage. She glared at the locals entering the clubhouse and began to complain suddenly about stinky shanties, the hateful fog, and how she couldn't wait to get back to New York.

Over the next few days, tuna boats motored in with empty sterns, which finally made her decide to leave. She bought Estelle and me one last ice cream each.

When she left, the skies turned a deep blue. Three boats came in, each boasting tunas of over eight hundred pounds. There was standing room only on the wharf. One tourist equipped with a fancy pair of binoculars inquired about bird watching.

"Look at the sky and you'll see plenty," Eddie Pockshaw told him.

Pierre called the man over. "In the marsh behind the dunes."

Another fellow, wearing shorts, heavy boots, and big woollen socks was looking for a place to hike. Having spent his childhood in the cliffs, André was happy to oblige. "You can start at the lighthouse and follow the cliffs right through to Bear Cove. There are caves all along the way."

Another wanted to know when the big *tyme* was—a party in Clare was called a *tyme*. I told him, "This Saturday night." How I wished I were a fly on the wall at one of those wild parties at the clubhouse. From the messes I cleaned up, they sure seemed like fun.

Mrs. Coney would not be going to the *tyme*. I missed her terribly, though I had to smile at her fickle love for my village. We had a saying about the Cape: *On a sunny day, heaven could be no better; on a foggy day, hell could be no worse.* Then there was Basil's advice to all the tourists: *You have to be from here to weather the Cape.* That certainly held true in the winter.

But the Cape was graced with a freedom that Mrs. Coney hadn't taken for granted. On that point, her sentiments had been as genuine as a prayer, my own prayer, which she had inspired.

Holy Mary—
Patroness of my village,
Watch over this virgin land on which we,
Your children, ramble so freely,
Along its shores, my feet caress the sand,
Along open fields, the winds I command,
I touch my Saviour's hand.

Beloved Mary—
Gentle Mother of my people,
Guard over my father's woods,
Where he flees the veil of gloom,
And the precious shed of his ailing mind,
Where he now so sadly idles all of his time.

Protect our vast ocean, our boundless skies,
My own mother, who God knows really tries.
Hail Mary, full of grace,
Could you soften a smile on that frustrated, angry face?

Blessed are you Mary. Blessed is your infinite love,
Blessed is Cape St. Mary, gently watched from above.

Sunday morning. The big *tyme* was over. Bucket in one hand, mop in the other, I started down the hill and halted, as always, in front of Estelle's house. Why was she sulking on her front lawn?

"Oh, oh!" I exclaimed, when I learned she wasn't allowed off the property. "Zita told your father about you and Paul-Emile."

She nodded. "I can't even go to the friggin' post office by myself." She lambasted the gossip with the same vengeful accusations I had heard before, but added a new one which was quite funny. "No wonder her husband disappeared on her wedding night. It was the first time he noticed the size of her mouth."

"She said to tell her if men bother me at the clubhouse," I remarked, causing Estelle to fume.

"You should! She's good at getting rid of men." Her dimples stiffened from one mean, threatening scowl. "I'll get her."

"I'm sure you will," I grinned, then continued on my merry way, contemplating where I'd spend my next three dollars. My father had lots of tobacco left from his carton. I didn't need any Kotex. At long last, a padded bra from Fred à Bill. I unlocked the door to the clubhouse, ready for the most disorderly mess imaginable.

There were empty beer bottles scattered everywhere, even floating in the toilet bowls in a scum of cigarette butts and urine. Drinking glasses were smeared at the rims with lipstick, some still half-full of warm stinky beer. My shoes stuck to dried-up puddles of spilt beer, splatters of pop, and bubble gum flattened under dancing feet. Where to start? The seashells along the window sills were overflowing with cigarette butts. While I scurried about emptying them, prying eyes gazed through the windows, curious locals killing time before lunch, I thought. No, Paul-Emile! How stupid not to lock the door behind me.

"Should I take my shoes off?" he asked, scanning the filthy floor. "I may get them dirty."

"Better keep them on," I advised. "You're not staying."

He scanned the displays inside the glass showcase. "What a stupid colour for a buoy, purple and yellow. Ugh! And what's that garbage? Don't they know tourists have seen driftwood before? What a lousy job," he said of the giant-clawed lobster mounted on the wall. Then he set his gaze on a corner shelf that displayed a collection dear to my heart—little sailboats and tiny birds perched on driftwood, the result of long hours of N'Oncle Joseph's time. "Who'd want to buy those?" Paul-Emile scoffed.

I gestured towards the door. "Since there's nothing in here that you like, you can go now."

"I thought I'd help you stack beer cases," he said, and the rat disappeared into the ladies' washroom. "Hey Zoé! Come see the mess in here."

"I've seen it," I said, "and if you think I'd go in there with you, you're out of your mind."

He came out grinning. "You're not very friendly today."

"Nor any other day," I replied, as the snake slipped past me, trying to rub against me. I slammed the door on his obnoxious smirk.

Thoroughly annoyed, I immersed my long-haired mop in

sudsy water and sloshed it across the massive floor, zigzagging to reach corners, and eventually making my way to the ladies' washroom where a lipstick had rolled under the sink. For Mam', was my first thought. It had hardly been used. I erased the film from the mirror and followed the outline of my valentine lips, coating them bright red. Not bad, I thought, proud of the soft curls that I had beautifully managed with Pricille's rollers. A knock on the door interrupted my self-admiring pose. That darned Paul-Emile, I thought. I'd surely tell Mr. Muise of the pest.

"Go away!" I called, but the knock was persistent. I couldn't stay in the bathroom for the rest of my life. I grabbed a handful of toilet paper and wiped off the lipstick, then with my arms swinging madly, I marched to the door. I glanced up, and my knees went rubbery. I opened the door to a tall, strapping hunk of a boy clad in an army jacket and standing with a tuft of hair in his eyes—Cedric of my secret fantasies, exposing an even set of snowy white teeth in a teasing smile.

"Do you always lock the door?"

My heart raced. "I should. I mean no, not always."

Shy Cedric moved deeper into the room, straddling a chair close to the picture window. "Did you see the tuna they caught yesterday?"

"I've seen so many," I told him, "that I don't even look anymore." He chuckled and I smiled shyly. "What's so funny?"

"Boy," he said, "you sure know how to flip-flop that mop around."

"I have to wash this floor twice," I told him, and the foolish urge to laugh seized me as he moved his long legs out of the way. Y *l'était toute en jambes.*

It was his turn to flush. "What's so funny with you?"

" 'Member the time you and Paul-Emile threw his cat off the wharf, and your father took off after you, with his size twelve boots?"

Cedric started digging shakily at his nails, a sudden, sober expression erasing his grin. "Yeah, well I'm sure he'd love to give me his boot right now."

I jammed my knife under a chunk of gum stuck to the floor. "You mean you're still throwing cats off the wharf?"

A short silence followed his nervous sigh. "My old man and I had a big row. I told him I was quitting school, that I wasn't going mossing anymore."

"Quitting school!" I must have sounded like his mother. "You got one year left. Are you crazy?"

"If joining the army's crazy, then yes, I guess I'm crazy. Hello Shilo," he said.

I stared, uncomprehending. "Shilo?"

"Out West," he clarified, "for my basic training." He must have noticed my frown. "In Manitoba," he added. He stood up, banged his chair against those along the wall. "I hate mossing, and I'm never going back! I'll get a job at the boatshop until I can join up."

"You could always do farm work for Deni Fournier," I jested, but the tease was ill-timed.

Chewing his jagged nails, he gazed towards the wharf. "Nobody's gonna change my mind."

I realigned the chairs and surprised myself at how daring, how authoritative I sounded. "You got the rest of your life to join the army. You belong in school!"

I glanced at his robust physique and at the strong arms with which he now lifted a stack of beer cases. "Where to?" he asked.

He followed me outside. "Set them here," I pointed, and *tête-à-tête*, I could feel his eyes focus on my soft curls. My lips quivered a faint smile as I trembled at the touch of his hand.

"Anything else?"

"No," I nodded, not quick enough to invent another job.

I would have melted under his gaze if he hadn't surprised me with a mighty punch on the shoulder which almost sent me flying. "I told Paul-Emile I'd go handlining with him. What time is it anyway?"

"Wait!" I called, and he halted, his long legs backtracking to the beer cases. The words were stuck in my throat. "Don't come back. I mean, I don't think it's a good idea ... without André. *J'veux dire, sa pourrait'm mette dans du trouble.*" Blushing, I swallowed hard. "It's only three dollars, but I need it badly. If Mam' ever ..."

Cedric made a sign to stop with his right hand. "Don't even

mention it. Lock the door," he said, and then he grinned. "You never know who'll show up." His long legs strode past the shanties. He was gone.

I waxed the floor and then gave my work the "Martine inspection," gazing proudly at the beautiful shine. I grabbed my pail and mop, gingerly bouncing across the room in long leaps. One last look. Had I missed any spots?

Ugh! I couldn't bring that grimy mop back home to Mam'. Down at the shore, I gave it a good rinsing in salt water and then let it soak while I relaxed my aching back and fantasized about Cedric.

I ambled up the long hill, leaning forward like Grand-père Dominique, fit for nothing more taxing than a nap. But first I had to stop at Zita's, consult with her. "Do you have an atlas?"

With a most curious stare, she handed me one. "What on earth for?"

I raced through the provinces, found Manitoba and there it was—Shilo. "Found it," I said, and I slammed the atlas shut, driving her mad, I was certain. I stood at her front door, admiring the yard transformed with blooms that made everyone gape on their way up the Cape road. There were bright, big flowers open to the sun, and tiny flowers, still struggling to awaken, flowers of all colours, maybe prettier than Charlotte's, though I knew better than to mention that to Zita. She'd tell Charlotte.

"It gives my mother something to look at," Zita said, "now that she's no longer mobile.

I lugged my heavy mop and pail across the road, then looked back. I could see La Caquette in the window, and the clothesline in the back of the house, lined with diapers for her worsening bladder problem. Her face was illuminated by a smile, just like Grand-mère Sophie's when she inspected her lupins. Nothing like flowers, I concluded, to put a smile on an old woman's face.

Chapter 20

Tante Marceline arrived and the first thing she did was inhale a whiff of cool ocean breeze. "Aaaaah," she drawled, "to get away from the suffocating heat." Such a gleam in her eyes, such a thrill to be home. She embraced Grand-mère Sophie and, as always, she looked me over. "Can't believe you, Zoé. You're a young woman!" She glanced over at Estelle "And you, Estelle. Look at you." She rolled her envious eyes at my friend's head of curly locks. "I sure could use some of that mop of hair."

Though plagued with Grand-mère Sophie's sparse coiffure, Tante was nevertheless an attractive lady, vivacious, with a laugh that bounced off the walls. She had a *joie de vivre* that she adopted in Boston, but it was scowled upon at the Cape. Women had no business talking to the men on the wharf, or checking out the shelves at the liquor store. Sometimes Tante used words that were years ahead of Cape St. Mary.

Hippies? Weren't they pants worn on the hips? "I think I would like some," I said, and my aunt hooted.

"I'll ask your mother how many pairs."

Tante Marceline was fussy, claiming that when she set her table in Boston, there was a certain way she positioned knives and forks. I couldn't have slurped my soup at her house. She travelled with a cumbersome iron. She hadn't a wrinkle in her clothes, having jumped out of the car as if all set for church. Like the models in pattern books, she stood tall and erect, wearing well her tailored dresses and brimmed hats—with a bearing of high society. But, oh, how thin she was, sickly thin!

Grand-mère Sophie's concern was contained in a mute stare. Grand-père Dominique's impassive eyes peered from behind his round wire-rimmed glasses. He glared at Uncle John, who was already examining the shingles on the old homestead in grave need of paint.

Mam' arrived at a gallop, time only for a hurried greeting and to caution Estelle and me. "Now don't you two be making pests of yourselves."

Tante did have the fatigue of a long drive etched on her face. "Make sure to rest," I cautioned, " 'cause tomorrow, we'll be here before the chickens are up. *Avanq'les poules saiond'boutes.*"

"You're not gonna spend all your time here," Mam' warned. I glanced over at Estelle. That's exactly what we had in mind.

We were up at dawn and waited what seemed like forever, until Mam' let us out of the house. Grand-mère's kitchen was alive, never at a loss for fun when Uncle John wasn't about. Tante was frying blood pudding, her tea was brewing on the stove. She gulped tea as though she had invented it, favouring one orange teacup, which was never idle long enough to make it to the dishpan.

Grand-mère Sophie sat at the table, inspected her new jams and once in a while stared hard at my father who competed with Tante Marceline at drinking the teapot dry.

"You drink far too much tea, Antoine," she reproached, making my father grin. It was Tante Marceline who had had the heart attack and who had been warned by her doctor that tea accelerates the heartbeat. So did cigarette smoking, but that didn't stop her. I suspected there was a bottle of rye tucked inside her suitcase. Was she allowed liquor?

Grand-mère gloated over the large-size, white sneakers from the States. Tante always chose perfectly. Well, except for the cotton housedress of white and flashy red stripes, rather risqué, too short, so that poor Grand-mère kept tugging at the dress to cover her strapped knees. "It's too bright," she fretted.

Tante sent a furtive wink my way. "Rubbish! It makes you look younger. No one wears dark colours in Boston. They're too 'old woman.' *Trop vieille femme çâ.*"

N'Oncle Joseph thought the dress was too flashy and yes, downright short, but if Tante said it wasn't, then it wasn't. Only two beings could walk on water—Jesus and my Tante Marceline.

My Tante had also brought home a collection of expensive hand and face creams. The skin on Grand-mère's face was droopy with sagging jowls in dire need of a bit of sun for colour, but incredibly smooth. Her arms and hands were also wrinkle-free, though heavily pigmented with age spots. She was eighty-four, after all. I tried not to gawk at the black blotches over her scalp, another toothbrush tinting job that had failed miserably—all the more reason for Tante to fuss with large ribbons like the bright red one which she tied around the fine, limp hair. She had brought Grand-mère more brooches, a red one to decorate her new dress. Grand-père would have scowled at my grandmother; to him pampering was such vanity.

Tante looked out the window, towards the shed. "Where *is* Dominique?"

"Aaaaah," Grand-mère gestured with her hands, the perfect time to broach the subject. "In the attic. Where else? He spends hours up there, searching for what, I don't know. I can hear planks creak as if he were lifting them, and then he comes downstairs grumbling, with a puzzled look on his face." Her blue eyes were serious. "What do you suppose he's looking for?"

Tante hurled my father a glance. "Well now, the old miser must have money stashed somewhere."

I had heard it all before. He had worked in the shipyards until age thirty-five, when he had married Grand-mère Sophie and then moved to the Cape. He was well-established, what with the livestock and land that he sold. Then he fished.

Tante's anger flashed as she looked at Dad. "Didn't pay you a cent in wages, never fixed anything on the house, never bought a darned thing. What did he do with his money?"

N'Oncle Joseph grabbed the opportunity, chiding his mother, "And he certainly didn't give it to you!"

"While we're on the subject of money," Tante Marceline motioned, "we should have Dominique do up his will. What do you think?"

Grand-mère was taken aback, causing my Tante to rebuke, "You're the one who says his memory is going. He hardly recognized me when I walked in here."

"That's because there's nothing left of you," N'Oncle Joseph jested. "You gotta put some meat on those bones."

Tante had such a hearty laugh, and when she smiled, her eyes smiled too. "Ever since my heart attack," she defended, "I don't have any appetite." She leaned forward with a wink. "Except for those mighty fine creatures crawling on the bottom of the ocean."

"We'll get you some lobster," N'Oncle assured her, unable to resist another tease. "At least there's colour in those cheeks now that you're back in fresh air, away from city smog. I bet you can't even see your neighbour's house."

Tante hooted. *Des grousses éclats d'rire.* "You mean like on the Cape, when it's foggy?" The two had such fun carrying on.

Estelle and I made ourselves scarce, until our turn alone with Tante came, one lazy afternoon after the kitchen emptied of people. My father was happy to just rock and gaze towards the wharf. Grand-mère was in her bedroom, testing her new creams. So it was just Estelle, me, and Tante Marceline with an endless supply of pink popcorn. Tante beat a path from the kitchen to the back bedroom, returning with more popcorn from her suitcase. This time she emerged with a bright smile and an ornate wooden container that concealed something we anxiously awaited—tarot cards!

Seated eagerly on the edge of her chair, the fortune-teller pushed her teacup aside, opened wide her mystical eyes, then raised her head, as if drawing spirits to a séance. "I suppose we're interested in romance." Primed for a fun afternoon, Estelle and I giggled. "You two had better be quiet," Tante cautioned, "or you'll break my concentration. Who's first?"

"I am!" cried Estelle.

Tante riveted her gaze on the cards. "Now there are many ways to read these." Her way was simple—a lengthy shuffle with dexterous hands, and she turned over the top card of the deck and pondered at length the psychic image. She tarried, adding an aura of mystery to the interpretation. "Hmmmm, not a very good start." She gazed intently through the bottom half of her bifocals. "I see a broken heart, tears, and sorrow."

Now Estelle, bound for the lustful life, was not overly moved, except to exclaim, "So that's what three swords piercing through a heart means!" She pulled out a card at random and passed it to Tante. "Now give me some good news."

Tante could readily oblige. "I see a very handsome young man, blond." Estelle shrugged at the unsurprising truth. "Is he the one I'll marry?"

"No," Tante verified, "but he plays an important part in your life."

Estelle was now half-sprawled over the table, eyes wide with anticipation. If her thoughts were of Paul-Emile, she wasn't mentioning him. Her dimples flashed. There was more in the cards— wealth and prestige.

"Makes sense," Tante Marceline figured. "You'll inherit the boatshop and, who knows, you may become rich."

"But what good is wealth with a broken heart, tears, and sorrow?" I pursued. From the look on Tante's face, I had just touched a nerve.

There was a curious tone in her voice, "It is far better to be rich and miserable ..." she paused, "than to be poor and miserable." Estelle and I sat back in our chairs. If my Tante was miserable, she concealed it well. We were as silent as a graveyard when she cut the deck of cards. "Now, for you, Zoé." There was a sun on my card. "You," she announced, "are going to have a happy marriage."

But she winced as she examined another card, one with lots of cups that looked like chalices. "I see a choice here. Two men in your life. How about that."

The card provoked her puckered brows. "A trip overseas? One must be in the navy."

"The army," I thought out loud, causing Estelle to perk up like a rooster.

"I knew it. I knew it. It's Cedric! And don't deny it, or you're full of shit."

I shoved her rude finger away from my face. "Is not."

"Is so. Why else would he hang around the clubhouse?"

We had distinguished company. I backed off.

"Cedric?" Tante grinned, clearing the air and recapturing strict attention. "A trip on the water," she confirmed from several other cards, and when she swirled the remaining tea in her cup and drained the liquid into the sink, her gaze lit up. "Here it is again, a trip on the water."

"To the Trinity!" I exclaimed, and I rose from my chair. "We're going fishing with Pierre. It's the tournament, and he wants you to see a tuna being fought."

Tante ignored my outburst, turning her cup in the palm of her hand to examine the leaves stuck in clusters on the sides. "I see a man."

I couldn't help but grin. "According to the cards, two of them."

She straightened her tall slim physique, no time for farce. "But this is an older man." Her expression became dead serious, explaining the significance of the two leaves joined together in the teacup. "It is this older man who you will learn to love from the heart."

Cedric was three years my senior, hardly an older man. Tante and I both glanced in the same direction, towards Dad.

Dad would have normally chuckled at the silly fortune-telling, but he was preoccupied with his own thoughts. When Tante pushed the cards and tea leaves aside and asked how the fishing was, I seized the moment.

"Not too good this summer."

Dad's white head was bent to gaze into an empty teacup. He was behaving himself well. He was either rich and mouthy, or sober and timid. I preferred the latter and, maybe, just maybe, Tante wouldn't notice the dementia taking him over. She might eventually question his idle whittling in Dominique's shed when all the boats were at sea. And then Mam' would tell her. Tante had a right to the truth. What if she lectured my father with sermons that would do no darn good? Maybe Uncle John would call him lazy, and then I would surely hate my uncle. Some relatives were already looking at Dad as if they were angry at him. Even Mam' rarely smiled at her Antoine anymore. Her heart was growing tired.

Not mine. All the love within me I had surrendered on the day he had carved my wooden ox. My heart would never grow tired. It was easy to love him because I knew he loved me, too.

I looked at him now as he sat in his chair, his weary head still bent while he graciously accepted a fresh cup of tea from Tante

Marceline. I saw a brother who had slipped away, outfoxing his sister over time and distance; a son who should have been booted off to school to discipline his mind; a husband whose wife would never understand him; a father my siblings would never know; and I saw an older man—an older man whom I had learned to love from the heart a long time ago.

Chapter 21

It wasn't easy to approach Grand-père Dominique at the best of times, let alone to ask him to sign over his house. My father, the proposed heir, was better left out of it. N'Oncle Joseph didn't feel it quite his place either. Grand-mère Sophie would have been grumbled to hell and back by the miserable old man. And Uncle John could mind his own business. That left Tante Marceline, but even for her this was a sensitive issue. She chose an evening when Grand-mère had retired early to bed. She didn't mind that I was there, nor Uncle John. Tante prepared a fresh pot of tea, then sat at the table, staring Grand-père Dominique in the face. "I think I may get Walter à Blanche to come to the house tomorrow." She didn't tarry with words. "Might be a good time, now that I'm home."

Grand-père circled his kitchen, taking a few minutes to glance about before looking at Tante in a long stare. "There's nothing here for you. What could you possibly want?"

The biting remark was deeply hurtful coming from the old man, and though Tante tried to repress her resentment, the ungracious dig provoked an outburst. "I want nothing!" she made clear. "Not a thing." She swallowed hard. "I was fourteen when you threw me out. You cut me off then." If memory was failing Grand-père, she quickly refreshed it. "It was in the middle of January that I went begging to relatives in Boston. I had to give up my baby." Uncle John's face flushed red, but she warned him with one of those daggered looks that read, Stay out of it. Turning to face Grand-père, she continued, "If it hadn't been for John's folks who gave me a job waiting on tables ..." She paused to calm her voice lest she waken Grand-mère, "No, I don't want anything. If there's anyone who deserves the little bit you have, it's Antoine. He started fishing with you when he was just a kid ..."

"*Oué, oué, oué,*" Grand-père interjected, his face guilt-ridden from the bitter reminder. But Tante wouldn't let him go until he finally made eye contact and, by his own words, agreed that Walter à Blanche be called to the house.

The terrible ordeal was over, but the fatigue of a full day in the fresh air and sun, gallivanting on the beach and all over creation overcame Tante Marceline. She fell into profuse sobbing, catching her breath so that I thought she was having a heart attack. "Do you think I was too harsh?" she wept. "All these years, and I wait until the man has a foot in the grave to blow up."

Uncle John had only one thing to say about the confrontation, not the least bit intimidated by my presence. "The miserable bastard deserved it." He still ached for the son he would have gladly raised as his own, an heir to his lucrative chain of restaurants.

I scrambled home by the light of a bright moon glimmering on the soft ripples of the cold Atlantic—a spectacle to behold from my attic window. The revolving light from the lone lighthouse flashed intermittently, illuminating the whole upstairs, guiding fishermen from sixteen miles away on such a clear night. I wished them a safe journey as I snuggled into bed and closed my eyes to the chirping of crickets. Whether encouraged by the light of the moon, the heat of the night, or the urge to copulate, their high-pitched trills were incessant. I was fourteen, Tante Marceline's age when she was evicted from her home. Where would I go if it were me? I shuddered at the very thought. Never before had I felt so privileged that the Cape was mine, the wide-open fields were mine. Never before had I fallen asleep so peacefully, to the songs of crickets. I belonged.

Next morning was eventful. My family congregated next door. Estelle was there. Walter à Blanche walked into Grand-mère Sophie's kitchen, his nostrils flaring at the sweet aroma of home-made bread. "Um-Umm."

Mam' explained. "Every summer, Marceline puts in her order. Perhaps you would like a loaf to take home."

"Very kind of you," the Justice of the Peace smiled. He retrieved a deed from his leather case and turned to Dominique. "I wonder if I could talk to you and Sophie for a few minutes."

Tante Marceline escorted them to the privacy of the living room, then returned to watch her golden brown loaves being drawn from the oven. Mam' sliced an end crust, plastered it with molasses, put it on a plate and pointed to a chair far removed from the table. "Here Thérèse. This might keep you quiet."

"But I didn't say a word!" she objected.

"Squirming like you wanted to," Mam' rebuked, and we all understood the squinting look: Compose yourselves or else! *Vous ferriez bain mieux d'vous comporter, ou savâler mal.*

"*Les kids,*" she called us, half apologizing to Walter à Blanche as he and my grandparents returned. "They wanted to watch."

She offered the Justice of the Peace the finest chair in the house, one of a high-back, hand-carved set of four reserved for special occasions. The gentleman took his seat, read the contents of the deed to my father, running through the meets and bounds description of the property, and then pointed to the dotted line. Dad marked his X, and then Grand-mère Sophie signed as having witnessed the movement of her son's pen. The Justice added his own scribblings, then he handed over the deed for Grand-père Dominique to sign, with the admonishment, "Register this right away."

Ten minutes of legal paperwork, and the old man barely owned the shirt on his back. He shuffled up the attic stairs. N'Oncle Joseph's misty eyes became fixed on my father. He was resolved, "Never was there a settlement so just."

My father merely grinned, having inherited a dilapidated shell of a house. The little tyke by the rockers of his chair flashed a great big, teasing smile, wanted to be picked up. He wiggled his way to Dad's shirt pocket.

"Careful, Antoine!" Mam' cautioned, but Joel got to the tobacco and then to the peppermints, causing her to sigh her usual disgust. "They could walk on your head and you'd never notice!"

"But he's my last," Dad defended.

Mam' wiped her brow with her apron. "Doesn't mean you have to let him eat tobacco." She covered Tante Marceline's loaves with tea towels and hand-combed the last of a sweated-down, straggly perm from her face. "Now I have to go home and bake my own," she remarked, as she snatched Joel from Dad and urged Thérèse, "we have to go."

Just then, N'Oncle Joseph had an announcement, "I'm driving Marceline to Wedgeport. She wants to visit our old home, if it's still standing. I've arranged for a boat. Thought we could visit the islands at the same time."

Who wanted to go? Surely Grand-mère Sophie. Not for the boat ride, but to visit a few remaining relatives and the graveyard where her beloved Nicholas rested.

"Estelle and me!" I blurted, and N'Oncle glanced at my father. "*Toi, Antoine?*"

If there was ever a time that my father's mind was resolved, it was then. "Not me. I have no desire to go back there." He still carried bitterness over his begging days.

Joseph glanced over at Mam', but knew better than to ask. My father's worsening jealousy discouraged her from ever leaving the house, except to check on the old folks. She sent me to greet the meatman on Saturdays now.

Zita had told her, "You're crazy to put yourself in a cocoon for a man."

But Mam' had dismissed the meddling remark with a shrug of her shoulders. "I knew he was jealous when I married him."

Tante Marceline gazed fixedly at the big oak tree by the side of her childhood home in Wedgeport, reminiscing about Dad, his treehouse, and his dog Wimpy. "Joseph and Antoine were always together," she recalled, "but Louis, ... he was a loner."

The mere mention of Louis' name drained Grand-mère Sophie's face of its colour. "Louis was the one who looked most like your father."

And he had never returned from war, Tante knew; she didn't want to hear the story again. " 'Member Théophile à Joe down the hill?" she asked, to change the subject. "I heard he became a missionary, somewhere in Africa or one of those hot places." Grand-mère didn't care about Théophile à Joe, so Tante reverted to the treehouse. " 'Member when Antoine fell and broke his arm?"

The reminder carried Grand-mère back to the fateful day when a stranger came to her door, the bearer of devastating news. Her Nicholas was at the Shelburne Inn, dying and incoherent. She had heard the last muffled mutter on his lips. "Peases ..."

Peases Island, he had been trying to say—where Grand-mère Sophie and Grand-père Nicholas had tended a lighthouse when they were first married.

Tante Marceline killed the chilling silence with a knock on the door of her old house. A frail woman invited us in, introducing herself as a Cape Bretoner. "Of course you can go through the house!" She appeared a bit embarrassed. "Not a lot has changed. You see, I have only a small pension."

The inside of the house was screaming for paint and repairs, and true, nothing much had changed according to Tante—still the steep flight of stairs to the attic, the nooks and crannies up there, a dwarf-size door that opened to a small cubbyhole, possibly meant for storing quilts. "Where I hid from my father when he came in from fishing," Tante grinned, "and when he found me, I wouldn't come out. He stunk of fish." Her tone softened, "Always, he had something for us when he was gone a long time."

She sat on an old bed, tears welling in the corners of her eyes. "He died so young." Her face was sad, remembering a happy childhood and the hard years that followed. On the bureau were pictures of graduates, brides and grooms, babies—smiling generations of Cape Bretoners.

We moved to Dad and N'Oncle Joseph's room. It was strange to see the very corner where my father had slept as a child. There was a houseful of nostalgia to recapture had Grand-mère Sophie not been so adamant to visit the cemetery. Deaf as an oak tree, she couldn't hear Tante Marceline's call, "We're coming!" Tante had no choice but to descend the stairs and thank the kind lady. "Another time perhaps."

We feared Grand-mère Sophie would never leave Nicholas' grave; she had enough binding around her rheumatic knees to bear the prickly weeds and their sharp spears. The thicket allowed just enough light to encourage a few tiny blossoms in the underbrush.

She found two white flowers that she plucked and examined for a long time. Even in the deepest darkness, there was promise of life. She laid the blossoms on Nicholas' grave for the soft breeze to caress. Grand-mère lifted her gaze to the faded lettering on the lonely tombstone: NICHOLAS LEBLANC 1886–1923. FOREVER IN MY HEART. Tante Marceline and N'Oncle Joseph waited patiently, until finally Grand-mère pointed to the reserved plot next to Nicholas'. They had heard already the supplication, "This is where I want to be buried."

Not a problem, yet, I could read the difficult question on their faces: What if she died before Dominique. They helped their mother through the long graveyard, drawing attention to the names they recognized. Tillie Jacquard. N'Oncle Joseph halted. "That one sounds awfully familiar."

Grand-mère blushed. "Sylvain's wife. You know. Sylvain Jacquard who kept all those horses."

"Yes, yes, yes," he remembered now.

What he didn't know was that Sylvain was from his mother's past, long before her Nicholas and Peases Island. "When you pass by the lighthouse," she pressed, "think of your father." She repeated it three times during the car ride to her relatives. We dropped her off then proceeded to the wharf to meet our chartered boat.

Grand-mère's obsession became mine. We had hardly left the Wedgeport pier when I started asking, "Where's Peases Island?"

"A long way yet," N'Oncle grinned.

So I asked, "How far to Harris Island?"

"About twenty-five miles," he frowned, having to refresh his memory as we steamed along. "Green Island over here to the right. That one over there, I'm not sure. Lobster Island maybe. Yeah, Lobster Island."

"Peases Island to the left!" we all exclaimed, upon catching sight of the lone lighthouse. My face fell. Sophie and Nicholas on this island, all alone. Doing what with their time, I asked myself, on an island with not even a pack of cards to their name. But then, they were sweethearts in the sunrise of their life together. I had seen pictures of Nicholas: a man of medium height, slim, dark, with a mustache. He reminded me of a handsome dude in the western movies.

Grand-mère Sophie didn't have stovepipe legs then. I imagined a head of thicker lush hair, restrained by a pure white ribbon. The blushing Monsieur and Madame LeBlanc.

In my reverie, I gave them back their youth, recreating their first night on Peases Island. "Passion at Sundown." I had read too many love stories. My imagination ran wild.

They watched the sun go down. Sleepy shades of orange hushed vibrant blends of pink. A peaceful splendour lingered, yet discouraged their eyes from blinking. They lingered over the final glimpse of the setting sun, their silhouettes timid against the softly painted western horizon. They counted stars, welcoming the darkness that cloaked their nuptial bed of grass. They shivered in the setting breeze that penetrated the virgin white fabric of Sophie's cotton gown.

She nestled by her lover's side, rested her sweet head against his, and trembled, as she touched his face, her delicate fingers caressing his shoulders. The abstaining martyr, never before touched by a woman, gave an agonized howl, "*Je t'aime!*" again and again, until the chaste words were but a pleading murmur that laid bare their desire, the two separated only by his impassioned breathing, a moaning sigh, a climaxed cry that came from deep within, "*Ma belle Sophie!*" Under a starlit canopy, Nicholas gave all of himself to the only woman he would ever love.

I emerged from my fantasy smiling, the very thought of Grand-mère Sophie, well ... doing it. How about Grand-père Dominique? *Never!* N'Oncle Joseph was staring, as if he could read such disrespectful thoughts. His gloomy mood only broke once we had docked at Harris Island. He led Estelle, me, and Tante Marceline to the cabin site where Grand-mère Sophie had been assigned to feed the fishermen after Nicholas died.

"Where were you?" I asked Tante.

She had to think for a moment. "With relatives in Boston."

"And N'Oncle Louis?"

"At Grand-mère's. He was small."

I studied the empty surroundings, full of questions for N'Oncle Joseph. "What did you and Dad do all day?"

"Rowed to Big Tusket Island." He pointed to where our boat

was docked. "Once a week, a big steamer came with food supplies. Antoine was too shy to go on board so he waited on the wharf. A boat also arrived every night to take the day's lobster catch into Wedgeport. We watched the fishermen count the crates to be taken away. Now they have holding tanks to store their catch for as long as they want." It was amazing how technology had improved everyone's lot.

"How long did you stay here?" I asked.

He replied, "A few seasons, until Grand-mère decided to work at the lobster factory. Fifty cents a day. She fixed lobster while Antoine washed the tails. She got fired."

"Fired!" I gasped.

He nodded. "When there were only seven or eight tails left in the big tub, Antoine would drop them through a hatch and I would fetch them under the factory to bring them home for our supper. The boss caught on."

"Then what?"

"She looked after the kids of a wealthy family in Yarmouth. They found out that she was leaving Antoine and me in the house alone all week and reported her." When N'Oncle Joseph got excited, he rubbed his hands together vigorously. "By the crackie, when the authorities came to the house, we were ready for them. We had my father's shotgun."

"What did they do?"

"They got the hell off our porch. Made my mother give up her job though. Then Antoine went fishing in the Tusket Islands, and our mother met Dominique."

Grand-père Dominique had distinctive roots, having inherited attractive high cheekbones and dark skin. "His grandmother was straight from the cabin," N'Oncle could attest, as he retraced a history. "Along the shores of St. Mary's Bay, there were mixed marriages with the Micmacs. Bet you didn't know that Meteghan used to be spelled M-i-t-i-h-k-a-n; it meant 'blue stone.' " No, I didn't know.

"Do Indians grumble?" I asked.

N'Oncle threw me an amused grin. "I think that's strictly a trait of Dominique's."

He was drained of energy. There were no more words from him until we steamed home, past the lighthouse on Peases Island. "Stop the boat!" he hollered to the captain. He relished a last long stare at the honeymooners' island. "We'll probably never do this again," he told Tante Marceline, whose own eyes were moist with a final, sorrowful look.

"They were happy."

"Had it all," N'Oncle uttered mournfully, "but on earth, Paradise is short-lived."

Chapter 22

Accustomed to getting up at four, Pierre felt it had been morning for hours. He checked his watch. Seven o'clock. "That's it," he figured. "Tante Marceline should be up by now."

He stalled to glance once more out our living room window at the pitiful flowers across the road, uprooted from their thriving beds and scattered haphazardly across the lawn, some still half-buried under dug-up sod.

The work of dogs, Zita had deduced, but my brother knew better. The job was slick, definitely the prank of some *"malfeasant."*

"Gave the old lady something to look at," he muttered, disheartened. I followed him next door where tea was brewing and homemade bread was toasting. Tante was up.

"Where's the blood pudding?" my brother tormented.

She rubbed her sleepy eyes, "Not this morning. I don't want to feed the fish with my breakfast."

Pierre moved to the window. There wasn't much activity at the wharf. All the boats were at the Trinity, either deep-sea fishing or gearing up for the first day of the week-long Bluefin Tuna Cup Tournament. The fisherman was anxious, though good-natured in his teasing, "Didn't you hear the rooster's crow? Meant it was time to go. You're not gonna get codheads by standing over the stove in a housecoat."

"Ha, ha, ha," echoed Tante's vivacious laugh. "A rooster's crow is much too early you know."

She left Pierre fretting at the window. When she rushed back from the end bedroom fully dressed, only a camera could have captured the look on his face. *"Astheure-là.* Where do you think you're going, to the Legion?" His rubber boots encrusted with fish scales, Pierre scanned her nicely pressed plaid pants and her angora sweater. "Do you have high heels to match?"

Tante's hearty laugh was swell therapy for her ailing heart. The smile in her eyes told who was her favourite—our Pierre.

"What about Uncle John?" he asked, and she almost choked on her mouthful of tea. "For loving sake, I can't coax him to the wharf because it stinks. Leave him in bed. We'll have more fun." She gulped the last of her tea, set her cup on the back of the stove, and smiled, "Looks like it's time to go."

We hastened down the Cape road, headed straight for the wharf, when Charlotte, out with her watering can, beckoned us. "Marceline, come see my dahlias and marigolds, how beautiful they came this year."

Pierre scowled at the significant size of the flower garden. "We'll never get out of here."

The stop afforded time to rouse Estelle from the house. "Aren't you coming?"

Putting on a sour face, she dragged me into her sun parlour. "I'm not allowed," she groaned and I frowned, confused.

"But you came to Harris Island. What's the difference?"

"Paul-Emile," she fumed. "He's out there on the ocean. We just may run into him."

The boatshop's huge sliding door was wide open, allowing Basil a perfect view of the house while manning his power-driven saw. He was slicing boards for a new boat, throwing the occasional glance our way. Estelle wasn't going anywhere. Her eyes were aflame, as she furiously chewed her gum, which reminded me.

"Have you seen Zita's lawn lately?"

She blew a large bubble, and when it snapped, she hurled the meanest look, meant for Zita. "She's the reason for this, and she's gonna pay for it."

"Unless I'm mistaken," I countered, "she already did." I looked hard at Estelle. "I don't suppose you know anything about uprooted flowers."

"You sound just like your mother!" she lashed.

I smiled. "But my sermons are shorter, to the point. It's the old lady that you punished, not Zita."

Estelle was now incensed. "That witch of a snitch told my father that she saw Paul-Emile climb down from my bedroom window. Now how in the hell ..."

"She may have informers," I deduced. Estelle just stared, angry enough to want to tear the eyes right out of that Zita's head ... and the flowers right out of their beds.

"Zoé!" Pierre called impatiently.

I reached for the door. "The difference between you and Zita," I concluded, "is that she's not aware when she's being destructive. You knew what you were doing. Or should I say, you and Paul-Emile?"

She snapped another bubble and wouldn't look at me. I raced down the hill, just in time to watch Cedric. He untied Noah's ark from the wharf, clearly embarrassed, either at the dory's bright red colour that could be seen a mile away or self-conscious about his vow I had heard: "I hate mossing, and I'm never going back!" He did manage a sheepish grin, my assurance that the miserable look on his face had nothing to do with me. Gustave was eager, with his rakes, burlap potato bags, and a new rig, spacious, with high flaring sides, ready for all the moss he and Cedric could toss aboard—a marked upgrade from the leaky sieve he owned before. There was a slight breeze from the northeast. The red dory was pouncing on the waves, set to go. So was the *Cape Marguerite*. I climbed down the narrow stairs to the scow, barely making it aboard on time.

"You were gonna leave me here!" I accused, allowing my brother a sportive grin.

"I thought you might enjoy the swim. Unless you look like a herring or a mackerel, the tunas won't bother you."

Tante Marceline's laughter echoed in the rocky cliffs as we left them behind, those below the lighthouse where Gustave's dory was heading, where Irish moss was plentiful. Tante inhaled a whiff of salty air, tilting her head back. Flocks of white-bellied seagulls flapped their grey wings over the wake, scavenging for any fish we could spare, preferably fresh herring. Pierre opened a five-gallon can of the bait. "Here," he motioned, "feed your friends."

Tante and I were mesmerized by how precise the herring gulls were in their graceful dives, their bills slightly hooked for a firm grip, emerging every time with a piece of bait. But they had to be swift. Tante flung her bait at one gull that didn't get a morsel; he was beaten to it by a more experienced adversary. She scowled at the gluttonous gull. "*T'es trop haglette toi.*"

Half a can of bait later, Pierre cautioned us, "As long as you're willing to feed, they'll eat. Eight miles to the Trinity." Tante put the lid back on the five-gallon can.

I invited her down the cuddy, but she made a squeamish grimace. "The last time I was down there, I followed a five-gallon can around and threw up everything in my stomach, including part of my guts."

"I do remember," Pierre chuckled. "You were kinda green."

He drew her attention to the fleet on the horizon. I counted twenty boats, all proudly flying their national flags. Tante took out her binoculars. Who were the big-game fish anglers of the world? Americans. British. French. She squinted at the less familiar flags: Cubans. Mexicans. West Indians. Some had no flags at all—judges' boats, camera and press boats, spectator boats, like ours with a very special guest from Boston.

Pierre eased the throttle of the *Cape Marguerite* to a slow burble, drifting near the two Canadian team boats to holler to Captain Melbourne Comeau whose boat had a white flag flapping in the breeze. "I see you got a strike!"

With the motor of his grey boat running at high speed, Melbourne flashed a smile. He was busy catching signals from the guide, who was communicating with hand gestures: few feet to the right. Now to the left. The objective was to drift sideways to keep the racing tuna at the back of the boat.

"Boat manoeuvring is very important," Pierre informed Tante. "Sometimes the captain is ordered to move it forward, backward, occasionally in circles to clear the line from the boat. At the same time he has to discourage too much slack which could unhook the tuna."

The rod at the stern of Melbourne's boat was bouncing, taking awful bends. I couldn't see the giant tuna, but it was obvious that he was a fast-running fish, wild to get rid of the hook in his mouth. The angler, strapped in the swivel chair, was handling his reel like he knew what he was doing, playing with the fish, tightening up the drag when so directed by the guide.

"I hear of tunas being fought for five hours and more," Tante Marceline commented. "Why can't the angler just reel the fish to the boat, gaff him, and raise him aboard? Why all the fuss?"

Pierre grinned at her naiveté. "The angler is fighting a powerful fish, maybe an eight hundred pounder, with a sixty-pound test line! Not only is he powerful, but the tuna is one of the fastest fish in the world, and he loves to race, run away. If that angler tried to reel in the line tight now, the fish is too energized and would break free. The idea is to tire him, and that can only be done by letting him race and not letting him rest. The angler reels in a bit of tension to coax him back. It's a skilful game. The idea's to drown the tuna."

"Drown?" Tante queried.

Pierre finished his story. "As he tires, he swallows more and more water, weakens, and eventually drowns. That's when it's okay to slowly reel him to the boat. Now don't misunderstand. The tuna that's gaffed aboard can still have plenty of life left, just like any fish that flaps all over the place, except a tuna is like a giant mackerel. I've seen some smack their tails and break boards once they're hauled on board."

"Why don't they use a stronger line?" Tante was curious.

Pierre's reply was straightforward. "Rules. Also there'd be less to brag about if you caught an eight hundred pounder with a one hundred and eighty pound test line, let's say, compared to a sixty-pound test." While he had Tante Marceline's gape-mouthed attention, he pointed to the fellow next to the angler. "That guy's called a chummer. His job is to keep throwing herring overboard to tempt the tuna close enough to take the pole bait instead of pursuing the loose fish in the water. The rest of those guys are visiting anglers who'll probably get their chance in the fighting chair sometime during the tournament week."

Tante Marceline didn't get it. "Can't they all take turns *now?*"

"No. The angler who hooks the tuna has to fight it. They can only help gaff and raise it into the boat."

"Look!" she pointed.

Pierre turned to the cloud of fish leaping out of the water. "Herring."

Tante Marceline knitted her brow, "I didn't know herring could leap so high."

Pierre had a smile split from ear to ear. "There are hundreds of tuna chasing after the herring. You'd leap too if you had those hungry jaws at your tail waiting to swallow you whole." He was about to say something else when we heard a loud snap, followed by a string of curses from the now disqualified contestant. Pierre stretched over the side of the *Cape Marguerite* and shouted across, "A busted rod? What happened?"

The angler looked up, shrugging his shoulders. "Don't know. That was a sonofabitch if I ever hooked one."

"Does that happen often?" Tante asked.

Pierre pulled back from the side. "Not too much. But a line can get messed up in floating kelp and then break. If there's a nice tuna at the end, you've lost it. Same if the line chafes against the boat. *Snap!* And everything's gone."

Tante noticed a second rod on the stern. "Would the same tuna return to the same boat?"

"It's possible," Pierre figured, "though I doubt that he'd stick around. Tunas are very clever, and none of them want to end up on display on the wharf."

She was as disappointed as the angler in the fighting chair. "I thought I was gonna see a tuna."

"Relax," my brother encouraged. "You'll see one landed before the day's over. We'll be back."

Pierre revved up the motor of the *Cape Marguerite* and headed straight to the Trinity where we joined other boats handlining, including the *Little Esther*. Estelle could have jumped aboard and handlined with her Paul-Emile. What a pity.

"Let's get those codheads," my brother urged.

Tante looked around, puzzled. "Where's the big rock that everyone talks about? The Trinity Ledge?"

"Boudreau's Rock," he corrected, pointing to the bobbing

buoy which marked the spot. "To see it, you have to make an appointment with the tides. In all my trips out here, I've only seen the rock awash twice, in extreme low-water spring tides."

I threw in my tidbit of knowledge, the obvious. "Called Trinity because it's three rocks stuck together. Grand-père Dominique said that fishermen in his time sometimes hit the ledge."

"And were drowned at sea," Pierre added. "Even knowing the area, we almost hit it in this boat a few months ago. You see, most of the time the boat clears the rock, passes over it or is swept away from it by the current. The tide was risky that day. *Fiou!* Close call," he grinned as he untangled us each a line. Tante threw hers in and, as luck would have it, claimed the first catch.

My brother quickly put a damper on her enthusiasm. "A dogfish. Throw it back in." Pierre caught a cod, then another and another, until there were fish slapping the deck about our feet, and not one was mine. It took a long time before I felt a pull on my line. "I got a bite!" I exclaimed, bouncing up and down like a yo-yo. "I think I caught a tuna, a record thousand pounds!"

Pierre grabbed my line and dragged it to the side of the boat, glancing at the red mark imprinted across my hand. He yanked up sixty feet of the line to free the hook, which had snagged a bunch of seaweed weighed down by suckling mussels. "The trick," he explained, "is to release your line until you feel a soft thud. That means it has hit bottom. Quickly, you pull it back about nine or ten feet. You'll get the feel of it."

He had the feel of it all right—eleven haddock, sixteen cod, seven pollock. Tante Marceline claimed five cod of her own. "Just what I wanted," she acknowledged, "but a flounder sure would be nice."

"Flounder need a smaller hook," Pierre noted. "You can catch them right at the wharf."

She examined the catch of the day. "Aren't there any halibut in this ocean?"

"Kinda' rare," Pierre answered, "but I do take a fair number in my nets."

With buckets of seawater, he cleaned the bloody slime from the side of the boat and then revved up the engine of the *Cape*

Marguerite. I dissected my dogfish while Tante Marceline dished out the remaining bait to the hungry seagulls.

When we got back to the tuna fleet, six of the boats were flying white flags: six tuna being fought. Pierre manoeuvred the *Cape Marguerite* to the left, to the right, until it was alongside Captain Melbourne's boat, allowing Tante Marceline to jump aboard to watch the fight up close. The angler at the stern was from Wedgeport. So was Tante. How to separate two *par-en-bas*. They opened their mouths and a camaraderie instantly bloomed, their conversation consisting of *ouain* for every second word in the Wedgeport lingo. The two sounded like energized ducks, in synch with the tuna running at high speed behind the boat.

"It has been two hours," the angler yelled to Pierre. "Just can't seem to tire the damn thing. *J'lavons quasiment pardu.*"

A splashing wake marked the course of the racing fish, which swam in five hundred yard dashes for twenty minutes before he finally slowed down, turned towards the boat, then ran off again, with about three hundred yards of line.

"Tighten the drag!" the guide yelled. The angler, short on temper, started giving everything the tackle could stand until he got the tuna fighting on the surface, within about three hundred feet of the boat. Tante Marceline had a perfect view of the giant, which was hooked by the corner of the mouth. His dorsal fin and tail were exposed. His great blue back occasionally surfaced. The angler cleared the line from the boat, and the fish raced off, smashing the water with his powerful tail. That called for extra tension again, and a new glove to replace the one that was chewed through on the thumb guiding the line. Captain Melbourne slowed up the engine, and we waited, waited, until the angler started reeling the line in short pumps, as tight as he could, and the tuna surfaced. It began to circle. The giant was weakening, his spirit breaking. Melbourne revved the motor again, moving forward cautiously until the angler was able to hold the tuna within a hundred feet of the boat, but the stubborn fish would not come any closer. His great tail worked back and forth in smacking splashes. He circled, further tiring himself, exactly as the angler wanted ... but where had he gone?

"Under the stern!" Pierre hollered. The angler threw off the drag on the reel and jumped up. "Move the boat forward!" yelled the guide to the captain. The angler began to reel the line tighter until the tuna smacked his powerful tail and resurfaced now within fifty feet of the boat, flapping wildly. Soon the angler had him within thirty feet of the boat, on the surface and trapped. That fish was going nowhere, even though he continued to smack his tail, wearing himself out. When the tuna was within a few feet of the stern, the angler swung his chair around to coax him alongside. That's when the guide grabbed the eight- foot leader wire on which the tuna was hooked, taking extreme care not to touch the line—a sure disqualification.

Captain Melbourne stopped the engine and one of the crew, ready with his gaff, drove it into the tuna's side. "Three hours and twenty minutes!" he yelled, and the angler grinned, flopping back in his chair. It took five of the crew to get the tail rope on the monster and pull him into the boat. What a spectacle!

The press people were snapping photos from every angle, but the magnificence of a tuna close-up could never be captured in photos. Tante Marceline, sprawled over the side of the boat, gaped at the sparkling richness of colours. She was dazzled by the iridescent hues, like the rays of a jewel, which formed an intricate part of the tuna's living tissue: stripes of gold on the side and around the fins—golds richer than the precious metal itself; beautiful yellows; a rainbow of grey, white, green, and pink under the tail; radiant silvers and pinks on the belly. But the tuna's eyes were glazed, and the living colours were quickly dying with the fish as it began to turn blue-black, the colour everyone sees when it hangs on the wharf.

Back on the *Cape Marguerite*, Tante Marceline asked how many pounds it weighed. Pierre took a rough guess. "I'd say about eight hundred."

"Then it's gonna win!" she cheered. He shrugged. "I've seen some landed of over a thousand pounds. Besides, even if this one proves the biggest, there's a point system."

"You mean it's not just the biggest fish that wins?" she protested.

My brother shook his head. "Goes by points. Something like:

one point per pound of fish taken, two hundred points each time to the team that takes the largest number of fish in each day's competition, the largest single fish in each day's competition, the largest number of fish during the match, and the largest single fish during the match. I don't know how many," he concluded, "but generous points as well for the least time taken to land a fish. This one will gain the Canadian team some points, at least for its weight."

Tante Marceline wouldn't budge from the wharf until all the tunas had been weighed and the winning team was announced— the Cubans, who had landed two tunas, one at seven hundred and twenty-five pounds, and the largest single fish, tipping the scales at eight hundred and fifty pounds—forty-five pounds over the one caught aboard Captain Melbourne's boat. Darn! Fresh blood was dripping from a total of seven tuna mouths. The Cubans were the only team with more than one tuna, closing the day with nineteen hundred and seventy-five points.

"They better take it easy on the rum," Pierre grinned to Captain Melbourne. "Points can accumulate fast with four days left."

Tante Marceline wobbled up the hill, tired, hungry, and terribly disappointed. She stopped to rest and chat with Gustave. He was excited about his covered driveway, thick with Irish moss drying in the sun, ready to be sold.

Cedric was puttering about in the barn. His grin set my heart aflutter, but the gloom in his eyes worried me. Oh, how he hated mossing.

Chapter 23

It was a time for leavings. First Philippe. He had poached lobster all summer, spent his savings on nice clothes. Grand-père Dominique had bought him new shoes. Grand-mère Sophie had served his favourite fish and potato "hash" as often as she could. And heaven forbid, my mother had excited him with enough "big city" talk at our kitchen table. You'll like it, she had promised, totally ignorant of what Toronto could possibly be like, let alone university. He couldn't wait, he told her.

Yet, on the morning of his departure, a veil of gloom descended upon him. He was barely downstairs when he began to cry in his porridge. Only days before, he had lashed at Mam' because there was nothing to eat in the house, "Why did you have so many children if you couldn't afford them!" He was now staring at her, teary-eyed, regretting his flippant words.

"I hate my temper. It doesn't let me think when I'm angry." The look on Mam's face assured him that she loved him nonetheless. "I like the way Tante Marceline leaves," my brother sobbed. "She sneaks away in the night. It's fast, easy."

And necessary to spare Grand-mère Sophie the agony of hateful good-byes. Mam', however, was fine. Mothers didn't worry about their boys. Confident that my brother's determination would yield him success, she handed over his valise without a tear. I checked in Grand-père Dominique's shed, searched the attic of the two houses, looked everywhere. My father was nowhere to be found. Mam' wasn't too concerned, as she glanced towards the fields. "He'll be back."

The rest of the family assembled by the old homestead where N'Oncle Joseph had parked his car. Eyes dazed, Grand-père

Dominique was pacing about, his good-bye grin misdirected at Tante Marceline. "Senility comes with hardening of the arteries," Docteur Theriault had told us. "He'll have his good and bad days." Who was really going away?

Grand-mère Sophie's legs were heavy, slowing her shuffle out of the house. She had been shedding tears for days. Her face was blotchy and swollen, her voice raspy, barely audible to Philippe. "Please write me," she begged. "Just a little note. Once a month if you can."

Sobbing, my brother embraced his old grandmother, accepting from her trembling hand some cash she could ill afford. Solemnly, he promised, "To write is the very least I can do."

Pierre extended his contribution—a roll of bills. Philippe shook his head, "I can't take this."

A boastful grin spread across our fisherman's face. "Take it. There's more where that came from. *C'est riânne.*"

There were no proper good-byes as such for a brother like Pierre, just a handshake and Philippe's voice overcome with emotion, "I'll pay you back when I'm an engineer."

He lightened his farewell with Thérèse who glowed at the mere mention of school in September, her hopes and aspirations every bit as ambitious as his. "I'm gonna be the smartest one in the whole class," she assured him.

Joel straddled Mam's hip, his inflamed gum reducing his communication to a constant whine. That darn tooth was cemented in there, never to come out. Philippe extended his arms, but the child buried his face in Mam's shoulder, prompting my big brother to turn to André.

"I'll be practising on my punching bag. When I come home, you better be ready." He had another message, uttered under his breath. "Watch the old man when he's been drinking."

What better parting words for Pricille, a sister with whom he had spent his youth fighting: "Don't take any shit from those guys in Boston." His voice broke with the loyal reminder, "If any one of them ever lays a hand on you, he'll answer to me." The reconciled rivals embraced.

And then the classic tease that would forever link me to my

criminal record. "I trust you won't be washing any more puppies."

"Not while you're around," I could safely jest, allowing our Philippe a hearty grin, a rest from his tangled nerves. He tarried as long as he could, talking trivia with Uncle John and Tante Marceline, savouring last looks at the wharf, anything to contain his emotions until he got into N'Oncle Joseph's car. The tears flowed, though, as he gazed towards the woods. I could well picture my father, sitting on a fallen tree, whittling away, thinking about God only knew what.

"The train won't wait," Mam' urged. Philippe looked around at all of us. His last look lingered on Pierre's gentle face.

Grand-mère Sophie shuffled back into the house, chagrined at the thought of yet another date fast approaching. If Tante Marceline was organizing a get-together, then she too was leaving soon. Besides, she had asked Docteur Theriault to drop by and check blood pressures, a sure sign of last-minute things to do.

The doctor arrived. He fastened and inflated his grey nylon cuff around Grand-mère's upper arm—one hundred and twenty over eighty, perfect for her age and size. "You want me to check Dominique and Antoine?" he asked Tante. His glance rested on me. "Antoine's little girl. How many times you rocked on that man's knees. Do you still have the wooden ox he carved you?"

I nodded. "Joel tries to eat it, now that he's cutting teeth."

The doctor smiled. He checked Grand-mère's vial of diabetes pills as he spoke to me. "You must be going into high school this year."

Again I nodded, this time with a smile split from ear to ear, "Yes, I am."

"How's your arthritis these days?" he asked Grand-père, who had just entered the kitchen, offering a civil grin for a change.

"Never felt better. Long as the *maudit* fog stays away."

My father arrived next. The doctor's voice was teasing, "You're piling on the weight Antoine." Then a frown furrowed his brow. "What's that huffing and puffing? Still a pack a day?"

His lie was easier spoken scanning the floor, "No, no, no. I cut down a lot."

With the same frown, the doctor tracked the pointer as he let the air out of the pressure cuff. "Yours is a bit high," he told my father. "Sophie tells me that you like salt far too much."

My father's grin was hardly an answer, his attention drawn back outside where he quickly rejoined N'Oncle Joseph and Uncle John. N'Oncle and my father chatted about fishing and small village trivia, Uncle John about lucrative business in the big city. I loved to listen to their talk, which often turned to heated arguments.

"My restaurants do well for me," said Uncle John.

But N'Oncle Joseph wasn't the least impressed with the figures, raising his head as if to deliver a lecture. "Money's not everything."

I found the expression out of place coming from N'Oncle Joseph, who was saddled with a crew of ten. And I could remember having a dental cavity so huge that I could pick at the nerve with the eraser end of my pencil. After days of crying in pain, I finally made it to the dentist and had the troublesome tooth extracted. Now I needed glasses, but I couldn't mention it to Mam'; we simply had no money. It was always the same story, so it was not at all strange that I sided with Uncle John's philosophy.

Eyes fixed on his Chrysler New Yorker, he pondered his comeback, perhaps remembering the wretched days of his youth and the shack in Maine where he had been raised. "Money's not everything," he readily admitted, "but it sure gives me a choice." He knew when to walk away.

"Maybe you said too much," my father fretted, causing N'Oncle to jerk his head back.

"He brags about his money and can't even bring you a carton of American cigarettes. I didn't say *enough*."

The day of Tante Marceline's get-together arrived, and Mam' strictly warned my father, "Now don't you and N'Oncle Joseph go drinking and mouthing off with Uncle John."

My father assumed his most serious expression, though flawed with a devious grin. "No, no, no. I know how crazy I get. Besides, there won't be anything to drink."

When I arrived at the soirée, Uncle John had practically transferred the Meteghan liquor store into Grand-mère Sophie's kitchen. He poured N'Oncle Joseph a jigger of gin, easing into friendly conversation, perhaps to smooth the differences. "You'll never guess what I saw today."

N'Oncle graciously turned his head. "What?"

"Potatoes, on the side of the road."

The statement drew a blank on N'Oncle's face. "You find that odd?"

"Yes, when no one's at the stand. I dropped my fifty cents and left with the potatoes. Can you imagine leaving a jar of money on the side of the road in Boston?"

"But we're not in Boston," N'Oncle reminded him, turning his gaze on sweet Pricille, who was attired in a lovely white dress, especially attractive against her jet-black hair. My sister was vain, tainted with the vice because of Tante Marceline who kept sending her nice clothes, and N'Oncle Joseph who poured on the flattery. True, my sister was striking when her hair was not restrained in a ponytail, but she hardly looked like Elizabeth Taylor. On the other hand, she sure was pretty. "*La belle Pricille,*" N'Oncle loved to torment. "You'll forget about Mr. Clyde once you get to Boston."

All eyes on her, Pricille glowed. "Who knows? Maybe I'll meet and marry an American."

The comment was hardly meant as fuel for a sermon.

"Marry your own kind," N'Oncle Joseph lost no time in rebuking, turning deadly serious. "Marriage is difficult enough without taking on a different culture."

Tante Rosalie could only scowl at the hard liquor on the table, lightning for negligent tongues. "We'd be honoured to have an American boy in our family," she admonished, and we all grinned, except for Mam' who had recently lost a front tooth. False teeth were not designed for tugging on dried fish. Dried cod. Uncle John said the stuff smelled like the shanties. He wrinkled his nose at the Acadian favourite.

When Mam' opened the oven door to display a crusty brown rappie pie, his mouth didn't water like ours. Instead he winced, pausing before he mocked, "That stuff looks like it has already been eaten."

Mam' readied the frying pan for Uncle John's steak, while N'Oncle Joseph fumed in outright annoyance. "You've never even tried rappie pie. Maybe you'd like it."

Busy attacking a steaming lobster, Tante Marceline ignored her husband's loose comments, downright reckless with her paring knife. She was digging and devouring with noisy gusto all she could salvage of the green pastelike stuff that made Uncle John wince even more. She sucked the tiny legs to savour morsels, then tried to slit open the hard shell of a large claw, an arduous task better left to the skilled experts. She passed the stubborn claw to Dad who simply crushed it under the rocker of his chair. She pulled out the succulent meat, chewing voraciously and wearing a blissful smile. The lobster finally devoured, she started licking clean all the shells.

"You don't have to eat the shells," Pierre cautioned, pointing to the stove. "The pot is chuck-full, and there are more where those came from."

Tante looked up, her eyes mischievous, her pause full of challenge. "I bet you didn't know that a lobster listens with its legs." The wide grin on Pierre's face led her on. "And did you know that it tastes with its feet, and has molars in its stomach."

"Where's its brain?" my brother now queried.

She hooted, "I should have known. Where?"

"Near its throat. And its kidneys?"

"Give up."

"Behind its forehead."

Primed with an audience, Pierre wasn't stopping there. "I bet you never noticed that flounder, plaice, and halibut all have eyes on the upperside of their heads."

"Well I'll be damned," Tante half apologized. "Of all the ones you bring home, and I never noticed. Why is that?"

"Because they swim close to the bottom of the ocean."

"Just flatfish?" she asked.

Pierre nodded. "As far as I know. Now when they're born, they look like other fish. It's when they're older that they flatten out and their eyes move to the top of their heads." Tante was fascinated. She didn't notice my father using his stocking feet to absorb the lobster juice dripping on the floor. But Mam' glared at him and at the glass of hard liquor he had snuck beneath his rocking chair.

"*Ma p'tite Zoé,*" he gestured with a sweep of the arm, "this trip will buy another leg for your ox."

He had a glassy stare. All eyes on me, I reluctantly jingled the last bit of clubhouse change in my pocket, but once in the shed, I cursed the long walk. "*Dinche de sacré marde.* Will I ever see the end of his damned tobacco? *Maudit* pest," I raged. "Why can't he get his own tobacco?" I grumbled all the way down Dominique's driveway, all the way to the post office. How many friggin' legs did an ox have anyway?

If the postmaster was fishing for information, he was pumping the wrong person. "I hear Pierre's got a girlfriend. *Une p'tite Saint Bernard.*"

"Not that I know of," I curtly retorted, and I slammed my change on the showcase. "A package of Export A." I stormed out of the post office and charged up the steep hills, gasping hard. A girlfriend? Pierre? I got back to the old homestead and Dad didn't even ask for his tobacco, caught up in aimlessly strumming on his old guitar, and trying to sing—yes, sing—a slurred and mutilated imitation of sentimental favourites by Hank Snow and Jim Reeves. Then came the stories of his supposed wealth, sending Grand-mère Sophie to her room.

"If only Martine would come to the bank with me," he pressed, set for a row, which would have erupted if Pierre had not risen from his chair. "Four o'clock comes early."

My father's eyes acquired a sudden, drunken madness that had everyone holding their breath, especially Mam', the object of his crazed stare. "Both leaving at the same time, eh?"

She didn't dare move just yet.

André sprang to his feet, fists clenched at his sides, the size of him, glaring at my father. "One more word, and you'll find out who's leaving!" My irate brother made a clean sweep, pouring everything in sight down the sink, "There! I never want to see another bottle of liquor in this house!"

Pierre could go. He had left Mam' in good hands. She tarried a while before she dared leave. I followed. Back at the house, she gazed out our kitchen window, waiting for the fool to come home.

"What was Dad like when you met him?" I asked.

She started folding clothes, grinning at the timely question. "Insanely jealous, mouthy when he drank."

"How did you meet him?" I probed.

She sighed, long and hard, returning to that long ago Saturday night in Meteghan. "All the girls were crowded around this young man who was strumming on his guitar, immaculate looking with his polished white shoes and cuffed grey trousers. Every once in a while, he took out a peppermint from a paper bag, too shy to look at any of the girls." Her voice was almost apologetic. "I guess I was taken by the blue eyes. He offered me a ride home on his bicycle."

"What about this Philippe Delaney?" I interrupted

She embarked on that story. "I worked at the Super Lunch in Dartmouth, his favourite place to eat. He was a lonely sailor and I was far from home. We went to the movies." She stopped folding clothes to grin nostalgically for a moment. "Until Antoine found out. He ordered me home and met me at the train in Meteghan Station, with a jealous, drunken streak in his eyes, set to raise hell if I didn't accept the ring he handed me. 'We're getting married,' he ordered, right there on the station platform. I was nineteen."

"Nineteen! What did your mother say?"

"She warned me that Antoine liked his drink far too much."

"And your father?"

"He advised me that there were plenty of fish in the ocean, to find myself another one."

"Wish you had listened?" I ventured, but Mam' got suddenly absorbed in folding her clothes, then retrieved a pail from under the sink. There was barely a speck on the light pink tiles, but she washed the kitchen floor every night. I was going to bed, out of her way, but not before satisfying my curiosity. "Do you ever think of Philippe Delaney?"

She was on her knees, the silence in the kitchen broken only by water splashing in her pail. I was on my way to the attic when she called me back. "Yes. I think of him." A smile penetrated the hollow eyes of my mother's haggard face. "But I married the man I loved."

Pricille came to bed, repeating word for word what Dad had said about his money and about me. "Imbecile! *Danche de trou d'chu!*" I exclaimed. "He told everyone I wasn't his?"

My sister confirmed that yes, he had, and then she fell into an exhausted sleep. It was still dark when she raised her head to see the clock and shine her flashlight. Five-thirty. There was no time for wordy farewells. She had to jump into her clothes and grab her suitcase. She beamed her light across the attic. Pierre was long gone. My father was lost in a drunken snore. André seemed small in a big bed by himself, his head propped on two pillows, having already claimed Philippe's as his own.

"See you," Pricille whispered to my brother. "Say something serious for a change."

He rubbed the sleep from his eyes. "Take all the fog with you, dump it in the Boston harbour, and we'll have ourselves a party!"

"If only I could," Pricille bantered, "but what about your invention of a fan in the dunes to chase it away? Work on it while I'm gone so that I might want to come home once in a while." She proceeded to the window where my father's silhouette had tarried so many mornings before heading down the stairs to light his fire. "Zoé," my sister said, unsure where to begin. "I know you're angry at Dad, but you know what liquor does to him."

Her words got me crying. "Sure. Makes him tell everyone stupidities that aren't true."

"Call it an *irony*. You'll learn that in English this year."

"Irony?" I pondered out loud.

She explained. "That he says you're not his, and yet …" she took me in her arms, "you were always his favourite. No matter how bad things get, you bring a shine to his eyes. And he to yours. The years passed me by," she lamented, "and I hadn't the time to know him. Mam' started telling me her problems when I was still playing with dolls. Too young to understand, I'd stand at this window with her, waiting for him to come home." She sighed heavily. "Sometimes the nights were awfully long." Her tears were warm on my face. "I was the only one Mam' could talk to. Now you'll have to listen for me."

Anger seized me once more. "But now Tante Marceline knows everything!"

"Tante's known everything long before now," my sister assured me, her perceptive words a powerful balm to our parting. "But she loves Dad," she allowed a slight pause, "just like you do."

Our Pricille was all grown up. She proceeded downstairs to gaze at Joel, who was sleeping in his crib. Thérèse was nestled next to Mam', in a cosy niche that should have been my father's.

"You look after Joel," Pricille whispered to her, "and I'll buy you the most beautiful doll you've ever seen. Okay?"

Thérèse had to restrain the quiver in her lips. "A walking doll?"

"Yes, if you promise to sleep with Zoé, so she can take revenge for all the times I stole her warm side of the bed. Now she'll do it to you." We all cried, binding a sisterly moment.

At a time when Mam' should have said much, there was little she had prepared. She sat in bed, bravely itemizing: "Don't go out in the dark by yourself. Watch your money. Act like a lady. If you don't like Boston, you can always come back." She blinked, her misty eyes savouring one last look. "Go to church!"

With a thousand nods, Pricille promised, reassuring her as she tiptoed out of the bedroom and into the kitchen to check for car lights beaming in Dominique's driveway. "I promise I'll go to church."

"Are you gonna serve rappie pie in Uncle John's restaurant?" I asked, and she had to smile.

"The big boss prefers steak. Watch those boys in high school," she sternly warned, "especially that Cedric. I see how he stares when he comes looking for André."

I gently shoved her out the door and hastened back to the attic where grey light from the window was now shaping shadows. André raised his head at the muffled grunting coming from my father's pillow, a slurred call for Pierre to get up.

"Pierre's at the Trinity," I responded, still plenty annoyed at him.

"Is that you, Zoé?" he asked, but I pressed my forehead to the window, until the tail-lights of Uncle John's car had disappeared over the hill.

"Yes, it's me." In no time, he was snoring again.

I snuck back into bed, reached for the lucky rabbit foot that was now mine and stroked my face with it, wiping the tears that rolled down my cheeks. I had also inherited my sister's hair rollers and her red nail polish. Everything in the orange crate night table, even her signet ring engraved with a P. Shame it wasn't a C. Maybe I'd give it to Estelle.

I had something from Tante Marceline too, a divine silver bracelet that she had brought me from the States. It somewhat matched the locket from Anna at the hospital. I had forgotten to tell Tante that the Cubans had won the tuna cup. I hoped she knew.

I had nothing special by which to remember Philippe, but then again, how could I forget those snapping black eyes of his? He had such power to incite extremes of emotion in me. Sometimes, I downright hated him. Other times, I loved him so much it hurt. The vengeance of hell he had for a temper, the gentle heart of a kitten for his family.

Chapter 24

Amos stretched his neck, lifted his head high and honked, just like he did the day he had taken flight to the beach—only this time he wasn't going far. The strength in his thin and knobby legs was fatally weakened. He strutted back a few yards from the woodpile and honked again—his angry protest to an untimely end. Feathers were flying about, a tiny one, graceful in the breeze, nestled in the pleats of my skirt. I cringed at the trickling blood streaking his white feathers as the goose staggered past me, and then stumbled to a senseless death.

Pierre had a new girlfriend all right, too madly in love to descend from the clouds and too enthralled with his new car to have noticed where he was going. Backing up, he had pinned the goose against the woodpile. I asked him, "Didn't you hear me yell for you to *stop?*"

He climbed out of the car, hardly glancing at the bloodied goose. "Why didn't the stupid thing get out of the way?" It was so unlike him to be callous.

"Because he had a lame leg!" I yelled, infuriated by his recklessness. "You're the stupid one!"

Mam' had heard the commotion and would have no doubt slapped me across the face if I hadn't been crying.

"Stop that foolishness," she immediately commanded, "all because of a silly goose."

"What if Joel had been crawling about the woodpile?" I sobbed, and her face turned deadly white. My father loved to watch his little scrimp crawl on the grass. Perhaps Pierre was in for a sermon after all.

For now, she just glared at him. "Fix that goose before Thérèse sees it."

Fix it? To cook? Who would eat Amos?

The day was overcast, stressed by a fair breeze that threatened the smaller boats tied at the wharf, though the rolling swells that crashed against the breakwater would soon be pounding if the winds gained any momentum.

"Not a cupful for the *Cape Marguerite*," Pierre entered the house to boast, "but I think I'll wait and see." Tormented by the heaving sea farther in the rip, he dallied about. The winds were not expected to abate. He had been rebuked by the other fishermen more than once for the high winds he chanced. But he had expanded his fishing grounds to the Lurcher, Bay of Fundy, and Browns Banks, so he was out dragging for three days on end and coming in loaded to the gunnels, reaping big money. He had a car to pay off and a new girlfriend's expensive taste to appease. We had caught just a glimpse of her, tiny next to Pierre's muscular frame. Pretty? A closer look had yet to determine that. He had met her at a Comeauville dance.

Zita was visiting more often, entirely curious about the new flame. "Who is she?" she pumped. What did Mam' know?

"Augustin's daughter. Whoever that is. *Ça's trouve une fille à Augustin à Bernard à Dâvid à Cyriac. J'ché point quisse que c'est.*"

Whoever she was, this new gal had Pierre spending long hours in the attic, strumming on my father's guitar and yodelling his lovesick songs. Every chance he got, he Brylcreamed his hair stiff, jumped into his black-and-white Pontiac, and headed for Saint Bernard—likely what he now had in mind if the winds didn't abate soon.

But girlfriend or no girlfriend, the *Cape Marguerite* couldn't afford to bob at the wharf. If I don't go out, I won't catch any fish, was Pierre's slogan. Maybe a shift in the wind would defy the weather report. My brother returned to the window to study the situation. He grinned, sure of his decision. "What's a little wind? Nothing for the *Cape Marguerite*." But then he lowered his eyebrows, doubt creeping back. "Quite the swells. I don't know." Still staring towards the wharf, I heard him exclaim, "Lord Jesus!"

I fled to the window. "What!"

Pierre put on a stone serious face. "That can't be Gustave!"

Though my eyes were failing me, I could see blurred forms on the scow. Was Cedric one of them?

"Gustave checking his punt," Pierre figured. "Or going mossing," he speculated. "In that saucer?" Pierre was making me crazy with his fickle judgement. "The wind is picking up. No, I think it's shifting. The hell with it. I'll just go to the Trinity."

I kept my nose pressed to the window, squinting for a better look. Where in the dickens was Paul-Emile off to? He was propelled up the Cape road as if the devil were after him. I didn't like the look of the burlap bag. Villagers threw their trash down the cliff behind Zita's house, not so unusual, but with Paul-Emile, God only knew what he was up to. I hastened across the road to find out. "You didn't go fishing?" I queried.

He merely smirked, trying to peer through my threadbare cotton blouse. "A slight breeze and everyone panics, but I'm not complaining."

"What's in the bag? Cedric gone mossing?" I asked.

Paul-Emile lowered his gaze, sending sly glances along my legs, which were sinfully bare with the trendy pleated skort I was wearing. "My, we ask a lot of questions," he smirked. "It will cost you for answers," he bargained, and I cringed at the thought of him laying his hands on me.

Taking a few hostile steps backwards, I made myself quite clear. "Then forget I asked."

"Cedric's gone to Yarmouth," the scoundrel now divulged. "Said something about tests for the army. Now about the bag ..."

While Paul-Emile's roving eyes tried to undress me, I sprang forward and grabbed the mewing burlap bag, yanking it open. By the time the scoundrel could react, I had already discovered three kittens gripping the meshed burlap to get out.

"There are enough rocks in here to sink the *Titanic!*" I wailed. "You're drowning them, aren't you!" Paul-Emile lunged for the bag, but I made a grab for the kittens, managing to rescue one.

The murderer tried to seize my arm, but I could run down the hill faster than he could stamp out of the tall grass.

What do I tell Estelle? I wondered as I panted all the way down the hill. Terribly afraid of falling, I avoided even the tiniest pebble.

"Come!" I summoned at my friend's sun parlour door. "I have something for you."

"For me?" she glowed. I recovered from under my armpit a half-smothered purring ball of fur that wouldn't meow until I frantically shook it.

"Ow!" I hollered. "He's alive all right, and gripping my arm. Take him!"

But Estelle would only stroke the rescued kitten, in no hurry to take charge, not just yet. "Where did you get him?"

The rush of excitement that had flushed my face dampened. "Does it matter? You wanted a fluffy white kitten, didn't you?"

"Where?" she demanded, adamant that I tell her.

"From Paul-Emile. He was going to drown ..."

"Paul-Emile!" she interjected. "I never saw him go up the hill. You knew where he was going?"

The cutting inference that I was chasing after the snake only served to nauseate me. "You want this kitten? Yes or no."

How could she reject anything that her precious Paul-Emile had touched. Of course she wanted it. I had my afternoon planned, and she wasn't ruining my fun, not if she was going to act like a jealous witch.

On such a windy day, there was no greater sense of freedom than to wander along the beach, to savour the waves pounding on the shore, music to the soul. At the end of the summer, there was a shallow stretch of warmer brownish ocean to wade in, coming from the dykes, *les dalles*, away from the numbing, icy water where huge swells were forming. I saluted the majestic ocean and would have surely plunged in to ride the waves if Estelle had been with me. Instead, I devoured every leaf of dulse that had washed ashore. I splashed around in a rippling tidepool, my thoughts diverted by the seagulls soaring overhead, their screeches adding melodrama to the windswept beach.

I gazed at the little grey schoolhouse that had held ten grades in one room, turning back time to the sweet and the bitter. I remembered the echo of my girlish giggle as I had ignored the schoolboys' whistles—their name-calling at times sugary-sweet to excite a crush, other times cruelly devastating. "Hopalong Cassidy" had been Babette's persecution. I could live with *"La p'tite Zoé,"* a friendly euphemism for a skinny girl, a term of endearment invented by my father.

I headed towards the Diner, the wind in my face, kerchief snug under my chin. I sucked in deep breaths of the heavy, salt air and marvelled at the low-lying clouds rolling by, eerie, yet exciting, inciting my imagination as I neared the sand dunes so that I could see a head bobbing in the tall blades of wavy grass on the steepest of the three dunes. I could see an army jacket, too, and pretended that I actually climbed the towering, sandy hill, sliding back two feet with each effort upward, but finally I reached the summit—only to come tumbling down the steep incline, head first in the sliding sand.

My imagined Cedric was still at the top, my fantasy running wild. In a few flying leaps he was breathing on my neck, our race to the ocean intoxicating as his long legs overtook me. He had almost reached the water when he tossed back his jacket and urged me to follow. I was taken by his voluptuous smile, his strong chest darkening through a wet shirt, but I could not join him. The smashing breakers drowned my call.

Careful! I imagined calling, all caution wasted on the vehement winds, for he had already plunged into a monstrous wave which enveloped his body and propelled him deeper and farther, until my voice was hoarse and useless. *Ced-riiiic!!*

Dazed from my emotional reverie, I stood there, still staring at the sand dunes. I glanced towards the ocean, briefly fearful that Cedric had drowned. No, it was a fantasy, after all. Still dazed, I sauntered back along the shore, pausing to contemplate the utter stupidity of such a useless fantasy. Cedric would never want me. I sunk my feet into the wet sand, played among my own footprints until I reached the Cape road to face the long trek home. I hugged the shoulder all the way as cars whizzed past me, much too fast, I thought, for such a narrow road.

Grand-mère Sophie had promised me a pie with the blueberries Mam' and I had picked. Hungry now, I hastened to the old homestead and entered her kitchen to find a pie shell empty on the table. She was obviously too upset to move from her chair. Grand-père Dominique seemed confused. Every time the phone rang, he would make furtive steps towards the hall, the temptation to eavesdrop on the party line too hard to resist. As it rang again, he shuffled over to pick up the receiver, causing Grand-mère to snap, "That wasn't two long rings!"

With bewilderment furrowing his forehead, he rehooked the receiver and retreated, pressing the brim of his cap against the kitchen window. For a change, he wasn't grumbling, just worried. "Something's going on at the Pointe."

The Cape was in a hurry. Cars were continuously parading down the road. The phone wouldn't stop ringing. There wasn't a soul on the wharf. They were all either on the Pointe, or standing on their lawns, communicating in hand gestures. When I noticed Estelle, Charlotte, and the boatshop crew take to the road, I knew something was dreadfully wrong. I stormed out of the house, yelling to Estelle all the way down the hill, "Wait! Wait for me! *Jette moi.*"

If she heard me, she didn't turn around. A strange sensation gripped me as I neared the first shanty and noticed the crowd and an ambulance. Standing at the back of it were two men in black rubber suits, trying to chase the people away. Even the Justice of the Peace, Walter à Blanche, was there. I felt a shiver of goose bumps. Pierre! Had he gone out after all? I ran back past the shanties. The *Cape Marguerite* was not at the wharf.

Keep calm, I told myself, so I wouldn't start to hyperventilate. Docteur Theriault and Père Lucien each had a restraining hand on Lina. Where was Cedric? *Yousse yavait Cedric?* Maybe he hadn't gone to Yarmouth after all. Maybe the covered body in the ambulance was his! My fantasy. It was a premonition!

Zita was thrashing about like a hen in our chicken coop, gabbling to an already distraught Lina. "How stupid to have gone out. *C'est doummage.* The weather report certainly gave enough warning."

Acting the gentleman he was, Percy coaxed Zita away from

the ambulance. Estelle glared at her, doses of hatred lumped into one final stare as she cupped her hands to my ear. "Nosey, that Zita. *Nez partout. Faut sa save toulle'chu d'la mouche.*"

I dragged her away, past Emma and Babette, to mingle with the mob overlooking the cliff. Sharp, slated rocks protruded from the ocean, where the violent waves were washing ashore the remnants of a red dory. Scattered broken boards told a grim story.

N'Oncle Joseph pointed to the very spot. "They pulled Gustave from there."

I almost fainted. *Cedric* was all right! N'Oncle was as puzzled as everyone else by Gustave's rash decision to have left the wharf in such a gale. "He should have known better," my uncle mourned. "Only a fool ..."

"Not for us to judge the poor man," Tante Rosalie surmised. "*Foudrait point asseyer'd'comprend çâ.*"

I kept my mouth shut. Pierre was the other fool, an idiot, to have chanced this gale. Except the *Cape Marguerite* wasn't a saucer.

Paul-Emile zigzagged his way back to the ambulance and, of course, Estelle had to take to his heels, breaking away from my grip. "I want to see!" I could do nothing but follow her.

Impatient, she ploughed through the crowd, almost knocking over Eddie Pockshaw to get to the white sheet shrouding the body. "I want to see the face," she persisted, and my knees turned to jelly.

"You're crazy!" *Deranged* was the word. "You're gonna get in trouble!" I exclaimed. But Estelle stood transfixed, paying no attention to the ultimate warning, "Your father's coming!"

There were a few seconds between the time Père Lucien coaxed Lina away and the moment when the attendant closed the ambulance doors, allowing Estelle to jerk back the white sheet. Horror-struck, she gasped, then barged past me, stepping on feet and bumping into people.

"Wait!" I called, as I chased her to the doorstep of a reeking shanty where she collapsed, her eyes as big as saucers.

"Did you see the gash!"

"Are you going to faint?" I fretted.

"Right across the face!" Basil was coming, and she panted for air, anxious to finish the horror story. "One eye was out of its socket! There were white blotches on his cheeks. Something had sucked his face. A shark!"

I helped her up and she hung limp. "Move!" I had to yell. I gave her arm a yank. "We have to get outta here."

A panicked glimpse at her father fast approaching got her moving—up the Cape road, past Cedric's house, where the scent of death had already permeated the ground. We hastened up the hill, past her house. Neither one of us dared look back.

"Get into that house!" Basil hollered after her.

Estelle tugged on my skirt. "If you turn around, I'll never speak to you again."

"In the house!" came the second command.

She only quickened her pace, nudging me in the ribs with her clenched fist. "Don't look back, I said."

When we entered Grand-mère Sophie's kitchen, she let herself fall on the floor, breathless, causing Grand-mère and Grand-père to gape. Utter confusion chilled their faces.

"It's Gustave," I informed them. I helped Estelle to a chair by the window, where I could follow activities as I told the story. Every pause was punctuated by Estelle moaning, "I can't go home!"

"Then don't!" I charged, my attention towards the rip, where a boat was approaching. When I squinted hard, I could make out an ugly canary yellow that instantly transformed into the most beautiful yellow I had ever seen. Just like drama in the silent movies, it took forever for the *Cape Marguerite* to clear the rip, but it did, and I breathed a sigh of utter relief. "Thank God! *Pour l'amour des esclâves.*"

Nearly all of the villagers had moved to Lina's yard, and finally, finally, Gustave's car went down the Cape road. Everyone was waiting for Cedric. He stepped out of the car and seemed to take an eternity to embrace his mother. I saw her raise her face to his and I could almost hear the despair in her voice, the depth in what I imagined was her cry, "It's your father. *Ton père çâ néyé.*"

Chapter 25

The whole Cape was in mourning over Gustave. Poor Eddie
Pockshaw. He couldn't go to the funeral home, stuck as he was
in the hospital with a bleeding ulcer and no family to visit. *Les
quates pattes en l'are.* If only Mam' could drive Pierre's car. Did she
dare bother N'Oncle Joseph again to go to Yarmouth?

"I'm always out fishing," Pierre reasoned, time and time again.
"The car's in the driveway, doing nothing all day."

Dad also pushed for Mam' to learn to drive, but for more
specific reasons. To go to the bank in Meteghan or to park on Main
Street in Yarmouth to watch the sights—his concept of an exciting
Saturday night.

"Must be like New York," he said dreamily.

Hands anchored in dough, Mam' blew her straggly bangs from
her eyes to glare. "You and your Yarmouth! Don't you have anything
else to think about?"

Well, yes, he did. Grand-mère Sophie could barely shuffle
herself around and didn't know how much longer she could cope
with Dominique going senile. Also, Docteur Theriault didn't like
the look of Grand-mère's big toe, the object of Dad's present worry.

Mam' kept on kneading her bread. "Nothing wrong with your
mother's toe. Something she's imagining. *Chequa fare qu'a çâ fijuré.*"

"Maybe we should move next door," Dad merely suggested as
Mam' rattled the lids on the stove to coax a smouldering fire.

"Move next door! And live on what? Their meagre pension?"
Chunks of dough flew as she raised her head to the window, looking
towards the Trinity. "I don't have a red cent for school stuff, the
pantry's bare, and I can't show my face at the post office—not when

we owe forty dollars." The next lash wiped the careless grin off my father's face. "You should be out fishing with Pierre, rather than grinding your ass on a chair. *À la place de't fare grâler'l chu s'une chaise.*"

"I don't have to go fishing!" my father lashed back in frustration. "If you weren't so damn stubborn, you'd get my money from the bank." He dragged on his cigarette butt, unconcerned as to where the next smoke was coming from. "You're a rich woman if you only knew it."

Mam's sudden outburst had mellowed to a sneer, causing a fury to burn through me as she mocked Dad. "And just where does all that money come from?" She sighed, disgusted, patted two doughy balls into a pan that she rammed into the oven, then looked my father in the eye. "I'm not crawling to the old folks. And I won't take Pierre's money either. He has a future to think about."

My father's impassive gaze didn't surprise me. It had been clear for some time that the man would never board a fishing boat again. Not Zano's. Not Pierre's. Not anybody's. And hounding him was as useless as harassing Eddie Pockshaw who would eventually kill himself if he didn't stop drinking.

Mid-afternoon, Mam' pulled her hair back with bobby pins, put on her best housedress, dabbed on some red lipstick, and ordered me to look after the kids. "As long as I have two hands and two feet, I can earn my own living." She headed towards the Cape View Diner.

I headed next door to check with Grand-mère Sophie. "You wanted your kitchen floor washed?" I sat Thérèse and Joel in the rocking chair, "Not a peep from either of you!"

I was rooting for a pail in the shed when I heard the gruff voice, "Get out of that jar!" Jar? What in the Moses …

I stormed into the kitchen, grabbed Thérèse's cookie and flung it back in the jar. "Get back in that chair and don't you move!" Great! Now I had two kids crying.

Grand-père shuffled out of his bedroom, clutching a bottle of holy water, as if nothing had happened. "Could you open this?"

I grabbed the bottle from his arthritic hands and unscrewed the cap. "Here!" Fuming over my pail of sudsy water, I formulated my list: Grand-père's clothes, laundered in Mam's washer; his hair, neatly barbered on her time; his meals, as of late from her kitchen; and now his actions, deliberately mean towards her children! Grouchy over a lousy cookie! He shuffled past me, and I let him have it, "Don't you ever do that again, old man!" He wouldn't look me in the face, which made me even angrier. "Who do you think is gonna look after you? Hein?"

Dominique halted, belched, then shook the bottle of holy water, spilling half its contents on the floor. "As long as there's holy water sprinkled in every room," he figured, "lightning will never hit."

He knew how Grand-mère Sophie was terrified of thunder. Her head was now bent, jowls sagging. She was clutching a crumpled handkerchief.

"I'll get your black dress after I finish the floor," I promised, but she just stared. Damn me with my temper, having upset her so heedlessly. I could almost hear Père Lucien from the pulpit, his roman collar stiff, forcing his neck erect, Patience! Patience with the old people. We'll all get there.

I finished the floor and went rooting through the attic for Grand-mère's black dress from Tante Marceline, the one with the beautiful high neckline, likely the exquisite dress she'd be buried in someday. I helped her choose from a hideous selection of bargain brooches. Her attire assembled, she scowled at Grand-père, her jowls flushing pink, "You're being stubborn. The whole Cape will be at the funeral parlour."

I had to shake my head at how contrary the old man could be.

"Gustave should have been laid at home," he protested.

Grand-mère paid no attention to his grumblings, until the next morning. The chickens were hardly awake before she was howling for people to get up. André and I thundered down the stairs and ran into Mam's bedroom. "Grand-mère's at the door."

"Well, open it!" she ordered, disgusted at our standing there. She made a mad dash to the door ahead of us, opening it to a horrified look on Grand-mère's face.

"Dominique's mouth is funny," she informed us. "He's mumbling something about his oxen in the woods. I'm not sure what he means."

When Mam' arrived next door, he wanted to go to work.
"Work where?" Mam' questioned.
He pondered for the longest while. "At the shipyard." Then
he was looking for his mother. She had been dead for ages, we knew.
He was drooling from one side of his mouth, and his speech
was slightly slurred, more confused than usual. "Where's my cap?"
he asked. It was on his head. "Don't make me go," he fretted.
Grand-mère Sophie understood the allusion. "He means the
funeral home."
It took Docteur Theriault no time to arrive. "Any problem
moving about," he asked, coaching Grand-père at the same time.
"Can you walk a straight line and hold onto this?" Grand-père
dragged his left foot then painstakingly coaxed his left hand to grab
onto the glass.
"Uh-huh," the doctor observed.
He examined the affected side of Grand-père's face while
Grand-mère fretted, "Will he be okay? I mean his mouth?"
The compassionate doctor slipped his hand into hers. "What
he's had is a mild stroke. He's confused. It will take time."
"How much time?" she wanted to know.
"Hard to tell. A few days. A few weeks." He stopped there.
She had already fallen into a *sanglot* of tears. "I nagged him about
going to see Gustave. Told him he was a stubborn, contrary, old
man. Do you suppose …"
"Now don't you be thinking like that!" Docteur Theriault
scolded. "The stroke was more than likely caused by hardening of
the arteries, a blockage. Would have happened anyway." He waited
at the door until she stopped crying. "I have another call. Zita's
mother is not well." He grabbed his bag, then summoned Mam' into
the shed. "They shouldn't be left alone."
He asked her when Gustave's internment was to be held, and
she told him, "Tomorrow morning at ten."

Estelle and I had barely entered the funeral parlour when she spotted Paul-Emile and left me stranded in a roomful of hushed tones. I
hugged the door frame, eyeing chairs along the safest wall, where
Emma Goodwin was sitting.

"Is that you Zoé?" she asked, feeling the chair next to her. "Sit here."

She was such a nice lady, and yet, I only lent half an ear to her invitation up the lighthouse road.

"But your cat doesn't like me," I jested, though I had plans to visit again, soon. I wanted my locket.

Emma's voice was troubled. "Lina's not taking this very well." She talked non-stop about sweet Babette, but I kept silent, my gaze fixed on a loose button on Tante Rosalie's blue trench coat. N'Oncle Joseph's brushcut and mustache were getting awfully grey, but his face wasn't aging. Holding my gaze too long, I had to blink to erase the blur and focus this time on Lina, who was sobbing in the arms of everyone who approached to pay due respects, so terribly desperate she was to talk. Her Cedric was fixed to his chair, his stare boring into the floor. I had seen the disturbed gaze before. Past differences with his father couldn't have rested easy on his mind. He rarely raised his head, except to loosen the tie that was choking him, or to shrug his shoulders, as if his navy, V-neck sweater was itchy. Meticulously pressed trousers fell neatly over his shiny black shoes. He looked like a soldier, stiff, commissioned to carry the world on his shoulders, gallantly suffering guilt, but miserably trained in expressing feelings, as I was about to find out.

I clicked across the room on Pricille's high heels which were rigidly stuffed at the toe with Kleenexes. The shoes hoisted me taller as I reached Cedric's chair. I had my coat draped over my arm, and was fumbling with the buttons, searching for something to say. Wasn't he going to ask me to sit? Cedric tilted his head back. The passionate eyes that had fostered a warmth in my imagination were now hardened in a cold-hearted stare.

"God's will," I blurted. Immediately I knew I had uttered the wrong cliché.

Darned good thing there was enough noise in the room to drown out his gruff rebuke. " 'God's will.' If I hear that one more time, I'm gonna punch the person who says it!"

I stood dumbfounded. "You don't believe that?"

He glanced over at the closed coffin. "God's will that he die the way he did?"

I cringed against the wall. "Maybe I don't know what else to say."

"Then don't say anything!"

Fighting back tears, I put my right arm into the wrong sleeve of my coat. "Let me guess," I exploded. "If you had gone mossing, this might not have happened. Maybe your mother should have stopped him. Maybe you should have cancelled the army tests. Maybe forget about the damned army. Period!"

Cedric wouldn't budge, so I threw in another maybe. "Maybe you should have burned the friggin' dory." He looked at me so morbidly. "Well," I concluded, "you hated mossing, didn't you? Maybe this. Maybe that. Well the heck with you. Now you have plenty of good reasons to rot in guilt, but I'm not gonna help you, though I do understand what you must be going through."

"Oh, you do!" he lashed, but at least he was talking. "How many fathers have you lost?" He sat erect for the final blow. "Leave me alone! *Quitte moi tranchille.* You *don't* understand."

"You're right," I said, fuming at his words. "I don't understand, I don't understand you!" I scuffed my high heels back across the floor.

Cedric's head sank. His anguished face bore a hellish guilt that rudely shoved everyone away, even his best friends.

André and Paul-Emile had retreated to a dimly lit room where Estelle had attracted an audience with her tall tales. She even had Paul-Emile glued to his seat. I sat next to Babette, who wouldn't twitch an eyelid as Estelle spoke.

"When my great-grandmother died, they used coppers as big as silver dollars to keep her eyes closed, a prayer book under her chin to keep her head up."

"You're making that up!" chastised Babette.

Annoyed, Estelle sassed back, "Am not! Ask the undertaker. He'll also tell you that they drain the blood and replace it with that stuff that keeps you from stinking. And," she haughtily added, all eyes riveted on her, "they sprinkle holy water to keep the devil away. Did you know that the devil smells like sulphur?" Her eyes were big, her dimples flashed. "Pilotte à Sirois smelled of sulphur, after he gave himself to the devil."

Babette lowered her voice, lest she offend Estelle again. "I've never heard of him."

"Of course you have!" returned Estelle. "He's the one who told his maid, 'Don't make my bed today.' He left for work and her darned curiosity lured her to his room. Guess what she saw lying on the mat?" Estelle afforded a short pause, "A big black dog!" She swore the truth with a sign across her busty chest, "Cross my heart."

"Pilotte's dog!" Babette surmised. "What's the big deal?"

Estelle's dimples grew more pronounced. "Pilotte didn't have a dog." There was more. A *câ'piqué*. "One time Pilotte wanted to go to a wedding, but he didn't have a car, and those who did wouldn't drive him. Pilotte settled the problem. He and his friend went to the wedding flying on a piece of bark. But the friend wasn't supposed to say a word, not one word. 'It's going like the devil!' the friend howled, and they crashed in somebody's field, which darn near killed them both."

Estelle inhaled long and hard. There was more to the wedding story. "Now Pilotte was taken with the blue eyes of a beautiful girl who was equally charmed by the tall, handsome young man, so they danced the night away. Whenever the girl appeared tired, Pilotte just had to say: 'We're dancing like the devil,' and she livened up, especially when she stepped on his feet. She looked down and guess what. A fit of horror rocked the dance hall—he had horse's hoofs!"

Babette nearly fell off her chair. "You're making that up!" In the same breath, she just had to know, "What did the girl do?"

Estelle keeled over in laughter. "She ran all the way back to Salmon River, and when she got home realized she had shit in her pants. *A l'avait chiée dans ses hardes.*"

Babette gaped at the storyteller. "Now I remember! Wasn't Pilotte the one whose coffin wouldn't go through the church door? The priest threw his stole on top, and with the help of five men, managed to drag it in."

Now Paul-Emile, who had been deprived of attention far too long, grabbed his chance. "That's the one! I saw the devil once," he divulged. "I had gone out fishing on a Good Friday. Now you know how that's frowned upon, fishing on Good Friday."

"Pulled your first trap," I interrupted, "and there was Satan, come to visit his kind." If looks could kill, I would have been sharing a coffin with Gustave. I retreated from Paul-Emile's glare. "Come Estelle. Your father's waiting."

People were going home. Lina was sobbing in Père Lucien's arms. It was as if Cedric had never moved, his gaze still empty, his eyes tearless. I observed the tuft of hair that hung over his eyes and couldn't keep from staring. There was something about the width of his chest, the size of his arms, the sensuousness of his mouth. Finally, he did get up, to speak to Père Lucien. He helped his mother with her coat, and then he glanced my way. I could have sworn that I detected a smile, however faint, a smile.

Estelle said she saw no such thing on his face. "Something you're imagining, as usual," she rebuked. Perhaps, but she had to drag me away.

Chapter 26

Finally, finally, Clare District High. A new school. Brand new faces. Kids from the French shore, all the way from Salmon River to Saint Bernard. Estelle and I were eighth graders, forbidden up the long flight of stairs where the higher graders resided. Those corridors were out of bounds. Estelle coaxed, threatened, called me chicken, but I remained steadfast at the bottom step. Until one recess, she grabbed my wrist and pinched, hard, forcing me up the unauthorized stairs to Cedric's classroom. The daredevil came to a halt, poked her head in, and motioned, Follow me.

Ignoring prying looks, she moved the desks that were blocking the aisle and headed straight to the back, where Cedric had claimed the last seat against the wall.

"To make room for your long legs, or to raise hell?" she queried. He could have at least grinned back. She leafed through a fat chemistry book. "*Ou ma-ma!* This stuff hard?"

He shrugged his shoulders. "Haven't opened it yet."

"You going for a smoke?" she ventured, and again he shrugged.

My turn to talk. "Are you going to help kill our pig?" I asked.

He did move a few facial muscles, though only to mock me. "Pig? Kill the pig?"

"Pig?" one of the big boys a few desks away reiterated. "Kill the pig!" Laughter rippled up and down every aisle. Shamed to tears, I didn't need Estelle's help to find my way out.

The grade twelve students were playing basketball at noon. However embarrassed by the pig incident, I still hastened to the gym and jumped up and down whenever Cedric scored a basket. I applauded vigorously when his team won, but my hoorays were drowned by the loud cheers of the pretty girls wearing short skirts and waving pompons.

I followed the boisterous heroes to the cafeteria and sat one table away, gulping down a peanut butter sandwich and hoping, praying, that Cedric would notice me. "*C'étane quite-a game,*" I remarked when he bumped the corner of my table. He kept right on talking to his teammates.

Mid-afternoon recess, I lingered, hoping to catch a glimpse of him barrelling down the stairs for a smoke. He was running ninety miles an hour, passing so close that he almost knocked me down, but he accorded me the same apology as everyone else. "Whoops!"

Bouncing her beautiful locks, Estelle arrived at my house after school, analyzing the cold-shoulder treatment from the stonehearted, stuffed-shirt, aspiring army asshole. *Un trou d'chu d'la prâmiere classe.*

"It's the straight hair!" she deduced. "Find me Pricille's rollers."

She rolled my hair so tightly that the plastic bristles were gouging my scalp. How to sleep with those? To spare my temples, I lay paralysed on my back, raising my head between dozes to relieve the unbearable ache. It was a night in purgatory, but necessary to curl my poker-straight hair. As soon as light edged its way through the window, I ripped the murderous things out in a flap to run down the hill. I devoured my porridge, not knowing quite what to make of my father's furtive grin and his bashful eyes. "Can I touch your curls?"

"No!"

By the time I reached Estelle's, the curls were falling limp. She grabbed a comb and teased for half an hour, then untangled the beehive, backcombing and squirting on the hairspray until the ends of my shoulder-length hair yielded a beautiful flip, stiff enough to weather a hurricane. She slammed the comb on the counter. "You need a perm! That's all there is to it."

"Forget it!" I told her. "Deni Fournier doesn't need another sheep."

"I won't make it too curly," she coaxed and coaxed. Finally, the aspiring hairdresser cuddled Foufou to her neck, pouting to the snow-white kitty, "I have no one to practise on."

I had a fantastic idea! "I told Zita that you gave your mother a beautiful perm. Stuck in the house with her own mother quite sick and all that, Zita was wondering if you'd give her a perm."

"And you said?"

"That I didn't think you'd mind."

I shrank from Estelle's ferocious glance. "Never!" she screamed. "I hate Zita. I'm not giving her a perm. And if you ever suggest something like that again, you'll do your own hair!"

"*Oké. Oké.* You don't have to take a fit. How do I look?"

She turned her anger to the nylons wrinkled on my lanky legs. The runs had been arrested with dabs of clear nail polish. "These are one size too big," I fretted.

My friend cast me an annoyed glare. "Garter belts are no friggin' good. They don't hold stockings up. Or is it because of those hanging threads that you call legs?"

With her thirty-six-inch bust swelling forward, she next sized up my chest. "And you must grow some tits. Two eggs," she observed. "And *don't* be flattered. I mean fried. Careful," my cruel friend advised, "keep your distance with that padded bra in case someone should accidentally bump into you and leave a dent."

"Sometimes, I hate you," I snapped, but she simply kept on patting Foufou.

"You don't have time to hate me. The bus will be here any minute."

Ladies should dress like ladies, was Sister Clothilda's motto. Estelle jeered saucily, "Who'd want that rig she has on. It flattens them to pancakes. Imagine being itchy and having to claw through all those layers."

"Waltzing Clothilda," she nicknamed the Sister the day the nun grabbed one of her darling boys and lumbered to the blackboard, waltzing him forward in large leading steps, and then letting go of his arm. A sudden turn sent the many layers of her habit softly whirling. The boy glanced at the lengthy equation, the challenge supposedly far above our heads. He zigzagged his chalk across the board and had the value of *x* figured out before I realized the boy was a genius.

He got a spirited clap from Sister, then an ecstatic beam. "Excellent, William."

"He likes you," Estelle figured, having observed the charming smile when he handed me his scribbler. But I caught him staring at Babette—an instant connection between the two was obvious. Both got on the good side of Sister, agreeing with everything she said, though they could not support her exaltation that the brilliant Dickens was the finest novelist who ever lived.

"I do enjoy his books," William readily agreed, "but I shouldn't have read *Oliver Twist* and *David Copperfield* so close together. The characters were too similar."

"I had a problem with his *Tale of Two Cities*," Babette added, making Sister flash a crooked set of teeth.

"Oh. Can you tell the class why?"

The lighthouse girl blushed. "I didn't think it came across early enough in the book just how much Sydney loved Lucie Manette, so that when he marched to the guillotine ..." Babette threw her hands up in disgust. "All of a sudden he loves the girl enough to have his head cut off!"

Sister Clothilda fell into a trance. "Oh, but to have sacrificed his life so that she could have her Charles. Do you remember his last words?"

Babette's stare was firmly fixed on supersmart William as she spoke: "*It is a far, far better thing that I do, than I have ever done; it is a far, far better rest that I go to, than I have ever known.*"

Seated behind me, Estelle jerked her busty frame forward. "Showing off, that Babette. She reads all the crap Percy gives her, has nothing better to do."

Estelle didn't know that I had been sneaking up the lighthouse road, and that the sweet girl was edging her way into my heart. "You're right," I said, feeling a sting at my deception. Sister Clothilda stepped out in the hall, and Estelle rose from her desk, greeting Babette and William with a gaping yawn. "You guys bore the *dickens* out of me."

Wild laughter erupted, an outburst of silliness from the boys who giggled uncontrollably, belched and broke wind, and strained their eyes to get a glimpse through Estelle's tight sweater. A few shamed faces appeared relieved when the door slammed and heavy footsteps lumbered back towards the scratched oak desk. Waltzing Clothilda's lips were pursed, her nostrils flared. "Oké. Who started it?"

She clapped her hands in numerous attempts, making the class cower beneath her glare, her arms resting on her huge bosom. "I want to know." Pale with rage, she hurled a glance my way, "Zoé?"

"Don't know."

"Don't know, or won't tell?"

Estelle was squirming in her seat, for just reason. Most every class has a blabbermouth.

But the next day, Waltzing Clothilda had calmed down. She scanned the room, "Quick! Let's get some hands. What's an irony?" She certainly allowed enough time. "I would have preferred hands from the back," she sighed, disappointed, but she could read the eagerness on my face. "Go ahead, Zoé."

"Isn't it ironic," I said, "that a lobster cannot be made to bite on a hook, yet it will crawl through the narrowest mesh entrance of a trap for a piece of bait."

Sister grinned, applauded, then opened her English text to fun time—alliterations. She burst forth from behind her desk. "The repetition of an initial sound."

Then she rumbled forward to face Estelle head-on, "For example: Sister settles smart alecs simply. Find that a funny fabrication?"

Estelle didn't dare look up. Still holding her stare on my friend, Sister introduced us to rhythm and meter. "Limerick. A nonsense poem of five lines, with a rhyme scheme as follows: aabba; the first, second, and fifth lines having three stresses, the third and fourth two. Let's give 'em a try."

The girls kept theirs clean. Of course, the boys had to outdo one another. One rascal from Little Brook outwitted them all:

I once ate some blueberry tarts,
But, boy, did they give me the farts!
I shrugged, "It'll pass,
When I've run out of gas,
If I don't explode into small parts."

Sister Clothilda couldn't have controlled the bellowing

laughter if she had tried, so she simply smiled through it. But when the tumult subsided, her toothy grin disappeared. Oh! Oh! She pointed her finger in Estelle's face. "Since you haven't participated, you will write one for next class." She continued her fun:

The examples you'll find in the text
Are only in jest—yours is next;
And it better be right,
With the syllables tight,
Or you'll find I can really get vexed.

No one dared move an eyelid, in case we all got nabbed for a limerick. At home I told André, "Sister's deranged. You should hear what the boys get away with, yet, Estelle opens her mouth, and she jumps on her. *A l'est point toute lâ.*"

"I had that penguin last year," he recalled. "She didn't find *me* darling. Told her I was gonna give myself to the devil, and she ran and got her ruler. I warned her, 'Hit me with that thing, and I'll be the last person you'll ever hit.' "

"And?"

"She left the classroom. When she came back, she looked like she had been crying. *A s'en nâ'té pianquer.*"

And now, for the question driving me mad, a change of subject to satisfy my curiosity. "Is Cedric helping with the pig?"

No matter how much I probed, bribed, or threatened, André the tormentor had one thing to say, "We'll just have to wait and see."

The morning of the great slaughter, Cedric entered the kitchen and walked directly to the sink. His business was seemingly pressing. "Where's André?"

My expression stiff with anger, I pointed to the fields. "Gone to feed the dogs."

"And Pierre?"

"In Dominique's shed, looking for a sledge hammer."

"Mind if I wait?" he asked.

I shrugged. "Suit yourself."

I rushed to the pantry to stack dishes on the shelves. I had my arms extended over the top shelf when I felt a large hand on the back of my neck. "You angry?"

The dumb question stirred a pang of bitter resentment, making me whirl around and glare. "My name's Zoé. Think you could say *hallo* when you pass by me in the corridors? I know I've been chasing you," I admitted, "but I just wanted to be friends."

Cedric looked ashamed. "Guess I've been a bit of an ass these past few weeks."

"A whole lot of an ass!" I corrected. "At the funeral. At school. Well now, I don't want to talk to you." He didn't move. "You treat me like dirt," I blasted, trying hard not to cry, "and then you have the nerve ..."

"To come and apologize?" he finished, his tone repentant.

He grabbed the stack of plates from my hands and set it on the counter. "Should I get down on my knees?" Impossible to escape. He pinned me against the counter and locked my bony frame into a tight squeeze. "What can you do now, hein?"

Of course, my anger turned to tears. "I had even curled my hair for you."

Cedric loosened his hold, and I understood from the deep lines etched on his brow and the fatigue in his eyes that his father's death had damn near destroyed him. He embraced me tenderly, and however many times I had fantasized about the moment, I was too shy to meet his gaze. I could feel my cheeks on fire, my smile trembling. His lips touched mine and it was like ... At first, Cedric was tame and gentlemanly, becoming of him, and I melted beneath his seductive gaze. It was like the wind caressing the leaves of a tree, softly at first, then passionate, as in a sudden gale that rips the sapling from its roots. My first kiss was far more romantic than I had ever imagined. I was now a part of Cedric's intimate life and therefore had the right to chase him up the fields.

I watched grimly as our heavy pig grunted for a meal, his muddy feet anchored in the trough, waiting for the potato peelings, apple cores, and vegetable leftovers that I always brought. He immersed his snout in my pot of water. When it was empty, he turned his suspicious eyes on me—as if he knew that I'd be back, accompanied with well-armed men, the eyes of ferocious hunters closing in on him.

Pierre balanced a sledge hammer on his right shoulder. My Cedric flashed a butcher knife. And André swung a meat saw in one hand and swirled a lasso in the other. "If that fat bastard tries any tricks, he won't go far."

Clearly, the pig was doomed.

Pierre unlatched the gate. "If a pig dies too fast," he cautioned, "he doesn't bleed as much."

Cedric shrank back with his pan of swill. "By the look of that thing in your hand, I don't think he's gonna live very long."

He no sooner had struck his pan against the gate than the beast was at the door, lured into the mud-soaked yard where Pierre had positioned himself for the fatal blow. As the glutton dug his snout into the pan, my brother swung his hammer through the air and caught him smack in the middle of the forehead, rendering him unconscious to the sharp knife that Cedric thrust in his throat.

Feet pressed against the pig's shoulders, he held it squarely on its back while Mam' collected the blood, sprinkling it with table salt as she stirred. "Blood pudding's no darn good if the blood curdles. *Ca f'râ point des bons boudonnes.*"

Dad helped Pierre immerse and rotate the pig in scalding water, which massaged its way into the scummed pores and wrinkles, loosening hair and dirt so that by the time they hoisted the carcass up, it was already flaunting a clean, white skin, made leathery smooth with Cedric's shaving knife. He ripped the belly open and removed the internal organs and the mass of entrails. André stood by with his saw, sizing up large chunks of meat to be salted for boiled dinners. He trimmed the fat for lard, and picked out the tender meat from around the bones of the pig's head for headcheese, mouth-watering mince pies, and the blood pudding that constituted a king's breakfast, when accompanied by a thick slice of Mam's homemade bread and, for my father, a cup of tea. Pierre loved pigs' feet in rappie dumpling stews, a dish that made him lick his plate clean.

André salvaged every morsel of lard to be salted in tiny barrels. How good was an Acadian dish without little cubes of pork fat—as tasteless as an Acadian dish without shallots. Mam' threw square lumps of the fat in baked beans, rappie pies, hash, stews, most everything. Her renowned dish of cod heads and turnip sizzled in fat. When she was growing up in Meteghan, she had even smeared pork fat on bread.

Her kitchen was now saturated with odours from a boiling mixture of blood, delicate ground meat from the pig's head, seasoning, gelatin, and lots and lots of onions—the *mélange* to be boiled a long time before it was poured into a shallow pan to chill into a jellied mass. Grand-mère Sophie would be looking for her headcheese.

In a large bowl sat a raw mixture of blood, chopped tender meats blended with lesser choice cuts, spices, flour, minced onions, shredded suet, and edible entrails. Yuk! The *mélange* was poured into a cake pan. Later it was extracted from the oven looking like a cake, dark in colour due to the high proportion of blood. *Du boudin noir.* I liked that blood pudding better than the kind stuffed in the casings of the small intestines. Though scraped, washed, and cleaned to the satisfaction of Mam's finicky eye, the casings had once been stuffed with what?

The mincemeat smelled delicious—a boiling, aromatic blend of valley apples, choice meats, molasses, spices, nutmeg, raisins, cider, cinnamon. Ummm! There'd be enough pies for us, Zita, Grand-mère Sophie, and perhaps Eddie Pockshaw ... if Mam' could dodge the big bad wolf and sneak up the lighthouse road.

My job was to clean the sty—scrape the trough of dried-up food from our victim's last meals and lay fresh straw on the floor, not a job to be hampered by a chatty little miss who absolutely loved school and was now learning to socialize.

"You're gonna get that thing all dirty," I scolded.

Thérèse held up her arms over the muddy yard. "Watch how you talk about my very special walking doll! Pricille paid lots of dollars for it." The chatterbox could be so darn inquisitive, starting with a thriller, "Why does a chicken still jump around in circles with its head cut off?"

"Because the heart keeps beating and pumping blood," I figured, "but not to worry. She'll eventually drop."

"Guess how long our goose would have lived if the foxes

hadn't gotten him?" she asked.

I feigned interest, knowing the real fate of Amos. "Gee, I don't know."

"Thirty years. That's what the teacher said." The clever little girl had it all figured out. "By the time it died, I would have been married and have gooses of my own." The next question. "Why does Pricille have a new boyfriend? I thought Clyde was her boyfriend."

I merely shrugged. "She wasn't married to him."

"Why doesn't Philippe have a girlfriend?"

"Because he studies day and night, according to his last letter. Engineering is hard."

"Then when he's finished school, he'll know everything," she concluded.

I grinned. "Not quite, but he should have no problem changing a light bulb."

"I'm not moving to Grand-père's house," my little sister stammered. "There's rats in the cellar. If Mam' makes me, then I'll go to Boston and live with Pricille."

"Then you better start packing your suitcase," I warned, " 'cause the way Mam' and Dad have been arguing since Grand-père had his stroke, it looks like we're moving real soon."

"Are we getting a new pig?" she asked.

I could barely muster a tired, "Yeah, think so. *Tait'terbonne.*"

Thérèse had saved the big surprise for last. "I got Dad some tobacco, and guess what?" Her eyes were wide, "He's gonna buy me an ox!"

I gave a full-toothed smile then. "Let me guess. That trip paid for the tail."

"I talked to a man," she said, and I dropped an armful of straw. "What did you say!"

"I was walking to the post office, and a man asked if I wanted to go to Yarmouth. He said he had toys in his car."

I grabbed Thérèse by the shoulders and shook her vigorously, frantically, her curly locks flying over her face. "What did you tell him?"

"No! That my doll was waiting for me."

I trembled as I hugged my precious sister, for I could only

imagine the worst possible scenario—a four-foot coffin, surrounded by ravaged faces.

"Did you tell Mam'?" I pressed.

"No," Thérèse explained. "She's always so angry.

"Because she has a lot on her mind," I felt it my duty to clarify. I stooped down, ensuring stern eye contact with my little sister. "Then you tell *me* everything, all your secrets. Promise?"

The child looked perplexed, about the strange man I thought, until she beamed for her last question. "Is Cedric your boyfriend? That could be our secret also. My doll and I saw him kissing you."

I escorted her and her doll through the tiny hinged door, out to the muddy yard. "You ask far too many questions. And I don't want you walking the Cape road by yourself. Understand?" My knees still trembled as I stood there and watched her walk back to the house.

Ironic. People came all the way from New York to bask in the tranquillity and safety of my village, yet I could have lost my little sister to a maniac—right here at the Cape!

Chapter 27

The day of reckoning had arrived. "Limericks," Sister Clothilda noted on her timetable. She opened her text and amused her darling boys with more nonsense poems. She touched on Ireland, the birthplace of the humorous verses. Then she remembered.

"Let's hear your limerick!" she ordered.

Estelle sat erect, ready. The daredevil pushed aside her scribbler. "I know it by heart."

But she didn't say anything, stretching Sister's already thin patience, "We don't have all day!"

Left with no alternative but to blurt it out, my friend cleared her throat, drew a deep breath and simply ignored all stares on her. This she recited:

Old Miss Zita Maidenhead,
Was married in a big brass bed;
Her husband found her frigid,
He stood semi-rigid,
She never knew where he fled.

Dead silence. Everyone observed Sister, who seemed to suffer facial paralysis. And then she growled between clenched teeth, "*Estelle à Basil à Joe.*" All heads turned as Waltzing Clothilda flounced up the aisle, grabbed Estelle by the arm, and charged towards the door. "Let's see if the principal likes your limerick."

She shoved my friend out, then clapped her large hands together, as if clearing dirt from her class. She slammed the door behind her. English period was over.

"I'll *never* apologize to Sister Clothilda," Estelle told me. "I don't care if I'm thrown out of the class. I won't!"

And she didn't. Though under her thick skull, I knew she was concerned that she would no longer be in my class, perhaps clearing space for Babette to move her desk closer to mine. Estelle was transferred to Monsieur Cottreau's class, another teacher with a severe look, but not opposed to smiling at big-busted girls. She was sure to be happy in his class.

Basil grounded Estelle for a whole year—she was not allowed out after school. Not a problem. All she had to do was sneak up the Cape road, and when the workers left the boatshop at suppertime, she had plenty time of time to race home. Basil always puttered around before he locked up.

But the scheme didn't work so well the day that Pierre proudly claimed the first kill of the hunting season, a buck two hundred and forty pounds with ten points, the biggest one ever paraded in our diggings. "You have to come see!" I hailed Estelle at her sun parlour window. She almost got away but Basil suddenly arrived with a client. He seized her by the shoulders, turned her around and marched her right back into the house.

Pierre drove up and down the Cape road with the buck sprawled over the hood of his Pontiac, and his Louise snuggled next to him, so close that Mam' scowled as she strained her eyes. "It's hard to tell who's doing the driving."

She wasn't about to unglue those two. The lovers were seen linked arm in arm, walking across secluded fields by the cliffs. I had caught them in the pantry, in the heat of passionate kisses. Louise waited at the end of the wharf every time the *Cape Marguerite* came in, making Mam' scowl even more.

"You'd think she'd wait until he cleared the men on the wharf."

Pierre must have sensed the hostility. He drove his Louise back to Saint Bernard before he fixed his buck. After it had been gutted and the meat apportioned between us and *les p'tits Josephs*, he entered the house to wash his hands. "Where's a clean towel?"

Mam' pointed to the bottom drawer of the sideboard in the pantry. "Where I always keep them."

"Any bread?" he asked, eyeing a steaming pot of homemade

beans, seasoned with floating cubes of pork fat.

But Mam' kept scrubbing all too vigorously her blood-splattered sink. "I didn't hear you come in last night."

My brother grinned. "No, I guess you didn't. Any bread?"

"Where'd you spend the night?" she probed, as he found the brown bread, cut himself a generous slice of the favourite and smeared it with molasses, running a sticky trail on her clean floor. She was too angry to notice. "Where'd you spend the night?"

Pierre was now sitting at the table, smirking. "At Louise's. On the couch," he freely added. "Or was that part of the question?"

An amused grin broke out on my father's face. Mam's eyebrows stiffened. "You have a bed upstairs."

"So."

"So that's not how I brought you up!" she lashed.

Depriving her of a full-fledged sermon, Pierre pushed his supper aside, grabbed his jacket and kicked my schoolbag out of the way. He was halfway down the hill, making brisk headway towards the wharf, when I picked up the bag and suddenly remembered, "I need pencils."

Mam' swung her head away from the sink. "Again! School's barely begun, and this is the second time you come home begging. You must chew your pencils and eat your scribblers ..."

"Swallow my erasers," I added. She hauled off and *smack!* right across my face with her wet hand.

I never knew my father to rise so quickly. He grabbed the poker from the stove, vicious with rage as he raised it. "Hit her again if you dare!" His eyes were jaundiced, poisoned by a demon's bile. "Sonofawhore! Who did *you* come home with last night?"

Facing the tiger head on, Mam' didn't move an inch. "You mean *how* did I come home? With Anne, like I always do." I thought the conversation was over, until she pointed next door with the most ungodly vengeance. "I wouldn't give a darn if your mother had gangrene on all toes, I'm not moving!"

Dad got up and took his tobacco makings to Dominique's shed.

With her broom and duster, Mam' rampaged around the kitchen. Once the floor had been swept of the last speck of dirt and the walls and windows wiped clean of tiny finger smudges, she piled blobs of lard on a rag and polished until the top of her stove could have reflected a fly on the ceiling. Finally she collapsed on a chair at the kitchen table. Dad's accusation had drained all spirit from her gaunt face. There was despair in her eyes and voice. "I don't know how long I can take it, slaving late hours at the Diner, then coming home to this. You think I can move next door and subject them to his crazy talk? *Du parler d'fou.*"

My cheek was still on fire. "Don't know," I said. "*J'ché pount.*" What I really wanted to say was, I hate you!

Pen and tablet before her, Mam' started writing. Her letter to Pricille would be depressing, drenched in problems.

I ran all the way to Estelle's house and found her upstairs in her bedroom.

"I can't stay in that house," I gasped, but she kept staring out her window, caught up in a madness of her own.

"It's getting dark, and I just have to meet Paul-Emile." She stroked Foufou, then raised her head. "I've got it!" she exclaimed. "I'll climb down the window, and you stay here and guard the door. If you hear Mam' ..."

"Or your father," I protested. "What are you fishing for, the first murder on Cape St. Mary?" I showed her my cheek, which was still imprinted and tingly. "If I got this for asking for pencils, then surely I'll be killed for helping you escape."

A dilemma plagued me; I needed her help. "How am I gonna tell Mam' that I need glasses?" I pleaded. "She's been in a savage mood ever since she started working at the Diner, hollers at everyone, about everything. Even for lousy pencils!" I fell into profuse sobbing. "Mam's having an angry day."

Estelle jumped off her bed and hastened to the window. "How am I gonna open this stupid thing? God knows what Dad did to it."

"You opened it enough times," I reminded her. She grabbed a pair of scissors from her bureau, dug and gouged and pried at the casing until the window opened. More than halfway down the side of the house, she jumped to the ground, not the least interested in my problems. I carried them with me back up the hill.

Problems! In my absence, Grand-père Dominique had taken a plunge down his attic stairs, nearly killing himself. When I arrived,

Mam' was dragging him from the hallway, through the kitchen, and into his tiny bedroom. She looked on the verge of a stroke herself, out of breath, her veins throbbing in her neck and bulging under the strain of lifting fat Grand-père onto his bed.

"Can you hear me?" she asked.

She did get some facial expression, a faint sound emanating from deep within his throat. "*Unn-ettes.*"

His glasses, or what was left of the twisted frame and shattered lenses, were out of service on the kitchen table. The doctor arrived, winced at Grand-père's bruises, poked at him, then came to a quick diagnosis. "His left side is totally paralysed."

Mam's face fell as if she had just been handed a death sentence.

She travelled back and forth between the two houses, feeding and bathing Grand-père and changing his bed linen, which accumulated feces, urine, and regurgitated liquids. My father looked after Grand-mère Sophie, who had regressed from the trauma of the incident. Unable to walk, she wanted her chair dragged across the kitchen, with her in it. Even an ox would have tired from towing the oppressive burden.

"You need a wheelchair," N'Oncle Joseph determined. She became even more disturbed, frantically howling when he returned from Yarmouth with the chair. "Put that in the attic!" She wouldn't eat.

"To hell with the wheelchair," my father said. So she stayed huddled on a kitchen chair by the stove for long hours, layered in two sweaters. As the fall days shortened, supper was barely over before she guarded the window, as if to hurry the close of day.

Mam' and Dad braced themselves to shoulder Sophie's weight into the small bedroom off the living room where they dropped her teeth into a glass and unwound yard-long gauze bindings from around her knees. They tucked her safely away from a staring Dominique.

"I'll sleep here," I had offered the first night, but when the sky turned dark, a feeling of terror seized me, and it was my father who burrowed under the covers on the old couch in the kitchen. It all seemed so wrong.

"We're gonna have to move." Mam' agonized, as she contemplated the turn of events.

N'Oncle Joseph made a long-distance call to Boston. He offered Tante Marceline no choice. "You have to come home." When she fretted over Uncle John being left alone, his voice turned aggressive. "We need you here. Martine and Antoine are overtired. Rosalie and I help whenever we can, but we have ten kids at home."

Tante arrived, affording Mam' a much needed rest. She recovered her sleep, and the dark circles under her eyes disappeared. But the few pounds she put on did nothing to fill her hollow cheeks or to pack flesh around her protruding collar bone. Occasionally, she gave us a grin. On clear evenings, she sat at the window, watching the string of lights dancing on the horizon—the herring seiners. Pierre was out there, fishing with gill nets at night.

During the day he could teach Mam' to drive. She sat behind the wheel of his car and practised, down to the wharf and back, sometimes chancing the entire Cape road, down to the Pointe once, causing my brother to get out of the car a bit worked up. "I have no desire to plunge down the cliff in a car!" I understood she wasn't quite synchronized in using the brake and the accelerator.

But she got her license, arriving home with a cocky smile. "It was nothing. Two wrong on the written. I had to drive along Saint Martin's road and park on the shoulder ..."

"Back up in the firehall," Pierre teased, though his grin was directed at my father. "Now you can park on Main Street in Yarmouth and watch the sights. I think the show this Saturday is John Wayne."

The show! Dad needed a full day to get ready, a fuss and a half. The breakfast dishes had barely been cleared before he attacked a bar of soap, using his shaving brush to whip up a mound of white foam in a saucer. He lathered his face, then put new Gillette blades in his safety razor, which he tested through thick stubble. He paused between strokes to feel the silkiness of his caved-in cheeks. He admired himself in the mirror with such an open grin that Thérèse and Joel gaped as if it were the first time they had noticed his toothless gums. Perhaps they were sizing his nose, or had noticed his eyes, pure blue for a change, unspoiled by jealousies or false riches— just dilated with plain vanity.

"Now you have to get my suit," he pestered, throwing Mam' into a huff as she checked behind his ears.

"For lovin' sake, the show's not 'til tonight." She scowled at the dirt accumulated in the creases of his neck. "You could use a bit of that soap on a facecloth."

He scrubbed a bit, smoked a lot, cut his curved and brittle toe nails, and rocked in his chair. After lunch, he wanted his suit, five hours before it was time to leave. He wore a path from his chair to the mirror. By six o'clock, he wanted to leave. "*Astheure! Allons-ye.*" He wanted to park on Main Street before the show.

Mam' scooped the rest of the beans in a bowl. "He's not gonna wait." She touched her lips with bright lipstick, pulled her wispy hair in place with bobby pins, and slipped on a summery housedress; the scant sleeves made her arms look so thin. Her coat was sixteen years old, as old as André, and starting to look threadbare. She dangled her empty purse on her wrist, and I caught Dad glancing sideways with the same flirty look as when she rigged herself for church on Sundays. "Not bad for an old swig," he proudly grinned.

Looking squeaky clean in his dark blue suit and brown suede shoes, he stole one last look in the mirror before he headed towards the door. Quite the feature presentation. With a haughty raise of his head, he straightened his shoulders, held his breath, grinned back at his wife and children for the almighty announcement— "The Sheik of Araby."

I couldn't help but grin, at the "high-water" pants belted below his paunch, and the white shirt, stretched in open gaps between buttons that could pop any minute. The royal highfalutin' from the backwoods of Wedgeport did have the right protocol though, walking in front of his woman—though I doubted that an Arab chief would have farted on his way out.

The Sheik of Araby was going to town.

Chapter 28

Grand-père Dominique ebbed out of life in grunts and groans. Docteur Theriault checked his weakening pulse and other vital signs, then sternly cautioned. "No more liquids." The old man's swallowing reflex wasn't responding.

Fear erupted in Tante Marceline's eyes. "What can we do?"

The good doctor moved away from the bed. "Keep wetting his lips with a face cloth."

Grand-père's breathing slowed and shortened to weak abdominal respiration. Père Lucien came and sprinkled holy water about the room and on Dominique's face, but the old man just stared, looking more at death than at life. Days later, the priest returned, unsnapped a small case and retrieved the oil of the sick. There was a series of prayers associated with the last rites, then a final sign of the cross on Grand-père's forehead, "By this holy anointing, may the Lord forgive you whatever sins you have committed."

Grand-père's breathing was irregular and rhythmic: three breaths, then nothing, three breaths, then nothing. When Docteur Theriault's hand tightened on Grand-mère's shoulder, her face grew pallid. There was a final murmur in the old man's throat, one short exhalation, and then nothing.

André hung a wreath on the door of the old homestead, and the following afternoon, one on Zita's door. La Caquette had also passed away.

"She had everything wrong," was how Zita interpreted the loss of her mother. Grand-mère Sophie had her own translation about Dominique. "*Ka-be-de-rang* down the stairs, and that was it. *Y yâ déboullé' en bas des escaliers, et ç'â t'est fini.*"

"No brooches and no hair ribbon," she stipulated.

But Tante Marceline affixed ornate and colorful accessories to the exquisite black dress. "Life must go on," Tante affirmed, but she wasn't having the wake at the funeral parlour. Grand-mère's jowls had turned fiery red, insisting that the old man's wish be respected, that his coffin be displayed in the living room. And Tante could forget about flaunting the most expensive one in Clare. Even with the cheapest, I felt Grand-père would spring up any moment and grumble about the price.

Sheltered between N'Oncle Joseph and my father, Grand-mère wept at the church service every time the organ played, through the inflated eulogy that the priest delivered, and through Holy Communion, barely containing her sobs when she returned to her seat. I saw her crying in her handkerchief. I cried too.

She'd miss my Grand-père. Maybe his constant grumbling was his way of resisting old age, of cursing aches and pains, of detesting kids. Maybe he had always been plain miserable. Maybe Sophie *had* married him because there was no widow's allowance. Or perhaps, … perhaps she saw another side of Grand-père Dominique that a young girl would never know.

Come winter, Dad moved next door, plugging the stove and poking at wood, forever consumed in a lamentable sweat. Grand-mère's face blazed red, yet she shivered from the cold. *A l'était ferdillouse'ste femme là.*

I entered her kitchen, and a stifling heat almost knocked me to the floor. "*Fiou!* You like the heat!"

Huddled by the stove, she had a warm smile. "Yes, I like this seat." Getting deaf as a two-by-four.

Gusty winds created whistling drafts; a current of frigid air that escaped from the shed door settled in her rheumatic knees. Blizzards smothered windows with powdery snow, making her anxious when she couldn't see my house. My father didn't like repeating himself, so he simply didn't talk. He threw potatoes with muddy skins into a pot of boiling water, and when Grand-mère wasn't looking, he shoved ungutted fish into the oven. Vegetables were too much fuss. He insisted that we all simply had to move.

"Soon," Mam' promised, but winter slipped by and, before we knew it, Easter had arrived and, with it, some wonderful news. Louise came to the house flaunting a "rock" on her finger.

"Pierre and I are getting married."

Mam' translated the shocker as meaning soon, as in the summer. She grinned the appropriate grin. "Will there be orchids at your wedding?"

"Hearts," the elated girl announced, her eyes twinkling like little stars. "Ever since I was old enough to fantasize about a wedding dress, I've wanted to be married on Valentine's Day." Another eleven months!

"I'll never leave the Cape," Pierre made it known, which gave Mam' pause for serious thinking—a decision made final. She hastened next door to negotiate.

"I'll move if you sign our house over to Pierre."

Instantly, Dad pointed to the phone. "Call Walter à Blanche."

The papers all signed, Mam' assembled our meagre possessions, though quite insistent about leaving the picture of Saint Theresa hanging in our downstairs bedroom. As tactfully as she could, Louise wrinkled her nose at the icon. "No, you take it."

"Should I leave some crucifixes?" Mam' asked hopefully.

The girl made herself perfectly clear. "Take everything."

Once in our new home, we raided Grand-mère's attic. Everything that wouldn't burn took a plunge down the cliff—metal frame beds, matching washbasins and pitchers, jugs, a washboard, records of the great Jimmie Rodgers, a gramophone; things that would have made antique dealers cry. Burning feather mattresses hurled a black smoke under a cool, spring sky. My father pitched in chairs with missing spindles, a weaving frame from the days of Moses, a butter churn, and nearly threw in a hand-carved picture frame that I grabbed from his careless hand. "Not that!"

I wiped away half a century's accumulation of dust from the glass, and gaped, awe-struck, "Look!"

I ran into the house to show Grand-mère, but she gave the large print a most disgusted glance. "I had told Dominique to throw that out."

The guardian angel was wearing a crown of white roses over a wavy mass of golden hair. Her face was so innocent and rosy pretty, like that of an angel. I just couldn't imagine. "Why don't you like it?"

"Hmmm," Grand-mère groaned, the image's blasphemy affronting her vision. "They could have dressed her." The maiden's white gown fell in gentle folds, flattering a firm bosom and youthful hips—outlining a virgin beauty kneeling on a cottony cloud.

"Take her away," Grand-mère scowled, so I hastened to the attic. Thérèse and I needed a guardian angel next to our bed.

Grand-mère wasn't overly concerned that her past was going up in flames, too worried about my father, who was gasping with the least exerted effort. "You smoke far too much," she rebuked when he entered the house looking for his tobacco.

"Look at the size of him," Mam' admonished.

As if proud of his protruding paunch, Dad merely grinned as he rubbed it. "All ocean blubber. Starting to put on the lard. *Ça coummence à fare d'la panse.*"

Even his relaxed breathing was short and raspy, tobacco-impaired, making Zita scowl. "From the sound of that chest, I'll eat my shirt if you don't have emphysema."

Since her mother had passed away, the gossip was constantly at our house, keeping us abreast of Estelle's whereabouts after dark. She had been caught parking in the dunes with the snake to whom she was addicted. Later in the summer, we got an update. "She's been seen in the cemetery in back of the church in Saint Alphonse!" Zita looked knowingly at Mam'. "And I don't mean counting tombstones."

Estelle didn't give a sweet hoot about Zita. She turned sixteen in September and freedom bloomed at the stroke of midnight. No more rules. I turned sixteen in October and could wear nylons without having to hide.

"No going out on school nights and no Paul-Emile," Basil ordered, not that it made any difference. Charlotte covered for Estelle. I usually left their house with all three hollering among themselves.

"In grade nine, every girl has a boyfriend," I told Mam'. She rolled disapproving eyes, though she loosened up, the strict autocrat of the firm conviction that the majority will do behind the barn far worse than what they'll do at home. And so, Cedric spent all his free time at my house … visiting André. She was no fool.

She eavesdropped on teenage conversations the night that we were clowning around about the good ol' days at the little schoolhouse on the Cape. À *la p'tite école.* Cedric was straddled across a chair in the kitchen, engrossed in an ear to ear roar over the time that Estelle had stood in the corner with a chunk of bubble gum on her nose.

"That's the day she smacked you across the face," André interjected.

The sudden reminder cut short Cedric's laughter. "I don't remember that."

"Oh, yes you do," my pesky brother graciously reminded him. "You lifted her dress, and she hauled off and slugged you one."

Supposedly knitting mittens, Mam' lifted her head to glare at Cedric. "I hope that if you should try to lift Zoé's dress, she'll have the good sense to do the same."

His face flushed a flaming red. I couldn't wait for Mam' to leave so I could tease, "And you don't remember lifting Estelle's dress? I bet! Ah, ah, ah."

The kitchen now clear, Cedric made a comment as offensive as the crooked grin on his face. "I bet she wouldn't mind now."

I cringed. "What kind of remark is that?"

"Zita's not the only one talking," he attested. He and André knew something, which they shared with me.

A quarter of a mile beyond the end of the Cape road, towards Saint Alphonse, there was a gas station where older men gathered to talk politics, fishing, and hunting, and younger men gathered to talk about fast cars and girls. Little boys bragged about their virility with a running total of how many times they had made out and with whom. One such braggart was Paul-Emile. The snake had made it perfectly clear to the guys, "When I marry, I want a virgin."

In the confines of her bedroom, I warned Estelle of what the cesspool rat was broadcasting at the garage, but she merely shoved me in front of the mirror.

"Straighten your shoulders," she ordered, "and repeat after me."

Dumbfounded, I gaped, as she rocked her flexed arms back and forth to work the muscles of her chest, her full-size bosom magnifying nature's failure to provide equally for all of us. She had on a full-size smirk also as she recited:

I must, I must,
Fill out my bust;
I better, I better,
Fill out my sweater.

I pulled away from her penetrating stare. "I'm not saying that!"

"Fine," she stammered, "then stop being so jealous."

I stood dumbfounded. "Are you nuts! You really think that's why I told you?"

She flopped on her bed, and jeered, "You sit in the front seat at school and still can't read the writing on the board. Seems to me you're the one with big problems."

"Yeah, well, I can't buy glasses with rocks," I snapped.

My friend had adopted the popular attitude, "Pierre will buy you some."

"He needs his money," I retorted, and then my eyes widened. "You should see the inside of my old house as *his* house now."

Before interior decorating magazines reached Clare, Louise's taste in colours livened and enlarged small rooms, especially the living room which had given way to a delicate mauve, covering a crude purple. Cardboard partitions had been ripped off the studs in the attic and the openings walled up with plaster of Paris. The downstairs bedroom was now a dining room. The kitchen had shrunk to make room for a bigger pantry to accommodate a modern sink. Louise talked about a bathtub and her plans to move the tiny bathroom from under the stairs to the attic. "I want a new roof," she stipulated. "And those gray, asphalt shingles around the house have to go."

But we knew Pierre was not Vendor Bill.

Zita observed the ambitious Louise from behind her kitchen curtains, surfacing when a monstrous rig backed up to my brother's house. The fat words HALIFAX FURNISHINGS were printed across the lengthy trailer. The gossip arrived at a gallop. *A la grand race.* She eyed Louise up and down, hastening past her into the house to agree with Mam'. "By the crackie, she's tiny all right." She examined the bone china that Mam' was unpacking, then stooped down to whisper, "It's gonna take something to keep that girl happy. I hear she's an only child, used to having everything."

She had other news, sure to be of interest. "Cedric is leaving."

I jerked my head back. "Leaving?"

The gossip grinned, blissful at being the first to tell me. "Leaving for Manitoba, in January."

Mouth wide open, I could only stare. "How do *you* know?"

"Lina told me," she said. I should have known. Ever since Gustave's death, the two had become awfully chummy. Mam' didn't look the least surprised. I supposed she knew about Cedric. And André knew. And God knows who else. Paul-Emile!

I rushed to Dominique's shed and had barely sat down before the hinged door creaked open. It was Dad, scratching the bottom of a flattened Export A package, salvaging a few strands of tobacco.

"Forget it!" I snapped, "I'm not going to the store! *Eje va point'la shoppe.*" I told him about Cedric.

He popped a peppermint between his hardened gums and proceeded to rearrange a row of tiny wooden whistles on a shelf.

"Why do you keep carving those?" I lashed. "Thérèse says they're for boys, and Joel's too small to blow in them."

He merely grinned, claimed his side of the lobster trap and attacked the finishing touches on a bovine wooden figure. He whittled and I watched, recoiling as I followed his knife in the fine indents of the face. "Some ox! It looks like a cow."

"It *is* a cow," he said, and tears welled up in my eyes. He interrupted his delicate carving to raise his head. "Maybe Cedric forgot to tell you."

"Sure," I growled, "it slipped his mind to tell me he's going to Manitoba."

I needed a long walk—to think.

"I'll see if Grand-mère has change," I said, and his grin widened to a smile sure of tobacco.

I cried all the way to and from the post office and had a few more crying spells that afternoon, so that by the time I went to bed,

I had drained my tear ducts.

Like a little old woman, Thérèse got on her knees and stroked my tear-stained cheeks. "Sissy and I don't like it when you're sad."

I lifted my head. "Sissy?"

"My doll," she clarified, reaching for the chain of the dimly lit bulb dangling from the ceiling. "I can only pee in the dark."

When I yanked on the chain again, she was staring at me, two tears welling in the corners of her eyes. "I think I missed the pot. Mam' will be so angry."

With a large flannelette rag, I soaked up the puddle. "Then we won't tell her."

"Tell me a story," she pleaded, and I had every good intention, holding on to the damp rag.

"First, I have to go burn the evidence." I descended the stairs, found the poker and lifted the stove cover, all without a sound. When the shed door opened, I dropped everything. *Bang! Crash!*

"Is that you, Zoé?"

"Just a minute," I whispered, then poked my head into Grand-mère Sophie's bedroom. "Yes, that noise was me."

"Who just came in?" she wanted to know.

I shot a glance at the long legs. "Cedric."

"*Qui?*" she wanted to know. "Medric?" Wow, getting more deaf by the day.

I moved deeper into her room, away from his pleading stare. "Cedric."

Grand-mère was in bed for the night, needing to talk, as if she were getting ready to die or something. "You know the quilt in my chest."

Having examined her mother's nine-point star quilt at least a hundred times, I could nod a definite yes.

She smiled the sweetest of grandmotherly smiles. "I want you to have it. For when you marry." But then she looked so sad. I knew Tante Marceline had undergone a series of electrocardiogram tests, but her heart was fine. Why the sudden sombre mood?

"Philippe's never written," Grand-mère said.

I immediately came to his rescue. "That's because he's always studying." My voice broke with the excitement. "He met a girl at a 'downeast' party, and we may get to meet her at Christmas! Her name is Arlene."

"Sixteen!" my grandmother understood.

I shook my head. "No, no, her name is Arlene."

"Aaaah," she grinned. "*Une Acadienne?*"

I nodded. "Yes, from Saulnierville." Her face lit up. Catholic was understood. But through all the excitement, there was still a terrible bit of news. "Pricille's not coming home," I said, as I lined up Grand-mère's hand creams in a neat row. "Did you know?"

She avoided my gaze. "Yes, I did."

I picked up a stack of sympathy cards that had gathered a year's supply of dust. "Should I put these in the top drawer?"

"If you like." She called me over and singled one out, laying it on the black rattan chair next to her bed.

She yawned, and I was quick to suggest. "I'll turn your light off now." It was so easy to slip the card under my blouse. "*Bonsoir* Grand-mère." I left her door ajar, on purpose.

Cedric was still sitting at the kitchen table.

"Could I talk to you?" he asked.

Graciously grinning at his puppy-dog face, I merely replied, "Don't think so."

He didn't dare follow, especially since I shut the hall door behind me. I reached for the card I was hiding. It smelled of Sophie's perfumed hands, even in a living room where the scent of death still prevailed a year after Dominique's wake. Stricken by tremendous guilt, I reflected over the eleventh commandment, *Thou shalt not read other people's mail.* But I was sinfully curious.

I squinted, straining to make out the sloppy writing. Sylvain Jacquard? "Sylvain, Sylvain, Sylvain," I sounded out. The graveyard in Wedgeport! Grand-mère had made such a fuss over a gravestone bearing the inscription Tillie Jacquard. This was her husband, Sylvain Jacquard. But how did he know that Dominique had died? *Le P'tit Courrier* perhaps? *The Vanguard?*

A series of doors slammed, and a tall silhouette hastened past the living room window, heading down Grand-mère's driveway. I tiptoed back to the kitchen, past my father, who noticed the card I was clutching. He grinned as he sipped his tea. Grand-mère's door was still ajar, so that I simply dropped the card back on her rattan chair, where it rightfully belonged. Neither my father nor I said a word. I climbed the stairs to the attic. Thérèse and Sissy were fast asleep.

Chapter 29

Everybody knew. Estelle was throwing a party to celebrate the Christmas school break. She had already blabbered her invitations in the school corridors. If Basil had any objections, well it was too late.

Even the postmaster knew. He handed me mail from Grand-mère Sophie's cubicle. "How many people are invited?" As if it were any of his business.

"A few," I replied, my immediate interest on the letter in my hand from Sylvain Jacquard. Safely out the door, I turned the envelope at different angles to the light, probing for a fingernail opening, but there was none.

"Moses," Grand-mère remarked when she noticed the back flap, scotch-taped right across. She flushed, shrank in her chair as she slipped the letter into her sweater pocket. She was glued to "Another World," not sure where to rest her embarrassed gaze as two lovers shared a passionate kiss. But the gaze had a fresh glow, surely sparked by Sylvain's letter. My invalid Grand-mère now wanted to walk. She wiggled herself to the edge of her chair and extended her arm to Dad, who went along with the silly notion. A long-established diabetic, the red inflammation that had started in her big toe had now turned the yellowish-white colour of decayed tissue starved of blood. Defeated, Grand-mère sat back, frustrated at her stovepipe legs that were too painful to walk on. She was reduced to pointing. "Then drag me over there."

Dad braced himself. The biggest hurdle was where the carpet was torn and curling at the seam, but he made it to the window, where she watched the *Cape Marguerite* come in. Every time the bow plunged, I was sure that a big wave had swallowed the boat, but then she'd resurface to tackle another breaker. That was our Pierre, pressing home at the last minute. He barely had the boat moored before tall breakers started to crash against the wharf. He unloaded his catch and headed straight up the line to pick up Louise in Saint Bernard. *Foudrait ça fut charcher la fumelle. La galle.*

Our fisherman safely back with his girl, the wind could howl all it wanted. In the comfort of his rocking chair, my father finished off a pot of tea, often rising to check at the windows. "*Quite-a gale,*" he muttered to himself. "Wonder how long Louise will stay in that attic once the wind starts whistling around her ears."

Mam' halted what she was doing to snap her big eyes at him. "Maybe she's *already* tried that attic." She hurled a glance next door, "Maybe that new four-poster bed is a bit too comfortable." She spent the latter part of the evening at her bedroom window, pulling down the shade only when it became obvious that Pierre wasn't taking his girl home to Saint Bernard. The next night, she didn't go home. Nor the night after that.

With hindsight, Mam' could very well reproach herself. "If I had known that Pierre would use that house to harbour Louise, it would have been signed over *after* his wedding day."

My father could only grin. "They're young. *Faut qu'la jeunesse se passe.*"

Zita showed up and didn't overly fret either, except to speculate, "Makes you wonder what kind of girl that Louise is."

"A good match for Pierre," Mam' retorted.

"Mr. Man," she addressed him, delivering her call-down one day in the shed, but I caught only part of it when she opened the door to re-enter the kitchen. "By the crackie, I have other children here."

Pierre started driving his Louise back to Saint Bernard, and came home in the mornings, just in time to board the *Cape Marguerite*. Mam' stayed away from her bedroom window, spending her time writing to Pricille. I noticed that when my sister wrote back, Mam' read the letters and pitched them in the stove to be burned. She went around the house with a new frustration on her face, obviously something to do with Pricille. It was not a good time to approach her about my increasing need for glasses. With what money? Business at the Diner was slack. Grand-mère's meagre pension could hardly sustain staple items. And Pierre, he was laden with bills.

Maybe Babette had a suggestion for the desperate. Maybe she'd persuade her sweet mother to talk to my mother. "Your eyes are changing," she had jested. "It's time to start looking at the world with sharper senses."

While she could jest, all I could do was fret, staring out the window. Should I? Shouldn't I? Finally, I grabbed my coat. A freezing rain had iced the grass to a transparent sparkle, causing the stiff blades to snap under my feet. I crunched a path across my lawn, followed the Cape road down the hill, up the lighthouse road, but nothing was moving at the Goodwins. No one home. It was such a sparkling fun day.

I headed for the Pointe. Carefully, I edged along the cliff, coming to an abrupt halt where I had once shuddered at the remnants of a red dory. Soft ripples were slapping against the slated rocks at the base of the cliff. How could an ocean that had so viciously consumed Gustave ripple so peacefully? A seagull soared overhead; its only concern was to shriek louder than the one perched on a rock. Oh, to be as carefree; they hadn't a worry in the world. What if I never got glasses? I closed my eyes, pretending to see an ocean in total darkness. I bet, yes, I bet I could walk up the Cape road, all the way to my house, with my eyes closed, as if I were blind. I moved away from the cliff, shutting my eyes tightly with stubborn determination. I cleared the Pointe, stepping in only one puddle. Now for the Cape road. Follow along the shoulder, I reasoned. Nothing to it. I had walked a fair way up the road when I decided to test my sense of direction, turning half a dozen times in fast-motion swirls. *Whoa!* Dizzy. Where was I facing? Towards Eddie Pockshaw's? The beach? No idea whatsoever. I stooped down and felt pavement. How far to the ditch, to the embankment on the other side of the road? To Estelle's house? Unable to guess, I opened my eyes and found myself standing in the middle of the road, within inches of ramming into Cedric.

"Having fun?" he grinned. He could look as puzzled as he

wanted. I wasn't talking. I gave my strict attention to the steep hill home. "I owe you an apology!" he admitted.

I cringed, snapping back, "For someone who's going away, that's an excellent start. Now if you don't mind, I'll be on my way."

"I can explain," he pleaded, but with my arms swinging vigorously, I kept a clear view ahead. "Let me explain," he despaired and begged until I marched back to where he was standing.

"Then you better make it quick!"

"I wanted the time to be right," was his defence. "Mam' wasn't supposed to tell anyone."

"Well she told Zita," I reminded him. "That was like telling the whole Cape and half of Clare. Anyway, what would have been the right time? Five minutes before you boarded the plane?"

Distress filled his eyes. "I didn't know how to tell you. You know me, I'm not very good with words."

"How about, 'I'm joining the army. Will you write me.' "

He levelled his gaze to meet mine. "Will you?"

"No!"

"Can I come to Estelle's party with you?"

"No!" It was final. Though I added rudely, "Actually, I'd rather you didn't come at all."

"Then tell me why," he pressed.

I simply imitated his grin. "I'm not very good with words."

I hastened up the long hill, my vision for the moment perfectly clear. He could leave that very day for all I cared.

At least half of Estelle's grade nine class showed up at the party, plus kids from other classes, friends of friends that I had never seen before, and late guests—Babette and her William, causing Estelle to scowl in annoyance, "I suppose you two had to discuss English literature before you could leave."

Babette looked stunning in a green velvet dress that enhanced the olive green of her eyes and her honey-blond shoulder-length pageboy. Her bubbly smile was captivating, a telltale sign of the happiness that William had brought to her life. She took me aside, wondered if I had approached Mam' about glasses.

"Not yet," I informed her. She wanted to know everything

about Pierre's wedding, of which I knew only a few details. "Louise mentioned bright colours, lots of reds, Valentine reds."

"Wow!" exclaimed Babette, "a wedding sure to be the talk of Clare."

She was all ears, oblivious to Paul-Emile's sidelong glance at her party dress. Estelle's tight sweater and mini skirt didn't stop him from sizing up the other girls, or from harassing me about Cedric. His tone could have nauseated a vulture. "He's not coming. But then again, we don't need him, do we?"

I poured myself a soda. He was right behind me. I sat in the sun parlour. He followed me. I slumped into a chair in the living room. He appeared in the doorway. Then to heck with him! I left the blaring music of the Dave Clark Five to sneak upstairs to Estelle's bedroom, a safe haven from Paul-Emile's pestering. Perhaps the scoundrel liked my curly hair, the party coiffure held stiff with a ton of hairspray. Or was it Mam's red lipstick, which made for voluptuous, valentine lips? A short, black skirt highlighted my suddenly shapely legs, a late-developing asset. The lacy ruffles across the front of my pink blouse nicely camouflaged my flat chest. Even Foufou was staring.

"When did you become king?" I asked him. He was sprawled over Estelle's silk bedspread, having clawed it to shreds where he habitually gripped to climb up. I patted him to start the motor in his throat, and then anchored my ear to the vibrations in his stomach. But the anxious cat pricked his ears to a new sound of someone climbing the wooden stairs.

Maybe Estelle, I thought. I stroked his soft fur as I picked him up. "I have an idea! Would you like to join the party?"

The answer didn't sound anything like his purr. "Not really."

I jerked my head up, beheld the beguiling smile of Satan personified, standing at the foot of the bed.

"What are you doing here?" I blurted. He slammed the door shut. Paul-Emile's voice sweetened to a whisper. "Relax. You sound like I have no business in here. I've been in this room so many times."

"Not with me you haven't!" I corrected, leaping to my feet. But the beast wrestled me back on the bed and *uggggh!* slopped his mouth on mine, making me gag.

"Have you ever heard of a French kiss?" he asked.

I had to struggle to speak. "No, but I've heard of a French asshole."

The insult would have cost me dearly if Mademoiselle Estelle hadn't been standing in the doorway, her glare stabbing me.

"It's not what you think," I gasped, but she looked like she could chew my skull between her teeth.

"I can see for myself!"

Paul-Emile could explain, quite simply. "I came to the bathroom. Zoé called me in here."

"That's not true!" I yelled, and when she wouldn't believe me, I fell into frantic sobs. "He's lying! *C'est riânne aute qu'une mentrie!*"

The scoundrel stood there smirking. It didn't look like he was going to leave, until almighty thunder roared through the doorway. "Out! *mon p'tit bastard!*"

Mr. Paul-Emile refastened the buckle on his belt, and would have flown down the stairs if Cedric hadn't stopped him with a bone-cracking whack on the side of his jaw. When he raised his fist to strike again, I let out a blood-curdling scream. "Stop it! *Arrétez vos affares.*" It allowed the snake a quick exit.

"Should of killed the sonofabitch," Cedric openly regretted. "He'd go after his own mother if she were alive."

Rag-doll limp, I could only sob in the comfort of such caring arms, a bear hug that bore me no grudge. "And to think I didn't want you to come to the party," I wailed. Cedric walked me down the stairs and outside to his car. I couldn't stop crying.

"Shhhhhh," he whispered. "I'll take you home." But then he drove right past my house, a silly little grin on his face. "I didn't say when."

He parked the car in the dunes. As I stared out at pitch-darkness, a most curious thought crossed my mind. "How did you know where I was?"

"I didn't," Cedric attested. "Estelle went looking for you, and I heard the yelling and arguing. And if you had-a let me … "

"Never mind!" I rebuked. "I don't necessarily want Paul-Emile dead."

Cedric fumbled about the dashboard for the light knob. "Well you may want this," he said. I squinted in the bright light, at the black velvet box he handed me.

"What is it?"

"Open it!" he urged.

I just stared. "For me?" Yes, for me. The daintiest ring, a cream-coloured stone speckled with flecks of pink and green. An opal! My birthstone.

Cedric blushed, and for the first time, his eyes filled for someone other than his deceased father. "You don't like it?"

"I love it! I'm just shocked."

"Then try it on!" Ever so clumsily, he slid the ring on my finger. Then he gazed into my eyes. "Will you wait for me?"

"I'll write you," I promised, and he had no choice but to grin.

"Guess I'll have to settle for that."

"I want you to wear it for the rest of your life," he said and, before I could refuse any rash promises, he kissed me, sealing my heart with the magic of an early Christmas.

"Now," he concluded, "I'll take you home."

"Sundays are reserved for the *Bon Djeu*, not to pick fights." That's what Mam' said, making herself perfectly clear as she thrust her forefinger in my face. "Mass is at nine-thirty!"

I strode out of the house and headed towards Estelle's, with no time to kick stones along the way. I knocked at her door. When nobody came, I banged, until Basil peeked around the kitchen stove, his pants half-zipped, his chest bare. He was terribly slow in reaching the sun parlour door.

"Isn't it a bit early?" he asked, yawning his annoyance in my face. Early or not, I had business to attend to.

"Is Estelle up there?"

I stomped up the creaky wooden stairs and barged into her room. My friend was utterly miserable; her bloodshot eyes focused with much difficulty. "What are you doing here?"

"We need to talk," I insisted, as she wiped sleep from her eyes.

Now fully awake, her face was defiant. "If it's about last night, you can go home, because no explaining is gonna change my mind.

Paul-Emile and I talked for a long time, and he said it wasn't the first time."

"First time for what?"

"You were after him," she shot back, her loyalty indeed commendable. "It's him that I trust."

I smirked sadly, regretful of her mindless gullibility. I was now compelled to tell the poor girl. "Speaking about trust. Do you know who Renette is? Very pretty. From Meteghan."

"Who cares?" an irate Estelle replied, aware that unpleasant words would surely follow. She raised her head. "Who is she anyway?"

I borrowed one of her very best smirks. "I suggest you ask Paul-Emile. He knows her very well."

Estelle's face now registered anger. She dislodged restraining blankets to lean forward. "Paul-Emile said if he had wanted to, you would have been pretty easy."

Easy! Of all the low-down, trashy things to say. I paced back a few steps to her window.

"You're not saying anything cause it's true," Estelle reproached.

I looked down into Charlotte's backyard, remembering the thriving garden, not so long ago blooming with prized flowers—rhododendrons, tea roses, *mums.*

"I hate you!" Estelle shouted, her face now radiating a flaming rage.

I observed the burlap bags that shielded sleeping bushes from the angry ocean spray and the merciless winter winds. The bitter chill that had settled into the ground was seeping into this room. I had neither the energy nor the desire to defend myself because nothing, *nothing* could have changed Estelle's mind. Nothing could have altered the look on her face. "*Oké. Oké,*" I motioned. "I'm going." But my whole body was numb, as I stared at a face gone arctic cold, with dimples turned to blank hollows, a disfigurement to a once spirited smirk.

The ache in my heart had nothing to do with her sneering at my reversible skirt, or making fun of my orange pants with a boy's fly. It was far more serious than my ruining her hopscotch game or hacking at her long, beautiful locks; much more damaging than her stealing my part in a Christmas concert, or the two of us snuffing out the lives of four tiny puppies. It was an ache far more dreadful than watching my Cedric waging bets behind the outhouse, or her Paul-Emile coaxing a cow to its death; far, far more hurtful than when she simply mocked what I looked like. The ache in my heart was about a friendship that had started over baby bottles and was now coming to a bitter end.

"Close the door behind you," was her final order, punctuated with the exclamation, "and don't ever come back. Ever!" And then, the iodine to the open wound. Estelle grabbed my school photo and ripped it to pieces. "There!" she concluded. "I don't want your ugly face on my bureau. Now, go home!"

"*Oké. Oké*," I said, retaining my composure until I hugged Foufou. I got his fluffy white fur all wet with tears. The cat purred at my good-bye pats, his cute face somber. After all, I had saved his life.

I left Estelle's room and followed the baseboard heater along the hall, a clamorous rig that banged all night, but it heated. What a luxury! That, and the four-legged tub in which I loved to soak. I counted all fourteen steps down the stairs, wishing they could swallow me up, for I still had to walk through the kitchen and face Charlotte and Basil. They were sitting at the breakfast table, lingering over their morning tea. Their facial expressions weren't cold, but they weren't friendly either. I knew of their awkward predicament, leaning the only way parents can, and should, when loyalty calls. I understood.

A smile trembled on my lips as I cut through the longest kitchen I had ever known, and then into the sun parlour, the cosiest place in the whole world to play in the soothing warmth of the sun. Here Estelle and I had coloured for hours; we had fought over Snakes and Ladders and games of jacks. She had to be first, always. We argued and then made up, a routine in our daily play. We caught flies and pulled off their wings. We caught grasshoppers and killed them *all*, whether or not they gave molasses. When we got older, her mother bought a record player and all our favourite records, like "Down in the Boondocks." I had played the single so many times that I had worn out the grooves. Then I had played it some more while watching Gustave's house, innocently hoping to catch a glimpse of Cedric. And then there were the secrets Estelle and I told in this very sun parlour, like the one Mam' had threatened of late: "Someday, I will leave the Cape and never come back."

It took every bit of strength I had to open and close behind me the door of the sun parlour that I loved so much.

Chapter 30

Christmas Eve. Basil arrived at my house, behaving as if nothing had happened. He mentioned that Estelle was helping Charlotte with a rappie pie, and did I want to join in their *réveillon* after midnight mass. *Réveillon!* I felt as if I had just been put to sleep in World War III.

"Don't think so," I forced myself to smile. Père Lucien would have to throw in quite a few sermons on forgiveness before I could enter that house again.

It was sweet Babette with the olive green eyes who had consoled me. "Estelle is bound to come to her senses. Give her time." She had comforted me over Cedric's impending departure. "You can't hold back a dream." And her parents had offered thirty dollars to buy me glasses. But I knew Mam's steel pride would never allow it.

Babette put Christmas Eve in my heart. With her friendship, I would heal; I would become strong. And I would never look back.

Basil's invitation was kind, but I wanted to be with Babette. He took note of a rather quiet kitchen. Where was everyone?

Mam', Joel, and Thérèse were next door. André was down the road with Cedric. Philippe was in Saulnierville with his girlfriend. Grand-mère Sophie was in her bedroom, likely mooning over Sylvain's Christmas card. And Pricille, she was in Boston, broken-hearted that she couldn't come home, often sick to her stomach I had overheard Mam' telling Philippe.

My father and N'Oncle Joseph returned from the shed, their breath reeking of liquor. Just having a smoke where it's cool, was their excuse. Basil delved into boatbuilding and all three had a lovely chit-chat, until Basil turned to politics. The discussion was cut short by my father's sudden announcement. "Next time, I'm voting for those D.N.P."

"N.D.P," Basil corrected, looking rather shocked. "I thought you were Liberal!"

An evil look crept into my father's eyes. "That Paul-Emile is a pimp," he blurted, utterly changing the subject. I gave Grand-mère's door a shove, shutting out vile talk contaminating her kitchen. The string of accusations that followed were directed at Basil but meant for Paul-Emile. "Dirty rotten sonofa ..."

"*Hé. Hé. Hé.* Antoine!" N'Oncle Joseph scolded. "Come on brother. We don't need that on Christmas Eve."

But nothing could curb my father's tongue once he had tipped the bottle. "You believed Estelle," he lashed at Basil. "You really think Zoé would have gone after that good-for-nothing hobo."

If Dad's outrage had been sober and directed at the pimp himself, I would have surely applauded, but he was knifing innocent Basil, at whose table I had shared many meals. The man was wise to make a move towards the door, turning and facing us all before he left. "Estelle's my daughter, regardless of what Paul-Emile is."

He walked out, and another visitor walked in—Eddie Pockshaw carrying a large stew pot. Mam' ventured in at the same time with Joel whining at her heels; he screamed to be picked up when he beheld the scarred face looking down at him.

"Haw'dam de haw'dam, I don't blame him," Eddie chuckled, exposing a black saliva gap where two front teeth had been knocked out. He set the pot on the table and Mam' lifted the lid to release the smell of fresh homemade beans. Ummm. A rich aroma hit my nostrils, but I could see black scum floating around huge chunks of lard. Perhaps Mr. Pockshaw had missed the spittoon. While he was hacking and spitting in the bathroom, N'Oncle Joseph got up to inspect the chef's concoction. He gave a nauseated grimace. "Didn't Pierre say that his hound needed a good feed?"

Grand-mère had heard the commotion and claimed her place by the stove, just in time for the bathroom door to open. Out came Eddie, with his fly wide open to the elements. He hobbled ahead a few feet, rolled back his glazed eyes, and flopped on the couch, with a nice drooling smile. "What do you think of those hippies on TV?" he teased.

Grand-mère made a sour face, "By the *farnell*, it's ugly that long hair. *C'est ti point laid sté grand joeux lâ.*"

The runty weasel took a coughing jag, choking on a chunk of tobacco that he went to spit in the toilet. He returned to the couch and lit a cigar. What a treat for Grand-mère. She perked her head up like a rooster. Her jowls flushed when he started blowing his smoke towards her curtains and in her face. She spent an agonizing half-hour before Smokestack Eddie left.

"Him and his *farnell de cigares,*" she blasted. "He only comes here to smoke my curtains. *Ca vin'citte boucaner les rideaux.*"

Mam' hadn't thanked the Good Samaritan for the beans. Lord forbid, she had noticed my father's jealousy simmering again.

"What were you doing next door all afternoon?" he questioned.

She cast an icy stare. "I wasn't there all afternoon."

My father's accusing look just wouldn't quit, causing her to swing her head away from the stove. "I was visiting my son! You have anything against that?" She tossed chicken pieces in a pot to boil and then grabbed a paring knife and started peeling, splashing the wall as she hurled potatoes in a pan of cold water. "By the crackie, I've been accused of many things," she glowered, "but this takes the cake—chasing after my own son."

There were many things to do, but none that I could do well enough. I put the icicles on the tree all wrong. I spoiled her shine on the stove with a clumsy spill of greasy chicken broth. I tried to peel potatoes and ended up removing half the potato with the peel. And I would never, ever learn how to sweep a floor properly. My father was even less useful, better off in his rocking chair, or better still, out of the house. The door slammed behind him.

Mam' should have been paying attention to her grating rather than gaping out the window. "Now I bet you anything he's going to Eddie Pockshaw's." That no sooner said, the jagged razor-sharp grater slashed two of her knuckles, causing her to jerk her hand away. Oozing blood was already streaking through the bunched-up fabric of her cotton housedress. What to do! I froze at the sight of blood.

At that moment, Arlene arrived. What a greeting for the new girlfriend. She grabbed the cheesecloth reserved for squeezing the juice from the potatoes, bound it around Mam's gashed fingers, then applied pressure.

"Bet you're a nurse," Mam' deduced.

Arlene simply grinned, "I work in an office."

She rinsed the blood-spattered grater under cold water, grabbed a potato, and picked up where Mam' had left off. Philippe helped, but with his usual temper. He nicked his knuckles and cursed our vicious grater to hell and back. "*Enfare de rig de sacré marde.*"

Arlene repossessed the grater and waited until my brother had simmered down. "You need patience," she admonished. "Slowly. Like this. Try it."

My mother grinned at the gentle hands disciplining her son. Who was this sane character he had brought into our family? A very modest-looking girl. No lipstick. No rouge. Plain, plain, plain, with straight hair, but not as straight as mine. Her short cut had a bounce to it. She was of medium height, too thin, though she had a nice figure. Well, except for her legs, which were knobby, like those of our dead goose. *Des jambes de bois collier.* She wore glasses. Was she pretty? Yes, already, in our hearts.

Philippe was getting too thin, causing Grand-mère to gape at his elbow-worn sweater and at the shoes that couldn't possibly be resoled one more time.

"Breakfast and one meal a day," he jested. "That's all I can afford."

Arlene smiled at my perturbed Grand-mère. "Don't listen to him. I make him rappie pies and *fricots*. And if he behaves himself, I buy him blood pudding at the market." She squirmed on her seat. "He has to eat it when I'm not around."

"Do you like Toronto?" Grand-mère asked.

Arlene shrugged. "Philippe says it's too big, but I don't mind it. I adjust easily, happy anywhere." I loved her smile.

Grand-mère complained about her rheumatism. She talked about Grand-père Dominique and showed Arlene her wedding ring, worn down to a thin band nearly lost in folds of flabby skin. Arlene touched the old hand to more closely examine the ring. I was scared of old hands. And I didn't have the kind of patience Arlene had to repeat herself two to three times. Philippe grated while the two chatted.

Our after-Mass *réveillon* had been doused with enough blood to transfuse a hemophiliac. "Gives it taste," Philippe jested, determined to eat his rappie pie without one word from my father, who had arrived home, judging by the racket in the shed. My brother looked up, his big black eyes shining when Dad appeared in the kitchen. "You're not spoiling our Christmas Eve. *Tu vas point v'nir icitte ravager.*"

Dad staggered across the kitchen floor and rammed into the hall door, staring at it a few long seconds before he realized he had to open it. He found the stairs with no problem, but he didn't quite make it up the steep incline. *Ka-be-de-rang!!* just like Grand-père Dominique. Except my father crashed his two hundred pound frame into the wall, punching a jagged hole through the plaster of Paris. I was glad then that Grand-mère was half deaf.

"Dad *est mort*," Thérèse yelled. "Dad *est mort!*"

My father wasn't dead, just a bit stunned. Massaging the back of his head and his right thigh, he dragged himself along the floor to the kitchen sink. "For Jesus sake, was I asleep?"

Broom in hand, Mam' hurled him one of her looks. "If you were, you're awake now." She hastened to the hall to sweep the crumbled plaster.

Dad glanced up, grinning sheepishly at Arlene and then at Louise, two very uncomfortable guests. "I guess a man can miss a step."

He hoisted himself up to the sink and was about to wipe the sweat from his brow when Mam' grabbed the dishcloth from his hand. "Not with that!"

He found his rocking chair, and began to perspire anew when he checked his shirt pockets. "*Ma p'tite Zoé.*"

I was in the hall, gathering scattered peppermints from off the floor. I certainly wasn't going to the post office at one-thirty in the morning!

"You'll get your ox for Christmas," he pleaded. "Tomorrow when you get up, your ox will be under the tree." Arlene had a perplexed smile. The story of the ox made for an amusing conversation over rappie pie, though not for Mam'.

"By the crackie," she assured me, "he'll wait for his tobacco."

Christmas morning an empty package of Export A and a bag of white peppermints occupied Dad's place at the breakfast table. They were still there at dinnertime. I picked at my food. Arlene picked at hers. "Shouldn't you get your father?" she asked.

Philippe continued slicing the turkey. "He's fine in the attic. It's a nice quiet place to think."

Louise's lack of appetite was understandable; her mind was consumed with wedding plans. Pierre's mind was in the woods. He had barely gulped the last bite off his plate when he asked, "Is U of T bigger than the vocational in Yarmouth?"

Philippe turned his head, giving him the humblest grin. "A little bit."

"Well they don't have woods like we do here," Pierre concluded. He went rooting for his red plaid shirt and orange hunting cap. "I'll get the dog while you get ready," he called, as he headed out the door.

There was a thin coating of snow on the ground, enough to see rabbit prints, perfect for a short-legged hound that hated the deep snow. But Pierre couldn't have been gone more than a few minutes before he reappeared, totally bewildered. "What the hell's wrong with Spot? He threw up all over his yard; I can't get him to move."

Total silence. The fate of Eddie Pockshaw's beans was sealed in Mam's smirk.

"I guess we're not going anywhere," our distraught Pierre decided. The rabbits could scuttle through the woods in peace, for that afternoon anyway.

Everyone disappeared next door to check out the marvels that Pierre and Louise had effected in their future home.

"Go on over," Philippe told Arlene, "I'll be along."

Textbook in hand, he sat at the kitchen table, an opportune time to steal a few moments with my big brother.

"What's Pricille's boyfriend like?" I probed, as I riffled through page after page of weird mathematical calculations in

Philippe's scribbler.

"You mean *husband*," he corrected.

My eyes nearly popped out of their sockets. "She's married!"

Almost apologetically, my brother nodded. "Rather a quick ceremony."

"Why didn't Mam' tell us?"

"Because," he explained, she needs time before she can face Zita." He paused before revealing even more shocking news. "Pricille's having a baby. In April."

"A baby! In April!"

Again, he nodded. "Zoé," he said, and I sensed a little talk coming my way. "Mam' has a lot of pressure these days." The rest followed after a laboured sigh. "I know you're serious with Cedric. I guess what I'm trying to say is that she doesn't need any more problems."

"What do you mean?"

Philippe came to the point. "She doesn't need any more babies."

About that, I could readily assure him. "You needn't worry!"

"What's Pricille's husband like?" I asked.

He didn't need an hour to answer. "Boastful!"

"Like Uncle John?" I persisted.

He grinned. "Exactly. It's his nephew."

"I can't understand these funny symbols," I grumbled, and my brother creased his forehead. "Greek alphabet, and unless you plan to take electrical engineering, you don't need to understand them. Why do you hold everything so close to your nose? You need glasses, don't you." Philippe gave me the creeps with a studying look that went right through me. "Well?"

He wouldn't quit about the glasses until I confessed. "Yes, I do, but that's not why I'm upset."

"Is it Pricille?" he queried.

"No," I assured him. Mam' had always said that girls who got pregnant were no worse than the others, just unlucky. Pricille had just been unlucky.

"What is it?" Philippe probed.

I glanced towards the hall door. "Can't you please call Dad to come down?"

My brother rose from his chair, flashing me one of his dark looks. "I will, but don't think for one minute that I feel sorry for him. There's hardly a Christmas that he hasn't ruined."

Head bent low, my father rocked for a long time before he could lift his gaze from the floor. He limped to the stove to fill his teacup, then veered to the cupboard for the last piece of mince pie. He grabbed a cold piece of turkey from the fridge, then sat at the table, painstakingly sipping his tea. Finally, he lifted his afflicted face to look at me. "Did I insult anyone last night?"

His sick insinuation about Mam' and Pierre quickly came to mind. But then I mulled over what he had told Basil about Paul-Emile, and a wicked grin spread across my face. "No, you didn't." He examined the few barley and ribbon candies which Santa had brought Thérèse and Joel, and I showed him my ring. "Cedric got me this!"

Of course, he examined it as he did everything else, with a price tag in mind. "How much?"

"A lot of money," I guessed. "I couldn't have gotten anything I'd like better." Instantly, I paused and made smiling eye contact with my father. "Except for an ox. Wasn't I supposed to get a real one for Christmas?"

My Dad's glum mood lifted. He grinned. I asked him if he liked Cedric, and he nodded. "Nice lad."

"Do you like Arlene." I asked.

Again he nodded. "Seems like *quite-a gal.*"

"Do you like Arlene?" I asked Grand-mère, who was fussing with her purse in her bedroom.

Her trembling hand searched the bottom of the handbag for the change that she handed me. "For Antoine's tobacco."

I glanced over at the top of the bureau, smiling at my perturbed Grand-mère. "You got a nice card from Sylvain." Her eyes shone like tinsel in tree lights. "He's coming for a visit in the spring. When the roads are better."

"Do you like Arlene?" I asked anew.

This time she answered, her face blessed with a renewed peace now that Dad was grinning again. "I always knew," she alleged, "that when Philippe chose a wife, she'd be very special."

"Soon Cedric will be thousands of miles away," I told her and I left the room, grabbed my coat from off the hook behind the stove. I cried all the way to the post office. He was leaving very soon.

January was a bitter cold, long month that kept me snuggled to my recruit, and dreading his departure that came too quickly. Cedric couldn't have chosen a worse blustery frigid day to leave, but a strong-minded dream has no season.

"It's like something calling me," he said, affording me a timid embrace and a whisper of caution, away from his mother. "Don't expect long letters. You know me with words."

He kissed me, told me that he loved me. Then he ruined it all with a teasing but disturbing thought. "Someday, I want to marry you."

His words resounded in my ears long after the slow-chugging train pulled away from the platform in Meteghan Station. His mother broke down in my arms. Gustave was gone forever, and now her Cedric would be far away.

I should have been crying too, but I didn't know what I felt. A slow, churning discomfort clouded my emotions.

"Cedric is getting too serious and it worries me," I later confided to Babette.

As always, she listened intently. Secure in her own mind about her darling William, she fumbled for words. "I'm totally baffled by you, Zoé. You were so distraught …"

"I know. I know," I interrupted. She stood before me, waiting for an explanation. I simply didn't have one.

Chapter 31

Faces filled with awe as Louise followed her flower girl and five attendants down the aisle of Saint Bernard's church, an endless aisle sprinkled with heavenly-scented rose petals of a deep velour red, like the petals on the bouquet trembling in her hands. All eyes were on the petite figure approaching the altar. Chantilly lace edged the V-shaped neckline and the long pointed sleeves, but did not overpower her elegant dress, leaving the emphasis on the shoulder-length veil, held in place with a tiara-like headpiece. Satin-covered buttons trailed to a satin bow at the back of her dress, somewhat like the dresses of the bridesmaids and flower girl, except theirs were of a stiff silk, the winter green immensely rich against the bride's white ensemble.

Louise paced her steps to the chiming tempo of the wedding march, played by a parishioner who knew how to manipulate the two thousand pipes on the massive *Casavant* in such a way that the towering granite church vibrated with music.

And what a church! I had to squint for a better view. I sized up the walls and ceiling that had consumed ninety-six tons of plaster, all mixed with mortar hoes and then hoisted by two men raising it one bucket at a time on a pulley. Louise's grandfather had applied the first trowel of plaster on the back wall. I marvelled at the gothic ceiling and the huge arches curving over domino strings of plywood pews, their seating capacity one thousand. There were well over two hundred people here now, Babette and I figured. Three hundred had been invited.

I studied the faces of Louise's people, few of them familiar, save for the occasional kid from high school. I gazed up and down, all around, at the loft in the back, then at the marble altar in the front.

"Pay attention!" Babette nudged when it was time for the vows.

It was the one moment that Pierre had everyone's undivided attention. "I do," he pronounced clearly before God, and before Mam'. A wide grin lingered on her face. She would no longer have to watch the house from her bedroom window. My brother now had divine blessing to take his Louise home to share his four-poster bed. The service over, he could relax his shoulders as he and his bride made their way back up the aisle. He beamed to all his fishermen friends.

It was a bright February fourteenth, cool but the sun was shining strong and low, hinting at the break of winter—a perfect day for the ladies, with not even the slightest breeze to ruffle their lovely hairdos.

I stood in front of the towering church, the architectural masterpiece that all tourists look for while motoring along the shores of St. Mary's Bay. I raised my head in wonder at the spires reaching into the blue sky and marvelled at the façade of the structure. Over eight thousand blocks of granite had been used, hauled by railroad from Shelburne, and then carted by ox teams a distance of one and three-quarter miles on a gravel road. The church had taken more than thirty years to build during the Depression and war years. Why a church of such extraordinary size? Because the Acadians were known for their big families, and the parish would grow, and grow, and grow.

"Imagine shaping those blocks, or doing the interior woodwork when there were no electric tools," Percy Goodwin grinned, as he, too, stared in awe. "If I could only make Emma see and feel the magnitude of this structure."

Percy described to Emma the red-and-white streamers that criss-crossed the huge reception hall and met at the centre of the ceiling. The theme of the wedding was hearts—cardboard valentine hearts plastered over the walls; heart-shaped silver necklaces and ear-rings for the bride and her attendants; a Just Married red-and-white crepe paper heart affixed to the trunk of Augustin's Lincoln; and of course, my heart, skipping beats from all the excitement.

Percy described the winter green silk dresses of the bridesmaids, something he was sure would interest Emma. "Short sleeves, square necks, tight skirt, bow in the back, that's about it."

"How long?" she was curious to know.

"You mean how short?" he corrected "Above the knee, though not short enough."

Emma gave the clown a nudge. "Stop it, you fool."

He called Louise over, fooling around some more. "This is my wife Emma. She wants to feel your cape."

Emma stole long, gentle strokes up and down the exquisite cloak, sighing over the ultrasoft fabric. "It's so beautiful."

Percy grabbed the honour. "A velvet cape over the most beautiful dress eyes have ever seen."

"What colour is the cape?" Emma asked, and he hugged the blushing bride, making her face flush all the more as he described, "It's blood red, passionate red. The little red riding hood has long, white fur all around, which sways when I breathe on it."

The stunned look on Emma's face should have been captured on camera. "What are you doing in the bride's neck?"

"Oh, but it's so young and soft," the clown grinned, and everyone at the table burst into laughter, except Mam'. Constrained amidst the pleasantries of carefree lovers, she sat like a statue, seemingly relieved when the wedding party seated itself, and the clinking of cutlery against glasses commenced. She and Thérèse found their places at the head table.

I wanted to sit with Babette and with poor Lina, whose mind and spirit were in Shilo, Manitoba. I had beat her to the first letter.

"What did Cedric have to say?" André pestered, as if I wanted the whole table to hear.

"You know Cedric," I smiled coyly. "Does he ever say anything? That Shilo's very flat, cold as hell; that he's forever waist deep in snow; and that you should get lost, to the head table, where you belong."

My pesky brother thrust his face forward. "Anything about kiss, kiss, kiss. Too bad he couldn't fly home to his sweetheart with a box of chocolates."

Clad in a black dress and white apron, a *Dame de Patronnesse* finally served André his turkey dinner, which he gulped down, more interested in the tall, slender glasses that arrived after the meal.

"Crème de menthe parfait," one of the *Dames* informed him, and he raised the short-stemmed glass to examine the multicoloured ice cream. With his long plastic spoon, he stirred the mixture and brought it to his nose.

"Ummm, smells like Dad's peppermints."

On behalf of Mam', I gave him the eye, and he knew to wait for everyone else.

"What's the wedding cake like?" Emma wanted to know.

"The usual," Percy muttered, "with a plastic bride and groom on top, but *huge*. You'd have to be blind to miss that cake ..."

"Or to fall in it," she added, and they giggled.

Babette turned to explain to a frowning William. "The last wedding we went to, Mam' tripped and flattened the cake."

Pierre and Louise arrived at the table and they heard the whole story, causing Pierre to grin. "Well she could fall in this one, and there'd be plenty left over to feed all of Clare."

Augustin arrived and embraced his daughter, boasting to anyone who would listen, "Isn't she the most beautiful bride?"

Beautiful? Perhaps, to some. Her shoulder-length, thick mop of hair overpowered her tiny face. Though the dimple in her chin accentuated her smile and gave her face character, I had grown to dislike dimples. Louise did look royally sweet. She was lucky to have inherited her mother's genes. Augustin was a humpbacked, heavy-set man with no spare looks to pass on to an offspring. He and Pierre spent a long time at my table, chatting about, what else, but boats. Pierre described the sixty-footer he was hoping for, and Augustin narrated a story about the *Acadian Queen* he had once navigated in the chancy waters of St. Pierre and Miquelon.

"Me and another guy," the heavy-set man began. "We set sail from Meteghan wharf, always with a tight schedule to reach St. Pierre, load, return to Meteghan, and unload before the full moon gave us away, always pressed for time." He winked at N'Oncle Joseph. "After all, the bootleggers from here to hell were waiting for us." We had all heard of Smugglers' Cove, the cave where he hid his contraband liquor. The story intensified as he continued, "One time, we were nearing the Cove with five hundred cases of rum on board, and we noticed the cutter, closing in on us ..."

Darn! To be left dangling in suspense, but it would have been impolite for Augustin to continue his smuggling story when his lovely wife was at the head table, calling for everyone's attention. There were telegrams.

Not all of the wishes were from Louise's relatives. Pricille and Tante Marceline had remembered Pierre, their heartfelt *félicitations* making him grin. Philippe's cable brought an emotional mist to his eyes.

A TOAST TO THE BRIDE, it read.

All glasses clicked.

A SALUTE TO THE CAPTAIN OF THE *CAPE MARGUERITE*.

All right-hands saluted.

And so, the message to Pierre read: MAY YOUR DAYS BE FILLED WITH AS MANY SMILES AS THERE ARE FISH IN THE OCEAN. MAY YOU NOT FORGET TO GREASE YOUR GUNS, BUT MAY YOU BE AS ANXIOUS TO RUN BACK HOME AS YOU ARE TO RUN TO THE WOODS. REMEMBER IT IS FAR BETTER TO LAY AROUND THE HOUSE ALL MORNING AND BOAST OF PLENTY THAN TO SCREW AROUND THE WOODS ALL DAY AND COME HOME WITH NONE.

There was a pause for grown-up chuckles. The message ended: MAY THE YEARS BE AS KIND TO YOU AS YOU HAVE BEEN TO US. BUT THIS, MY BROTHER, I WISH MOST OF ALL: THAT YOUR HAPPINESS BE YOURS TO KEEP, YOUR SORROWS OURS TO SHARE. I WISH I WERE THERE.

All eyes filled. Even Augustin's.

N'Oncle Joseph knew the man from way back. "He's made a pile of money," I heard him tell Percy Goodwin. "On rumrunners, yes, but also on scallop draggers. One of the best shuckers in the fleet." N'Oncle scanned the reception hall, grinning. "He can afford to give his daughter a wedding."

N'Oncle Joseph wouldn't dance. No way. "That's for young whipper-snappers," he declined, his eyes fixed on Pierre and Louise, who were locked in a sweethearts' embrace, gazing at one another with dancing flames in their eyes. "Young and in passion," he mused. "*Des jeunes réchauffés.*"

Tante Rosalie's wink accompanied her flirtatious chuckle. "I like to think we have some bit of life left in us." She urged N'Oncle to ask Mam' to dance, but he knew better than to disturb my pensive mother.

If there was a time when Mam' had danced, she no longer had an ear for music. Her days were now filled with aimless tunes and her face bore fatigue from too many accusations. And there were more when we got home. Dad barely gave her time to hang up her coat. "Who did you come home with?"

Drained by the big event, she half-heartedly muttered, "Why wouldn't we come home with Joseph? We left with him."

"Who was there?" he wanted to know.

I rolled my eyes at the loose question. "All of Clare. Far easier that you ask who wasn't there. Only Estelle."

Mam' stiffened. "I noticed!"

I let her in on a little confidence. "Basil and Charlotte said that she didn't want to go, that she's been so darned irritable lately."

I could tell what Mam' was thinking, that Estelle felt remorse, resulting from the row that had finished our friendship. Maybe, though I doubted it. Estelle didn't want to go to school anymore either, and that had nothing to do with the row.

I shouldn't have gloated over Augustin's Lincoln. It only served as fuel for Dad to begin raving about his money and his annoyance with Mam' for not cooperating with him. I tried to distract him by describing Louise's dress and cape. I told him about Louise's mother's dress, which caused him to stare at the yellow suit Mam' was wearing, a lovely outfit with matching hat, but one of which Tante Marceline had grown tired.

"You could have had the nicest dress there," he growled at Mam', "but you're too damned stubborn." Utterly disgusted, my father shook his head. "What a darn shame, married to a rich man and you don't even know it."

What a darn shame that Mam' was too tired to listen to that. She opened the hall door to escape to her bedroom. But there was more. Not the usual goodnight, instead an order that emanated from deep within Dad's throat, meaning that she had best carry it out. "Tomorrow, I want you to go straight to the bank and get my money!"

Chapter 32

By the dark circles under her eyes and her dishevelled hair, I could tell Mam' hadn't slept. She closed the hall door for a private call, ran a comb through her hair, got Joel dressed, and asked if I wanted to come. She knew exactly where she was going. Not to the bank. I knew that.

We borrowed Pierre's car and headed towards Meteghan. When we arrived at Docteur Theriault's office, my mother pressed the secretary, "I need to talk to the doctor."

With small talk, he urged her in. He rambled on about a new Canadian flag, flown for the first time on Parliament Hill. "Don't you just love the maple leaf?" he asked, but what did Mam' know about a new flag.

She helped herself to a chair. "I came to see you about Antoine. He's getting worse. Much worse."

Docteur Theriault was a short man, even when sitting up straight in his chair. His slow drawl minimized this serious matter. "You've mentioned before that Antoine thinks he's rich."

Mam' hardened her tone. "Yes, but before he was only rich when he was drunk. Now he's rich when he's sober, all the time." She shrugged. "I don't know what to do. It's not just that he won't work; he doesn't want me to work either. You see," she began, her eyes hopeful, "people tell me that if you'd sign a form saying that Antoine's unfit for work, then maybe I could get a pension. His jealousy and that foolishness about money can't be normal."

She cited a few of the scandalous falsehoods that my father had spread in the village, at which the doctor lowered his brows. "And where does all this money supposedly come from?"

My mother could only sigh at the absolute nonsense. "For bringing up Zoé. He claims she's Eddie Pockshaw's daughter."

"You mean he thinks Zoé's ..."

"Eddie Pockshaw's," she grinned, uncomfortably, as did he at the sheer absurdity.

"You see, Martine, it's not all that simple. You would need signatures from two doctors." He raised his head apologetically, tidying papers as he spoke. "Myself, from what I've known of the man, I couldn't sign that there's something wrong with him. If I did, I'd be lying." He relaxed his tone. "However, there's a psychiatrist who comes to Digby twice a month ..."

"Forget it!" Mam' blurted, point-blank. "Antoine would never agree to that. He says that I'm the crazy one, not him." She paused. Her voice became plaintive, "You can't take my word?" She shot a glance my way. "Or Zoé's? She's heard him enough. Antoine is sly," she hastened to add. "Sober, he doesn't talk his foolishness to just anyone. *C'ain fou rusé.*"

Sheepishly, the doctor stared, as she picked up the papers that Joel had crumpled and dropped to the floor. "About Sophie ..." he said, and she leaned back.

"Sophie?"

"Yes," he continued, "I'm concerned about her; we may have to put her in the hospital."

Mam' knew of Grand-mère's black gangrenous toe, of her bluish stovepipe leg starved of blood. And she had heard of people who had first one and then the other leg cut off due to poor circulation. These sufferers of severe diabetes had all died shortly after the procedures. Her face turned white. "The hospital? To cut off her leg?"

Docteur Theriault glanced through the top part of his bifocals. "I didn't say that. The specialist will decide."

Astounded, my mother stood up and backed away from her chair to move towards the door. "About Antoine. Maybe you could check his blood pressure and make him talk."

The doctor merely grinned. "He and I talk every time I drop by; I was there just weeks ago, and he's never as much as whispered one word out of line."

Mam' fumbled for the doorknob, painstakingly holding her respect for the family doctor who had always served us well. "I'll tell Joseph about Sophie."

Driving home, her defeated expression gave way to a silly grin that frightened me. "Well, Zoé," she attempted to joke, "I guess we're gonna have to stop at the bank and get his money, hein?" Then her expression turned bitter, her words directed against the doctor. "A psychiatrist in Digby. And exactly how does he expect me to move a two hundred pound man who never leaves his rocking chair?" Her hopes extinguished, her dark eyes sunk further in their sockets. "At least a pension would have kept us together."

Her despair shattered my conviction that if Jesus had raised Lazarus from the dead, then surely he could heal a deluded rich man. Regardless of the many times Père Lucien had attacked bitterness as nothing better than fuel for hatred, I rode home with the same bitterness that ate away at Mam'.

We stopped at N'Oncle Joseph's and there was none of the usual chit-chat with Tante Rosalie. Mam' simply repeated what the doctor had said, her tone brusque, our leaving hasty. When we arrived home, she cleaned and she scrubbed, and it was well into the afternoon before she relaxed her frown.

Pierre arrived at the house swinging a five-gallon can which he slammed on the table. He talked about one fisherman whose catch had been lost when crates of lobster were left out in the cold and wind.

"Are yours okay?" Mam' asked.

He grinned. "They're in barrels of salt water aboard the boat, doing perfectly fine. Do these look dead to you?"

The lid on our large pot popped up and down as struggling claws banged against the sides. Mam's face registered relief. Pierre turned to her, "Lobsters left in a breeze, especially in this cold, suffocate because their gills dry up." He pressed the lid down, then flopped in an easy chair, exhausted and lulled by the heat of the stove. He had barely rested his head when Louise popped in.

No greeting for anyone, just a humourless tease from the new bride. "Wouldn't you sleep better in your bed? Someone's at the house looking for you."

Pierre coaxed himself up and shuffled towards the door as if his rubber boots weighed a ton. "Well, I suppose."

Shortly after his departure, N'Oncle Joseph arrived, letting in another stream of frigid air that didn't help Grand-mère's miserable cold. Dad could poke at the stove all he wanted, nothing could have snuffed the chill that my uncle brought with him. He had serious talk, and he had evasive talk. "The doctor wants to put you in the hospital," he informed Grand-mère, "to regulate your blood pressure."

My grandmother merely raised her frail arm, pointing to the window sill, "I have pills for that."

"But it's too high, dangerous for a stroke," N'Oncle pressed, as he reminded her of Grand-père Dominique's plight.

This didn't abate her suspicion. "Docteur Theriault didn't say a thing about my pressure." She was too sick, too feverish to argue, except to order my father. "Help me to my room."

The next day, she wouldn't leave her bed. Nor the day after that. Nor for the rest of the week. The doctor came and warned her, "You have to get up, or you'll never clear those lungs." Neither would the bottle of cough medicine that he left on her bureau.

With alarm on her face, she stared. "My sore is not going away." The doctor dabbed the gangrenous toe with ointment, to no avail.

He left and I rearranged the things on her bureau, with cheerful reminders that would surely get her up—Sylvain coming in the spring, the lupins that early summer would bring—but her head remained sunken in the feather pillow. She said that everything was wrong; the most upsetting ailment was that she couldn't see well anymore, having fallen victim to cataracts.

"Her breathing is full of gurgles," Mam' fretted over the phone. "Like a rattling," she further explained, and the doctor arrived with his stethoscope. Grand-mère complained of a pain in her chest. Pneumonia, he feared. The penicillin he left proved far too late against a stubborn lung infection. My father couldn't face up to the obvious. He hid in the attic or in Dominique's shed, until Grand-mère asked for him. Then he fled to the woods.

She weakened and became reduced to soft murmurs and

congested breathing. With fatigue etched on his face, N'Oncle Joseph kept faithful vigils by her bedside, but he became exhausted, jumping off his chair at the least sound.

By the time Tante Marceline made it home, he was disoriented. When Grand-mère asked for Nicholas, N'Oncle looked up at Marceline in a daze. "Nicholas? Who's that?"

"Your father," Tante reminded him, and they both took to giggling. She chased him from the room and claimed for herself the rattan chair, dozing off periodically herself. One evening she fell into a deep sleep. I was fussing with hand creams when Tante woke up. "Where am I?" she asked, then looked around the room, first glancing at me, then at her mother's eyes, which were wide open and fixed.

"Mam'! What is it? What do you see?"

"Louis," Grand-mère responded, her voice perfectly clear, her eyes a dreamy blue. Her entire face beamed in a blissful smile for Louis, the son who had never returned from war and was now paying a visit to his dying mother.

"God's blessing," my elated N'Oncle Joseph claimed. His mother died with her Louis, probably clad in a soldier's uniform standing beside her, and with the sweet name Nicholas on her lips. She could finally claim her place next to him, in the Wedgeport cemetery.

My Grand-mère wouldn't have been smiling in her coffin if she had known that her precious creams and hair-tinting kit had taken a ride down the cliff, and that her ribbons and knee bindings had gone up in flames. I salvaged her brooches for Thérèse to play with, and I strictly warned Tante Marceline, "Grand-mère gave me a quilt, the one that her mother made."

But Tante kept on burning things. "Junk," she said, and Sylvain's letters turned to ashes. I could well imagine the shock on his face when he visited his Tillie and fell upon Grand-mère's tombstone, or if he heard about her passing simply by chance. Perhaps he'd read the obituary in *Le P'tit Courrier*.

"It just doesn't seem right," I told Mam', but she said to mind my own business.

"Tante Marceline's really changed since her last heart attack," she told me. I found out just how much after she'd left. When I checked Grand-mère's cedar chest, my quilt was gone. No amount of sobbing could convince Mam' to write a letter. "We're not gonna cause trouble for a lousy quilt," she reasoned. "It should have been hers anyway."

My father was too unhappy to help me. His grief was at times pronounced, dulling his blue eyes; other times, it was not evident at all. He'd walk over to Grand-mère's bedroom door and then turn around, looking totally lost. He took up strumming on his dusty guitar, and before long had begun to pester Mam' again about his money. When she returned to the Diner he continued to fling abuses at her, so that when spring arrived, her usual surge of enthusiasm passed her by. She didn't bleach her sheets. Rather, she ignored spring cleaning, and instead sorted through clothes in the attic, setting some aside in cardboard boxes. She was up there almost every day, muttering to pieces of clothing: "Would Joel need this? Does this still fit Thérèse?" She unpacked and repacked, driving herself crazy. "I don't know how much I can bring on the train."

She was going to Boston, supposedly. Pricille had written that Nanny should be there for the first grandchild.

Going for the rest of her life, I judged, by the boxes packed in the attic.

But first, Mam' had a disturbing issue to settle. "Back in January," she divulged, "Philippe sent a money order to buy you glasses."

"Glasses!" I exclaimed, and my eyes filled, causing her expression to turn sheepish. "I spent the money."

She glanced up. "How could we go to Pierre's wedding and not bring a gift?" Before descending the attic stairs, she paused, the apology difficult to make. "No matter what," she said, and she could barely look at me, "I was wrong to use that money. Before I leave, I'll make an appointment."

But I forgot about the glasses. Pricille had her baby, two weeks early.

"The cutest little girl in the whole world," my sister reported over the phone, then followed up with a picture in the mail. Agatha had slanted eyes set above swollen cheeks, a flat nose that enlarged her nostrils, shapeless lips, a large head, and she was practically bald, except for a bit of blond fuzz. Clearly, the infant had inherited her American father's looks. Mam' showed the baby picture to Zita and, for once, the gossip was tactful with my mother.

"She has a nice forehead."

To Pricille's great disappointment, Mam' didn't go to Boston. She spent a lot of time in her pew after Mass, praying to her *Bon Djeu*, or kneeling before the grotto, praying to Our Lady of Lourdes. Her sudden moods of irritability made it difficult to approach her. She growled when I mentioned that it cost fifty cents for my impending school bus trip to Grand Pré, "They must think that money grows on trees!"

I told her that William had been chosen as the tour guide, and she rolled her eyes mockingly. "I'm sure there's a lot to explain and see—a couple of cows in the fields. Why him?"

"Because he knows everything about Acadian stuff," I told her. "Someday, he wants to study history at Dalhousie."

She put on a nicer face, "Aaah. Now you know where Babette will end up."

She talked about a trip much farther and costlier than Grand Pré, a short vacation in Toronto with the two small ones. My face paled as she callously tried to soften the blow. "Summer's not an eternity! Perhaps Antoine will open his eyes and start thinking. You'll come to the presbytery with me," she ordered. I didn't say a word.

Mam' needed to talk to Père Lucien. I listened as they conversed about trivia, and then Mam' used the same preamble as she had used for Docteur Theriault. "I came to see you about Antoine. He's getting worse. Much worse."

"I know what's going on in my parish," the kind priest assured my mother. Though he did not profess to be an expert, he had some training in psychology, enough to recognize my father's symptoms. "My Tante Suzanne also had delusions," he confided, "that she was a famous singer." He lowered his bushy brows, as he dared jest, "Not a bad delusion, if she could have sung past a monotone screech."

Mam's stone face quickly wiped away his jovial grin. "My guess is that Antoine started having responsibilities too young—bringing up a family."

"True," Mam' acknowledged, but with the firm reminder that her life, too, had been hard. "At thirteen, I had to quit school to look after my mother who was bedridden with a kidney disease." She told the priest how her mother used to cry in bed because she couldn't do her housework. Now I knew the roots of Mam's sickness for cleanliness. She came to the point. "Everyone had a hard life back then."

"*Oué*, Martine," the priest nodded, pausing before he added, "but for some people, building sand castles is child's play, while for others, it's an insurmountable task."

I began to understand how my father's boyhood plight, reduced to begging with a tiny pail, may have helped to destroy his mind.

Mam' continued. "I've tried working. I went to see Docteur Theriault for a pension." She glanced my way. "You can ask Zoé."

The priest rested a sympathetic hand on her shoulder. "You're a good woman, Martine. Heaven has a place for you."

"But on earth I have children to feed," she said impatiently, surrendering with a hand gesture. "I can't see that I can stay here."

"Where would you go?"

"Toronto," she replied. "Philippe's written me."

"Martine," the pensive priest began, and then he paused, contemplating the difficult compromise, "my job is to save marriages, not to break them." His gaze met hers, "But you have to do what is right and, in this case, it's to look after your children."

Mam' rose from her chair, the weight of the horrible decision now removed from her shoulders. With pride in her face, she looked Père Lucien in the eye. "And that's what I plan to do, look after my children." She thanked the priest profusely.

I would always remember their parting words to one another.

"I don't know any other way," Mam' said.

The priest shrugged his own shoulders, fetched his holy water, and blessed us out the door. "Neither do I Martine. May God forgive me."

Chapter 33

The eye doctor used the term "myopia" for my shortsightedness. He defined astigmatism. "The cornea is 'a little out of round,' so to speak. Doors may be curved for a few days." He juggled a number of possible lens combinations, scribbling a high minus prescription, twenty/sixty. "What you can see at sixty feet, she can only see at twenty," he explained to my mother, hurling an accusatory stare. "It is time your girl got glasses. How in the world could she function at school?"

"Quite well," I thought fit to answer. "I was good at squinting and not telling."

"I'd say," he muttered, his face just a putrid breath away from mine as he stared into my eyeballs, blinding me with his tiny flashlight. "You don't want large frames," he cautioned, "or the lenses will be too thick."

I examined his meagre selection and chose the least ugly pair which arrived in the mail, just in time.

"Can you see the wharf?" Mam' wanted to know.

I gazed far across the ocean. "Yes," I determined, "the one in Yarmouth—and I can see a fly on a crow." I bubbled over with excitement. "Now I'll really enjoy my bus trip!"

It was an immaculately clear, sunshiny day, and I could see a mile of lush green fields before me. The month was May, the start of the Annapolis Valley Apple Blossom Festival. Finally, our class trip to Grand Pré.

William made it perfectly clear, having to talk above the noise: "In one day, we can't possibly do all of the Evangeline Trail, which starts in Yarmouth and ends in Mount Uniacke."

The bus had barely left the school grounds in Meteghan River when Babette's eyes became fixed on him.

It was too early in the morning for Estelle. Nose glued to the window, she yawned irritably. I had noticed her dimples, lost in chubbier cheeks, and the floppy white blouse, a radical change from the skin-tight sweaters. Her long, beautiful locks were tied back in a dishevelled ponytail. I couldn't stop staring at her, and so I missed the spiel about Comeau Seafoods in Saulnierville and whatever William said about Comeauville. I asked Babette, "Do you find Estelle looks different?"

She shot a glance across the aisle. "No, she looks the same, like she can't stand me."

French villages stretched out, one after the other, quaint with their large wooden houses, many of them flying the Acadian tricolour flag. I counted the houses with sun parlours. William talked about Little Brook and its mink ranches, soon pointing out the towering steepled church in Church Point. "The tallest and largest wooden one in North America," he announced, but my attention was now on the massive edifice next to it, Collège Sainte-Anne. *Aâh les collegiâns.*

We passed through Grosses Coques, known for its big clams, and Belliveau Cove, where the tides of the Baie Sainte-Marie are among the highest in the world. William explained, "Because the Bay of Fundy is shaped like a funnel, billions of cubic feet of water are squeezed through a narrow space, forcing the water to rise very high when the tide comes in, and to recede very low as the tide goes out." There were other reasons having to do with the timing of the tides and the moon's and sun's tug on the ocean, but I was far too chatty to care.

"Mind if I ask you a stupid question?" I leaned over to whisper.

Babette grinned, "Not at all! You mean I haven't already told you everything?"

She had had her first period at age nine. She had first felt butterflies for William in Soeur Clothilda's class. And she had gotten her first kiss in the crammed top of the lighthouse, nothing too thrilling. William was too nervous, though he had been all hands on the second date.

Babette was grinning. "What is your question?"

"It's about falling asleep on my arm and cutting off circula-tion," I explained. "My fingers feel rubbery and fat, and if I pinch them, there's no feeling. Is that what your polio leg is like?"

The lighthouse girl let out a chuckle. "My leg is not paralysed. If you pinch it, you'll surely hear me." She paused. "It's just shorter. Is it that noticeable?"

"Oh no!" I assured her; my friend had greatly perfected her walk. I had another stupid question. "If you had kids, could they have short legs?"

Her olive green eyes widened. "My mother's blind, and I can see. But," she added, most determined, "I do plan to have a houseful of kids and find out for myself."

We missed the highlights of Saint Bernard and Weymouth, as she told me all about her polio, which was caught by a virus, not inherited. She was three years old when she became afflicted, five years old when she moved from Argyle and, yes, she had hated the Cape because no one would play with her. "But I know it wasn't your fault," she clarified. "Estelle never liked me."

Shamefully, I met her gaze, the moment opportune to confess. "You're very forgiving," I told her. "It wasn't all Estelle, I have to say. I found you slower than molasses."

"But molasses usually sticks," she jested back, the hurt on her face stabbing my conscience, causing tears to come to my eyes.

"I ignored your friendship for a long time," I apologized, "but today I hope we can start fresh." I opened my locket, and a smile beamed on Babette's face. A tiny picture of her had found a permanent niche next to mine.

The bus pulled up in front of the Scallop Diner in Digby, but we were too emotional to eat. We had too many things to talk about.

Estelle ordered French fries and stared at them, as if she were going to be sick. William rambled on about the Digby scallop fleet, one of the largest in the world, and she leaned back in her seat. "Who cares?"

Our tour guide had a rowdy bunch of girls who were downright unruly when they got back on the bus and then passed through

Cornwallis. They hooted and hawed and yelled at the handsome recruits, attired in crisp navy blues and shiny boots, precise and cute in their naval salutes. I stole my fill at Greenwood, gawking at the older men in their Air Force blue, tall, dark, and thick-chested ones, though none nearly as handsome as my Cedric of the army. In his last letter, he had just gotten rid of the drabby green uniform of a long winter in favour of a summer tan uniform.

Estelle slept through the military hunks, almost missing the breathtaking apple blossoms. We had entered Wolfville when she lifted her pale face, leaning her head against the window. She wouldn't descend from the bus at Blomidon Lookoff, the best view of the Annapolis Valley and Minas Basin.

"Are you okay?" I tarried behind to ask, as she wiped droplets of sweat from her brow. "I hate the Valley," she groaned. "It's always so suffocatingly hot."

"Sure beats the fog," I said, trying to make conversation.

She simply rested her head. "I don't care about anything."

How could she not care about Grand Pré, the climax of our trip! William positioned everyone in front of Evangeline, Longfellow's fictional heroine. "This is where she and her fellow Acadians gathered the night before they were exiled," he told us. "For those of you who haven't read the poem *Evangeline*, it's a must. You will *live* the Deportation of 1755."

If I had been the tour guide, I would have simply described the Expulsion of the Acadians as a time when the English threw the French off their lands. William referred to it as a complicated dispute involving religion, politics, Indians, an international fight for land between English-speaking Protestants and French-speaking Catholics. Husbands and wives and children were boarded on ships and exiled, separated from one another, like Evangeline was separated from her betrothed Gabriel. Sweet Evangeline. She spent the remainder of her life searching the New England states, and at last, when she was old, found her dying Gabriel at an almshouse in Philadelphia. William recited Longfellow's words about her tireless search:

> *Within her heart was his image, clothed in the beauty of love*
> *and youth, as last she beheld him, only more beautiful made by*

his deathlike silence and absence.

"Do not confuse fiction with reality," Babette later warned me on the way home, as if she had been through a series of love affairs. "It would be so easy to pine for someone you barely know. That is why many silly dreams are born in courting days, when the Gabriel is so sweet and perfect. Evangeline remembered him from then." My friend apologetically smiled. "I don't mean to be cynical."

"Cynical?" I frowned, and she explained. "Don't go thinking that all love affairs end up like that of your parents. Your mother was a very strong woman, and would have survived if ..."

"My father hadn't been crazy," I concluded, turning my face to the window to watch the green fields go by. My parents' life together was over.

The bus pulled into Annapolis Royal, and William took us back to Samuel de Champlain and his fellow French colonists who arrived in 1604, braving hardships and struggles, laying claim to land for those who would follow.

I returned home exhausted, but headed straight to Dominique's shed to sit next to my father on the lobster trap. I couldn't recount the story fast enough. "I saw the most beautiful flowers! Far more beautiful than any in Charlotte's backyard, or those at the funeral home; fields and fields of orchards, more than you can ever imagine." I stopped to take a breath. "Somewhere outside of Wolfville, we drove up a side road, and there were miles and miles of trees, tons and tons of blossoms, like it was snowing in May, filling the air with perfume! That's what the flowers in Paradise look like, I just know it." I stopped short, suddenly realizing, "You've seen those trees! Full of apples that you peddled door to door in the Valley. The trees must have been beautiful then, too."

My father kept hacking at a block of wood, and when it became too small, he found another, and he hacked some more. I told him about Estelle's miserable trip, but he didn't even raise his head. Fine then. I would shock him. "I think she's going to have a baby!"

Head bent to the wood chips, he kept on whittling, expressionless. I wasn't sure if he had heard a word I said.

He had heard Mam's words, though, that she was going away. He had seen the cardboard boxes, proving her dead serious.

"You're crazy not to get my money," he pleaded, but as time hurried by, he faded into thinking spells, his focus distant. He stopped telling his rat stories to Thérèse and Joel, a cruel detachment since they both cried for their story at night, wanting to sit on the arms of his rocking chair. I rooted through the attic and found their winter coats, mittens, and boots all neatly packed by Mam'. Just going for the summer? I dug out my reversible skirt, and I cried as I squeezed it into one of the boxes. Someday, it would fit Thérèse.

As if to preserve the past she'd take with her, Mam' reminisced about the carefree first ten years of her marriage. She spoke about a handsome lad in polished white shoes and cuffed grey trousers.

Again, I asked her, "Do you ever think of Philippe Delaney?"

And again, she assured me, "I married the man I loved."

She grew pensive, started scrubbing and dusting everything in sight. School finally over, she thought she might show me how to bake bread, but when she beheld the *sacré* mess of flour all over her clean floor, she shooed me away from her kitchen.

"Then I'll learn from Zita!" I lashed, and my outburst threw her into a teary silence. That night, while watching TV, she took puffs off my father's cigarettes, an old habit long abandoned. She paid a visit to Zita and came back looking as if she had been crying.

"Leaving is very hard," she confided, but as the time grew alarmingly close, a peace settled on her face. It was a decision with no turning back. The night before she left, it was barely nine-thirty when she started guarding the clock for a fair time to steal away. At ten, she opened the hall door and cast a brief look at my father, but he was hypnotized by the TV. He stayed fixed to his chair until the station signed off, then proceeded up the stairs to bed, where he fell into coughing bouts. His congested breathing worried me.

Thérèse woke up and started crying, the horrible thought of leaving now vivid. "You're gonna miss me," she sobbed. "This bed will be too lonely." Like a little old lady, she raised her head, had the solution. "Maybe I could leave my doll."

I thought about the plastic feet and hands gouging me in the back all night. "I'll miss you to madness," I could vouch, "but I think you better take Sissy with you."

I fell into a fitful sleep long after Thérèse, waking up to screams from the kitchen below. It was Thérèse yelling—likely Joel was pulling her hair. This was the day. I sat up in bed. Where was my father? I hastened downstairs to find the teapot empty, as he had left it the night before. His tobacco was gone.

"Dad's not here!" I told Mam', but she had already delved into the pressing chore of scrubbing Joel shiny behind the ears, licking her finger to tame his silky curls. She was obsessed with curls, wrapping bunches of Thérèse's hair around her finger and letting the beautiful ringlets spring back. At seven, my sister found the ringlets far too babyish, but Mam' was determined with her comb, ripping through stubborn snarls and ending with a head of long, hanging curls.

N'Oncle Joseph arrived, and she showed him the boxes in the attic. She passed the comb through her own hair, which was knotted in a tight permanent wave.

"All set?" N'Oncle grinned, after she had given her kitchen a final inspection, the top of her stove a final polish. She draped her coat over her arm and grabbed her purse.

A knot tightened in my stomach as I opened the hall door. "André! Hurry. They're leaving,"

He came down the attic stairs carrying a clumsy brown suitcase, which he lugged outside to N'Oncle's Joseph's car. Mam' seated the two children in the back seat, and then stood on Grand-mère's lupin bank, gazing first towards the wharf, at the small draggers on the horizon, and then at the woods. She took in a deep breath of salty air, as her eyes traced the houses dotting the Cape road, pausing at the house across from ours. Driven by the challenge of reaping nicer flowers than Charlotte's, Zita was forever working the soil in her yard. The gossip had gotten wind that Estelle was expecting a baby in October, and she knew that there had been a powwow down the hill. Paul-Emile was forbidden to set foot on Basil's property, five months too late. Mam' would surely miss Zita.

"Look after your father," she said. My gaze lit on Thérèse's and

Joel's innocent faces, bursting with excitement. They were going on the big train.

"Be good to your brother," I urged Thérèse, and she turned her head to Joel, swinging a head full of ringlets and screaming. He was pulling the eyes from her doll. Once Sissy was moved to the window, Thérèse divulged the electrifying news that she had almost forgotten to tell me.

"In the big stores in Toronto," she gasped, "there are 'skel-lators,' like our attic steps, but they move! Philippe says it's a rig for lazy people."

I grinned at my sweet Thérèse, looked over at Joel, who was so divinely cute in his short-sleeved white shirt and little bowtie. And then, I stared at Mam'. "There's a lemon pie in the pantry," she said. She reminded me there were beans soaking in the shed— as if I knew how to bake beans. I caught the lie as her voice trembled, "It's only for the summer. Before you know it, we'll be back."

Blinking tears from my own eyes, I nodded. She searched the treeline, a last long look before she again pleaded. "Look after your father."

I backed away, no longer able to look at her. "I'll look after Dad," I promised, and she climbed into N'Oncle Joseph's car, turned around to wave at me. I waited until the car had cleared the driveway, then fell into a deluge of tears as I ran to the lupin bank. I waved back, until I could no longer see my mother's face.

O Martine. Sweet Martine. Fool of innocent hearts,
To have deceived yourself from the very start.
Antoine was never yours, could never be,
Fool of innocent hearts,
Why could you not see?

Could you not have known from his first embrace,
That a dull stare flawed his demented eyes?
That offending blemishes lay naked in his restless heart?
That seasons of crazed delusions would come to be?
That perpetual ecstasy was but a girlish fantasy?

Even the Heavens would mock the fabled illusion,
Of a Martine fed from a paradisiacal dream,
Fallen in lust, for beautiful blue eyes,
Cuffed grey trousers and polished white shoes.
The white-candy peppermints, masking the scent of
drunken jealousies, fermenting to later molest the soul.
His love had no rhythm. His love had no rhyme.
Short was the passion, ravaged and uprooted with time.

O Martine. Sweet Martine. Fool of shattered dreams,
And yet, you've always professed your love for him,
That all seasons have a reason,
May God bless you, and keep you well my dear mother,
And yes, yes I will look after my father.

Chapter 34

Arriving too late for good-byes, Babette was apologetic. I reassured her, "It's okay. Really. Mam' understood, and I hugged the kids for you."

She sat beside me on the lupin bank and allowed me a good cry. "It really hurts, doesn't it," she spoke compassionately, as she supported my limp head on her shoulder. "I want to know your deepest, darkest thoughts. Right now," she stressed, "and don't leave one thing out."

Looking fixedly towards the ocean, I thought hard, wanting to word the truth just right for my best friend. "Right now," I reflected, "I feel as if I've just been tossed into high seas, suddenly master-in-charge of a ship, but left with no compass for direction, no landmarks for guidance. There's no trace of any log book, not even a lousy oar to help propel me to shore." I looked up at Babette. "But I *am* master of my destiny. I am Martine's daughter. By the crackie, I'm a survivor!"

"Go on," urged Babette. But the strength in my voice faltered. "I feel like an orphan, cast in a storm of swift currents and left to perish, … unless I can chart my own course, through the thick haze that's fogging my vision."

Babette stared with such translucent green eyes. "Zoé! You're a poet! Hanging around my father suits you well."

"But do you understand?" I asked, and she grinned.

"I think so. Sounds to me like you're both excited and horror-struck right now."

I absorbed the warmth of her smile. "You know Babette, with you as my best friend, no matter how difficult the voyage, I *will* make it to port."

"And after that," my best friend concluded, tears glistening in her eyes, "there won't be an ocean you can't navigate. You want me to go into the house with you?" she asked, though she already knew my answer.

"I need to do this alone."

A grin trembled on her lips. "I feel so helpless."

"Believe me," I could vouch, "before the journey's over, I'll have called on you many, many times. Just not this time."

With a laboured limp, she proceeded down the hill, stopping repeatedly to look back, hoping, no doubt, that I would call her back.

No greater challenge had I known than walking into that empty house. Matriarch of a diminished household, I felt overwhelmed, chilled to the bone. I walked through the shed, into the kitchen, and everywhere I stumbled upon disturbing traces of my loved ones: there was Mam's sweater left hanging on a nail behind the stove; here, tiny whistles, carved for a two-year-old; there, white, plastic shoes that fit a walking doll; and on the window sill, my wooden ox, so terribly indented with Joel's teeth marks that my father figured it now belonged to the child. I stood it on the shelf above Dad's dilapidated couch. The shine from the stove reminded me that the stove was now mine, to have and to hold, forever polished. To cook? I couldn't boil an egg, but perhaps Zita would teach me how, in exchange for some gossip.

Already, changes were needed. There was a brand new bed in Grand-mère's room. I shoved the door open, all set to rearrange what would become my father's bedroom. I moved the bureau and found a red hair ribbon. Lucky to have dodged Tante Marceline's clean sweep, it had fallen behind the bureau, a keepsake come to renew my mourning. I picked up the ribbon, let myself fall on Grand-mère's bed, and I cried—for the scent of hand creams, for more colours of lost pretty ribbons, for the vanity of brooches, for my Grand-mère Sophie. How I now wished to feel her old hand in mine. I cried for my mother and for my younger siblings. Nearing the window, I saw my father emerging from the fields. He would be famished. I dried my face, ran to the phone, and dialled across the road. "Quick! How do I make a corned beef hash?"

Of course, Zita had to mix her opinion with the corned beef and potatoes. "Just fry everything together. You're pretty stupid if you can't make a hash!"

I assembled the ingredients, dropped two bags into the teapot, boiled the water until it turned rusty, and waited for my father, who had probably detoured into Dominique's shed. Finally, he staggered in. Because his eyes often teared and burned and itched from too much TV, I couldn't tell if he had been crying.

"You must be hungry," I said, and he found his place at the table. His stare circled the deserted kitchen.

"Yes, I am." I dumped some dried-up hash on a plate that I tossed before him. "Where's André?" he wanted to know.

I rolled my eyes. "Where do you think? In the cliffs or at the wharf."

It seemed such an onerous task for Dad to simply dig his fork into the hash, each bite followed by a gulp of water.

"Is it salty?" I asked.

He raised his solemn head. "A bit dry. Did you put in any butter?"

"Was I supposed to?" I asked.

There was a slight pause, the kindest of grins on his weary face. "Some people do."

"I've decided to drink tea!" I announced, and he gazed at the fancy orange cups, plucked from Grand-mère's "good dishes" collection. The handles were far too dainty for his fat fingers, but he would manage for this time. He stared, anxious to witness my first mouthful, which soaked for a couple of long seconds before I mustered the courage to swallow. I made a few grimaces, but the flavour improved with each determined swallow, so that by the time I gulped the last few sips, my father had gained a tea-drinking partner.

Our hearts far too fragile, we spoke not a word about Mam' and the children, at least not intentionally. Dad called me Martine a few times and, when the kitchen door opened, he perked up, but then his face fell. It was Pierre, dropping off the fish he had fixed aboard the boat and a fifty dollar bill, which he snuck into my hand, embarrassed to have to warn, "Don't tell Louise."

He left and I countered the monotonous ticking of the clock with the clatter of dishes, already growling about the disgusting strands of tobacco all over the table. I swept the floor and told my father of my intention to take over Mam's job at the Diner. As I stood at the window, a fantastic idea materialized. I pointed to a small parcel of land across the driveway. "We need a garden! Right there!" I exclaimed, "and we can sit here and watch it grow. We could start with fast stuff like lettuce and Swiss chard, and maybe next year, add potatoes and carrots." Like anyone in a state of depression, my father didn't comment. I'd purchase seeds at Fred à Bill and we'd plant them together. I'd learn how to cook.

I thanked the Lord for Zita's suggestions over the phone, for I was starting to recoil at the sight of fish. I would soon grow gills if I didn't learn how to vary the menu.

"The trick is to get your grease sizzling hot," she cautioned, as I attempted potato pancakes. André stuffed himself with the golden brown creations, but he wasn't at all impressed with Sunday's roast chicken. He had to tear the meat off the bones, and he would have become quite irate if my father hadn't cooled his temper.

"Nobody's forcing you to eat it. *Un houmme se soutte.*"

My angry brother stormed out of the house, and I stared at the rubbery meat on my plate. "I cooked it for an hour and a half. Wasn't that enough?"

My father raised his white head, affording me another of his patient grins. "Martine cooked them all morning."

I tried not to nag too much, emphasizing only the most grievous points. "Clean that tobacco off the table, and stop wiping the floor with your stocking feet!" (Did I sound too much like Mam'?) I caught him wiping his sore eyes and hurled at him another yell, "Not with the dishcloth! Where are all the hankies?" I growled, until I found them glued together in his pants pockets, overdue for next wash. What a dreadful, *Moses de job!*

I hated to disturb Dad from "Sinbad the Sailor" and "Gumby," his Saturday morning connection to the kids, but he could darn well get off his chair and fill the washer. He helped pull the heavier clothes through the wringer and he emptied the huge rinsing tub. I was still at the washer. The dirty water nearly all drained, I passed my hand over the metal filter, but instead of grabbing the usual lint, I lifted a lumpy mass of mucus, the remnants of his dirty hankies!

If the man wanted to nauseate me out of the house, he was off to a good start. First thing every morning, he opened the outside door and pressed down on his nostrils to dislodge the insides of his nose. What if someone had emerged in the line of fire? And what made him think that he no longer needed to change his underwear? I burned one pair and then I laid down the law, "From now on, you change every Saturday!"

Shaving was not a problem—he could hardly stand a day-old beard. He sloshed water all over his face, wet his hair back, and that was a bath, leaving intact the dirt in the creases of his neck and the grime in his hair. "Look at your pillowcase!" I growled, but the oily nest didn't bother him. I gave him a fresh "*souzzi*" dried in country air and he grunted as he buried his nose in the clean pillowcase, emerging from his pillow with a contented smile. Dad appreciated cleanliness, he just didn't mind dirt.

He walked barefoot between the rows of his small garden, then came back in the house leaving a trail of dirt on my clean floor. But the garden and the tasks that I delegated absorbed his loneliness and occupied his time. Once I landed a job at the Diner, I warned him, "If I'm to work, you're to help with the housework."

"Yes, yes, yes," he agreed, all encouraged.

Poorly organized for my first day of work, I left the house in a frenzy. "Maybe you could wash the floor. And don't forget to throw out the leftover fish," I emphasized. Once outside, I tapped on the window, reminding him again, "Don't forget the fish!"

"Yes, yes, yes," he said, but I knew his ways.

With fish on my mind, I served tables all night, staggering back to the house very late and very tired. I was quickly awakened, sickened, when I opened the kitchen door and beheld my baseboards, splattered a grimy grey from splashes off the long-haired mop. Such a massive floor and he had not changed the water, streaking it dirtier than before.

"Go to bed," he coaxed.

But I knew I wouldn't sleep, not until I got on my knees and cleaned up the mess. I cried over my pail of suds, muttering as I scoured the baseboards. "By the crackie, things will have to change."

"You're too darn fussy," growled Zita the next morning, when I told her how late I had gone to bed. She watched me parade around the kitchen, duster and broom always in hand. She had seen the fields beyond my house, punctuated by the blinding white of freshly bleached bedsheets.

"You're Martine's daughter," she rebuked. "Happiness for your mother was measured by how clean her house was." She glared at the shine on my stove. "And I can see that you've inherited the same sickness. A clean house will be your obsession, too."

Head bent drowsily over my dishpan, I yawned from sheer exhaustion. "Yes, I suppose it will. Too bad my father couldn't catch a dose of the same sickness."

A hot spell drew a putrid smell from the far pantry. I witnessed the ultimate of his insouciant ways. I was used to finding spiders crawling in the pots in those old cupboards, but here was a fermenting mass of leftover fish, teeming with maggots. I emptied and rinsed the cast-iron pot, then lugged it across the road. With one heck of a temper brewing, I shoved it under Zita's nose. "How can I clean this stinking pot?"

She quickly drew back, "Not even with Javex. Throw the darn thing down the cliff."

"Sure," I said, swinging my arms wildly as I crossed the road home. "And buy another one with what?"

"This has got to change!" I raged at my father. "If not, I'm moving in with Pierre, and I mean it! *God Zounce, faut ça change.*" Having acquired Philippe's and Mam's tempers, I raged on about his being too lazy to simply flush the *Moses de fish* down the toilet. Then I pointed to Grand-mère's bedroom. "You're sleeping in there from now on, because that couch is going to the dump."

From the look on Dad's face, I knew that Grand-mère's bed could very well stay in her room, with the door shut tight. He escaped further wicked nagging by fleeing to his small garden. As a grey mist enveloped the vegetables, a melancholy entered his eyes. Mam' hadn't written him.

Tired of the relentless fog lingering at the windows, I became dreadfully lonely myself, though I was careful not to cry, lest I depress him even more. However, it happened that during one meal I finally broke down. There wasn't the least hint that the sun would ever cut though our thick Maritime fog. Weary over the prospect of more swollen doors and windows, I could no longer stand the eerie sound of the wailing foghorn. It drowned the clicking of our forks as my father and I consumed yet another fish dinner. All of a sudden, I dropped my fork and burst out laughing, the kind of belly laugh that eradicates all cares, a hyena's laugh more suited to a lunatic. My father rested his own fork and stared.

"I'm not crazy," I hastened to explain. "Really. It's just so depressing that it's funny." Despairing tears rolled down my cheeks as I contemplated the oddest question, so odd that I hesitated even as I asked it. "What would you do if it got worse than this? Lonelier than this?"

My father took no time to answer. "I have a twelve-gauge shotgun in the attic."

Shotgun! He sure knew how to halt a conversation. I escaped to the attic and stared at the twelve-gauge. My God! What was he saying? If there's a purgatory like the priest said, then I surely passed mine when I went to bed that night. And for many nights after. My father's option was unthinkable. Catholics didn't take their lives, a sure send-off to hell. For long, sweat-filled nights, I tossed and turned in distress, causing Zita to scowl at the dark circles under my eyes.

"You're gonna kill yourself," she cautioned, and she itemized, "cramming schoolwork, coming in late on weekends, scrubbing this house silly, and now this worry that's taken control of your life."

But how to sleep? Zita foolishly advised me to drink strong tea. All night I was up, nearly voided the sea. Warm milk made be shudder, as if fresh from the cow's udder. My bedsheets were nothing but a tangled mess, until I finally came to my senses. Pray! When Tante Rosalie couldn't sleep, she prayed, and it worked. I got down on my knees and pleaded with my Hail Mary to produce a holy letter and to make the fog go away. Though the fog stayed, not one, but two letters arrived! I ran all the way from the post office, bursting through the door utterly elated. "I got a letter from Cedric, too!"

I ripped open Mam's envelope first, every bit as eager as my father for the sweet mention of the names Thérèse and Joel. "They miss the country," I read.

His face lit up. "I knew it! They'll never last."

Philippe had taken them to Niagara Falls and Mam' found the heat unbearable. She had gotten lost on her first trip on the subway, "to big downtown Toronto," I read, keeping from my anxious father that she was now working at Simpson's, in the packaging department. "You should see the size of the store," I read silently. "I eat my lunch in the bathroom, 'cause I'm too shy to eat in the lunchroom."

I grinned, causing my father to get impatient. "What else does she say?"

I read aloud. "Thérèse caught her flip-flops in the escalators, and Joel broke his arm!"

The bad news broke my father's grin, "How?"

"Fell down concrete steps," I read.

A sour displeasure clouded his face. "Those kids are coming home!"

The second letter contained more bad news. Cedric's wasn't coming home in October. "Imagine that!" I stammered. "To tour the West with his friends."

My father merely grinned. He was full of hope, until we received the next news from Toronto.

You don't know how I hate to have to write this, Mam's letter began, and the rest was obvious. They weren't coming home for school, not until Christmas.

"Don't you want to hear the rest?" I called, but Dad had already stepped outside and was now headed towards Dominique's shed. I finished the letter, so overcome by the last paragraph that I threw everything into the stove. "Forget it!" I cried out loud. "I'm not going to Toronto. Not for school. Not ever." I sat at the table and cried, imagining Thérèse. I could still see the expression on her innocent face, believing that she and Sissy would be back. I took my father's twelve-gauge and headed next door. "Take this," I ordered.

Though Pierre welcomed yet another gun, he hesitated.

"Are you sure?"

"He'll never go hunting again," I fervently concluded. "He can hardly make it up a flight of stairs. *Y peut hardlé s'déhauller en haut des escaliers.*"

"What about André?" Pierre queried.

But I had thought of that too. "He's never home long enough to think about hunting."

I bought my father gingersnaps to soak in his tea, but he left them on the back of the stove. He had no more chit-chat for N'Oncle Joseph. Neither Red Skelton nor Jackie Gleason could make him chuckle anymore. He just rocked, each movement of his chair wearing away hopeless time. When an Oldsmobile flashed across the TV screen, he stopped his chair, his tone determined. "I want you to go to the bank and get my money." Then his anger broke loose. "Those kids are coming home, where they belong, in the fresh air! She's unfit," he said of Mam', "and if she doesn't come home, she'll *lose* those kids." He spoke about the smog in Toronto as if it would surely annihilate his family, and he grew irate because I wouldn't go to the bank. But I never mentioned the dirty word "money."

When he talked about Christmas, I refrained from looking at him, in case he should discern the truth in my eyes. They weren't coming home for Christmas. Mam' knew that. I knew that. But my aim was to survive each troubled day, and once Dad grew strong enough, I'd tell him. But not before I got his grin back.

"Once people are old, they don't smile anymore," Tante Rosalie told me. Fifty-one was a far cry from *old*, though ugly streaks did run wild through my father's hair—streaks of a premature "pissy" yellow that would eventually overtake his white head. His nose was rudely spreading across his face, and his cheeks were *beaucoup* caved in, too long deprived of a set of teeth. Particularly prominent were his eyes that appeared possessed. With pants drooping below his heavy paunch, elbows always encrusted with dirt, and the bare soles of his feet hardened to a tough, scaly skin that he scraped with a penknife, I found it increasingly difficult to picture my father with cuffed grey trousers and polished white shoes.

Chapter 35

Grade ten started out with a major problem—André. He didn't open his books. He started skipping school, once, then twice a week, until finally he came home one day and flung his books across the kitchen floor. "I quit!"

The clown wasn't joking, not this time. "Are you out of your mind?" I howled. "What's this, a sickness that you caught off Cedric? One more year to go. You can't quit school!"

Defiantly, he scowled. "Watch me."

I spent costly time on the phone, pleading with Philippe, who couldn't do much from thirteen hundred miles away, except to fret about the terrible mistake. "Stay in school," he lectured my brother, to no avail.

Mam' yelled at me, as if *I* could stop André. She made it perfectly clear that if I entertained similar thoughts, I would find myself in Toronto, real quick. "I'll see to it that you get the things you need," she pressed. I slammed the receiver down, guilty as charged for failing to persuade André. A high school pal of his had just enrolled in an electrician's course, the spark that triggered my brother's sudden departure to Halifax.

This caused the villagers to speculate that he was forced to find work because we had nothing to eat. Zita showed up with a batch of bread. It took precious little time for me to sink my teeth into a steaming end crust.

"Does Antoine eat properly when you're at school?" she inquired.

I almost choked. "Does he look like he's starving, Zita?" I finished chewing and swallowed, grinning at her generosity, "He'll eat even better now."

Babette came by with a banana loaf. I buttered a thick slice, but my father wouldn't touch it. No sireeee. My best friend left and I glared at him. "Why not?"

Shamefaced, he divulged the truth. "I can't eat anything that a blind person makes."

Now there was a perplexing irony if I had ever known one: a man who could have lived in a pig sty, yet, he wouldn't touch the scrumptious loaf drying up in the pantry because it was made by a woman who couldn't see. But he certainly enjoyed Charlotte's molasses cookies, his favourite, to soak in his tea.

Not all visits were from Good Samaritans. Paul-Emile made me nervous, hanging around the woodpile while my father chopped our cords of winter wood. "Seems to me he's awfully friendly these days," I objected loudly, but Dad was clearly enthralled with the black leather jacket, heavily ornamented with chrome studs; the jackknife, which the scoundrel agilely manoeuvred between his fingers, making it flip several times before its flashing blade hit the ground, the knife standing upright; and the Chev Impala!

My father practically drooled, crazy with curiosity. "You need a lot of dough for a rig like that."

With a haughty shake of his head, the snake grinned. "A few dollars. How about a ride?"

Luckily, Dad had a rule: he only climbed in a car if Mam' was driving. Paul-Emile turned to me. "How about you Zoé? Yarmouth in twelve minutes. I did it the other night."

"I'm too young to die," I asserted.

The scoundrel jeered, "I suppose you've heard that I'm engaged."

I took a few steps back towards the house, thunderstruck. "Engaged! Who on earth with?"

"Don't get smart," he shot back. "You know who I've been seeing."

I was good at mimicking his smirk. "All the girls in Clare, from what I've heard. But Renette is the lucky one, is she?"

I entered the house and hid behind the kitchen curtains where I could observe the two at ease. With a leer akin to the devil, Paul-Emile opened the passenger door of his car, stole a glance towards the house, and handed my father a brown envelope. The business deal *accompli,* Paul-Emile left. My father headed towards Dominique's shed and came back to the house empty-handed.

"Why wouldn't you go to Yarmouth?" I probed. "Paul-Emile offered to find you a woman," I rolled my eyes at the kind of dame, "a night on the town."

Hardly in a mood for wisecracks, Dad reached for his tobacco and spoke real sense for a change. "How could I look at another woman, after your mother and I have been through so much?"

He rested his elbows on the table, in serious thought, as he amused his idle hands with cigarette makings, creating two and then measuring them one against the other. He built another two. Now challenged by the differences between the four, he packed a bit more tobacco in one, removed a bit from two, until all four appeared the same size, a task not easily achieved when rolling lumpy tobacco.

"When I met Martine," he said, "she was wearing a sailor suit." The nostalgic memory dated back to the spring of his youth. He turned his head to address me. "Your mother was pretty you know. Didn't always look like a rake."

I had seen pictures. "I know," I readily agreed, struck with a sudden curiosity. "Was Mam' your only girlfriend?"

"One other," he confided, "but she died of a blood disease." Leukemia came to mind. He resumed his cigarette work, thinking in silence before he spoke again, quietly. "No one had ever been with her."

I understood that she was a saintly girl, having resisted temptations of the flesh, which I imagined was far easier done when her days were numbered. "It would be horrible to die young," I said.

The vivid memory of his long ago girlfriend cast an anxious look over my father's face. "Yes," he mused, "but now look at me. I still have to die. At least it's over for her."

"If I'm not mistaken, we all have to die," I reminded him, my attention on his line of white-jacketed tobacco soldiers.

"Are they all the same size?" he asked.

I shook my head, for I knew how he revelled at the challenge of finding the culprit. I spent the rest of the afternoon staring out the window, wondering when I might sneak to Dominique's shed.

My chance finally came when his attention turned to the TV.

The brown envelope was hidden under the lobster trap. My suspicions about it were justified as I slid out the concealed contents. *Playboy!* I had found a similar magazine under Philippe's mattress—another boot in the backside for having snitched.

I riffled through the glossy pages of the magazine and cringed at the come-on smiles of the teasing beauties, the boldest sprawled across the centrefold, a feast for my father's hungry eyes. I had often caught him staring at me, and a strange suspicion gripped me every time I went to the attic. I could hear something, as though someone was peeking through the lath wall in the adjoining attic. Who else but my father? When confined with him in Dominique's shed, I started leaving the latched door open. The supper dishes barely put away, he'd subject us to near darkness in the kitchen, dimming the lights and closing the curtains to the wharf, blocking our best view. His excuse was legitimate, convincing. "Maybe Eddie Pockshaw will come." True, the man was a regular pest. His visits made it hard for me to study.

One evening, my father reached for the light switch, and I was left with the flickering light of the TV to find my way around. "That friggin' Eddie Pockshaw. If he sees light, he may come over."

My attention on a TV documentary, I paid no further attention to him, except to scold, "Close the door!" He never closed the bathroom door. It annoyed, disgusted, and frustrated me.

Stretched out on my stomach, with stocking feet tensely dangling over the foot of the couch, I became oblivious to Dad's prolonged absence. Totally absorbed in the documentary, I watched as mounds of skeletal corpses were bulldozed into a huge pit. As I stared into the horrified face of a Jewish girl the age of our Thérèse, I became aware of a hovering movement behind me. Two giant hands began to caress my back, followed by a whispered endearment, "Let me rub your feet."

My feet! I gave a violent kick and it took me no time to jump off that couch and find the light switch. I stood in a daze. A sickening panic ran through me at the realization that I had just been touched the wrong way. I could only glare at my father. "I'm your daughter!" I lashed, then I tamed my frantic voice. "You ever do that again, and you'll find yourself alone, you hear?" He didn't dare lift his gaze, which was just as well. Right now, he had a face that not even this daughter could love. Luckily, I knew the folly of too many hasty words. The lamb was easily intimidated back to his chair, head bent low as he rocked. He was punished enough.

Another sleepless night. I staggered down the stairs half-awake, joined at the breakfast table by Zita. Early or not, she had important gossip on her mind.

"You'll never guess what Estelle wants to call her baby."

"No," I replied, admittedly with interest.

"Emile," she blurted. "If you can possibly imagine! Basil said that no grandchild of his will be called Emile."

"Then I don't imagine she'll call him Paul either," I said, half-grinning.

"Are you gonna go see the baby?"

"Of course I'm gonna go see the baby," I informed her, "Babette and I. What about the recipe?" I asked, but she had totally forgotten. It took everything to coax me across the road.

She rooted through her cupboards for what seemed like forever. Finally, she passed me her simplest recipe for a birthday cake. "Get a good even heat in your oven," she cautioned.

Profoundly excited, I rushed back home to boast to my father, "Before this day is over, you will taste the best cake in all of Clare. Even better than Mam's."

I had my birthday party all planned, tea and cake for two, with our "good dishes" collection of orange cups and saucers.

Dad's TV was blaring. I had my attention on my mother's baking utensils, meticulously blending each thrice-recited ingredient and vigorously mixing, holding onto the bowl for dear life, when muscular arms suddenly encircled me from behind. A familiar face brushed against mine and I froze, transported into ecstasy. "Cedric!"

There was no lock of hair flopping over his eyes, but a familiar grin animated his face. My soldier boy blew the flour from my face. "I bet you thought I'd miss your birthday."

I wiped my tears. "How in the world ..."

"Did I get in?" he chuckled. "I was already in when you came back from Zita's, hiding behind the stove. Actually," he confessed, "I was home last night, but I didn't see any lights. I almost came ..."

"But this is a much nicer surprise," I interjected, and I lay limp in his arms; it was a wonder I didn't faint. I was glad that my father disappeared to the woodpile, for Cedric had come back an animal, barely able to control his kisses, playfully annoyed with me. "What are these? I leave for ten months and come back to find you with glasses. My mother's smoking a pack a day, she's a bundle of nerves! I'm never going back."

"*Une minute,*" I urged. I poked at the wood in the stove, then tossed my cake into the oven. I had a million and one things to tell Cedric in the privacy of the living room. I started with my best friend Babette and our trip to Grand Pré. I recapped Pierre's wedding and Grand-mère Sophie's death, the intricate details never properly captured in my letters. I told him all about Pricille's Agatha, getting remarkably cuter with every picture, and what I knew about Estelle's baby boy. "Zita says he looks just like his father, and that he's possessed like his father, screeches all the time." Then I added the inconceivable, "Paul-Emile's engaged! With Renette! I hope he marries her and gets the hell off the Cape."

Cedric put on a wicked grin, "You mean there's a girl in Meteghan foolish enough to marry Paul-Emile? How's school?" he asked.

I preferred to elaborate on my father's troubled life, which had become my troubled life. "He's excited about Christmas, and it's driving me mad. Mam' will tell him three days before that she's not coming, and I'll have another mourning hell on my hands. *Un n'auter deuil.*"

The time was right for Cedric to drop his bombshell. "I won't be here either. I'm being stationed to Cyprus." I could see real military duty dancing in my soldier's eyes. "It's what I want," he beamed. "I can't wait."

He slid my hand into his, to check if I was wearing my opal. "I almost brought back a diamond," he grinned, bashfully. "Would you have been upset?"

My tone was stern, "Very."

"Zoé," he began, and I knew that serious thoughts had been brewing. His brown eyes were impassioned, "I want you to be mine. Forever."

"You mean, will I marry you someday?"

He nodded, and I stared back, wide-eyed. "I can't promise you something like that."

"Why?" he asked, but I had no ready answer. There was, of course, the difference in our ages.

"What's three years?" he wanted to know.

"The difference between my restless heart and your settled one."

Already dreaming of a wife and the sound of a son's pitter-patter in a house with a sun parlour, he didn't understand my reasoning, so I tried again. "I haven't even finished high school. A lot can change. I may want to go to university. Babette thinks I should."

"I don't mean to marry you tomorrow," he began, but I cut him off.

"I smell something burning!" I raced to open the oven door and my face fell. The best cake in all of Clare was burned, mountain high on one side and valley flat on the other—a combination of uneven heat and two tablespoons of baking powder, rather than the two teaspoons required. I found a potholder, grabbed the blackened cake, and dashed outside. "*Bon appétit*," I hollered to the cows in the field. I returned to the living room where I resumed my place on the couch, somewhat perturbed. "So much for my birthday cake."

But Cedric's mind was on other things as he studied my face. "Sweet seventeen," he joked, "and never had me." His breath was warm on my face, "I've been stuck ten months in cramped quarters with enlisted studs who had two obsessions, real war and women. Sometimes, any woman."

"Don't get any ideas!" I cautioned, but then I felt my resolve weaken as his lips sought my neck. "I need you Zoé." He looked over to the forbidden threshold leading to the end bedroom, swept me off the couch, and landed next to me on Mam's bed. We talked about the possibility of university. "Go to school the rest of your life if you want," Cedric maintained. "I just want to be the honoured guest at your graduation."

He inhaled deeply and encircled me with trembling arms as he made a serious pronouncement. "I can't go back Zoé, not unless I know you're mine."

I nuzzled my head in his warm neck. "I was here this time, wasn't I?"

"But I want you forever," he clarified. I held back words that would have poisoned the moment, letting him lighten it with a sudden joking concern. "Imagine if your mother were in this house right now, and walked in on us. What would she do?"

"Put it this way," came my quick retort, "I wouldn't have to worry about your getting killed in Cyprus."

"Or your going to university," he added, as he pressed himself closer to me. "I need you Zoé—if not forever, then for now."

A mist of passion filled my eyes as I felt my body respond to his. Tomorrow, the guilt could very well kill me, I knew. I would wake up confused, regretting the *faux pas*, maybe forever. But for now—only seventeen—I blushed to my soldier the last of my innocent smiles.

Chapter 36

Cedric spent his Christmas with scorpions and black widow spiders, in a suffocating one hundred and ten degree heat—and that was at night. His altar boy *savoir-faire* served one happy padre. Somewhere in Cyprus there was a lovely midnight Mass.

Tante Marceline was the angel who saved my Christmas. She arrived with her vivacious laughter and opened wide the door to Grand-mère's room, allowing heat from the stove to thaw the musty smell. She drew the curtains wide open, inviting light to filter through the gloom.

"I'm home for a rest," she said. I grinned to myself, a rest from Uncle John? She had a stack of pictures of Agatha. The child was absolutely adorable, though her features showed no trace of her Acadian heritage. "Her father through and through," Tante said. She proudly added, "He's managing one of our restaurants now, doing very well."

Hmmm. Knowing that Tante Marceline and Uncle John had no children, I wondered who would inherit the lucrative chain of restaurants. Uncle John had only the one blood nephew, and he was married to my sister. Tante had pictures of Pricille's house, referring to the district as middle-class suburban, whatever that meant. The brick two-storey looked pretty high class to me—rich to my father.

Tante wanted to know everything about everybody, starting with Estelle. "I'm surprised she's not here having her cards read."

"Too busy with the little one," I said.

Her hand jerked, spilling tea on the floor. "Little one! She had a baby! *À l'âs ti a-yu un bibi?*" We had some catching up to do.

"Tante Rosalie had a tumour removed from her stomach," I said.

Tante nodded. "Joseph mentioned that when I last called him. Apparently it was the size of a grapefruit!"

I told her about Lina's bad nerves and all the nice things about Cedric, but when she poured the last of her cold tea down the sink, she wrinkled her brow at the tea leaves clustered haphazardly on the side of the cup. "I see a troubled relationship."

Impressed by the clairvoyant revelation, I borrowed her hearty laughter. "If they're King Cole leaves, then they're reading right."

My father was stretched out on the couch, grunting into his pillow, content. It was indeed a pleasure to have Tante Marceline with us.

The next morning had barely dawned when she emerged, bright-eyed, from Grand-mère's bedroom. "Today, I want a tree."

Sleepily poking at the wood in the stove, my father was not ready for Marceline in the black-and-white striped pyjamas as she appeared at the door—a convict. What little hair Tante had was sticking out in misbehaved pincurls, thinly distributed over a bare scalp.

"The ghost of a skeleton," Dad teased.

She took to laughing, covering with her open palm the loose skin and bulging cords in her neck. "I dare say that a skeleton would weigh more." She dug her thin fists into her waist. "Never mind this tradition about rigging the tree on Christmas Eve. That's Martine's style, not mine."

"Yes, yes, yes," my father agreed, having sunken into his chair to savour a smoke, "I'll get you one."

"*We'll* get one," she corrected.

He stopped rocking to glance outside at the knee-deep snow. "You can't tramp in those woods."

Fed up with bad-heart rules, Tante reiterated the doctor's orders, "Need my rest. Shouldn't drink tea. Shouldn't smoke. Can't exert myself. Can't—never mind. What's the sense of living?"

She was allowed pink popcorn and had brought a suitcase full of it. She shoved boxes of the treat in her coat pockets, then turned to my father. "You and I, for old time's sake."

They left the house like two turtles ambling towards the fields. As they disappeared into the thick forest, panic seized me. How would I get an ambulance into those woods?

But they returned, lugging the biggest tree they could find, my father hacking and coughing, my Tante pale and shaky. She had barely entered the kitchen when she hastened to the cupboard for her ginger ale. She rushed to her suitcase into Grand-mère's room. Rye mixed well with ginger ale.

The top of their giant tree was bent against the living-room ceiling, its cumbersome, far-reaching branches better suited for my school gym. Tante was downright reckless with her saw, first slicing away excess branches, then, after getting into more rye and less ginger ale, she brought down even the symmetrical beauties with loud snaps. Who cared if limbs kept falling. She backed away from the tree, wrinkling her nose in a gale of laughter at the awful gaps. "Nothing that garland and tinsel can't fix."

"Garland and tinsel?" I fretted.

Again, she wrinkled her nose, this time in a subdued grin. "Don't you worry, Zoé. Unless Yarmouth's moved, we'll get decorations."

Our living room boasted the best-dressed tree that Eddie Pockshaw had ever seen. Mesmerized by the dazzling lights, he sat on the living room couch and beamed like a child. He knew the rule: welcome anytime, as long as he was sober.

My father was at the kitchen table, examining his Christmas cards and counting his booty. "*Septante, octante, nonante,*" he tallied in Wedgeport twang, hoarding his riches in the black wallet with which he slept. He had ninety dollars.

Pierre arrived and slammed twenty smackeroos on the table. "One hundred and ten!"

"I'm rich!" Dad exploded.

But I cautioned him, "Winter can be long."

Whenever Tante Marceline drank hard stuff, she became emotional. Now she smiled at Pierre. "How about Christmas dinner with us? You and Louise." She spoke the absolute truth, "I'm a first-class cook."

But my brother had a chagrined look, all too common on his face these days. "Louise will want to go with her family."

"I can understand that," Tante grinned back, but I could read the extreme disappointment on her face. She could very well choose another nephew as a favourite—Pierre now belonged to Louise and no one else.

Tante spent time in the frigid attic, poking at loose boards and prying at them with a crowbar. "I'd give a fortune to find out what Dominique did with his money."

How many times had she ransacked that attic? She didn't find a thing, except for a cracked shingle that had slipped between the floor joists. Its rounded shape had served to dry the pelts of skinned muskrats.

"To think that I remember," I mused. "I was barely three years old when a man snapped our picture for a magazine. The table in the shed was covered with pelts."

I had watched my father skin many a "scrat" in Dominique's shed. With a penknife, he'd cut the tail off, and then make a large horizontal slit at the rear end so that the whole pelt slid over the muskrat's head. He then removed the fat deposits from the skin and stretched the pelt, fur inside, onto a rounded shingle. It dried in Grand-mère's attic for no more than three or four days. The general store didn't accept pelts that were too stiff.

"Dad was a good trapper," I praised, though I was more concerned with retrieving something else—a metal box from Grand-mère's cedar chest. It contained my parents' marriage certificate and unpaid doctor bills dating as far back as my deceased baby sister. What interested me were the receipts from the Courthouse in Little Brook. I passed one to Tante, dated July 1934. *Received from Antoine LeBlanc the sum of Three Hundred Dollars.*

"What for?" I asked, and I could tell that I had put her in a tight fix.

She sighed, giving the matter a few moments' reflection. "That's hardly my business to divulge."

I couldn't close the metal box, not until she told me. "I'm not a little girl. I want to know."

Tante pursed her lips. "You have a half brother," she said.

I stared back in shock, then took a few grown-up swallows. "A half brother! My father had an illegitimate child! He had to pay?"

"Rather than go to prison," Tante clarified, cutting short the subject. "Anything else, you ask your father—after I'm gone."

"Fair enough," I promptly agreed, now content to lower the metal box to the bottom of Grand-mère's chest. I folded some blankets over it, staring at Tante before I dropped the lid. I wanted so badly to ask her about my quilt.

André arrived Christmas Eve, with a rundown on his electrician's course and on Halifax—the city of trees. He was living in the North End, handy to Fort Needham where he could see the navy ships in the harbour. In Halifax, there was Citadel Hill, Point Pleasant Park, the Gardens, sailors and more sailors, and Kentucky Fried Chicken! Next visit, André promised us a bucket of the "finger lickin' " stuff advertised on TV.

He was certainly glad to be home, looking forward to a meal from Tante Marceline's cuisine. She roasted a golden turkey that made our mouths water, and prepared dressing that would have surely made Pierre lick his plate clean. It was a Christmas dinner to remember, our humble kitchen blessed with the bubbling spirit of Tante Marceline, who made my father smile more in those three weeks than any other time I could remember. He must have put on twenty pounds.

But he couldn't stomach all her foods. He flatly refused to eat lamb chops. Tante could coax all she wanted. "Lambs are God's pets," he strictly ruled. Fine then. Deni Fournier could keep his lamb, but she gladly accepted his free beef, and she roasted it just as Dad liked it, served with mashed potatoes that he saturated with Carnation milk, cold from the can.

When Tante Marceline left, my father's smiles dwindled to the occasional grin and then he reverted to a blank expression as he ached to see the faces of his children.

"I'm giving Martine until this summer," he decided. "And if she doesn't bring those kids home, then she can expect me in a brand new Cadillac." A hostile anger flickered in his demented eyes. "And if she won't get in that car, then she'll hear from my lawyer."

The mood in our kitchen was eerie, as if darkness had entered an asylum. He talked about having received a rhinestone belt from the Queen. The brown leather belt in his hand had a tarnished buckle and horizontal slits stretched to their limits to accommodate his distended belly. No rhinestones that I could see. I turned away from a foul-smelling sink. "A rhinestone belt from the Queen! I didn't know she was into Country and Western. Why would she give you a rhinestone belt?"

"Because I'm the great Jimmie Rodgers," he said.

I rolled my eyes, annoyed at him and at the stubborn stench in my sink. I sprinkled Bon Ami and scoured, vigorously, until I brought a white shine back from the yellowed enamel. Then I poured in a bit of Javex, which killed the vile smell. I gazed at my father, my patience at its limit. "Somebody's been using my sink for a toilet." When he didn't react, I asked him, point-blank, "Are you pissing in my sink?"

He continued to examine the invisible rhinestones on his belt. "Straight from England," he said.

I flung my cleaning cloth in the washer. "Where's that?"

"Overseas," he was quick to reply. "N'Oncle Joseph was there in the war." He hadn't totally lost his mind.

The great Jimmie Rodgers spent our bone-chilling winter nights plucking on his guitar, paying homage to his idol, though once in a while strumming Jim Reeves' smooth-toned, heartbreaking songs, making us both low-spirited. Often, while I was doing my homework, he'd take Grand-mère's place near the cosy warmth of the stove, and with his penknife, he'd scrape on a turnip, feasting on raw purée, cool and tasty on his gums. Raw potatoes were less tasty and often came out gnawed with fanglike teeth marks. One night, he opened the trapdoor, attuning his ears to the earthen cellar.

"Rats," he determined, and he set off with his box of white powder. Sure enough, before I left for school the next morning, he came up the cellar steps with a smile, dangling a furry culprit by its long, black tail. "This one won't eat any more potatoes." But it was only a matter of nights before the rustling of rats resumed.

Tante Marceline called, and her spooked-out laughter resounded over the wires. "Rats! Well I'll be swoggered!" she exclaimed, one of her unique expressions. "I'd much prefer mice."

"We have those too, squeaking behind walls," I assured her.

She talked about a great Christmas and wished me a happy 1967, crying, as if she had been drinking. "I hope things get better for Antoine."

It was the last time we heard from her. The next call was from Uncle John. The words "massive heart attack" sent chills up my spine. *A l'avait déboullé en faisant les plats. C'était son cheur.*

Pricille called, so terribly upset that I couldn't even ask her about my niece Agatha, or if she knew that we had a half brother. "Boston will never be the same," she wept over the phone line.

"I'll never be able to look at pink popcorn again," I, in turn, sobbed to my sister. "Or tarot cards. Tante's laugh will haunt my sleep for the rest of my life." A vicious headache pounded inside my skull.

"It was her heart," I told my father, but he wasn't any more moved than if I had told him that someone in Timbuktu had died.

"Martine's coming home," he said. "Call my lawyer and tell him that I want my money."

"Do I have a half brother?" I ventured. He kept rocking, so I simply rephrased the question. "Did you have a kid when you were twenty?"

"He was no more mine than the man in the moon," came the answer, as noncommittal as could be. "She didn't know whose it was, so I got framed into paying."

"She?" I asked.

He raised his head, "Call N'Oncle Joseph. He'll drive you to the bank."

That night, I headed down the Cape road. I had to talk to Babette about Tante Marceline, about death in general. The subject intrigued me.

"I think," my friend began, "that all souls go straight to heaven."

"How's that?" I asked.

"Because," she said, "everyone surely repents on their deathbeds."

"Oh," I said. What about the ones who die in a head-on collision and have no time for amends?"

"Never thought about that," she admitted.

I had a theory of my own. "I believe," I told her, "that *after* we die, we enter a limbo state, at which time we can repent—purge our dirty slates. In this limbo state," I speculated, "one gets to either accept or reject God."

Babette's comeback was quick. "Now who in their right mind wouldn't choose heaven once they've seen it?"

I shrugged. "Exactly my point. My way, more will be saved."

"There's just one little snag," she determined. "Sounds like we can live a life of debauchery and everything will be A-OK on the other end."

"That's the part I failed to mention," I grinned. "Some of us will be limping through the pearly gates."

"Some more than others," my sweet Babette joined in. I fell into a *sanglot* of tears, causing her olive green eyes to widen. "Zoé! What's wrong?"

"Everything," I sobbed. "Dad talks about a rhinestone belt, a Cadillac, a lawyer. Money, money, money! And he urinates in my sink. Now *that* drives me crazy! I feel like I'm living in an asylum, going absolutely mad. I can't concentrate at school. Sometimes, I just want to take off. You can understand that, can't you?"

"Anybody could," Babette responded.

"Then you'd understand if I should abandon ship and run away."

She grinned, "Yes, I'd understand, but you wouldn't go far."

"How's that?"

"Because," she reminded me, "only days ago you told me that the ocean would dry up of its fish before you'd leave your father. That tells me your heart is firmly anchored, and this is just a northeast gale. It too shall pass."

"Blessed you are, Babette," I sobbed more softly, all encouraged, "for you shall inherit my deepest darkest secrets."

"And blessed you are Zoé," she retorted, "for you shall inherit tomorrow, a brand new day." My friend's smile had a way of reducing rocky mountains to grains of sand. I dried my tears.

"I have a half brother," I confided. "I found out at Christmas."

Her jaw dropped, "How did that one get past Zita?"

"That's the one thing," I assured her, "that I wish she had known and told me. Imagine, all my life having to listen to Dad accusing Mam'. I can't bloody believe it, the hypocrisy of those raging unfounded jealousies!"

Babette revealed a jealousy of her own then—rather a surprise, coming from such a sensible girl. The foolishness had all started when William had appeared on "Reach for the Top," bringing victory to our Clare team. He had travelled to Halifax with three girls for the television game show. A breakup had almost ensued over that. "Aren't you ever jealous when Cedric is so far away?" she asked, then cringed, as if she had hit me with a ton of bricks.

"Given a choice between jealousy and the guillotine," I assured her, "I'd choose the guillotine."

"But a little jealousy can be good," she said.

I shot her a vile glance. "*All* jealousy is sick. I've seen enough at my house to last me a lifetime."

Jealousy. The mere thought of it drove me to madness. It was not a good time for Babette to broach the subject of diamond rings. Again, I told her, "I didn't want a diamond for Christmas, and I don't want a diamond now—maybe never, certainly not while I'm in school."

"I'm your best friend," she said, "and I'm not sure you mean that. There aren't too many girls around who wouldn't love to flash a diamond, if they truly cared for the guy."

"I *do* care!" I insisted, but Babette's piercing gaze forced me to clarify. "I really care for Cedric, but I want someone who can cry at his own father's funeral."

Her face went blank. "I have no idea what you're talking about."

"I didn't think you would," I snapped.

She limped to the bay window, pressing her nose to the pane. "Are you sure it's not because of your father?"

"My father!" I blasted. "Why would you think that?"

"Because you can't serve two masters at one time, not while one is demented and the other one is in an awful hurry to get married. And you don't have to yell at me. I'm just a few feet away."

I cupped my wicked face in my hands. "My God, what am I doing! You're my best friend in the whole world, for listening, for understanding ..."

"Then tell me about Cedric," she pleaded.

I explained as best I could.

"He's *robuste*, muscular, and determined, which will probably win him medals, and I must admit, all of it first attracted me to him. But I can't stand the 'tough guy' part of him that can't speak about emotions, the part of him that says *hallo* with a bang on the shoulder."

Aaah. Now Babette understood. She picked up Angus, patting his long fur, "Maybe you want a man who's a pussycat inside. Like my William." The image of an intellectual wimp came to mind.

"Most of the time," I confirmed, "Cedric is great—a teddy bear inside that steel-studded chest. But other times, I just don't think we're talking the same language, looking in the same direction."

Babette rolled her eyes at me. "Why didn't you say that in the first place?"

"I didn't think of it," I said, and we both grinned, *point final*.

I could finally pat Angus without feeling he wanted to gouge my eyes out. I brought him to the bay window. "It's getting late," I observed.

"Dad will drive you home. I'll go ask him, right now."

"No, no," I insisted. "Don't bother him." I left Babette and ran, ran, ran, down the lighthouse road, up the steep hill, arriving home with a heavy pounding in my chest, "Dad, go to bed! I mean, what are you doing up?"

I could tell by his furtive look that he had something to tell me. He waited until I had hung my coat behind the stove. "There's someone in the end bedroom. Jehovah's Witnesses."

I halted. "Jehovah's Witnesses! More than one?"

"Two," he confirmed, and I noticed the pamphlet on the table, rebuking our wicked world. "What did they try to convince you of this time?"

"That I shouldn't smoke," he said.

I threw up my hands in disgust. "Then they'll be here forever! Next time, put them in Grand-mère's room."

Such a cold night—my bed in the attic was freezing, unfriendly, and full of Thérèse's ghostly jabbering to her doll. How I missed the chatterbox. If only she were with me, I'd never again tell her to be quiet, or that I hated her Sissy in our bed. I longed for my sister's warm feet on my legs.

I tossed and turned, but a cosy position was difficult to come by with so many things on my mind. I raised my head off the pillow. I could have sworn that I had heard the hall door and footsteps up the attic stairs. Now I recognized a tall shadow.

"You're not sleeping up here!" I said, using my meanest voice. Quickly, I reached for the string dangling from the light bulb. "What are you doing here?"

As quietly as he had climbed the stairs, my father descended them.

A cosy niche was now impossible to find. What if the Jehovah's Witnesses ... no, surely not. If they refrained from smoking and from anything harmful to the body, then surely they wouldn't harass a poor girl freezing in her bed. What if Cedric knew that Jehovah's Witnesses were in my house? He would have simply grinned and wished them a good night's sleep. All the same God, he would say of all religions. Mam', though, would have surely shown them the door. We were Catholics!

Peace to the Jehovah's Witnesses. Peace to Thérèse with her doll. Peace to the Greek and Turkish Cypriots. Peace to my Cedric, was the pleasant thought that finally closed my eyes.

Chapter 37

Every spring radiates some sunshine. In my house, it transformed wintry stares into smiles and brought hope for two impatient souls that a letter would arrive or the phone would ring.

"We're all coming home," Mam' confirmed, and I could feel the earth thaw beneath my feet. "For the whole summer? What about Pricille? Have you heard from her?"

"Pricille too," she attested.

My exclamation stole the conversation. "We get to see Agatha!"

Mam' asked about Dad and I assured her, "He'll be doing just fine, once I deliver the good news." I hung up and then it dawned on me. She had never mentioned Pricille's husband.

I charged through the attic with Lysol, mercilessly crushing the flies that hadn't built up enough metabolism to escape Zoé LeBlanc. Those that lay dormant on the window sill, I drowned in my lethal suds. I swept the dustballs from under the beds and dismantled the cobwebs that had survived the last clean-up. There were quilts to air, sheets to launder, my father's yellowed shirt and dark blue suit to burn, or hurl down the cliff. He looked panicked. "You're getting a new suit," I promised.

Mam' was coming home in her new Honda Civic. They'd be going to Yarmouth.

If ever there was a store that closed the gap between the comfortable and the poor, it was Frenchy's. The second-hand "boutique" brought dignity to those in tatters. A certain fellow in my class at school had traditionally worn one pair of jeans and the same shirt until Christmas. Then Santa would bring him a change of clothes which he wore until June. The shamefaced boy discovered Frenchy's and started walking into class with brand-name shirts and pressed trousers *à la grand style*. He applied soap, spruced his looks, and it wasn't long before the handsome dude was seen in Yarmouth, arm-in-arm with a girlfriend. *La fille d'un fish plant owner.*

N'Oncle Joseph was only too delighted to drive me to Frenchy's. He helped me dig through the crammed bins, surfacing with an extra large white shirt, brand-spanking new. He examined the size and grinned his approval. Then he rattled the hangers along the men's clothing wall until he spotted a dark green suit with a ripped seam on the inside right leg of the trousers. Again, he grinned. "Rosalie's sewing machine will fix that in two seconds."

Nothing could quite have equalled the smile on Dad's face when we returned home. The Sheik of Araby modelled his new suit, admiring himself up and down.

"How much?" he asked.

N'Oncle kept him in suspense until it was time to leave. "Two dollars, including the shirt."

"Martine *et moi*," my father eagerly planned, "we'll park on Main Street and watch the goings-on." He talked about Joel, who would now be big enough to watch him whittle in Dominique's shed, and he sized up the shelf above his couch. "Thérèse must be as tall as that shelf by now."

They had been gone only a year, but it seemed like a lifetime. Dad had planted three rows of peas for them, and when he wasn't weeding his small garden, he was sitting at the window, watching it grow. When the sun got hotter, he covered the roof of Dominique's shed with cod, flattened to dry. Everyone would be ravenous for dried fish and all the fresh fish that Pierre could land at the wharf.

"I find it hard to review for exams," I told Zita. "I'm too excited."

She was anxious herself, working her front yard to coax the prettiest flowers for Mam' to praise.

"Cedric coming home?" she questioned.

Deep disappointment came over my face. "He's only got four days leave."

I left her yard and ran up the hill to catch up with Babette and William. "You guys going to the post office? Wait for me!" I had been itching to question William. "Cedric's going to Beirut on leave. Isn't that in the Middle East, where they're fighting all the time?"

"You mean like in Cyprus?" The history and geography buff produced a friendly grin. "There's no fighting in Beirut," he assured me, "and I can think of plenty of reasons why the whole world loves to go there."

Arms bare, Babette shivered in the cold mist rolling in from the ocean. "Name me one reason," she demanded, "why Cedric would rather go to Beirut than come home to Zoé."

William wrapped her in his skimpy jacket. "For a start," he joked, "there's never any fog there, and I wish there wasn't any here. It freezes my little darling. *La brume, ma belle p'tite Babette, c'est bain trop frette.*"

His little darling blushed. "Give me another reason," she probed, as he rubbed her arms vigorously.

"It's a beautiful city of friendly people, at the foot of the Lebanon Mountains—for those who like mountains. It's on the Mediterranean," he added, scowling at the frigid Atlantic, "for those of us who fear frostbite when we go swimming. And," he concluded, "for those of us who like history, there's an American university."

"Forget it!" Babette retorted. "Dalhousie will do just fine."

Dalhousie! I couldn't think past high school, dreading the Provincial Exams as if they were an evil rarely survived. Blessed with a brain of the gifted, William could afford the cockiness. "For those of us who know our stuff, sleep comes easy."

Babette gave him a little slap on the side of the head. "Yeah, well for those of us burdened with problems, sleep doesn't come at all." She knew that I had had a rough year.

Zita dropped off a loaf of her delicious bread. "I know you have to study," she acknowledged, but then she sat down and told me all about Estelle's baby cutting yet another tooth. It made me smile, but I wasn't interested to learn that Estelle had hemorrhoids. I now knew to hide my father's box of suppositories, lest the whole Cape learn about his. The gossip mentioned that Percy Goodwin had been walking up the Cape road and that Paul-Emile's car had almost sideswiped him, missing Babette's terrorized father by a mere few inches.

I fumed, "Can't wait for the maniac to marry. Then he can drive his car the hell off the Cape!"

"He's not getting married," Zita had found out. "Sleeping Beauty has finally woken up."

"Renette has called it off?"

She nodded and I had never felt so relieved—the girl had come to her senses. However, the garden snake (as Zita called Paul-Emile) would still be around.

The exams arrived, and I worked myself into such a frenzy that my father was barely allowed to roll cigarettes. It bothered me if he hummed, rattled the teapot, plucked on his guitar, or left the bathroom door open. The TV was down to a whisper. I warned him, "Unless you're dying, don't talk to me."

I studied late into the night, and when I went to bed, my brain was a live wire, even in my sleep. It fed me garbled data from the fat scribblers I had memorized—chemistry symbols and algebraic solutions that didn't make any sense and woke me up in a frenzy. I would surely fail math.

"Relax," Babette assured me, having spent productive hours as my tutor. "You'll pass."

I spent two weeks in agony, but when the postmaster passed me a white envelope, a surge of adrenaline shot through my veins as I ripped it open, held my breath, then hurled the marks in the air. "I passed! Babette said I would!"

I ran home to tell my father, who was as excited as I was—not that numbers meant anything to him—seventy-three in algebra, seventy-six in geometry, in the other subjects I scored low eighties. "First in her class," he told Basil, who arrived to check out his garden and to chat.

The next time I saw Estelle struggling up the hill, I dropped the bunch of Swiss chard in my hand and ran to her carriage. Her Gabriel was squawking, not the least enthralled by the birds chirping overhead or the beauty of our *paysage* under a clear, blue sky. The nine-month-old started screeching, delirious for his rubber soother. Estelle had to yell over his bellowing. "Just a small tantrum!" She found the soother and popped it into his mouth.

I told her about Mam' and the crew coming home, and a mother's pride overtook her face. "I must come and show them the baby. I'm going back to school in September," she announced, friendly. "My mother's gonna look after this little rascal, if she can handle him." Estelle was back to wearing tight sweaters. She invited me to her house. "Paul-Emile's not allowed anywhere near this baby," she made clear. She paused, "I was crazy to believe his lies. You tried hard enough to warn me." I recognized an apology when I heard one.

Her dimples were set in a genuine smile when she asked about Cedric and Babette. Though having a baby had hurried on some maturity, the smirk was all too familiar. "So, I heard that you were first in your class."

"Dad got the story mixed up," I grinned, "but I did quite well."

"Do come to the house," she urged, stressing once more, "you don't have to worry about Paul-Emile."

I merely stared back at her, remembering the wound that would never heal. She continued her walk and I ran back to the garden, intent on correcting Dad. "I wasn't first in my class— William was. I came nowhere near." My father kept weeding his carrots.

He had yearned for his children, yet, when they arrived, he watched from a distance as car doors burst open and they ran straight to the garden. Philippe and André fell into immediate chit-chat. An aspiring electrician and a promising electrical engineer had plenty to talk about, until Pierre arrived, and Philippe wanted to know everything about his sixty-footer in the works. Philippe's eyes were as expressive as ever. "Six hundred thousand dollars! Almost takes a rich man."

Pierre put on a haughty grin. "Takes a good bank."

My father didn't quite know what to make of our lively three-year-old. Joel had curls, curls, and more curls, and the child was never still long enough to watch Dad whittle. My sister's springy ringlets had given way to long, wavy hair. She was indeed as tall as the shelf in the kitchen. It took some time before the two stole up to the arms of the rocking chair, exchanging quick glances at first, as if my father were a total stranger. But Thérèse soon unwound, the chatterbox stipulating, "We want a story, but not about rats."

Dad could relate to the muskrats living along the marshy river banks. "One day," he began, "I spotted one with the nicest brown fur, shiny, thick, and long—the kind that the store paid big money for."

"What does a muskrat look like?" Thérèse queried.

He exaggerated a ridiculous length between his open hands. "This big, with a long tail trailing behind. Like a rat," he said—a terrible *faux pas*.

No matter how hard he tried to embellish the prized muskrat that he had caught in his snare, my sister was resolved. "Philippe tells nicer stories."

My father tried to lure Agatha to his chair, but the toddler had more interesting business on her mind—to eat the tobacco that she had snatched from the window sill. When that proved foul-tasting, she moved on to Pricille's periwinkles, making weird faces before she spat them out. She kept Mam' busy, picking up after her, and wet-mopping the floor every night to keep her frilly dresses clean. Pricille was too busy stuffing her face with dulse, which she dipped into vinegar and chewed and chewed, occasionally stopping to swallow and suck in a breath. Pierre arrived with cod heads, and she ordered pork fat and turnip to complement the feast, eating until she bloated. *A l'â manqué s'fare quervé.*

"I can see that Boston hasn't taken the Acadian out of Pricille," N'Oncle Joseph was glad to notice.

My big sister was as pretty as ever, her jet-black hair still coiffed in a teenage ponytail, but she flaunted Boston's latest fashions, spoke about closets full of shoes and clothes, and even owned a mink coat, bought in New York!

"Did you see any nice churches in New York?" Mam' was anxious to learn.

"None," my sister divulged. I had a sneaking suspicion she hadn't seen any in Boston either. She hardly ever mentioned her husband, except to remark that he worked day and night, and that she didn't think he'd like rappie pie. I didn't think he'd like us either.

N'Oncle Joseph teased Pricille about her Agatha. "Our little

American," he jested, though with a serious edge to his voice when the little one spit out a bit of fish. "Get her used to our food now, or she'll grow up turning her nose."

He and my father lured the child outside to where the grass was short, ticklish on tiny feet.

"Leave her shoes on," Pricille scolded.

But my father's grin was laden with mischief. "Babies love to wiggle their toes." He could watch the child for hours, mesmerized by the duck waddle, her small hands, and the dainty heels of her bare feet. Thérèse and Joel ate peas from the garden, frolicked around Agatha and hid her shoes in the tall grass, forcing my father to go find them.

Mam' watched from the window.

"Come see my garden," Dad entered the house to coax, but her obsession was not on vacation. He had to content himself with her usual behaviour—scrubbing everything in sight.

"Is Toronto bigger than Yarmouth?" he asked, and she turned from her shiny stove with a half grin. "Good Lord! Yarmouth would fit in one of its post offices."

She looked terrific, with her face filled in, false teeth that fit, a decent haircut, and an air of confidence that came from "*se débrouiller*" in Toronto. My father couldn't stop staring at her. However, one morning I came down the stairs and found him in his rocking chair, unable to lift his gaze from the floor. Mam' was her usual fussy self, though very talkative, having rested her *torchon* to chat with Pierre, who had banged at the door far too early. A few days later, I nabbed Mam' in the attic, needing to talk about the loneliness that had aged my father's face.

What else could she say? "How I wish things were different. Maybe someday ..." She paused, then inhaled deeply. "The kids won't always be small."

"Do you still love Dad?" I asked. She tilted her head back, rather shocked at the question. She sheepishly grinned. "Remember the other morning when Pierre was in the kitchen?"

Oué, I thought back. "What did he want so early?"

"Just to chat," she replied, then timidly lowered her gaze to the clothes she was sorting. "Your father and I were in Grand-mère's bedroom."

"And Pierre came in to chat!" I exclaimed. "Of all the rotten luck!"

I was silent for a moment, as I contemplated a more difficult question. "Do I have a half brother?"

Mam's face paled in annoyance. "Who told you?"

"Tante Marceline."

She wrinkled her brow. "Now why in God's name would Tante …"

"Because I found some receipts," I interjected. "But Dad said the kid wasn't his. *Another* one not his."

She grinned at my sarcasm. "He said that?"

I nodded and his denial made her smile. "Well if it wasn't his," she retorted, "he sure had *something* to do with it. I've never seen a kid look more like his father. Even the hand gestures."

"Why didn't you tell us?" I rebuked. "All those accusations from him and you never said a word!" I felt annoyed. "I think I'll apply to the Vatican to get you canonized."

She averted her gaze. "For the sake of the boy. His mother had threatened to send him to his grandmother's if he was ever caught talking to us. He knew who his father was. Sometimes, he biked the Cape road and he'd slow down when he passed our house." She paused. "I often wondered what would have been worse—to be sent away to New Brunswick, or to have to watch you guys playing outside and never able to play with you."

I couldn't, no matter how hard I tried, remember a strange boy on the Cape. "Where is he now," I asked, not quite prepared for her shocking answer.

"In New Brunswick. When he got older, he turned against his mother and ended up with his grandmother after all."

"Can we ever see him?" I asked.

Her tone was unyielding. "No. Not as long as Antoine is alive. You may not understand."

"Only too well," I assured her. "You have enough on your plate."

My mother reminisced about when her kids were small—the time one of us got into her chocolate pudding in the pantry and arrived in the kitchen with face plastered in chocolate. I could visualize it—Dad in his rocking chair, grinning from ear to ear, and Mam' frantically rooting for a facecloth.

She talked about the less happy times—when I had performed my own tonsillectomy with our TV antenna—and about the humiliating times—when some neighbour (Zita, she figured) had left boxes of groceries on our doorstep. "It wasn't always easy to cope," she said, and the grim alternative made me shudder. I knew of kids who had ended up in foster homes, to be used as barn hands, wanted only for the monthly allowance they furnished.

"However you did it," I reassured my mother, "you kept us together—a gift we can never repay."

Her gaze met mine, "You were always one to understand, Zoé. You should become one of those doctors ..."

"A psychologist?" I blurted. "Forget it! I'm not so good when it comes to figuring out my own head." Cedric came to mind.

"About my half brother," I changed the subject, "didn't Zita know?"

With all due respect for her friend, Mam' relaxed her grin. "Sure she did. She can control her tongue when it's necessary."

"The only time she ever did," I marvelled.

The dreaded day of Mam's leaving drew near, and Dad once more withdrew into his money fantasy.

"I'm Henry Ford," he said at the table, and Pricille shrugged her shoulders, frowning, as if she had forgotten that her father was rich.

"You have to go to the bank," he urged, but Mam' deflected his chatter.

"Henry Ford better buy some soap and clean around his ears."

Still angry that she had mocked him, when I next approached her, my voice was laden with hostility. "Dad has emphysema," I informed her. I touched on his bronchial problems of the past winter and revealed that he had come close to pneumonia.

"You never mentioned that when I called," she said.

My stare was wicked. "I didn't think it was important."

The cheap shot irritated her. "What kind of a dig is that?" she glared. "Just in case you think it's fun bringing up two kids in

Toronto, I have news for you. In fact, I *did* catch pneumonia, and I went to work for two weeks dragging my feet, doubled over in pain struggling to breathe. It's not a picnic—far from it."

"Well you should try living here!" I snapped.

She had a quick retort. "I have!" She asked if I wanted to move to Toronto.

"Never!" I said, and I escaped to Dominique's shed to cry—tired, confused, but determined. I wasn't going to Toronto.

The day Mam' left, words were so painful and the remorse so intense that even hand gestures were difficult. "Write to Dad," was all I could muster, as I scanned the fields leading to the woods.

Thérèse cried from watching Mam' and me. Joel banged on the car window with a toy gun. Pricille wept softly, her attention given over to a busy Agatha and the anxieties of her own trip back on the plane. Philippe was trying to fit too many suitcases and a cooler of fish into the very small car trunk, sobbing all the while. I hated his good-byes; they always ripped through the soul. He was crying when he left, and he cried all the way back to Toronto, according to Mam'.

Chapter 38

Grim-faced and weary, I stood at the window, contemplating the withered remains of my father's garden; much of it had perished under Joel's and Thérèse's tramping feet. Clumps of split pods marked the spots where the two of them had stripped the peas and feasted. I glanced down the Cape road. Charlotte's garden was no longer captivating to the eye; its flowers were wilted and hanging, waiting for the bitter frost.

The season's gone, I reflected, and when the season's gone, it's time to look forward to the next.

But for my father, the end of the summer left a chill. Mam' would never be back for good. Autumn days came and went, and so did he, sometimes attuned to this world, sometimes not. We played cards at night. He talked about Agatha, remembering the miracle of tiny hands and feet, but then in the next breath, he rebuked, "Don't you ever look at Estelle and think she has the life, stuck in the house looking after a kid."

I glanced up. "What do you mean?"

He picked up his playing cards. "There'll be plenty of time for a baby carriage. *Enjoy ta jeunesse.*"

"But someday I'm going to have two little girls," I told him, "one who looks like Pricille and the other like Thérèse. Now don't get me wrong," I continued, "if one, or both, end up looking like Grand-père LeBlanc, with blue eyes and thick, wavy hair, then that's fine with me. Except I want my girls to have tiny noses."

Dad checked for trump, grinning at my crystal clear future. "I'll be long gone by the time you have children."

"But you just said to take my time!" I retorted. He slapped

down the five of diamonds, which, of course, ate my jack.

The nighthawk was tired; he didn't want to play Auction Forty-five anymore and didn't want to know anything about my plans for two little girls. A little snooze on the couch would suit him just fine.

In the evenings, Dad would drink tea, watch TV, and, of late, audition for the Grand Ole Opry. I awoke intermittently to the concerts of the great Jimmie Rodgers, not at all entertaining on a school night. Finally, I stomped into the kitchen, slamming the hall door behind me. Gleaming with legendary fame in his rocking chair, Dad produced the most innocent smile. "I'm wearing this to the Grand Ole Opry. They tell me that's the place for rhinestones."

I glared at the *Moses de* brown belt that I had yet to burn, and I stammered, "Aren't you going to bed!"

"I'm gonna find me a woman," he said. I raised my head in surprise. "You don't think I can find me a woman, do you?"

A woman! "Well, euh, certainly not on the Cape. Can we talk about this tomorrow?"

I made sure Paul-Emile stayed far away from the woodpile, and that Zita minded her own business.

"Your father's not thinking right," she called from across the road. "I dropped off some bread, and he started to talk about a woman—and he didn't mean your mother. I tell you, he's not well."

A venom frothed in my saliva. "Neither are you! Repeating what he says to Emma Goodwin. *Botherer d'répéter d'la beurdasserie coumme çâ.*" Her jaw dropped, and I could read the look. How had I found out? "Babette's my best friend!" I yelled towards her shocked face, "or did you think she wouldn't tell me?" I dug my fists into my waist. "Now if you ever gossip anything like that again, I'm gonna get on the phone and tell the whole Cape, maybe all of Clare, nasty things about you."

"What could you say about me?" she asked indignantly.

I could feel my flushed ears on fire. "Oh I'll think of a story. And then I'll stretch it three miles. Isn't that what *you* do?" She backed off, clearly shaken.

We didn't talk for two weeks. My father missed her bread. I apologized, but only because N'Oncle Joseph asked me to. Every

Saturday, he dropped by the house. Since the great Jimmie Rodgers was often exhausted and snoozed away the visits, my uncle talked to me. This usually meant war stories and complaints about his rheumatism. Considering his handsome deameanour, he had, I felt, a premature fear of aging.

"You know you're getting old when you start regretting all the women you missed out on," he jokingly blurted, then turned to the window as if his tongue had betrayed his thoughts. I could only deduce that there were tempting beauties in Europe during the war, though I had never seen anyone quite as stunning as Tante Rosalie. In her youth, she was even prettier than the Judy Garland of the thirties.

"Pictures lie," Tante cautioned, whenever I admired her then "movie star" face. "Look at me now," she'd say. My aunt was so beautifully humble. She baked us pies and cakes, and got N'Oncle to call Docteur Theriault every time my father caught even a simple cold.

One of these developed into a wicked flu. N'Oncle's face became lined with worry. "When Antoine refuses a smoke, it's more than the flu."

The doctor arrived with his stethoscope and listened to the rattle in Dad's chest. "Bronchitis," he confirmed, and he meant business as he pointed a finger in my father's face. "You must stay inside." I gaped at the vial of caterpillar-long pills that he left on the table.

"Will he be OK?" Mam' agonized during our phone conversation. I assured her that I would nurse my father back to his whittling shed, which I did. I received a follow-up letter and was overjoyed to discover its contents. "She sent us money!"

But Dad just kept staring out the window. "I don't think Pierre will go out today. *Quite-a breeze.*" He hardly ever asked about Thérèse and Joel anymore. But he did ask about Cedric.

My darling came home at Christmas to bring up the subject of diamonds once again and to scowl at my mid-term grade eleven marks.

"Nothing to write Mam' about," I readily admitted, but he was in no mood for wishy-washy attitudes. "You can't sleep, can't study, and you barely passed!"

"But I *did* pass."

"Sure," he growled, with a concern better kept to himself. "Your father's too much for you to handle, Zoé."

I hurled him one nasty look, "My biggest complaint used to be that you didn't talk enough. Now that you do, I hate what you say."

Strolling down the Cape road later, he reopened the issue, and I halted to an angry standstill. "I'm fine with my father, and that's where I'm gonna stay! Now stop saying that he's the reason for my marks, or the cause of my not wanting a diamond. You're the cause, hounding me to death!"

Cedric picked up a stick and, braving a grin, tapped me on the head to jest, "In Cyprus, we have these clubs called 'puppy pounders' to keep the wild dogs from jumping into our jeeps. Now if that temper of yours gets any worse, ..." he retreated a few paces, "I'll have to bring one home."

As he talked about American, British, and Canadian acquaintances, I asked, "Is it strict in those compounds?"

"Like a prison," he confirmed, "with curfews that drive me goddamned crazy. Because of the war. It'll be so hard to go back," the dispirited soldier confided, too long frustrated at his gun lying idle. "This peacekeeping is for the birds."

He turned to the subject of his mother's bad nerves, how she had pleaded for him to ask for a transfer, closer to home. He halted. "Maybe I'll ask for Germany. What about Oromocto, New Brunswick! Close enough?"

I shrugged, indifferent.

Surely he sensed the troubled heart that accompanied my lack of enthusiasm. It was a very quiet trip back to the airport. Luckily, his mother's nervous jabber cut through the tension of good-byes.

"Flight 829 boarding in fifteen minutes," a voice over the loudspeaker intoned.

I shoved him to the end of the line. "Go on! You don't want to miss your plane."

Cedric couldn't help but grin. "The only plane on the runway, and I'm forty minutes early."

His mother broke down in his arms, robbing me of a proper

good-bye. I could have been nicer about the transfer, but my mind was consumed with worries about my father.

"I'll buy you an ox," Dad still bargained, whenever he wanted tea poured into his cup, a turnip from the cellar, his plaid shirt from off the hook, or tobacco. Damn tobacco! Each package was meant to finish off my ox—was more apt to finish off his lungs. Some mornings he coughed incessantly, so that I had to light the fire. He would be up all night, then sleep all day. When I came home from school I had to prepare kindling for the next morning and worry about kerosene and newspaper, but I never had to search for matches. He always had those.

Come Lent, I told him, "You're supposed to make sacrifices. If you could unglue yourself from your couch and help me, it would be a good start."

"And go to church," Tante Rosalie scolded.

He grinned, "Yes, yes, yes." But he snoozed away the forty days of Lent, and when she arrived at Easter to sermonize about the Passion of Christ, he rocked in his chair, humming Hank Snow tunes.

Cedric called, breaking his good news over a static-charged line. "I'm in Germany!"

Was I studying hard?

"Very much so," I assured him.

How was my father doing?

"Absolutely great," I replied, hastening to add, "he's planning a small garden."

But come May, the seeds stayed in the pantry. I had to study and review for exams.

Philippe called to express his utmost relief over my June marks. "I knew you could do it!" he rejoiced. He was chagrined to have to report, "We're not coming home this summer. Mam' landed a new job—manageress in a cafeteria—and I'm taking extra courses. I'll write and explain." He, too, had exciting news, "Arlene and I are engaged; getting married next summer, after I graduate."

"Married!" I howled, and I kicked open the hall door. But there was no spark in my father's eyes—not anymore.

I had plans of my own. "In September, I'm taking a secretarial course," I said, cutting short my brother's good news.

"Secretarial course! Why not grade twelve? You may want to go to university someday."

"And so, someday I may," I replied, but there was a long silence on the other end of the line.

I received another long silence a few days later, from Babette.

"I just want a simple office job," I explained, "maybe at a store."

"Maybe close to your father," she interrupted. "I do understand, Zoé. But is that what you really want?"

"Of course it's what I want! And stop looking at me like my life is over. Besides," I grinned, tongue-in-cheek, "being a secretary sounds like fun."

Come September, I found myself banging away on the keyboard of a rickety typewriter, often striking two keys simultaneously and locking them into position.

"I hate typing!" I muttered.

The good-natured teacher overheard me. "You're too impatient, Zoé. Slow down, and you'll see how easy it is."

She timed us: "Eyes on your copy. Get set. Go!" I got set, but I couldn't go. My cramped fingers were pressing all the wrong keys.

Bookkeeping was great, but filing was the bane of all creation. My partner was Charles Doucet. Very charming and extremely friendly, he sat with his chair jammed against mine.

"Cedric is filed before Charles," I reminded him, and his guffaw could have been heard down the corridors.

"Does that mean I don't stand a chance?"

"Exactly," I established point-blank.

He assumed a more serious demeanour. "Someday I'll control the fishery down here. I'll be the wealthiest businessman in Clare. Does that change your mind?"

"No."

"Then can we be friends?"

"If you move your chair."

"Imagine, a guy in my class!" I told my father, but he didn't exactly fall to the floor. "A *guy*," I repeated, "taking shorthand! Can you imagine, a guy as a secretary!" I felt like waltzing right across that kitchen and slapping my dad across the face, to see if I'd get a reaction. "Think of some words," I said, engaging him in a little game. "I'll write them in shorthand."

"Fish ... woods ... boat ... shed ... wharf," he dictated, but then he was out of words. The high-speed symbols only marginally interested him.

"I already have fifteen words per minute in typing," I boasted, as if it mattered to a man who could sit and stare for hours on end. No, he didn't want to see his name in shorthand, or in longhand for that matter. He just wanted to lie down on the couch.

"Don't you whittle in the shed anymore?" I pressed.

He nestled his head in his pillow. "When you're at school."

He caught yet another cold, which developed into another bout of bronchitis. N'Oncle Joseph split our cords of winter wood and ordered me, "Don't be scared to plug that stove."

It grew extremely cold. I lugged in snow-logged blocks that produced a black smoke, a choked heat. I did manage a fire every morning, but I made a pact with myself: First thing when I land a job, I'm buying a *Moses de* furnace!

Mam' sent me extra dollars, so I jacked up the oil flame on the Boston Breeze, while my father sat at the window, watching for my bus and waiting for the long winter to end.

The snow had barely melted when I started practising the ecstatic line, "Everybody's coming home, for the whole summer!" There was no sparkle in his eyes. "Philippe's getting married," I reminded him. "You get to wear your suit!" Silence. Totally complacent in our private little world, he talked about how I would someday buy a car, and then he and I would go to Yarmouth and watch the sights. He talked about the day he would turn sixty-five and would no longer need Mam's money—eleven years left to wait. But he didn't talk about *his* money, as if the aging brain cells of that delusion had died off to be replaced with a delusion of fame.

Spring came, and I nailed a calendar on the cupboard door. I marked every day, up to exam time, then handed him the pencil, "You keep count." But time and the pencil stood still.

"William wants to be a history professor," I attempted, but

that achieved hardly more than an empty stare. It was the same when I told him about Babette. "She wants to be a phys-io-thera-pist." Such a long word. "It's someone who makes people better with exercise, by stretching their arms and legs."

"Why?" I probed, when I next saw Babette.

Her green-eyed stare aimed straight at her feet. "So I can change the colour of these ugly brown shoes!" Then came the impassioned real reason. "Maybe I'll invent a dainty high heel for polio victims to wear to the prom."

I glanced at her shoes. "What's wrong with those? I had some like that."

"Because you were too rough on girl's shoes," she remembered, "not to raise you off the ground."

Babette would be going away soon, a morbid thought that hounded me day and night. "Couldn't Halifax wait until September?" I pleaded, grasping futilely at anything that could possibly stall her departure. "Maybe you're jealous that William will meet someone else if he's in Halifax before you."

My friend, now grown up, rejoined, "Good try Zoé, but given a choice between jealousy and the guillotine, I'd choose the guillotine."

The dull ache within me just wouldn't quit. "You're not even gone, and I feel like I want to die. Can't you please stay for the summer?"

My father read my despair. "Why don't you go with her?" he asked, making me even more sad. "Don't you want me here?"

With a sweep of his hand, he cleared the tobacco strands from off the kitchen table. "There's nothing on the Cape for a young girl like you."

"But this is my home," I protested. "I need the ocean, the wharf, the wide-open fields," a grin spread across my face, "Zita across the road."

It had been so long since Dad had grinned. "Then if that's what you want, this is your home. *T'es chu vous icitte.*"

The nerve-wracking morning came all too soon. Percy's car drove up our driveway, and Babette ran into the house, clutching a package. "You can open it later!"

I hastened to the attic, threw the rectangular parcel in the top drawer of my bureau, and hurried back down the stairs. I cried on my way out the door and all the way to the train station, just as I had done at her graduation. She took me aside at the station, found a Kleenex to wipe my tear-stained face, and fell into profuse crying herself. "Oh, Zoé! I'm not exactly going to Hong Kong. I'll be home so often you'll think I never left. I'll be home for Philippe's wedding."

"Minutes will turn into hours," I sobbed, "hours into weeks, weeks into forever." I fell into another torrent of tears and pleaded with William, "You can't take my best friend away. The Cape will never be the same."

The intellectual embraced me. "*It is a far, far better thing that I do, than I have ever done.* Who wrote that?"

"Certainly not me," I could vouch. "Good-bye, Charles Dickens." I wept, gave him a hurried hug, then turned to embrace my best friend. "Bye, *ma p'tite Babette*. You won't forget me in the big city, will you?"

The very mention started her weeping again. "If I ever forgot you, Zoé, you'd be visiting me at an asylum. It would mean I could no longer remember my own name."

She fumbled for the handle of her suitcase, bid farewell to her parents, and then turned to face me one more time. "You can always come too," she sobbed, and for a fleeting moment, I wished myself on that train. Instead I waved her away and watched her hasten to catch up with William.

"Go home and open your gift," she called and I hollered back, "I will." How I adored the ground that girl limped on. The persistent little miss had hobbled into my life at a snail's pace and, in so doing, had given me the greatest of all gifts—true friendship. Slow caterpillars turn into beautiful butterflies. I would never forget her.

First thing every morning, I opened my locket and there she was, smiling at me, my inspiration for the day.

"Only a week to go," I told my father, "and the crew will be here."

Arlene had come home early to attend to her wedding plans.

She visited, telling me secret bits about her dress, and talking a whole lot about Philippe. "An engineer," she said, and all the stars of a moonlit night were twinkling in her eyes. "Just imagine, my husband soon."

I had an announcement of my own, almost as exciting. "Tomorrow, Zita's showing me how to bake bread!"

My very special new sister helped me line up the ingredients on the table, then paused before leaving. "I'll be back tomorrow for an end crust. You'll need a good heat in the oven."

I cautioned Dad, "Now tonight, you have to let me sleep. I need to get up early and so do you—to start a good fire."

I went to bed, reread Cedric's newsy letter, then laid my weary head on the pillow. Visit him? In Germany? Me? I drifted off to thoughts of beautiful castles on the Rhine and to the sound of smooth-toned Jim Reeves songs, only to awake at midnight with the wind and rain rapping at my window, and the sound of my father on his couch, seized by one of his coughing bouts. "Are you all right?" I called, rushing to the kitchen. "*Quosque c'est q'les étouffries icitte.*"

"Lay on your side," I scolded, waiting until he had caught his breath before I cursed the darn stuff that was choking his lungs with phlegm. "That tobacco poison will kill you yet."

"*Ma p'tite Zoé,*" he replied. He now looked snug from what I could make out in the dim shadows of the night light. He lifted his covers invitingly, and I understood only too well the insinuation in his raspy voice. "Stay with me, and I'll buy you an ox." It wasn't exactly tobacco he was bartering for. I bolted out of that kitchen, leaving behind his wheezy call, "I'll buy you an ox." Back in bed, a shudder went through me, as I reflected that if my father had been a violent, physically aggressive man, my life could have turned into an incestuous nightmare.

The now angry wind drowned out my father's coughing, the banging door, and the rattle of the teapot. I could hear the great Jimmie Rodgers back up and about. I thought I saw a large man at the foot of my bed. I jerked the chain right off the dangling light bulb. No one was there.

I coaxed myself back to sleep, then later awoke and looked at the clock in the grey light—five after three. It had stopped raining.

But the wind was still rattling my window. I sprang out of bed, dashed through the living room and shivered in the hall, contemplating the one-inch crack at the bottom of the door. I lay flat on the floor with my ear attuned to the ticking of the clock. I heard snatches of congested snoring. *Fiou.* I opened the door a crack—enough to feel a cool breeze and to see in the dim light that Dad was lying on his side. I stole back to bed.

"Peace at last," I sighed. When I closed my eyes, thoughts of Cedric returned to harass me. Now why did he have to invite me to Germany? I'd have to lie, for I could never take his money. I'd tell him Dad wasn't well—too many bouts of bronchitis. Good idea! Now go to sleep, I silently scolded, and I tried to imagine Joel and Thérèse. How they must have grown. I tried to count sheep, but it was golden loaves of bread that leaped over the fence, among them Babette floated by, ever so gently. I fell into a deep sleep.

Chapter 39

For the love of Sweet Jesus, how long had it been light? I glanced over to the bureau. Nine o'clock! I jumped out of bed and into my clothes, drew back the bedroom curtains and shivered as I shot a glance towards Zita's. *B-r-r-r-r-r-r*. Why is it so bloody cold? With an ear towards the hall, I couldn't hear the crackle of kindling, so I opened the door to the kitchen and a gush of outside air came through, chilling me to the bone.

"Why are all the friggin' doors open!" I scolded. "It sure doesn't feel like summer yet." I grabbed my jacket from behind the stove, then picked up newspaper and kindling from off the floor, barely lending Dad a glance. "Tired this morning, eh?" Talking to myself, so it appeared. "We need a good fire," I emphasized. "And a little tea, to celebrate, maybe in our orange teacups. Philippe's getting married. And today, I'm baking bread! Kerosene," I muttered in a shiver, as I made a beeline for the shed. "Don't you feel well today? *Tut sens tu point bonne?*"

I hastened back to the stove, splattered kerosene over the kindling and finally, fully awake, glanced over to the couch. "Matches. Dad?"

Having ransacked the kitchen well into the night, the Great Jimmie Rodgers needed his sleep, his face snug in his pillow and facing the wall to ignore me. Not this morning. Bread was on the agenda. "Dad! Get up! Talk to me. *Vas-tu point'm parler'à matonne?*" No reply, so I gruffed the tone of my command. "Sheik of Araby, aren't you getting up!"

I gave Dad's free arm a nudge, but it stayed fixed, rigid at his side. I gave another nudge, then noticed the hand, wide open, having released a brown belt to the floor. The body that I touched was frigid, lifeless—the silent corpse of my father. "Oh my God! *Mon Djeu du ciel. Y l'était mort!*"

My own eyes frozen in their sockets, I backed into the stove, then made a mad dash into the shed. I had to tell someone. No! Not yet. Lock the door, I reasoned, and I hastened back through the kitchen, into the hall to dial across the road.

"*Hallo!*" echoed Zita's enthused voice over the phone. I had warned her I would call as soon as I was up.

All I could manage was to blurt, in a frantic gasp, "*Hallo*. This is Zoé. We'll have to forget about the bread. I've got the flu." I banged the receiver before she could reply, for surely there would have been a thousand and one questions.

I raced up the attic stairs and flopped on the last step. What if she came to the door and checked for herself? I steadied myself, kept a reasonable distance from the window overlooking the Cape road, where I could safely observe the gossip's house, and then it registered. The door was locked, and why was I tiptoeing across the attic, whispering to myself, when I was the only living soul in the house.

Why am I up here? I asked myself. Clothes, for … I glanced over to the antique bureau by the lath wall, and quickly remembered. Socks, any socks, good socks.

I opened the top drawer and grabbed a pair, then glanced around for Dad's brown suede shoes. I had almost picked them up when I suddenly realized. He won't be needing them. Socks? Of course not. The drawer still open, I tossed the socks back, my attention now drawn to Babette's parting gift to me—what else but a book—one that I had faithfully promised to read. So far, I hadn't gotten past the inside cover where she had scribbled her autograph. Every time I came to the attic, I felt compelled to read aloud the tender passage, except this time my hands were shaking.

May this poem Evangeline *serve to remind you that it was on our trip to Grand Pré that our friendship truly blossomed. Strange. I had never seen apple blossoms, yet I could imagine something of their beauty, just like I have never tasted the bitter core of your life, yet, I can imagine something of its flavour (how hard it must be, alone with your father).*

Best friends for ever and ever ...

Amen! my anguished heart cried as I pressed the precious book to my heart and shuddered. If only my best friend knew just how hard it was, just how alone I felt. My sweet Babette, so far away, and yet the mere recollection of her gentle smile was like a soft breath on my face, like the grace of an angel come to nourish the moment, but there were things to do when people died.

A sudden strength lifted my gaze to my father's green suit and white shirt hanging on a nail. He had last worn the ensemble to Yarmouth, so long ago that the wrinkles had ironed themselves out. I simply had to get up and check the trouser pockets. Just as I thought. From one pocket I retrieved three wooden matches and two cigarettes, from the other, four peppermints. No dirty hankies to launder. I draped the trousers over my arm, stood there contemplating what to grab next—the shirt and jacket. This called for a deep breath and every ounce of strength left in me—to walk back down those stairs, open the hall door, and re-enter my father's domain.

Actually, I was doing fine. I headed straight to his chair and sat in it, mimicking his grin as I rocked. Then I neatly draped his suit across the high back of the chair, gazed towards the wharf, and observed in his very tone, "I don't think Pierre will go out today. *Quite-a breeze.*"

Pierre! What would I tell Pierre? That Dad had hacked and coughed all night, like he did every night. That he was choking and I ran to check on him. Why panic, he always came around. N'Oncle Joseph and Tante Rosalie might not understand, they who would have surely called the doctor. I'd tell them ... perhaps I'd tell them ... I'd think of something. I turned from the window to observe the back of Dad's white head, the pitiful haircut that N'Oncle Joseph had effected. I scanned the full length of my father, his plaintive call having returned to haunt me, "*Ma p'tite Zoé.*" There'd be no tobacco today.

I flopped back in his chair, my whole body limp as I wept. Fool! Why in God's creation would he fabricate that I wasn't his daughter! I shivered at the very thought of his matchmaking. How could he have imagined Mam', a "fusspot" and a squeaky-clean woman, with Eddie Pockshaw, a runt of a weasel who lived in a malt-infested sty. Their conception of a daughter had been the most deranged of my father's delusions. I sobbed.

I was more Antoine LeBlanc's daughter than the stars were of the sky, the fish were of the ocean, his rhinestone belt was of his kingdom. Even when he was off in his own world, I was of him, his *p'tite Zoé*, the source of pride that coursed through his veins.

"Pray for me when I'm in purgatory," he had asked. I raised my head to the heavens, and in a hushed tone that his departed soul would hear, I recited my prayer: *That the Good Lord should let me live to bear two little girls, they will know their Grand-père.*

My strength diminished, I approached the couch and picked up Dad's belt from the floor, struggled back across the kitchen to his rocking chair. I gazed at the belt for the longest while before I slid it through the belt loops of his trousers. Rhinestones? I stared out the window towards the wharf. What a *Moses de* lonely life he had known. There were carved wooden whistles on the sill; I picked them up, to save for my two little girls. I looked over to the table, which was still lined with bread ingredients. My gaze paused here and there, finally rested on the shelf above Dad's couch, to the wooden ox of my childhood. He had replaced a missing leg with a nail to match the other three, and with a brown crayon, had concealed the teeth marks—all this intended for Joel. Had Dad forgotten that the ox was mine?

I mustn't lower my gaze. Far better to remember my father whittling in Dominique's shed or rocking in his chair, than lying as he was now, on his dilapidated couch. Oh my God! He must have called for me in his desperate attempt to open every door to the outside air so he could breathe. Outside! I could hear the voices of Pierre and his fishermen friends. Soon, my brother would come to the door. He always did, to check on Dad and me.

Hurry, I scolded myself, having dawdled far too long. I gave my kitchen a last "Martine inspection." Everything looked in perfect order, except … I shoved the bread ingredients back in the cupboard. Then I approached the shelf above the couch. Time to go. Should I? Could I? I did. I picked up the wooden ox, and escaping to the shed, I determined, "Joel can't have this!"

I dug my fingertips in the creases of the neck and bovine face of the chef-d'oeuvre, the very nicest thing that my father's penknife had ever carved. *Pour moi!* I vividly recalled exclaiming as he had passed it to me. I pressed the masterpiece tightly in my hand, remembering the proudest grin on his face and his very words, "*Pour ma p'tite Zoé.*"

I slammed the kitchen door shut and proceeded to unlock the outside door, all the while clutching the wooden ox, which I had slid into my jacket pocket.

The ox was mine. By the crackie, I had earned it.